TALES FROM

THE GREEN

By SHARON GEORGE

FOR BUDDY

WHO FILLS MY HEART WITH WONDER

Appendices
Months of the Year

The months begin with darkmoon, wax to brightmoon, then wane.

SEPTEMBER – Moon of Painted Leaves

OCTOBER – Moon of Falling Leaves

NOVEMBER – Moon of Sleeping Oak

DECEMBER – Moon of Bare Branches

JANUARY – Bittercold Moon

FEBRUARY – Ice Moon, White Moon

MARCH – Moon of Many Winds

APRIL – Skywater Moon, Birthing Moon, Moon of the Children

MAY – Moon of Many Flowers

JUNE – Green Moon, Moon of Green Leaves

JULY – Moon of Warm Winds

AUGUST – Moon of Warm Rivers

Glossary

All That Is – the universe and beyond

Barker – dog

Bed-warmer – denigrating name for a cat with a home

Bittercold – very cold weather, coldest months of the year

Bloodlust – an ancient era when kin slaughtered kin for sport

Boulderfalls – a cascade of boulders forming a Stonehenge

Brightmoon – the full moon

Brood kit – baby skunk

Bushytail – squirrel

Buttercup Root – Goldenseal, an herb to fight infection

Cactus Water – Aloe, soothing herb

Catling – adolescent cat

Chamomile – herb with small, yellow flowers for settling nerves

Coldmoons – cold months of the year

Commonspeak – shared tongue of body language, scent, intuition

Cramp bark – herb used for female troubles

Darkmoon – no moon in the sky, night before Newmoon

Death-Den – shelter where ferals are taken and euthanized

Den – where a cat or other animal lives, also called a nest

Denchurl – enormous fighting cat, palace guard for evil

Den-kin – pet cat, domesticated by humans

Deosil – clockwise motion, used to summon energy for spells

Dog Father – deity for canines, also called Lord Tooth & Tail

Dreamweed – Valerian, nature's Valium

Earth Mother – feminine, nurturing force of nature

Eight-legged – spider

False-stone – concrete, asphalt

Feathertail – bird

Feral – cat born in the wild without human connection

Fetch – a cat's spirit self, leads it to Beyond & Fields of Nip

Fields of Nip – where cats go when they die, cat heaven

Finback – fish

Flattail – beaver

Flatstone – diamond shaped stone for Darkmoon Gatherings

Furleaf – Comfrey, an herb to fight infection

Ghostdog – coyote, also called a gulchdog

Goldenseal – herb that fights infection

Graytail – gray fox

Great Mother – cat deity, loving spirit, mother to all

Green – huge nature park where the kin live

Guardian Stone – boulder hiding the opening to Hillside Pod den

Head-jewel – shape of varying colors on forehead between the ears

Ironstone Manor – home of the Royals, Ozymandias

Jinny – female skunk, sow

Kin – cats, also called Pelted Ones, Clan of Fang and Claw

Kit – kitten, baby cat

Leatherboots – animal control workers who hunt feral cats

Longear – rabbit

Longtail – rat

Lovename – secret name given with mother's milk, hidden in the purr

Malkin – essence of evil in cat form

Metal pelts – cars, trucks, buses

Milk Mother's Spill – the Milky Way

Moon – one night

Nightsoil – feces

No-fur – human being

No-pelt – human being

No-tail – human being

One oak – unit of measurement, the height of an average oak

One tail – unit of measurement, length of a cat tail

Plate-licker – denigrating name for a cat with a home

Playname – nickname earned playing with siblings

Pod – family of cats united by blood and/or friendship

Podcat – member cat of a clan, family by blood or friendship

Poppy Seeds – used for pain relief

Preypile – where all hunters put their catch to share

Provider – a human who feeds ferals, gives them shelter

Ravenspeak – the magic that lets all animals understand them

Redberry Tree – Guelder Rose, Cramp Bark, for menses bleeding

Redtail – fox

Ringtail – raccoon

Ronin – rogue cats who wander alone

Round-eye – owl

Rue – an herb to ease birthing

Rumble-road – street

Shelterveil – a magical place invisible to the uninitiated

Skywater – rain

Slitherer – snake

Smelltail – skunk

Snap-jaw – vicious dog

Snuggery – bed for queen with kittens, made of moss and herbs

Squawkbeak – crow, raven's smaller cousin

Standing Folk – trees

Sun – one day

Sunhigh – noon

Sunfall – sunset

Sweetgrass – slender-leafed, fragrant grass used for nests

Sylvan – water spirit of caves and forests, can appear feline

Tall-one – human being

Tall-walker – human being

Two-legged – human being

Two-legged den – where a human lives

True-blood – purebred Royal, the Persians of Ironstone Manor

Turn of the Moon – one complete moon cycle, one month

Upright – human being

Walk-In – spirit who steal bodies

Warmmoons – warm months of the year

Waterfall Boulder – huge granite slab above Hillside Pod den

White Truck – animal control truck, greatly feared

Widdershins – counter-clockwise motion, to banish, or lessen

Wildborn – feral, a cat born in the wild without human connection

Worldname – how a cat is known to the world

Youngling – adolescent cat

Cast Of Characters

CATS OF THE FAR NORTH:

Leafturn – female, brown, mate to Topbranch

Topbranch – male, brown, pod leader of High Home

CATS OF THE NORTH:

Bigpaw – gray-brown mackerel male tabby, white paws, face

Bravetail/Red – male, chestnut colored ticked fur

Browser – male, gray-brown tabby, white paws/face

Buster – male, black and white tux, Browser's 2nd

Kyra – female, solid black, Siamese lineage

Monkey – female, gray, beautiful face, strange neck fur, pot belly

Patches – black and white tuxedo male

Princess Rosamonde Whitewhiskers – female Abyssinian

Rosebud – beige fur, golden eyes

Shadow – female, black, Siamese lineage, blue eyes

WISDOM CATS OF THE NORTH:

Erasmus – Elder Cat of the North, male, gray mackerel

Ghost – male, small, silver-pelted, blue-green eyes

Robin – male, gray tux with peach blush on chest-bone

Rootheart – male, first Wisdom Cat of the North, great healer

Morsus – male, partial Sphinx descent, patchy hair, yellow eyes

THE PUPS:

Jasper – son of Sugar Pie

Shorttail – son of Sugar Pie

Sugar Pie – terrier mix, white/ beige/brown

CATS OF THE EAST:

Edgerunner – male, Sandpelt's second, sandstone-colored pelt

Sandpelt – male, leader of Windcave Clan, tan/white paws

Stonefly – male, brown & beige swirled tabby

WISDOM CATS OF THE EAST:

Flyingtail – male, dark gray, extra long tail, blue eyes

Indra – female, black, silver eyes

Nebula – Elder Cat of the East, black male, white stars

Skyleaper – male, white, silver-green eyes

Starpaw – male, black, white stars on front paws, blue eyes

Stormchaser – Windpaw and Windclaw's sire

Windclaw – male, pale gray/white bi-color

Windpaw – female, pale gray/white bi-color

Windsong – female, white

CATS OF THE SOUTH:

Blackpaw – male, black, Flat-tail Dam Pod leader

Broadface – male, chocolate brown, Southbridge Pod chief

Ember – male, red, golden eyes, Broadface's 2nd

Firetail – male, red/white with red tail

Goldenfoot – female, ginger-pelt

Graytail – female, calico/gray back & tail

Mistypaw – gray female, Cattail Island Pod leader

Pebblepaw – female, white and spotted calico

Rushpaw – male, beige, Mistypaw's mate & 2nd

Whitewhiskers – male, black/white tux, Blackpaw's 2nd

WISDOM CATS OF THE SOUTH:

Bent Whisker – male, red-ocher tabby/curly whiskers

Reggie – male, ginger pelt, green eyes

Smokepelt – male, dark-gray, black streak on back, blue eyes

Sosay – white female, blue eyes, crescent moon on forehead

Tinypaw – female, small brindle

CATS OF THE WEST:

Barney – male, gray tabby, long hair, slanted ears with tufts

Graypaw – female, gray-ocher crone, mate of White Fangs

Kiliarcos – young warrior

Rainpelt – male, silver-gray tabby, leader of Bigmarsh Family

Silverpelt – female, silver–black pelt, Birch Grove Pod leader
Threepaws – gray long hair male, ear tufts, born with 3 legs
WhiteFangs – Bigmarsh Family leader

WISDOM CATS OF THE WEST:
Annapurna Snowpelt – female, pale cream, blue eyes
Darktail – male, Elder Cat of the West, dark gray tabby
Martileena – female, choc–brown brindle, golden eyes

CATS OF THE SOUTHWEST:
Ozymandias – Emperor of Ironstone Manor, 6–toed Persian,
Sylvestes Felaria – the Grand Vizier, Siamese, 5–toed
The Chevalier – silver, polydactyl, Persian knights of Ozymandias

CATS FROM THE ALLEYWAYS:
Angel – female, gray–ocher queen
Big Spike – gray tiger male, huge, mangy
Cloud – Siamese colored & marked male, son of Angel
Diva – female, once black fur now white with age, one eye
Gentleman Jim – male, gray and white
Long Claw – male, gray with white belly, paws
Nit & Kit – black and white tuxedo twins

MORSUS' MINIONS:
Black Max – male, black pelt

DENCHURLS:
Hissfurr – huge black male
Scratchblood – huge black male
Snakeheart – huge black male

OTHER CHARACTERS:
Grimfang – skinny, scarred leader of seven coyotes
Nightbeak – Father of Ravens, shaman of ancient oak grove
Daisy – skunk mother living in Smallmarsh
Old Scaley – king snake living near pool of Hillside Pod

Redears – female coyote in Grimfang's pack. Has reddish head

Trouble – golden kitten @ Harmony Tree

HUMANS:

Bleggs – works for Animal Control, enemy of the kin

Miriam – Mee-am, Rosie's forever mom

The Mate – Miriam's husband

The Provider – feeds feral cats, practices trap/neuter/return

Wilson – works for Animal Control, friend to the kin

RED'S KITTENS:

Brightstar – male, black/white tuxedo, star on forehead

Petal – female, lion-hued

Tigertom – male, orange tiger

EARTH MAGIC

POLESTARS

NORTH: Polestar – Harmony Tree · Element – EARTH
Spirit Cat – Starlight
EAST: Polestar – Crystal Aerie · Element – AIR
Spirit Cat – Cloudrunner
SOUTH: Polestar – Sacred Yew · Element – FIRE
Spirit Cat – Solara
WEST: Polestar – Scrying Pool · Element – WATER
Spirit Cat – Ripplemist

FIRE IS ONE
WATER IS TWO
AIR IS THREE
EARTH IS FOUR

Beyond – Limbo after death for those not ready for Fields of Nip

Boulderfalls – naturally occurring Stonehenge

Cedar Trees – Harmony Tree, Sacred wood used for temples, altars, by oracles for prophecy, gateway to the divine

Ceremony of the RA – given by Elder Cat to apprentices after their vision quest but any Wisdom Cat can give an apprentice the RA. Imparts powers of that element and its secret lore.

Code of the Children of Great Mother:
Respect all life, living in service to others
Share with everyone, never taking more than you need
Never waste a life, kill only as much as you will eat

Commonspeak – shared tongue of body language, intuition

Darkmoon – night before new moon, no visible moon

Darkmoon Gatherings – wisdom cats bring apprentices to learn and commune, happens night of the darkmoon

Dog Father – masculine principle, protector of wolves, dogs

Earth Mother – Nature, feminine energy, compassionate

Elementals – Spirit Cats living in Polestars

Fetch – spirit self, all your deeds are recorded in your Fetch which
    comes at death to lead you to Beyond or Fields of Nip

Fields of Nip – feline heaven, blue skies, clear streams, catnip fields

Great Mother – female deity, eternal mother, nurturer of life

Harmony Tree – giant cedar, Polestar of the North

Milk Mother's Spill – the Milky Way

Polestars – vortexes of power, home to Spirit Cats

Prophecy – ancient poem about a quest that must be fulfilled to bring
    the Era of All Peace, ending the holocaust

RA – Essence of Great Mother, Dog Father, universal wisdom

Shelterveil – magic place the uninitiated can't see

Spirit Cats – liaisons between Great Mother and Wisdom Cats, there is
    a Spirit Cat for each element: Earth, Air, Fire and Water

The Three Names:

    Lovename: secret between mother & kit,

    Playname: given by siblings & playmates,

    Worldname: given by Great Mother @ the naming ceremony

Waking Dreams – meditative trance yielding prophetic dreams

Wisdom Cats – shaman cats, use the powers of the elements

GREAT MOTHER'S PROPHECY

A Queen discarded, saved by Clan,
Will mate with King of her command,
Will birth the future of the Green.
Then with Beloved, son, and Gray,
Will find the one tossed her away.

Earth for healing, Clouds to dream,
Visions of fire, Oceans that bring
Hearts of emotion, Four become One
And black wings most beloved son
Will guide us to All-Peace
Where Love is Legion and All Is One.

THE DARK PROPHECY

Who takes a life into his own
Grows strong of muscle, hard of bone.
And he who eats a beating heart
Will rule a kingdom, long and dark.

Behold! The greatest power comes
To he who eats the heart of one
Who is but spirit, body-free.
That heart bestows eternity.

And the finest heart to eat
Beats within the Mother Great.
A single bite of Her Sweet Flesh
And he can rule the Vast Expanse.

MAP OF THE GREEN

Contents

PREFACE

Earth has traveled many times around our sun since Sagan left me for Fields of Nip. I still miss him, my friend and companion, my guardian. Always napping nearby, he'd rouse himself to accompany me to the laundry room or dumpster, growling at people who didn't like me, rubbing his wide, golden head on those who did.

One night while resting on my chest, he asked me if I'd help.

Help who? I asked.

Let me show you, he answered, and Sagan's orange tiger-striped face floated before me, big and blue. He showed me his essence; how he felt, as cat, living beside me through the years. He took me into another world, a world where Great Mother and Dog Father ruled, where Wisdom Cats and Spirit Cats led the kin. I met ronin toms, pod leaders, queens, and kits, everyone from bed-warmers to the wildest ferals. Sagan shared his deepest joys and his secret suffering: how much he loved me and his home, how he'd been born wild, and he still felt its call. *That is cat,* he said. And he told me he was dying.

No! You mustn't, I cried.

Promise me you'll help, he answered. I promised.

Then he showed me, in this world, on our cities' streets, so many ferals live short, cruel lives of hunger and homelessness. *That's who you help,* he said, licking my hands with a raspy tongue.

Sagan taught me many truths that night. At the last, he taught me the most sacred Felidae secret — dreaming.

This is what he said:

All cats dream and many remember, some as philosophers, dreaming of a better world, some as adventurers exploring their own. Some are poets, spinning tales of plump mice and round moons. Others are warriors stalking the borders of their turf. Some conjure like magicians. Some pray like priests. And some are just simple folk, dreaming about dinner and a pet. Whether ruled by their hearts, their minds, or their senses, whether they sleep on soft pillows or hunker in alleyways...all cats dream.

1 – Tales Of Red & Rosie

"What is it, Red?" Miriam knelt beside her aging cat and ran her hand down his back. Once the proud bearer of a deep russet pelt, the years that had worn the muscle from his frame had also bleached his fur. He rubbed his golden head against her thigh and meowed. "You want out? You just got here." Red head-bunted her leg again, his tail quivering high. "OK, but the sun's almost down, and it looks like rain." Miriam rose and opened the door. Red padded to the edge of the porch but didn't leave its shelter, entranced by mountains of bruised clouds and jagged spears of light racing within them. When the sky rumbled and a few fat drops hit the sidewalk, he darted back to Miriam. "What? What is it, baby?"

"Neow," he explained, looking up with pleading eyes.

"Honey?"

"Yes?" A male voice rolled down the hallway.

"Red's acting weird. He wants something."

"Told you letting him out front was a bad idea."

"No, he wants something."

"Yeah, to chase Robo again." The voice sounded tired.

"Red, you won't chase Mr. Miyazaki's dog anymore, will you?" She caressed his back as she'd done for many years, years when his pelt had grown lush over powerful muscles, his skin resilient beneath her hands. She'd loved rubbing her palm down his back, ending with a gentle pull of his tail. She loved to still, although now she felt each bone beneath his skin.

Miriam had loved Red from the moment she saw him. A great wild prince, he'd marched into her life and won her heart. And despite all the experts who said he wouldn't, he'd loved her back with a ferocity that matched her own, with a heart as loyal as a warrior and generous as a

1

child. She'd aged since then, and he'd grown older still. Now her love was tinged with sadness, knowing their time together would end sooner than she could accept. Red pushed his head against her leg again, reminding her of his need. "He wants to show me something."

"I'm feeding the ferals out back. Call if you need help."

"OK," she said, following Red out the door and to the corner, wondering why she was crazy enough to let her cat take her on a walk while a storm brewed. Raindrops blew over Miriam's shoulders and she looked back toward the porch, thinking about her warm sweater and warmer cup of coffee, both inside. Then Red dashed up, complaining loudly and she forgot about her comfort and followed him for several blocks. He turned down an alleyway and Miriam stopped again, watching her little tiger lope to a dumpster at the far end. He waved his tail and yowled at her to join him. She did, just as the clouds ripped open and torrents of water soaked them both. A sweater would have been useless, but Miriam did own an umbrella, also in the house, probably next to her cell phone. Hugging herself for warmth, she tiptoed toward Red, wondering why they were there when she heard a faint cry, and a big-eyed scrap of rust-colored fur popped out then dashed back beneath the dumpster. The next cry was louder, ending with a growl. Miriam smiled as she lifted Red into her arms. "I'm proud of you. Yes, we'll help them," she whispered into his ear, and the old tom purred. She hurried home.

The pale stone house rose on the corner of two tree-lined streets. On the first floor, a bay window protruded left of the recessed entrance where large resin planters shaped like the tops of Grecian pillars and filled with rosemary and lavender bushes, lined each side of the stairs and crossed the landing to the oak door. The door boasted a brass handle, the kind where you put your thumb on top and press down, curling your fingers beneath. High up was a little window of leaded glass and below that hung a brass face of the Green Man, Lord of the Forest. One knocked by lifting his tongue. His leafy hair and beard, polished to a satin sheen, continued downward in a flourish that said 'Welcome'.

Red's humans meant that word. Every heart beating from front stoop to backyard garden wall was cared for. And tonight, thanks to Red, they would welcome three mewling orphans with a warm bed and all the nourishment and affection a baby needs.

Red's tail quivered with joy when the door burst open and in sailed the carrier holding precious cargo. Winding figure eights around their legs, Red helped his humans down the hall and into the kitchen where a basket waited, a bed for the kittens warmed by a heating pad beneath layers of blankets. Miriam had prepared a formula of mother's milk replacement, and she had drops to kill the fleas, and medications for the intestinal worms so common to babies born outside.

Red purred, pleased to help his humans raise another litter for adoption. He lived with them as a rescue himself, long ago abandoning the hunt for dinner in a dish, and sleeping beneath a tree for a nap on a pillow. As Red learned the ways of his uprights, the urge to race through tall grass faded. He knew he was loved. But sometimes, just sometimes, even now his legs would jerk when he dreamed he was running through tall grass with Shadow, rubbing against her softness. After those dreams he'd be sad for a while. The kittens helped. The kittens, with their runny eyes and swollen bellies gave him purpose, and they reminded him how lucky he was.

In the large kitchen, old enough to have a fireplace, on a night cold enough to have it lit, Red crouched before his three rescues, tipping their wicker basket with a giant paw. Out they tumbled, shaking sleepy heads. The ginger tabby hissed a warning. Red smiled.

"My name is Red," he meowed. "Red is my worldname, a gift from the tall-ones with whom I've lived for many turns of the moon." He gave the babies a sly look. "I've danced at two hundred and twenty-three brightmoons myself." The little ones trembled. They'd seen only one brightmoon and couldn't dance.

Licking their little bodies to reassure them, Red helped them scramble back inside their bed. "Long ago, I had other names. My mother gave me the first, but as you know, the name whispered with the milk is never spoken..." He licked their paws, remembering her warm softness and loving eyes. "I earned another name with my deeds. It was about my tail. Have you been given names?" The kits' eyes widened with worry. Had they missed something, done something wrong? Red licked each of their faces, starting their purr motors. "The uprights will call you something soon enough. Learn your names. It pleases them to think you're smart." With that, he stretched lazily across the floor and dozed. The babies curled around one another and slept too.

The kits suckled bottles of warmed goat's milk and were caressed by gentle hands. They grew. Red taught them to use the potty box and where the best toys were kept. He showed them the pantry drawer filled with soft towels and taught them how to squeeze through the secret opening in the rear above the potato bin. The drawer was dark and comfy, perfect for a nap.

"You've been rescued," he told them. "Tall-walkers saved your lives." Red nuzzled the little female. "You wouldn't have survived another night outside...but if by some miracle you did, after six brightmoons you'd birth a litter of kits and another one every four moons thereafter, whether you could feed yourself or not. You two," he tapped the boys with his tail, "would fight for food, or queens or turf. You'd fight until injured or killed. The strongest males have harems, but most of us are forced to wander alone until death takes us from the streets. You're lucky to be here and not in a death den.

"What's a death den?" the orange tabby asked.

"You don't want to know," Red answered.

The little male sat stiffly, pulling himself to his full height, chin up, whiskers splayed. "So why do *you* know all this?" he demanded.

Red chuckled. "Would you like me to tell you *what* I know?" The tabby nodded. "All right. I'll begin with a beautiful, courageous queen... Rosamonde Whitewhiskers."

The kits turned the circles of past, future, and now, each finding a perfect place to lie. Spreading and curling their tiny toes, they rested their chins on one another's bodies, the sounds of their new home fading as Red purred the story of his life.

🐾　　🐾　　🐾

Rosie dug at the blankets. The scratching and mewling woke Mee-am, who switched on her reading lamp with a nervous glance at her mate. He snored. Relieved, she focused on the lump rooting beneath her knees.

"What's wrong, Rosie-Posie?" Mee-am asked, lifting the Abyssinian kitten to her belly. Rosie's eyes were open wide, and her claws fully extended. Her eyes were open wide, and her claws fully extended. "Don't be afraid, baby. It's okay, It's okay," Mee-am cooed, holding her close and stroking her back. Gradually Rosie calmed, the red pupils and sharp fangs of her nightmare fading before her human's love. Mee-am and kitty sank into the covers and fell back asleep.

Princess Rosamonde Whitewhiskers began life as royalty. Her father, a magnificent sorrel named Thurgood Rubbelly the Fourth, garnered many awards including three Grand Championships and a Best of Show, and her mother, Victoria Thrice Silvertip, was a ruddy silver who traced her lineage back to Zula herself. Zula was a beautiful alley cat with a strangely speckled coat. Found by a British soldier in the port city of Alexandria and brought to England in 1868, she became the first Abyssinian on record. Rosamonde's ancestors had traveled from Egypt to England to a cattery in northern California that bred Abyssinian show cats. And there Rosie entered the world.

Rosie lacked some minor qualities needed to win at shows, differences so small only an expert could tell but they sent her life down another path. Rosie was treated as 'less than' by her peers, which caused her pain, and that pain made her think, and that thinking led to self awareness and compassion. By the end of her life, Rosie counted her physical flaws as some of her greatest blessings.

A ruddy like her father, her coat had the Abyssinian ticking, but it blushed too pale. Her ears were too small for an Abby, as were the tufts at their points. She had, however, a lovely face with a well-pronounced muzzle, and her plump whisker pads grew strong, white hairs with a sweeping downward curve. They were magnificent. Brilliant copper-colored eyes shone from deep black rims within spectacles of light fur, and perfect mascara lines ran from their corners down the sides of her face. Rosie's imperfections might assure she wouldn't win contests, but she was beautiful. Coupled with a strong personality and a reduced price, she quickly garnered a home.

Rosie's forever mom, a young female she called Mee-am, had been easy to train. She came when summoned, always kept Rosie's bowl topped off, her water fresh, and her business-box scooped out daily. Rosie was given an enclosed condo of soft fabric. It was placed on a chair in the sleeping room, but Mee-am let her climb into bed, petting her until they both dreamed.

Rosie loved her home except for one thing: Mee-am's mate. When Mee-am wasn't looking, he watched Rosie with hard eyes, whispering to her that he wanted a dog. Rosie thought he was lying. He was there when Mee-am brought Rosie home, holding her close, cooing to her while walking through their rooms. She placed Rosie on the floor, and the kitten explored everything, making her new home her own. After a nap behind the sofa, she wandered down the hallway, stopping at the only closed door. The scent of human kit emanated from beneath, so she scratched at the floor, then reached for the handle, crying to be let in. Mee-am came running, scooping her up heartbeats before the Mate reached her, arms waving above his angry face.

That room was forbidden, and *that* door was never again left open... until one day it was and she went inside. Nothing in the room had been touched for a long time. For so long she left paw prints in the dust on the table when crossing to the tiny human bed. The sweet scent of baby lingered and Rosie's heart quickened with the thought of nuzzling Mee-am's kit. She raised on her hind legs and peered over the headboard. *What? It's empty. Where do they keep their youngling?* She leaped into the crib, scenting with open mouth. A dark shape filled the doorway. *The Mate!*

"Get out of here, cat," he roared, stomping toward her with a face so red and ferocious she couldn't think. Hopping from one end of the little bed to the other, Rosie dodged the hands grabbing savagely at her fur. She somersaulted through a side bar, landing on the Mate's shoes, then dashed between his legs and across the floor with amazing speed. By the time the Mate bent over and grabbed the space between his ankles, Rosie was slip-sliding down the hallway. When he pitched cursing into the wooden bars she was diving behind the couch.

Her heart pounded for a long time, but eventually she emerged, surprised to see light from the kit's room still spilling into the hall. Rosie couldn't help herself. Pressed against the wall, she tiptoed slowly toward the open door and peeked inside. The Mate hunched on a tiny chair, his giant hands holding his face. *Tears. Their kit is lost!* And lost kits, she'd learned from her mother, don't come home. Feeling his grief, Rosie forgave the Mate, and brushed against his leg trilling condolences. He spread his fingers and stared. His foot jerked and she backed away, confused. She was almost to the hallway when Mee-am's hands closed around her belly, whisking her off for cuddles and treats. Never again would she find the door open, but after that day her encounters with the Mate grew ever more tense. The more Mee-am showed her love, the more jealous the Mate became. He only hurt himself. The more anger he directed at Rosie, the more Mee-am held her close. Sometimes Rosie heard him speak her name so fiercely Mee-am would cry. He'd leave the room, and Rosie would go to Mee-am and lick the tears from her cheeks.

One night she heard Mee-am scream, "No more! Leave!" The front door slammed. Suns rose and moons fell and the Mate stayed away. Life was peaceful, and Mee-am more attentive than ever, but Rosie sensed sadness within her, loneliness she couldn't heal no matter how much she rumbled her love and shared her warmth.

The Abyssinian Princess stretched along the top of the plush chair by the window. She seemed to be sleeping, but in truth she waited, smelling the Mate close by. She heard his car door slam. As he came up the walkway, Rosie called to Mee-am that her male had returned. Then she ran.

"What? What is it, silly girl?" Mee-am asked, lifting her head from a book as the kitten dove under the sofa. A knock at the door. "Who could that be?" *It's the Mate,* Rosie yowled. Mee-am opened the door.

Many tears flowed that night and tender words. Whitewhiskers learned *I'm sorry* and believed it was true. At least that night it was. She almost welcomed him, she was so happy to see Mee-am smile. She was happy even when they moved her bed into the kitchen and closed the door against her.

The Mate returned, but at least now he stared past Rosie, pretending she didn't exist. She could live with indifference.

Rosie matured. Gangling legs grew sturdy, her color deepened. Muscles developed on once thin shoulders and hips. Dozing on the couch, ears twitching while she listened contentedly to Mee-am talk, a single word made them swivel like radar dishes: VET. Rosie must go to the VET and be fixed. Soon. Very soon. *Fixed? There's nothing wrong with me.* VET meant having your stomach poked, your tail lifted for impolite intrusions and your skin pierced with stinging needles. VET she had endured when she first came to Mee-am. *Not again.* Then it got worse. Her humans spoke of a promotion at work, which made them happy, but also meant they must leave this home and find another. Rosie worried. In her short life, change had always come wrapped in danger.

Suns rose and fell and nothing happened, until one morning Mee-am reminded the Mate he'd soon be taking Rosie to the VET. *How could you?*

the little cat grumbled, glowering at Mee-am. But the Mate seemed pleased, lowering his paper to nod, then snapping it back before his face. Hidden from Mee-am, his gaze found Rosie. Their eyes locked, and into his crept the darkness still in his heart. Rosie bolted from the room.

"What's bothering my Princess?" Mee-am asked.

"Her brain," the Mate replied.

"Stop that. She's wonderful." Rosie warmed to Mee-am's love, but feared for her future, especially when their home filled with boxes and the boxes were filled with their things. All the things they used and all the things they didn't were packed away. Their books, clothes, movies and music, dishes, spices, pots and pans, even Rosie's china bowl went into a crate, not to be seen again until they reached their new home. Rosie didn't understand everything about the move, but she knew Mee-am always took her purse. She spent hours squatting in that leather bucket, butt planted deep, her top half spilling across the table. When Mee-am first saw her, she laughed so hard Rosie was insulted.

The morning of the move arrived. It was early when strangers filled their home and began carrying boxes to a truck outside. Soon their footsteps echoed through empty rooms. Rosie was stressed by their presence and the changes they brought, and on this day, the absolute worst day possible, she was scheduled to see the VET. She hid in a box that was taken to the truck, but Mee-am found her and brought her back inside, laughing again.

"Don't worry. Daddy's taking you to the VET, then he'll bring you to our new home. You'll love it. There's a room just for you with all your toys in it." She buried her face in Rosie's pelt. "I love you, Rosie-Posie." For a moment, life was as it should be, and Rosie purred, making bread on Mee-am's shoulder, careful not to use her claws. Mee-am giggled, dropped her into the carry box and closed the lid before she could protest. The Mate reached for it. "Wait!" Mee-am rushed from the room, returning with a white cloth. "I finished this today," she chirped, waving the PRW she'd stitched in the corner with golden thread before Rosie's eyes. Opening the top of the carry box, she placed the cotton towel beneath her, whispering, "There, sweetheart." Then out the door Rosie flew, into the car, landing with a bump on the front seat. Mee-am leaned in the window to kiss the Mate good-bye. Hoping for a kiss too, Rosie got only an outstretched arm, a wave and a "Love you, Rosie-Posie." From behind the mesh of the carrier, she tried to lick Mee-am's hand, but her human was already gone and without a glance or a word, the Mate drove away.

Whitewhiskers stared through the carrier's mesh top at the clouds. Gradually, the scent of water and trees faded, replaced with the smell of cars and machines. Rooftops crowded one to another, each block more cramped and crooked than the last, and more gray. The Mate hummed a senseless tune. "Da de da, da da de da," he muttered, tapping rhythms on the steering wheel with the heel of his hand. Rosie realized he was nervous and making noise to hide his thoughts.

"No! Bad, bad!" she yowled, when the vehicle slowed and turned down a narrow street where the rooftops on both sides seemed to bend inward, shutting out the sky. The stench of garbage and urine overwhelmed her, but worse was the stink of black mold, a malevolent undercurrent in a sea of sloth. Somehow a part of Rosie knew this place, knew it was hunger and pain, disease and slow death. The Mate stopped singing. He got out, came around and opened the passenger door. Then with a sweeping motion, he plopped her carry-box on the ground and flung open the end.

"OK, pretend baby, this is it for you and me. Get out." Stunned, Rosie cowered in the back of the box. "Get out, I said, and I won't say it nicely again." He lifted the carrier, tilted the opening down and shook. The towel landed in the grime. Moaning with fear, her claws scraping the plastic, Rosie slowly slid toward the open end, toward the filth, toward her abandonment and the loss of everything in her life. "OUT, you damned nuisance!" The Mate dropped the box, opened the top, and grabbed her by the scruff.

"Nee-owww," she cried as he pulled her free. She reached frantically for his jacket, but he tossed her away from his body and her claws flailed the air. Rosie hit the pavement, slipping in the grease and dirt. Appalled, she lifted her pristine paws in high, quick little hops with nowhere to go. The Mate laughed meanly, though he seemed to regret it as she sank down, so shamed she couldn't look at him. *Why does he hate me? What's wrong with me? What did I do wrong?* And lost in self-loathing, she crouched in the slime, paws tucked beneath her trembling body.

For a moment, Rosie's self-loathing tore at his heart too. He'd committed himself to this betrayal, however, and tossing the carry box into the car, slammed the door before she thought to jump back inside. From the driver's side, he turned for one last look. "Look, she won't...I can't..." He stared off into the distance, his eyes darkening. "She'd never give you up. Look, I want a real baby, OK?" Then in a voice more snake than human, he hissed, "You'll make it outside, you're a cat."

Tires squealed. A plume of exhaust and the life Rosie knew was gone. Staring down the empty road, she tried to believe it was all a mistake, a bad dream, that the Mate would return for her. But she knew he wouldn't, and hunkered on her towel, Mee-am's last kindness. The alley grew darker and the air chill. Outside the alley, streetlights winked on. Far above, windows glowed with lights too weak to reach the gloom at the bottom. Rosie's stomach stirred with hunger, but no bowl of kibble was placed at her paws. There was no Mee-am to put it there.

She flinched when a metal door scraped across the asphalt, and a pudgy human wrapped in white aprons shambled from a rectangle of warm light. Each fist clenched a black plastic bag, a heavy bag judging by the raised veins and trembling muscles of his forearms. He lurched forward, propelled by bent knees. The bags smelled delicious with bits of pork and beef, chicken and fish, all the flavors Rosie loved. But before she could rouse herself, the human had tossed them into a dumpster and slammed the lid shut. Rosie moaned.

Will I die of starvation, or cold...or loneliness? She dropped her head to her paws and curled like a snail on the towel, no longer concerned with hunger, cold, or filth soiling her lovely pelt. Grief became physical pain. *If I sleep, the pain will stop. If I sleep forever, I'll never feel pain again.* She lay in a heap in the middle of the alley and slept.

🐾　　🐾　　🐾

Paws stretched before her, Rosie hooked her claws into loamy earth. She yawned and rose, sunlight warming her back. The air was spiced with catmint, valerian and sweetgrass, and she was considering which to nibble on first when playful squealing turned her head. Three kits, her kits, tumbled through a maze of roots, climbing the tree bark with tail-swishing delight. *Am I dead?*

"Far from it," came the answer. Rosie looked up, into the enormous cedar. A white cat shimmered on a branch, blue eyes blazing into hers. He lay perfectly still in constant, glimmering motion, his long, feathery pelt shedding pale blue gems of light.

"Who are you?" Rosie asked.

"The question is...who are you?"

"Rosie?" she said with a lilt that turned her statement into a question. She felt foolish. Amused, the white cat rolled his whiskers forward then back, sending strings of lights spinning away.

"Who are you?" she asked again.

He shook his head and galaxies wheeled through space, fading into nothingness. "I'm your friend, Rosie question mark. You don't know who you are? Let's see. Are you Rosie Diva? Rosie Prima Catus? Are you Felis Rosieatis or Rosie Princess Felis?" Rosie squirmed. "Ah, definitely Princess. P...r...i...n...c...e...s...s..." He taunted, stretching the word, "Princess Fragilis Animalus? Would that be you, dear? On your silky pillow-throne with your china bowl of meaty nuggets? No mouse entrails for you, huh, kid?" The white cat licked his paws not caring if she answered. Princess Smoldering Heart flattened her ears and narrowed her eyes.

"Are you angry?" he asked coolly.

Rosie exploded. "You don't know what I've experienced! I've been violated!"

"You and so many before you and so many more to come...yet the question remains. Who are you? What are you going to do? Give up?" Rosie's pride was stung, but she recognized the truth in his words. In the end it didn't matter how unfair her abandonment; what lay ahead would be affected for good or ill by what she did.

Still, she couldn't stop herself from wailing, "I've lost everything!"

"You've lost your past." Joyful as a kitten, he pranced along the limb, somersaulted into the air and landed directly above her. Whorls of glittering stars fell around them, some landing on her pelt, infusing warmth and strength into her body. The white cat brought his face close to hers. His gaze was genuine and warm. "You are free to make your future, Rosamonde. Let us hope it is for all of us a good one." The kits squealed, flopping about the roots in a game of tag.

"How can this be?" she asked. "Where am I?"

"This is a future that can be yours, a powerful future along a path of healing magic."

"What should I do?"

"Live!"

The white cat, her kittens and the meadow faded.

Rosie opened her eyes and sat tall, scouring the dimly visible stars. Her face lifted above the desolation of the alley, she railed at the Gods of Fang and Claw. *I am not defeated! I will make my way and you will help me!* Then taking Mee-am's gift reverently into her mouth, she made a nest behind a tower of boxes, in the stoop of a long-locked door. She spread out the towel, curled and drifted into a dream. Until the Gods of Fang and Claw tested her faith, and Rosie woke in a snake pit.

"Mmmmmeeeow. Hssssss. Hsssssssssfft!" The tomcat spit.

"Yeow-ow-wow-wow-wow!" Wailed another.

Scruff high, she peered from her shelter at shadows against the far wall.

"I'm gonna find you," snarled the owner of an enormous shade prowling from one trash mountain to the next. "Big Spike's got sumpin' for the new girl." Rosie didn't move, didn't breathe.

"Leave her be," another demanded. "She's not yours." Big Spike's wide face split open, showing impossible fangs.

"Ye'r claimin' her then?" More hissing and moaning, raised pelts and unsheathed claws. Rosie crouched in her hideaway, hardly breathing until fingers of morning light chased Big Spike and his rivals back into their moldy nests. She emerged to a run of dirty asphalt and urine-marked piles of trash, her new home.

   🐾   🐾   🐾

The telling left Red exhausted. He yawned, crouched and lifted his legs behind him in a spine-limbering stretch. He spread his toes. Finally, "You must understand. Tall-ones cry tears. We cry inside. They mark their graves with stones. We mark ours with our pain. They build machines to fly in the sky or roar down rumble-roads. When we climb a tree or race through the forest, we're filled with joy. Humans don't know that. They think we have no thoughts or feelings. Makes it easier to kill us." Red sighed. "We threw our lot in with them long ago. We rid their villages of rats for scraps from their tables and a place by their fires." His voice trailed off. "Get some sleep," Red murmured, licking their heads, then curled up beside the basket and closed his eyes. The kits dreamed of their mother, whose fate they prayed was kind.

2 – ABANDONED

Thirsty and hungry, Rosie crept to the clanging door and found a leaky spigot on the wall. She drank deeply. She hadn't eaten for two days and the water hit her belly like a bomb. She waited before taking another swallow. That one didn't hurt nearly as much, so she took another, then another, hoping to outwit her hunger. It kind of worked. She fetched her towel and moved close to the spigot near the door. It was also near the garbage bin, whose odor, Rosie noticed, wasn't as rank as when she first arrived. Laying her treasured cloth behind more boxes, she spent the morning drinking, dozing and making small forays into her new surroundings until some sound or movement sent her scurrying back to her nest.

As the morning deepened, delicious scents of meat and fish seeped beneath the metal door. Rosie couldn't stop herself from standing before it, sniffing along its edges with her mouth slightly open, praying for scraps. With Big Spike and other toms prowling the alley all night, she should be looking for a better place to hide, but all she could think about was food. *When the man comes out, I'll ask for something to eat.* Yet she doubted she could; the Mate had shaken her faith. Movement in the corner of her eye. She slapped the roach scurrying along the metal bin, pinned it with her claws then swallowed it whole. *Ugh.* She ate several more. *Triple-ugh,* but they took the edge off her hunger. She'd caught feathertails in Mee-am's garden and could do it again but there were no gardens here. There weren't even those grass strips with planted trees where tall-walkers pooped their dogs. Beyond this alley was another alley just as dismal as this one, and another after that. Rosie was lost in a maze of human indifference.

The sun sank, and the sky grew dim, the air chill. A heavy thud against the door. Slowly it opened, scraping against the asphalt. Rosie bolted for her makeshift nest as the human lurched into view, again hoisting two plastic bags before him. He set them on the ground, opened the dumpster and tossed them in. Staring at his hand resting on the raised lid, Rosie prayed he wouldn't close it. A voice called from inside.

"Out here," he barked. A mumbled reply. "What?" More garbled words. "What?" the chubby cook looked annoyed, and giving the lid an inattentive thump, stomped inside. It dropped halfway, catching on debris. Rosie scrambled from her nest and stared up at the lid as it sank slowly lower. *Rat whiskers! I'll die one way or the other!* She leaped to the rim, braced herself beneath it and pushed as hard as she could. It sprang open, all the way open, revealing bag after bag of food, more food than she could possibly eat. Rosie took a deep breath. Odors of spoil mingled with scents of fresh meat and fish. Her emptiness overwhelmed her revulsion and down she leaped, ripping the plastic with the fervor of a lioness tearing into fresh kill. Delicious bits of pork, buttery shrimp and roasted duck were followed by a huge serving of rice soaked in fish sauce. Rosie ate every bite, then sat, licking her paws with deep satisfaction. She lay on an unopened bag and stared at the twilight sky. For the first time since her abandonment, Rosie had a sense of well-being. *Nothing improves your mood like a good meal.* Yes, the cook could return, she might get trapped, and who knew when Big Spike would appear on his evening prowl, but Rosie's greatest enemy was hunger. She curled her paws to her full belly, and fell asleep.

Four cats peered down with glowing eyes.

"I'm a fool!" Rosie gasped, leaping to her paws. Ears back and low, she bared her fangs. The largest intruder dropped into the bin and sat staring. She hissed, but the tom seemed unconcerned. He just stared. Rosie warbled a warning.

"We won't hurt you, girl," he said at last, and stood. With an undulating yowl she crouched, lowering her head in attack stance, slapping her tail furiously against the metal wall behind her. "I'm Browser," he trilled and moved toward her. With an ear-splitting caterwaul, Rosie flurried. "Nee-ooow!" he cried, barely escaping her daggers.

She peered up at the six glowing eyes and hissed another warning. *If they pounce, I'm done.* But the big male didn't signal his followers, and they didn't move.

"We could have jumped you while you slept," he said and sat tall, covering his paws with his thick tail.

Rosie also sat, waving her tail over primly placed paws. *Never show fear, always look strong.* But it was too late. Fear came upon her in heart-pounding waves, her brain chewing through escape plans, none of them do-able. Wondering why he talked so much, she heard only snippets of what he said, "...want to help...you must choose..." *Attack or leave, but all this useless chatter...*

The moon climbed high, shining into the bin, and when its light swept over Browser, Rosie gasped. She wasn't sure what she'd expected a feral tomcat to look like: perhaps something broken like Spike's distorted shadow, or a face upon which hateful actions had carved hateful features, but she wasn't prepared for the young lion she saw now. A short coat of black and brown stripes wrapped his muscular shoulders, back, and upper legs. He had white paws, long white socks on his hind feet, a white belly, throat and the softest cream down on his muzzle that came to a point above a brick-red nose. He had a decidedly handsome face. Browser glanced up at his friends and Rosie saw the scars, slender rivers of pink skin curving down his throat and chest. This cat was no coward, and frightened as she was of him, she couldn't help thinking maybe he could keep her safe. Her gaze wandered to his shredded ears. They'd been chewed on more than once. *Meow, he is good looking, but must he be so dirty? Surely he can wash those paws.*

"What do you want?" she asked.

"We saw you dumped. Tough break, kid," Browser said in a surprisingly gentle voice. "We want to help you." Again, Rosie's eyes traveled over the giant paws, shoulders and head, coming to rest on his honest face. She believed him. She'd never met a ruffian, but he wasn't anything like what she imagined. His deference surprised her. Rosie retracted her claws.

Browser looked relieved. "What's your worldname?"

"Princess Rosamonde Whitewhiskers."

A snicker echoed through the bin.

Browser ignored it. "May I call you Rosie?" She nodded. "We won't hurt you, Rosie."

"I'll hurt her," hissed the owner of the snicker, a slender female with silky black fur. She leaned toward Rosie with menace.

"Hush, Kyra," Browser growled, and Kyra pulled back, almost tumbling off the rim. She recovered her balance and hid her embarrassment by cleaning her paws. *I meant to do that,* she seemed to say, swiping a long tongue between gleaming claws.

"Sorry," Browser meowed. "Don't worry, she's harmless." Rosie looked unconvinced. He stepped toward her and this time they touched noses, his moist and cool. His scent stirred feelings within her she didn't know existed and they jumped apart, both quickly dropping their gaze. Neither had expected the spark that passed between them.

"Maybe Rosie would enjoy meeting the rest of us," another voice called, "...in the alley...where it smells better?" A thatch of whiskers bursting from his harlequin face, a black and white tuxedo leaned into the moonlight. "I'm Buster," he said and slipped back into the shadows.

"He's right. Let's get out of here." Browser floated to the top of the bin. "Come on." Rosie followed, but with a full belly and a heavy dose of anxiety, she lunged rather than levitated, hit the side of the bin, and had to pull herself up by her paws. Embarrassed, she was relieved Browser was too busy gliding to the ground to notice her clumsiness. But Kyra noticed, and wore the smirk to prove it. The cats sat in a circle.

"Introduce us, handsome," Buster teased.

"Oh yes, let us meet Princess Full-of-Grace," Kyra scoffed, her inky tail twitching across the asphalt. "I've never been in the presence of royalty."

"I can't help where I was born any more than you can!"

"Rosie, this is Kyra. Kyra...Rosie." Browser said awkwardly.

"Charmed, I'm sure," Kyra meowed. Rosie said nothing. She re-met Buster, the tux with the strange patchwork face. She stared at the little black chin-piece attached to his black helmet with black streamers that zigzagged past each ear. A wide black swath ran the length of his back, his sides and tail while a nervous white pinstripe ran down his throat, fanning into a ruffled shirt front. This jittery pen continued along his belly in varying widths, ending in mismatched white boots. Buster's personality mirrored his looks. He was a study in extremes, both rambunctious and mellow, shy and full of jokes, but one trait had no opposite: Buster was unfailingly kind.

Then Rosie met Ghost. "Soon to be a full-fledged Wisdom Cat, a healing master of herbs and waking-dreams," Browser boasted. Thin and small-boned, the spectral cat seemed tiny even next to Kyra, having been stunted by lack of nourishment in his wildborn mother's womb. Once on his own he'd found prey, however, for his coat rippled an iridescent silver when he moved. Sea-blue eyes smiled from a delicate face and Rosie intuited a gentle spirit familiar with worlds beyond this one. "He's our best hunter," Browser added and she nodded, envisioning Ghost fading from reality in the right light. She faced Browser.

"You said you want to help me?"

"You won't survive the streets alone. You need protection, and someone to help you hunt."

"Hunt?" she asked.

"You've heard of it, right?" Kyra chuffed. Rosie ignored her.

"We've been watching you and we want you to join us."

"You've been...watching me?" Alarms clanged in Rosie's head. Her scruff rose. She stared wide-eyed at Browser, who seemed suddenly, very embarrassed.

"Well, you need us. We're..." Browser began searching for fleas in his hindquarters. He looked so silly Rosie's heart began to soften. Then...

"The old boy's lonely," The tuxedo cheerily announced. "He likes you." Browser's head flew up. He looked furious. Rosie crouched. *What does this ruffian really want? What will he do?* Her mother had been full of stories about the fate of stray females at the paws of feral toms. Fear lifted her scruff again and she backed away from the circle, tensed to flee.

Browser started after her, but stopped himself. "No, it's not like that...I'm not stalking you...I would never...Great Mother's Pelt, you're almost a child..." he groaned, staring at his paws as if in pain. Rosie wondered if she felt relieved or insulted.

Ghost head-bunted her shoulder. "You'll be safe with us," he whispered.

The compassion in his voice calmed her and Rosie remembered her dream, the white cat and her kits. Were these the kin who would lead her there? She sat in thought for many heartbeats. "OK," she mewed. "But I'm *not* a child," she added with a pointed look at Browser.

"Right," Kyra sneered.

"Good choice," Ghost meowed, touching her nose with his. Then Rosie met them all, front and back, even Kyra, who couldn't help snarling when the newcomer sniffed beneath her tail. Everyone else approved of

Rosie's scent and with this ceremony Princess Rosamonde Whitewhiskers was accepted into their group.

"We must return to the Green," Browser meowed.

"Let's eat first," Ghost said, watching Buster sniff and paw at a stack of boxes, hoping a fat mouse would scurry out. None did, so Ghost, with Kyra beside him, crouched at the base of the bin, ready to leap inside.

"Anything special from the kitchen, my lady," the black siren poked at Rosie, who again ignored her. This infuriated Kyra, who, like Rosie, had the sleek good looks of a thoroughbred, though she lacked any papers to prove it. No one knew her story before she appeared on the streets as a young adult, imperious and cynical. Something had broken her heart. She never spoke of it. Ever. Not even to Buster. She was born on First and Broadway after twenty-one turns of the moon. Get over it. Right now, they needed to eat.

Up and in they went. Pieces of meat and fish hit the pavement. When everyone had something to enjoy, the scavengers leaped to the ground. Her jaws busy with a leg of roasted chicken, Rosie sidled up to Ghost. She had no idea what a Wisdom Cat was, but sensed mysteries behind his placid face and wanted to know more.

Keeping counsel with his meal, Ghost said nothing. The last thing he wanted was to share his fears, to upset others with things he didn't yet understand. He was troubled by changes in the Green, troubled by flowers who fell silent when he approached, by sighs of dread from grasses when he brushed against their blades. He felt a hidden purpose, forebodings not yet formed into thoughts, whispers flimsier than spider silk, yet real. They were signs of something, something not-good, rising in their midst. *Our world is dying before our eyes. The uprights, for all their wizardry, refuse to see we're all intertwined, that every life has value and a vital role in the web of life. They believe they create as beautifully as Great Mother, but She needed eons to weave this world, the world they're destroying in just a few human lifetimes.* He gulped his food, hardly aware of Rosie's presence as dark thoughts raced through his mind. He yearned for counsel with Erasmus, but his mentor had been clear: to prepare for your vision-quest, you must trust your own counsel. Well, maybe so, but decisions made now could change more than personal history. He longed for guidance.

Rosie's voice pushed his thoughts aside.

"What?"

"I said, Browser calls you a shaman. I have to know. Can you disappear? Make it rain or something?" Ghost chuffed.

"Browser exaggerates. I use roots and flowers to heal."

"Marvelous," Rosie trilled. "I would like to learn that."

The wizard smiled with his eyes. "Then I'll teach you." They returned to their food. *She has spirit. Strength. If she's who we hope she is, the Prophecy will unfold and with her, if she is...we just might survive.*

After eating and grooming, they set off down the alley, Browser in the lead with Buster beside him. Kyra permitted Rosie to walk at her side, while the little shaman dropped back to the rear. Rosie moved without fear. Her heart stung when she thought of Mee-am, but what could she do? How could she ever find her now?

"Wait! I almost forgot," She cried, dashed back to her spot near the dumpster and fished her prized possession from the debris. Her new friends followed, staring in disbelief when she turned and faced them, a grimy cloth hanging from her mouth.

"What's this?" Browser asked.

Reverently, Rosamonde placed the towel at his paws. She met his gaze. "It's all I have left of Mee-am. She gave it to me the day I was dumped."

"Mee-am?" he pressed.

"My human. My upright."

"You kept something from the two-legged who dumped you?" Kyra tittered.

"Mee-am didn't dump me! Her mate did!" Rosie hissed, and the black beauty stepped back, angry at being challenged.

"Here, let me help." Carefully, Browser gathered the cloth into his jaws and they set off again for home. Rosie warmed to his kindness, but her mood darkened when she thought about the Mate. *What did he tell Mee-am? I bolted from the carry box and ran away? And what of the towel? Did that run away too? Surely she won't believe his lies.* Without realizing it, she whimpered. Kyra glanced scornfully in her direction. *Cats don't cry,* admonished the golden eyes. Rosie remembered the white cat. *Live!* She didn't know what the future would bring, but it couldn't be worse than hiding in the alley, stealing scraps from dumpsters and running from Spike. Tail high, she gazed at the moon and star-laden sky. *This is good,* she thought. *This is good.*

3 – A Home For The Homeless

Silver light from a cloudless sky caressed their small shapes as they hurried home beneath the Moon of Painted Leaves. A chill breeze cut through Rosie's fur, stinging her skin.

"Coldmoons are coming," Ghost said and the group pulled together, moving down one alley into another. Stealthily they traveled the asphalt veins from the city's steel and concrete heart, coming to a crossroad of thundering monsters. They found a sleeping monster and scooted beneath to rest. Hunkered low, their eyes caught every movement, their ears every sound. Rosie could tell they were frightened by their spiked pelts, sensing they feared something worse than fast cars.

"Rule of Survival," Buster whispered. "Always check for two-leggeds. You must see them and hide before they see you."

Kyra hissed. "Yeah, their younglings throw rocks. I have scars to prove it."

Browser dropped Mee-am's cloth at his paws. "They can't hate us more than I hate them," he snarled, to which Kyra chuffed an amen. Shocked by the venom in their voices, Rosie couldn't imagine hating humans. She despised the Mate, but certainly not Mee-am and felt varying degrees of indifference to others. Then again, she'd never met humans who let their younglings throw rocks at homeless kin. Before tonight, she'd never met homeless kin. She crouched with her new friends, trying to understand.

Buster's trembling voice turned her head. "Look over there." All eyes followed his pointing tail across the broad street. A cardboard box leaned crazily in the doorway of an empty shop, trembling like a volcano. A puppy head erupted, yapping at the ankles of passersby. He chased a couple to the corner, his small brown face turned up, hungry for food and for love. But they hardly noticed him as they crossed the thunderous road the pup was too frightened to follow.

Sitting between Kyra and Browser, Rosie squirmed. "Why is he here?"

"Dumped." Came the unanimous monotone.

Rosie unsheathed her claws. "How *could* they," she whispered. Alarm became rage while she watched the little guy dance after anyone who passed, then waddle back to his cardboard home with a whimper, rejected again. At last he grew tired and crawled inside. Now he just watched when someone walked by.

The White Truck arrived. Leatherboots emerged, holding poles that ended in nets or loops of rope. The puppy's instincts told him these men weren't his friends, and he crammed himself against the back of his box, trying to disappear. They scooped him up, and dumped him in a cage. Rosie saw his wide eyes staring through bars until the doors of the truck closed with a finality that made her shudder.

"What will happen to him?"

A long heartbeat before Browser answered. "He has three sunfalls to find a home.

"And?"

"Not and...or..."

"I don't understand," Rosie meowed.

"They'll put him down."

"Put him where?"

Kyra'd had enough of the verbal dodgeball. "He'll be killed."

"WHAT!" Rosie jumped up, hitting her head on the car's chassis. "He's just a puppy!"

Buster groaned. "White Trucks hunt these pathways." He wound his tail tight to his crouching frame. "I'd rather be run over than taken."

"White Trucks?" Rosie asked.

Kyra chuffed her annoyance. "You just saw it, Litterbox Lilly. Two-leggeds throw you inside and take you to a death-den."

"My name is Rosamonde," Rosie chuffed as she and Kyra faced off, nose to nose, ears back and tails lashing. A blood-and-fur roll in the dirt was moments from happening when Buster began to keen.

"They come as an army, a family to take.

21

The weak and the hungry and helpless they hate.
Nets and lightning, struggle and sting.
Once touched and taken, you're nere 'gain seen."

Rosie crumpled, fear sapping the strength from her legs. "Is this true?" she warbled. The Mate was cruel, but Buster was saying uprights worked together to mass murder the kin, something she wouldn't have believed before her abandonment.

"Ghost sees Fetches following the trucks," Buster murmured. "A Fetch for every cat with no exceptions...a multitude of doomed."

"What's a Fetch?" Rosie mewled and everyone stared.

"It's the cat that comes for you when you die," Browser said. Rosie trembled.

"Nothing to fear," Ghost meowed. "A Fetch is like a mirror, with everything we've done, for good or ill, reflected there. When we leave this life, they guide us through Beyond to Fields of Nip and present us to Great Mother." Her own mother, Victoria Silvertip, had never told her anything about Fetches, only about a journey to endless, fragrant meadows beneath blue skies where bluer water flowed and prey was always plentiful, the paradise where Great Mother nurtured her charges.

"If you're a good cat and not unkind, you pass through Beyond to Fields of Nip," Buster added. Rosie's new friends said nothing about the other place, the suffering place her mother warned her about. The Fetches seemed so alien...and right after telling her humans are murdering puppies and kin...it was too frightening to believe.

"You can see these Fetches, Ghost?"

"I can."

"Like I said," Buster asserted. Rosie's gaze wandered between the two. *Impossible! Why should I believe these crazy stories from the court jester and Doctor Brood?*

Kyra lay on her side, giving Rosie a dead-fish stare. She rose to a crouch and crept close, pushing her sly face closer. "Listen, Bed-warmer, before you think we're crazy or lying, think again. We've seen the cages ourselves."

"When they caught my brother we followed his scent and found their death-den." Browser told her. "Fenced yards filled with caged barkers and kin. It reeked of feed, scat...and death. We hid and watched while the uprights pulled them from their White Trucks. Man-friendlies were put in outdoor cages; wildborn were taken inside. Their fear erupted like storms...lots of screaming. Bars on windows, leashes and locks. We've all heard stories about what happens there." Browser fell silent, staring into the distance, but despite the quiet that descended on their gathering, Rosie no longer heard the cars in the street. Then Browser wailed, "Great Mother's Pelt, we couldn't save them."

Ghost whispered into his paws, "My mother died in a death-den."

Rosie's world exploded. *Humans murder homeless animals! Humans murder kin! Lots of kin! Every day!* A cat with a home, she'd always been treated with respect or at least benign indifference by the uprights she met. Except the Mate, who she'd thought an anomaly. Only he wasn't. The wildborn who rescued her revealed a holocaust visited upon her kind! *My kind. I'm homeless too!*

The troupe rose in silence, nudging an almost catatonic Rosie to her paws. Urging her on, they crossed the busy thoroughfare and padded down several more alleys, arriving in an open field.

"Almost home," Buster called as they entered a stand of fir trees. In the quiet of their embrace, Browser turned left, taking them north over a sea of fallen needles. The moon sank below Rosie's latticework view of the sky, leaving her alone in the dark with her new, bleak view of humanity. Their march never slowed and her paw leathers ached almost as much as her heart when Browser finally stopped, lifted his slightly open mouth and sniffed.

"Harmony Tree," Ghost murmured as if greeting an old friend. Blowing in from the east, that *friend* probed Rosie's awareness. Its spiritual fingers combing through her thoughts, she bounced straight up into the air, landing on rigid toes. Kyra snickered at her discomfort as trills and purrs rippled through the rest of the group. Breathing deeply, Rosie told herself she wasn't afraid of a tree, even one that talked to her, and it answered her now. For the first time since her abandonment, she felt comfortable in her own skin, in control of her life. She would decide what her life would be. Harmony Tree agreed.

They continued through the woods until Browser halted at a clearing, and they stood transfixed before an ocean of moon-silvered grass. Wave after wave of rolling hillocks were lined with hedges tangled and thorned, kneeling knights guarding mighty oak kings and earls of elm. Regal birch and alder crowded behind, some leaning forward to greet Browser and his guest.

"The Green," he murmured with pride and in a flash of prescience, Rosie understood that entering this world would change her life forever. Gracefully, she glided down the slope into the meadow. Only Ghost felt her heart thrashing in her throat like a trapped bird. *Courage,* he thought.

They traveled toward a boulder-strewn hillside to the north. A rosemary hedge flourished at its base and Rosie wondered if her friends nested beneath its branches. She fixed her gaze on their goal...and then she didn't, or she...*what have I forgotten?* When she came to herself, she was standing still, alone. *I'm going to that hillside, right? Where's Browser? What's wrong with me?*

"Problems?" Kyra whispered in her ear.

Browser came up her other side. "I should have warned you. Sorry."

"It's better she found out for herself," Kyra snapped.

"It's all right," Ghost reassured her. "Everyone does this at first."

"Does what?" Rosie asked, trying to sound confident to thwart Kyra.

"It's Great Mother magic, the most powerful magic there is. She hides our home from intruders. Our den is a shelterveil, Rosie, hidden until you know it's there."

"What's where?"

"The entrance to our den. Long ago, when Browser and I were searching for a safe place to live, he fell into the opening. That tumble was a gift from Her. As you just experienced, the closer we came, the more disoriented we were." Rosie stared past Ghost. They were almost to the rosemary hedge, but she didn't remember getting there.

"A gift from whom?" she asked still dazed.

"Great Mother. Don't focus on the hillside, Rosie, or before you realize what's happened, you'll have moved past it." Rosie did exactly what Ghost said not to. She stared directly at the hill, and seeing nothing resembling the entrance to a den, turned right at was about to move on.

Browser was beside her. "You'll do fine," he trilled, licking her ear, guiding her beneath the rosemary, emerging on the slope side of the hedge. They climbed the loose dirt and gravel toward a ledge where a boulder shaped like an egg with a slice off it's upper side was sunk partway into the ground. The visible half of the egg was unnaturally smooth. The stone was light and bright, a pale ocher with darker veins branching down beneath the earth. *What hatched?* Rosie wondered, then asked herself if that might actually be true. *It's not stranger than Harmony Tree.*

Above the ridge holding the broken egg, monoliths pushed themselves from the dirt like half-buried beasts. At the top of the hill was a boulder split in two by a twisted pine. A waterfall sprang from the rocks below the tree. It splashed to the bottom where it fed a reedy pool, then cut a path in the meadow's crust, watering pampas grass and willows on its journey south. Close to the hillside, a stump hung over the creek's western bank, its tangled root-ball groping the current, sheltering giant frogs and tiny silver fish. Rosie stared. The stump bristled with life, as if the bole itself were breathing.

Ghost followed her gaze. "A Guardian," he murmured.

"A what?"

"The stump is a Guardian, a protective spirit." Rosie stared at the scarred bark, a favorite place, she would learn, for the kin to measure their stretch and sharpen their claws. She shook her head with disbelief, but couldn't deny the strangeness that clung about the stump...or the egg-stone.

The cats continued up the hill, past clumps of wild violet, fountain grass and yarrow until they reached the egg. Browser leaped on top of it. "Our Guardian Stone," he meowed. "Come, join me. I invite you inside." Rosie leaped to his side, facing the hill. *What does he mean inside?* Above her eye line a horizontal row of four scoops had been dug from the clay and to the right of that, another line of four scoops formed the bottom of a triangular symbol of ten. *What do the markings mean,* she wondered. Browser sprang from his perch directly at the hill. He disappeared.

"Yeow! Wha—what?" Heart pounding, Rosie rose on her hindquarters, fell backward and slid halfway down the hill. Kyra snickered, but Ghost hurried to her side.

"I'm here," Browser meowed, peering down at her. "Come up again and I'll show you," A trembling Rosie re-joined him. "Look at the hillside." She saw only a rock wall. "Look at it, but past it, with your eyes half-shut, and this is important: think shelter, think home, safe, warm..." Rosie tried, sensing more than seeing a blurry emptiness below the symbols. Hidden by the stone, it began at the base of the ledge, an entrance both wider and taller than a large cat. Rosie had never encountered such strangeness. She'd been horrified by the White Truck, astounded by the Fetches and Harmony Tree. Now she was challenged to accept shelterveils. She felt stretched in ways she could never have imagined; this world presented her with such new, strange things, and yet...it felt familiar, as if she were simply remembering a dream.

"What are these markings?" she trilled, pointing with her tail to the scoops.

"The four dots mean earth, one of the four elements from which all things are made," Browser said.

Ghost jumped up beside them. "Our pod is of the earth."

"Meaning what?"

"Meaning Ghost heals with roots and flowers. Now hurry!" Kyra chided, adding her body to the crowded Guardian. She pushed Rosie's rump with her shoulder, toppling her through the shimmering entrance to their den. Rosamonde landed with a thump on the packed dirt floor, staring at a domed ceiling high enough for an upright to stand. Light filtered into the cave from the entrance, and from hundreds of tiny holes tiny creatures had bored to the surface. A sweet aroma led her from the first chamber past three smaller rooms to an arched grotto where moisture trickled down the far wall into a basin of petrified stone. Sorted and dried herbs were stacked against the other two walls, rows of four scoops and triangular symbols of ten scoops etched in repeating patterns across them.

"What is this, Browser?" She asked, sweeping her tail side to side.

"Great Mother's altar."

"With its own water?"

"Ghost tells us the water is proof She cares." His voice carried a smile.

"What do these mean exactly?" she meowed, pointing her muzzle at one of the symbols. Rosie was fascinated by the scoops, so carefully drawn any image turned on its side would look the same.

"Our pod is *of the earth*, the row of four. Air is three, water two. Fire is one."

"There are pods aligned with each Element?"

"Of course. You'll meet them at Harmony Tree." He twitched his luxuriant whiskers.

Rosie's pelt rose from nose-tip to tail, electric with the

understanding she stood in the belly of Great Mother, the sacred She-Cat from whom all life began. This was a home blessed by Her, holy to the Felidae heart. The world Rosie came from seemed barren and lifeless compared to this realm where magic was the norm. Rosie felt alive, as if some long-buried part of her had awakened. *What I feel now is my true self.*

The hillside cats were young, but their journey had been long and they needed rest. Rosie followed Browser into the first room off the main, where he offered her a nest of moss and sweetgrass. Settling on her belly, she pulled Mee-am's cloth beneath her paws and lowered her head to them. The big tom lay on the dirt floor beside her. Too tired to fret over his assumption she would permit him to remain so close, Rosie realized she desired it, eyeing him lazily beneath slitted lids. He stared back at her

"What is it?" she asked.

Browser's nose crinkled and his whiskerpads moved as if he'd speak, but he didn't. Instead his eyes dimmed and he looked away. "It's nothing," he said at last, curling his back against her nest, wrapping his tail around his body with finality. Rosie let her paws brush his back, drawing his warmth and energy up her limbs. She felt safe.

In the blue pre-dawn light, hunters crept bellies to the earth through tall grass. A quivering rump, a pounce, and they returned to the den with two longear for the preypile. The pod formed a circle around the prey and Rosie wondered who would eat first: Browser, their leader, Ghost, their shaman, or the hunters, Buster and Kyra. Browser murmured a prayer of gratitude and they ate together as equals.

Rosie faced a longear's sightless eye. The other carcass already pulled to pieces, her new friends were lapping blood and entrails from shredded fur. The smell was overpowering. She'd caught a crunchy feathertail or two while living with Mee-am, even toyed with a few field mice, but this was so much greater. This was biting through skin and ripping meat from bone, it was raw flesh and flowing blood. Rosie lurched to the Guardian Stone, convulsing until the last of her dumpster dinner slid down its far side.

"What's wrong?" Browser asked with a gentle head-bunt.

Kyra flicked her inky tail. "Plate-licker's too prissy for real food," she taunted, and began licking her paws with exaggerated motions. Rosie yearned to drive her off. She unsheathed her claws, but Browser stiffened and Rosie backed down. Angry and miserable, she crept to her pallet, Kyra's snicker in her ears.

The following morning Rosie woke with a knot where her stomach should be. She padded to the main room and the preypile. Still unable to eat raw meat, especially raw meat that had been waiting all night, she padded to the alcove and filled her belly with water.

Browser came up behind. "Would you like to see the Green?"

"Yes," she said, hoping the outing involved food. They passed Ghost laying on his belly at the cave's entrance, paws tucked and eyes closed.. "Is this where Ghost usually sleeps?"

"No, he's having a waking-dream."

She nodded. "Neow, Browser. I've never heard a word for it before."

"I'll tell you whatever you want to know, but first let's have some fun."

"And maybe some food," she threw in, hoping he understood her distress. They slid down the hill and beneath the rosemary hedge. Tiny blue flowers came loose and fluttered about their paws, while resin from the needles coated their pelts with a heavenly scent. Rosie purred. Browser raced to the tree stump, stretched and sharpened his claws. She did the same.

"This way!" Browser yowled and tore across the meadow, Rosie close on his tail. Climbing a hillock, she gasped and sank down. To the east stretched a moonscape of sand and sun-cracked boulders, a desolation of scorpions, rattlesnakes and carnivorous mice. The air was dry. It smelled of sage and chaparral, good smells, but the desert-scape turned deadly in the dark. Manzanita groves lined the drop-off to the gorge, their branches curved like the spines of old witches with arms spread in a coven dance, gnarled fingers pointing at the star-laden sky. During the night, coyotes would slink beneath the twisting trees into the meadows and woods where kin lived. The kin could not outrun them and every family had suffered loss. The trunk of Harmony Tree held hundreds of claws torn whole from mourners honoring a stolen life. Harmony held more sorrows than Browser could count. But today he told Rosie none of this. He wanted her to stay.

"Where do you hunt?" she asked.

"Not there," he said, his voice a low growl.

28

"Will you show me?"

Browser guided her back to the main meadow. He showed her which thickets hid burrows of longear, which canopies housed colonies of roof rats, and where to dig for the fattest moles and voles. He took her to a stream bank pock-marked with tiny holes, the dens of plump little mice. Rosie paid attention. Then he taught her where the not-good-to-eat animals lived: timid possums in tree hollows and dauntless smelltails who burrowed in rushes by the marsh, sharing space with the mischievous midnight bandits. He told her about the dangerous redtails with their earths in deeper forest and about the badger's sett to the west behind Harmony Tree. Then he explained about the tall-walkers in the southern half of the Green with their false-stone, sleeping monsters and ball games. He warned her not to drink from their pool of blue water. Browser had little praise for humans but did concede the food they tossed into bins yielded good meals for hungry kin. Then he added, "But don't eat much. You'll get a sour belly." Browser must have been hungry too because that started an endless tirade about the cooked meat in the trash bins and how shameful humans were to waste it.

Rosie stared at her paws while they walked, smelling and tasting with her mind. She didn't want to think about her fierce need for food. Her stomach growled with every step, until at last she exploded. "Let's go there now! South where the bins are!"

"Now? South?"

"I could use some of that food, Browser. I'm used to human..." He looked so forlorn Rosie worried she'd harmed him. "Is that wrong?"

"No, it's just I was hoping you'd get used to ours." She stared. Was he really that insensitive? She was starving.

"Of course, but for now...we can go there, right? I mean, if you take me the first time, I can do it myself after that." She looked past him, imagining the trek. She had no idea what a trek south would be like, but she was so very hungry, and that made her brave. "What am I saying? I can do it myself. I just keep going south and avoid the White Trucks, right?" She padded away.

"Rosie! Wait! Of course I'll take you. I was surprised, that's all."

He loped to her side and they moved on, Rosie setting an even, determined pace, her golden eyes missing nothing. They came to Smallmarsh, where the water wandered sideways across the field, never deeper than a cat's thigh. Bordered by cattails and pampas grass, it grew and shrank with the weather and right now, at the close of the dry season, it was about half the size it would be. They skirted along its edge, pausing for a moment to rest. Rosie dipped her forepaw into the clear liquid, disturbing a carpet of moss full of tiny silver fish. They darted away. A frog croaked and her paw flew out at lightning speed.

Browser chuckled. "Rosamonde," he began. She met his gaze. "I need to tell you something." Perched on a rock, he shuffled his big paws.

"Yes, what is it?" *It must be serious for him to call me Rosamonde,* she thought, watching him dig in his chest for fleas.

Nervously, he faced her again. "You're going to meet creatures here you've never seen before."

"Really?" *You struggled for that? Great Mother's Tail you're a bad liar.*

Barely meeting her gaze, he shuffled and mumbled. Finally... "Remember, eyes to the front, danger; eyes on the side, dinner."

"What about tall-ones?" she threw out.

"Yes, exactly...danger." He mumbled, cleaning burrs from his tail.

"What about Mee-am?"

Flicking his spotless appendage, he chuffed, "Mee-am? What about the Mate?"

Head down, Rosie watched little fish flit around insect larvae. She sighed morosely. *Everyone eats but me.* "Yes, the Mate did an evil thing."

"And the White Truck?" Browser hissed.

"I'm sorry for your brother," she whispered and rose, ready to move on.

Farther south the water funneled into a narrow bed, tumbling over boulders into a moss-green pool. Fish swam from its shadowy depths in ascending circles, breaking the surface with a kiss. Rosie's belly clenched and she gazed hopefully at her friend.

"I'm not good at catching them. That's Kyra's hunt."

"Lizards will grow feathers before Kyra brings me a fish," she muttered, padding father south to the shallows where the stream flowed quickly over mossy stones and the water was delicious.

Browser followed. "How much have you hunted? I imagine you had little need." Unlike Kyra, he held no contempt for Rosie over her pampered past.

"I was hoping you might teach me," she said. Side by side, they stared into each other's eyes. They seemed hypnotized. "If you can...I mean, I know you can...if you're not busy."

"I'm not busy," he said, his gaze locked on her face as he absently walked into the stream. Wet to the bottom of his chest fur and feeling foolish, Browser didn't look down, hoping Rosie wouldn't either, and tried a casual backtrack to the shore. *I do this all the time,* he pretended. But the Gods of Pride refused his pleas. His paws slipped in the moss, his legs spread-eagled and he plopped face-down in the water. *Mother of Sharp Claws, this isn't happening,* he gurgled, eye to eye with a bewildered bluegill.

Browser thrashed his way out of the stream while Rosie rushed forward to help. His rear leg kicked out and caught her in the chest, propelling her into a furiously swinging tail. And that tail swung her right into the water. Browser landed ingloriously on his butt. Rosie scrambled out of the stream and stared at him with wide eyes.

"Are you all right?" they asked simultaneously.

"Yes," they answered together.

Browser stood, embarrassed and miserable. "I'm so sorry," he mumbled. She just trilled and began licking herself, then him. They licked each other dry. Hungry as she was, Rosie knew there would be no trip to the southern trash bins today.

The bedraggled couple entered the cave, and scenting the preypile, Rosie's empty belly convulsed. Tormented by hunger, she sniffed at a few mice but still couldn't eat the raw food. They shambled past the others to her cubbyhole where she collapsed in her nest, Browser close by. Neither moved until morning.

Rosie woke and found Browser awake, crouched beside her. "I want you to meet a friend," he said, thumping his tail.

"All right." Yawning, she stretched her paws out before her. "Is it far?" she asked worriedly, and when his eyes answered it was, Rosie deflated into a puddle of tired cat. He licked her ears. "I'll do what I can," she said and rose, discovering she limped.

Browser nudged her leg, but she kept moving, avoiding his curious touch. Finally he pinned a paw, and saw the cracks in her leathers, soothing them with his tongue. "Show Ghost. His herbs heal everything."

But when they entered the big room, the scent of food flooded Rosie's mouth. Hunger pulled her like a puppet to the preypile and all the while she was telling herself she couldn't eat raw meat, she devoured it. Crouched above a longear, she ate all of him. The others watched intently, half expecting the rabbit to reappear, but Rosie was stubborn in all things, and once she crossed a threshold, she arrived. After cleaning her fur of blood with an efficiency that belied it ever bothered her, she sought Ghost. "Can you help me?" My paw leathers cracked."

"Yes," he said, leading her to the alcove where the pod stored their herbs. He examined her swollen pads, and pulling a spiky succulent from a pile, slit it open with a claw, slowly peeling back the skin, careful not to ingest the gel inside. "Stand on it." Rosie obeyed and coolness oozed into her wounds.

"Blessed Mother's milk, this is wonderful!" she exclaimed. "What is that? Oh, I know," she answered herself, "Mee-am used this on my ear once when I cut it playing in the garden." She sniffed the plant. "Aloe. She called it aloe." Then remembering she'd never feel Mee-am's loving hands again, Rosie tucked her tail and fell silent.

"We call it cactus water," Ghost said, "But don't eat it. It's poisonous." Rosie looked alarmed. "Not on your pelt."

She thanked him with a lick to his ear and met Browser at the Guardian. "Let's go," she trilled, leaping down the hillside and under the rosemary with kittenish ease. They trekked along the stream past Smallmarsh, the waterfall and Northbridge. Skirting Bigmarsh, they continued south until Browser led her west through undergrowth, behind two-legged structures and over a field of false-stone where uprights lurched about with a ball. The cats slipped from the Green with tails high, passing many rows of dens before entering the destination alleyway lined with fences and small huts where the uprights put their monsters to sleep. Between the weedy yards littered with trash, grew vegetable or flower gardens, and Rosie would slow her stride to sniff the sweetened air, remembering her own garden where Mee-am turned the earth.

A thin barker yapped at them. His neck was raw from the rope that imprisoned him. Attached to a chain ending in a spike pounded into the ground he never had much freedom, and now he'd wound it around his house until he couldn't even reach his empty bowl or overturned water dish. His whimpering described a life of loneliness and pain.

"Shut up, dog," a two-legged yelled through his open window. Now Rosie understood Browser's hostility toward them. The cowed hound lowered himself to the ground. He thumped his tail wildly as she came abreast, but she passed without saving him.

Two large dens faced each other across the alleyway. A pattern of window, door, window repeated up three levels of rust-stained stucco and brown wood doors. Despite the dumpsters at the end of each building, garbage blighted the ground. There wasn't a single patch of green. Anywhere. No grass, no flowers, not a tree.

"Who lives here, Browser?" Rosie asked as wildborn appeared like haunting ghosts from under sheds, dumpsters and heaps of discarded junk.

"Lots of kin," he murmured, nodding to various thin, scruffy cats. "Some were abandoned, more are wildborn of abandoned parents or grandparents. Here comes Gentleman Jim. Careful, he's wrong in the head." A big gray and white tom limped toward them, favoring a leg with a festering sore. The skin on his belly hanging slack below his ribs, his pelvic bones threatened to poke through with every step. Rosie averted her face, helpless before his suffering.

"Nee-oww, Gentleman Jim," Browser called.

"Back off," Jim growled, limping past them without a glance.

"What happened to him?" Rosie asked.

"Dumped. Had a home until his tall-ones moved and left him behind. Broke his heart. He's crazy now." Watching the hapless cat mutter down the alley, Browser chuffed angrily but Rosie trembled with excitement.

"Why don't we hunt and bring him something to eat!" Browser looked dumbfounded.

"I don't have time to feed Jim *and* care for the needs of Hillside Pod." Rosie's eyes narrowed to slits, the tip of her tail twitching erratically.

"Can't he join Hillside Pod?"

"Rosie..." *Does she really not understand?* "He wouldn't."

"You're looking at this all wrong, Browser. What's so hard about bringing Jim some prey when we come here?"

"Nothing...I guess," the pod leader said, wondering how many homeless cats she'd insist he feed.

"Good!" Rosie leaped to her paws, then looking confused, quickly sat and scratched furiously behind her ear. Something traveled her pelt, biting as it ran. "Furballs! What?"

"Fleas, Rosie, Fleas!" Browser cried.

"Fleas?" she mewled. "How can you endure this?" She remembered the stinky drops Mee-am squirted on the back of her neck with talk of fleas. Back then, Rosie hadn't a clue what fleas were and was annoyed by the reek, but if these were fleas...well...she'd trade a tuna fillet for a smelly spot between her shoulders.

"Dirt baths help..." Browser began, "You know, a good roll in..." His voice dropped with the approval rating on her face. Then he got a better idea. "...the round leaves of the Medicine Tree. Fleas run from the scent. We'll bring some into the den." Rosie continued to rake her skin. "You get used to...if you're born with..." He'd never thought to be embarrassed about his fleas, but suddenly nothing seemed more squalid. *More dirt baths,* he decided, staring down the alleyway. Browser had been born in a place like this, forced to fang and claw his way through the world as soon as he left his mother's teat. Once proud of his survival, now he felt small. *How could a princess understand? In her world, warmed cream is served in china bowls while she rests on silk pillows.*

"What's wrong, Browser?" He could smell the sweetness of her.

"Nothing." Rosie was about to press him for an honest answer when movement caught her eye.

Angel scooted under a fence and loped toward them. Her small, sturdy body covered with gray-ocher fur, her warm eyes sparkled with intelligence. Strong with life-force, she was as soft as a field mouse and possessed the quiet, slow-dawning beauty of the eternal mother. None of this was lost on Rosie, who was surprised by her own jealousy.

"Browser," the newcomer hailed.

"Angel," he meowed affectionately. They touched noses and licked each others' ears.

"Angel, this is Rosie." Rosie squirmed as they eyed each other.

Angel was calm. "You're the one who's supposed to—? Why, you're just a girl!"

"I am *not* a child," Rosie proclaimed, strutting past the feral queen with tail at full mast, scruff ruffled and whiskers spread.

Angel's eyes sparkled with amusement. "My mistake," she trilled.

Browser changed the subject. "Where's Two Fang, where's Rocky?"

Angel lowered her ears. "White Truck. Bright Eyes is gone too and

Trinket...and Blake...Sadie-Lady and her kits. So many have been taken."

Browser faced her, cleaning the asphalt with an angry tail. "When?"

Angel blinked. "Sunfall last and the one before."

"Leatherboots came...then came again?" Browser stepped back and began pacing around the two queens. "I've never known them to do that."

"They've never taken so many of us before. It was as if they knew where we hid."

He stopped abruptly. "They *did* know, Angel. Some two-legged must have told them." He began pacing again, hissing and snarling to himself.

Angel scanned the windows of the large dens. "They took a family of barkers too. I'm not glad, even though they stole our food and chased us."

"Your kits?"

"I lost the smallest to green cough but the others flourish. Luckily, I'd moved our snuggery before the White Truck came..." She lowered her head, remembering, then took a deep, cleansing breath. "We eat well, those of us still here."

"Really?"

"We have a provider now."

The pod leader squirmed. *Anything but that.* "Okay," he said, trying to sound pleased, hoping she would talk of something else. She didn't.

"She comes when most two-leggeds sleep. When she came earlier, the other tall-ones," she pointed with her muzzle at a high window, "yowled at her for feeding us. I think she's brave."

"It's easy to be brave when you're so much larger than your enemy."

"No, Browser, she's brave against her own." Angel knew he detested all uprights, even the few who helped kin, but she couldn't help wanting his approval. "Last brightmoon, she caught a nearby colony in carry boxes, and returned them unharmed two sunfalls later." Browser's swinging tail said she wasn't getting what she wanted, but Angel was telling her story to Rosie as well. "She killed their fleas and ear bugs." Angel paused, shuffling her paws. "It's true they don't breed anymore," she murmured in a voice so soft Rosamonde had to stretch her neck to hear. "That's been hard for the queens...and the tips of their right ears are missing, but they're unharmed and safe. She feeds them and now she's feeding us."

"Yeah and she'll trap you soon too," Browser snarled. "And make you barren!" The fierceness of his tone surprised the females.

"I've birthed enough kits," Angel snapped. "Anyway...when their milk-feeding is done I'm giving my litter to—"

"Angel!" Browser slapped his tail on the ground so hard it raised a cloud of dust.

"No. Great Mother sent this Provider to save my babies. She told me in a waking-dream." Rosie pressed her body to Angel's in solidarity, and they licked each other's ears. Then the three cats plopped on their bellies, tails swishing in unison in stiff, irritable bursts. No one spoke.

Angel had experienced prophetic dreams all her life. All kin had waking-dreams, but most let them flow into the vast sea of the unconscious mind. Browser absorbed his visions like sunlight on his pelt. But Angel, like Ghost, lived with full awareness of her dreams, and Browser had learned to trust them. That made her decision all the more unsettling. Browser despised tall-walkers, even a Provider, even a Provider vetted by a waking-dream. He found their furless bodies ugly and feared their unblinking, predatory stares.

Angel broke the silence. "I'm alone, and now the White Truck patrols my alley. Coldmoons will arrive soon and my kits came late in the season. They won't survive!"

Browser lowered his gaze and muttered. "The strong will survive."

"Cruel!" Rosie hissed.

The tom glared at the queens, but when he spoke again, his voice was tender. "You and your kits need never go hungry. There's always room at my preypile."

Ears twitching and eyes averted, Angel murmured, "I think about that, then I remember Kyra." Rosie giggled despite herself. "The Provider is kind, Browser. She'll give my kits a home, a real home...inside." But the words she meant to end the argument, only made it worse.

His scruff rose. *How could Angel, of all kin, forget my brother's cries, forget they killed him. Angel betrays us.* "Real home...inside?" He snarled, lashing his tail. "You're a fool and you'll murder your kits!" Infuriated, Angel flew at him, swiping his face. Her claws drew blood. Browser didn't defend himself and surprised by her own behavior, Angel collapsed into a panting hunker.

"He's wrong," Rosie whispered. "If this upright is kind enough to feed you, she might give your kits a home. I lived in a home once. It's wonderful." Angel trilled hopefully and Rosie continued. "She might give you a home too."

Browser loomed over them, eyes flaring like little suns. "You talk as if no-furs are truthful," he spat. "You can't trust them. *Any* of them. They're liars." He circled the females, growling angrily to himself.

"You're the liar!" The little mother cried.

And Browser froze. *How does she know I haven't told Rosie my secret? I haven't lied, not really.* But he had, really. And Angel knew nothing of his secrets; she was talking about the tall-ones.

Browser backed away, but Angel came after him, whispering in his ear. "I saw our home in a waking-dream. It's safe and there's food and it's full of love." The pod leader turned and stomped off without a word.

Rosie gave her new friend a quick lick goodbye. "Hey, wait for me," she cried. Browser glanced at her, then away, remaining silent all the way home. His anger wasn't aimed at her, or even Angel, although their tolerance of two-leggeds was more than he could bear. He saved his rage for himself, for his cowardice, his unworthiness. *Rosie deserved the truth. I should have told her before I brought her to the Green, but her trust had been so fragile.* Now his silence could only be seen as deceit. If he told her now she'd despise him and Browser didn't think he could bear that.

It was no accident Hillside Pod had come to the alley where Rosie was dumped. Guided by Ghost' waking-dream, they were waiting for the Discarded Queen. They saw her abandonment, and when *Princess Rosamonde Whitewhiskers* introduced herself, her name itself was proof. Rosamonde of noble blood, Princess Rosamonde. Browser's task was to bring her to Hillside Pod where she would settle in the Green, mate with the king, and give birth to a prince, thereby stopping the genocide and saving all kin everywhere. So said the Prophecy.

Then he watched Rosie hide in the alley. She was so young and vulnerable, yet strong, demanding protection from their gods. Browser had feelings, and they led to doubt.

"It feels like kin-napping," he said, sitting with Ghost the night before the pod revealed themselves to Rosie.

"It will unfold as Great Mother wills," Ghost reassured him. "You've been given a great mission."

"But it feels like kin-napping," he said again.

"We'll ask. If she refuses, she's not The Discarded Queen. We're not hurting her getting her out of this alley."

"That's true...we're not."

Ghost shook his head. "We all live in ignorance of Great Mother's plans, Browser. None of us can really know The Truth." His eyes smiled. "Let her decide if this is her destiny. Either way, Great Mother honors you with a mission to save the Green." That rang sweetly in Browser's ears and his thoughts turned cheerful. Knowing he would help the kin, he bit down on his mouse with renewed relish, then took another from their preypile.

Born into its promise, most of the kin in the Green were aware of the Prophecy. The wise and curious recited the poem, passing it parent to child, but even those who'd never heard the words believed its fulfillment would bring an end to their suffering, a new era when uprights no longer murdered wildborn. Browser was honored to help end the genocide. The only thing not part of his plan was falling in love with Rosie.

Browser didn't know who his father was. No big daddy from their neighborhood ever came to meet him or his siblings, but he was certain his father didn't have a name like Thurgood Rubbelly the Fourth. *I come from common stock,* he'd told himself, proud to be strong and adaptable. Now the qualities that had seemed important, mattered little. He lacked the one virtue needed to reveal his love: the right birth.

Great Mother's Tail I'm an idiot! He tore down the alley, past the dens then through the thicket, wishing he could hide. He knew Rosie struggled to keep up, but refused to slow down, fearing to look at the one he so desired. *She'll see how much I care. Will she laugh at me? No, she has class. I need to talk to her. What are you thinking, fool? That she might actually love you, a flea-bitten street fighter? She's polite because she has breeding, but she could never love a brute like you!* Self loathing came in torrents. His paws thudded against the earth. *It's true! I love her! I love her...but I can never be the king she must marry.* He staggered forward, feeling as if his heart had been ripped from his chest and trampled beneath him.

After evening meal, everyone lounged about the preypile to share stories from their day. Rosie settled next to Browser hoping to talk, but without a glance he rose and crossed to Ghost. The little wizard and Buster didn't notice, but Kyra did. Rosie's scruff rose with embarrassment, and she stalked from the chamber, the black queen's smirk burning into her heart. She collapsed on her nest of moss and herbs, burying her face in Mee-am's cloth. Their separation had never felt more bitter, or Rosie more alone. *I'll survive. I've been through worse,* she told herself, tucking her tail and paws, but kept her ears high while Browser recounted the White Truck's death sweeps. From the silence that followed, she sensed they all felt bitter and alone.

🐾   🐾   🐾

The moon stretched silver fingers across the floor, casting Browser's shadow over Rosie's sleeping body, the only embrace he was entitled to enjoy. But she felt the touch of his spirit, and it woke her. His energy was melancholy and part of her yearned to comfort him. She didn't. Rosie dozed and woke many times, aware of his presence without letting him know. When he pushed his nose into her pelt and breathed her in, purring softly, even then she didn't let him know.

Later, Browser crouched on the Guardian, counting the last of the stars. He had loved Rosie from the moment he saw her yowling at the gods. He would love her forever and never call her his own. This was his punishment for lying, for bringing her here, an offering to their king.

4 – PLIGHT OF AN ANGEL

Angel crept through tall grass toward a wooden pallet where she'd hidden her kits. Shiny black spiders with red hourglasses on their bellies stood guard, swaggering along the mildewed planks to repel human hands. Angel trilled and three little faces appeared. Now six weeks old, every one of them had a full belly, felt loved and safe, and knew the price of disobedience. They wouldn't dare leave the nest without the permission she'd just given. Angel was an excellent mother.

Her own life had been hard; she'd barely finished her milk-feeding when her own mother was taken. Her father, she never knew. Surviving by wit and caution, she froze or fled with every sound, scent, or change in the wind. She taught herself to hunt and to forage in dumpsters, how to hide, how to build a nest, how to insulate it against the cold with whatever was available. She became a master opportunist and she survived. As seasons passed, Angel birthed many litters, but she never forgot her first, born when she was hardly more than a kit herself. Somehow she managed to feed and protect them.

Angel was tough, and she was smart, but life on the streets was dangerous. Without a home or human to protect her, she was fair game for the stupid and cruel. Hit by stones, chased by predators, she'd been wounded more than once. She'd fallen ill with nothing to save her but her will to survive. To Angel, Death was a trickster. Brushing her whiskers with a bony paw, it had gathered many loved ones and left her breathing. Angel had danced beneath seventy-two brightmoons, but since she'd lost her friend and mate to the latest sweep of the White Truck, she'd had enough. She was tired of being hungry, cold and frightened, tired of running, tired of hiding. She'd run from the Leatherboots for as long as she could remember and she'd be running until she couldn't. To the uprights being homeless was a crime and death the only punishment.

So after a romp to stretch their legs, she herded her litter back under the pallet. Other than the babies and her cousin Long Claw, Angel was now alone. And thinking on Long Claw, she wasn't surprised when he slipped into their shelter, green eyes glittering. "We have to leave," he whispered, fear scent rolling off his gray and white pelt.

"Why?"

"A tall-one, the heavy woman with mean eyes stalks the alley. She's shining a light into the sheds, looking for your kits. I'm sure of it!"

"What have we done to her? Why, Long Claw, why do they hate us?"

"I don't know, but we need to leave. It's not safe here anymore." Long Claw knew uprooting a queen from her snuggery was difficult at best. He licked Angel's paws with pleading eyes.

"When?" She asked.

"Tonight, after sunfall."

"What about the Provider?"

"What about her?"

"I don't want to lose her."

"Maybe she'll find us."

"No, she won't." Angel bathed each of her nursing kits, then stared into her cousin's sad eyes. Lying on her side, brushing her babies with a slow tail, she was content. "I'm not leaving," she declared and realizing his pleas were futile, Long Claw left. It pained Angel to deny him, but losing the Provider would be worse. She'd endured too much hunger to abandon a food source at the first sign of danger. She washed her kits again, then curled around them and dozed.

At sunfall, Angel again let her brood out to play. They stalked one another through the weeds and chased their mother's waving tail. She cherished her children's joy, dreading the days of bittercold when hunger came daily and beetles and worms and skinny birds became great swag in their haunted eyes. They couldn't lose the Provider. They just couldn't.

Gravel crunched beneath heavy wheels, pulling Angel from her thoughts. She leaped to her paws. The kits raced to their mother and were ushered beneath the pallet as doors slammed and Leatherboots stomped along the other side of the fence. Long Claw squeezed beneath a weathered post, scuttling toward them with fearful eyes.

"White Truck!" he hissed, as he and Angel slipped into the nest, peering between blades of grass at the gate. It creaked open and two tall-walkers entered the yard. One was heavy and red-faced with small mean eyes. He held the pain stick that sent shocks through your body when it touched you. The other, tall and thin, carried a net on a long pole. They were Leatherboots wearing leather gloves, the most dangerous breed of men.

"Is that where she said the nest was, Mr. Bleggs?" the thin one asked, showing deference with tone and body language toward the alpha male.

"Shut up already, Wilson. You're gonna scare 'em off." They advanced, the thick one grunting as he reached for the pallet, aiming the pain stick with his other arm. The tall one stood to the side and readied his net. Long Claw pushed Angel behind him and unsheathed his claws. With felid instinct, he focused on Bleggs' pulsing carotid. He hissed like a venomous snake and his powerful legs tensed to attack. *I'll die with this furless fatty's flesh on my fangs but Angel and the babies will escape.*

A shriek split the air. The uprights turned, staring as if frozen through the open gate at Gentleman Jim who perched on the hood of the White Truck, his body swaying side to side. His head trembling violently, his eyes rolled into his skull as he yowled again and again, raising furrows of paint kneading the monster's shiny surface.

This agitated Bleggs and Wilson greatly. "What the fur fly–" Bleggs cursed and forgetting the cats trapped beneath the pallet, both men bounded toward Jim.

"Yeeeeee-ooooow-wow-wow-wooooow-yeeeooww," the crazed cat wailed. Wilson slammed his net on nothing as Jim tumbled off the far side of the truck. Despite his infected leg, Jim raced down the alley ahead of the two men while Angel and Long Claw scurried from the nest and out the gate, kits dangling from their jaws. The largest kit was forced to run on his own, but fear made him strong. The fugitives put a safe distance between themselves and the humans before they checked on Gentleman Jim who sat with his rump against the last fence, all signs of frenzy gone. When Bleggs and Wilson rushed him, he didn't run. He merely looked up at Bleggs and the pain stick he'd raised to his shoulder, ready to plunge a shock to Jim's side.

"Wait!" Wilson yelled.

"Are you crazy? He'll escape!" Jim embraced them with soft eyes and Bleggs lowered his weapon. "What's that sound?"

"He's purring," Wilson whispered, laying his net on the ground. He lifted the bony tomcat into his arms, careful of his festering leg.

Bleggs watched as Wilson stroked Jim's head and under his chin with gentle fingers. "He's real skinny, boss," Wilson said, surprised when Jim's fur compacted beneath his hands and his skin slid loose along his bones. He cooed to the broken stray, who purred, loud and ragged before settling into a steady rumble of contentment. Years of struggle had carved a bitter grimace into the cat's expression, but the warmth of Wilson's hands erased those lines. Love was the gift that eased his suffering, and Jim forgave the humans who had betrayed him. He raised his forepaw to Wilson's cheek, then closed his eyes. His purr faded. Jim left the world that hadn't wanted him loved again at last.

The tall man carried Jim to the truck, wrapped him in a towel as if he were sleeping and held him in his lap. He turned to the window so Bleggs couldn't see his grief. He'd experienced worse in the two years they'd been working together, but Jim had touched his heart.

"We screwed up, losing those ferals," Bleggs said, glancing at the towel. "Didn't lose this one though," he chuckled, reaching for it. "I'll incinerate it."

Like a mother cat protecting her kit, Wilson's hand batted Bleggs away and he pulled Jim's body closer. "He's not an *it* and I'll take care of *him*," he said, his voice hoarse with emotion. "...sir," he added. A moment passed in silence, then by way of apology, "I have a big backyard." Bleggs didn't respond. They both knew what Wilson proposed was against the rules.

No matter, Bleggs told himself. *There's rules I don't like much either.* "I always knew you were a softy." He paused, then, "I guess it's all right to do a favor." The word 'favor' told Wilson one would be expected in return. He didn't care, not now, and Bleggs said nothing else.

Years of loneliness and hunger faded away and Jim felt no pain. He padded beside a stream through a meadow of nip and climbable trees. Bending over the water, he saw the reflection of a muscular youngling with sleek fur and a perfect build. Great Mother lowered her massive paw and lifted him to her azure eyes.

"Welcome, my beloved. I name you Radiance, for that is your true nature. Here you will know only joy." Radiance stood again in the fragrant grasses, his back warmed by sunlight. In the distance, he spied friends from long ago.

❀   ❀   ❀

Angel and Long Claw loped down alley after alley until the scent of uprights faded. They followed a tree lined rumble-road twisting down a hill, ending in a tall metal fence with a locked gate. Following the fence, they found a skunk-hole and entered a field of thistles and foxtails. Angel's largest kit, Cloud, spied a creek and bounded to it, bending his taupe head for a drink. He jerked away in disgust. The water smelled metallic and left a rainbow slick on stones. Angel and Long Claw, still holding the smaller kits in their jaws, made for the center of the field where they found a strip of asphalt covered with rusting monsters. Beyond that, rising from the weeds like an open mouth was a cave of broken glass and concrete, a skull with teeth of metal gears and a conveyor belt tongue. Farther in, exposed stairways rose into space, ending nowhere like unfinished thoughts, while cables dangled without purpose over machines littering the floor. Pieces and parts lay oddly about as if dropped when the humans suddenly departed. Coffee cups, overflowing with rainwater warped the desks beneath them and open boxes of papers had turned to moldy mush. The cavern smelled of mold and felt ominous, as if life had been canceled here mid-dream, and the uprights dissolved where they stood.

Windows ran the length of the building, their metal frames leaking rivulets of rust down the stucco outside. Inside, cubbyholes lined the walls, some with wooden partitions and doors with windows of milky glass. Some were just splinters and shards on the floor. It felt lonely here, abandoned, and Long Claw was sure it was haunted. He wanted to leave but exhaustion won. Dropping the kits into a dry box they found beneath a desk in a cubbyhole near the entrance, Angel climbed into the makeshift snuggery and nursed her babies to sleep.

"It feels so bad here," Long Claw moaned. "This land is wounded. It's not safe. That's why the tall-walkers left."

"We won't stay long and perhaps the haunting will keep others away."

The scent of dog filled their noses and Long Claw jumped up, his scruff on high alert. "Evidently not," he rasped. "I'll look around." Angel huddled over her kits, agitated until her cousin returned. "The barker's gone," he assured her, settling wearily on his belly. "But it might return.

Maybe it lives here."

"I doubt that," she meowed, curling around her babies' warmth. Angel slept as soundly as they did and didn't wake until moonlight shone through a gap in the roof and fell upon her face. Looking at her sleeping cousin, she felt uneasy. *Long Claw's right about this place. We can't stay. But* she was hungry now. She slunk into the field where she found several mouse holes in a patch of dirt and settled nearby. Soon a little creature crept out to forage in the bright and shadowy world beneath the moon. Angel killed it with a single blow, then ate it in two bites.

She crouched over a new hole. That's when she smelled the dog. Overwhelming, unmistakable, stinking foul feral dog! Angel whirled around to fetid breath and vicious yellow eyes. Yowling with terror, she twisted 180° mid-air, hurtled across the field, jumped the stream and rocketed toward the hole in the fence, the hound right behind her. She dove and he lunged, growling and snapping. Fierce pain! Her tail caught in his vice-like jaws, he shook and pulled and Angel began sliding backward through the hole. Hooking her front claws into the earth, she kicked dirt in his eyes with her hind legs. Demon-dog jerked backward and Angel's vertebrae snapped, delivering fur, skin and bones into his mouth. He released her, choking, spitting her parts as he dug deeper and squeezed through the fence, now several heartbeats behind. Angel ran for her life, screeching with pain.

Faster! They streaked into the maze of human dens. She cleared bushes, boxes and bikes, dodged hedges and monsters, faster, faster, down the center of the street. Angel lunged, faster, faster. She leaped forward, faster, faster, faster. And still the thud of his paws, the click of his nails, his sweat-stink and foaming jowls came ever closer, his growling louder than her pounding heart. Faster! Her paws no longer touched the ground and the world flew by in a blur but the creature would not relent.

Then she saw the fence. Bursting ahead, she leaped. Up, up, up, she climbed the linked chains until she danced along the top. Whang! Monster-dog slammed into it, tossing Angel into the air. But Great Mother thrust out Her Paw and Angel fell to the far side, landing in a cushion of weeds, cheating death one more time. Whang! Whing! The galvanized steel sang as the frenzied beast threw himself against it. Whang! Again. Whang! Angel lay with her heart pounding, too exhausted to move. The fence held.

At last the hound realized he couldn't reach her. He barked furiously, then whipped around and ran off. Angel worried he'd find another way, so she roused herself and limped down the road. She climbed a myrtlewood still in bloom, pressing her nose into its blossoms to calm her still-racing heart. Once her breathing calmed, she loped down the center of the road, looking for a safe nest to rest before returning to her kits.

Into a yard, down a pathway of smooth stones, Angel climbed the porch steps, opening her mouth to taste the air. A faded scent marker near the door told her kin once lived here; now she sensed tall-walkers inside, dreaming in their snuggeries. From the porch roof hung a swing. Angel crawled behind the bottom cushion, covering herself with the top. She closed her eyes, grateful Death had missed yet again. *There's a reason I'm spared,* she told herself and slipped into a dream.

Morning came long before sleep had healed her. Angel watched from behind the cushions as human kits burst through the door and scampered down the walk to the corner. A huge yellow monster rolled to a squealing stop, opened its mouth with a hiss and swallowed them whole. It roared away. A big daddy lurched from the den, climbed into a small monster and made it purr. He left, but Angel sensed the female still inside. As they tend to be kinder, she relaxed, permitting herself to rest on the swing's pillow rather than beneath while she licked dried blood from her tail. The wound was clean, snapped off, not shredded, and would heal. It was shorter by a third, but it would heal. Her teats taut with milk, the needs of her babies filled her thoughts and Angel leaped to the porch just as the door opened and she and the human mother faced each other, both surprised.

"Well, who are you?" the woman chirped. Neither moved. She saw Angel's tail and gasped. "Are you all right, baby? What happened to you?" Crouching and reaching with an open palm, Angel sensed she meant no harm, but almost nothing is as dangerous as letting a two-legged touch you. Anything could happen. Angel leaped from the porch and ran.

All night she had dreamed Long Claw kept her babies safe, but he couldn't feed them. She must hurry back. *What if the hell-hound returned to the field?* Angel ran faster. *No! Why should he?* She resumed a less strenuous trot. *What if he wanted revenge for my escape?* She quickened her pace again. *That's crazy. He doesn't know my babies are hidden in the building. Yes, but he can sniff them out. Perhaps he hunts there. What if he does live there!* Heart pounding, the anxious mother bolted toward the field.

Angel slid through the skunk hole, hurtling toward the hulking shell of stained stucco and broken glass. She froze before a wide swath of grass, beaten down and red with blood. Violence clung to the area like a tortured spirit. Trembling, Angel parted the tall blades with her muzzle and found the dog dead, his chest gashed and neck ripped open. His blood had sprayed the weeds. Warily she approached the hulk's entrance, and found Long Claw's lifeless body thrown against rubble, his broken neck twisted unnaturally, his blood staining the ground. Angel sank to the earth, overwhelmed with sorrow. The loving energy who had been her cousin was gone.

Angel rubbed her cheek against his lifeless shoulder, then threw back her head and keened. Little mews answered her wail. Great Mother Be! Noble Long Claw had given his life for her kits. Cloud bounded to his mother purring like an engine, the other two close behind. Angel ran to them, licking their small faces in a frenzy of joy. She led them to their box and nursed, trilling her gratitude. Long Claw had saved them. Every brightmoon for as long as she lived she would sing of his greatness.

Once the kits slept, Angel left to feed herself. She caught a mouse, quickly ate her kill, and set about burying her cousin. A recent skywatering had softened the earth and she dug a depression at the base of a straggly oak near the stream, then dragged the hero's body into the hole. She searched the field for herbs to cover him. His favorites, chamomile and valerian, she dropped around his face. Their bodies threw long shadows over his grave when Angel and her kits said goodbye.

"The Great Life wastes nothing," she told them as they listened with tall ears and wide eyes. "All is transformed. Long Claw's life in this body is finished and we are sad for it, but the light he emitted has only moved on. It can't be destroyed."

Cloud shuffled his paws. "I don't remember a life before this one, mother."

"Nor do I, but I've had glimpses of Spirit. I believe this, son." The kit gazed sadly at Long Claw's empty body. Now it would feed beetles and worms, for Great Mother loved all her creatures.

Angel sang the Song of Loss, followed by a poem she dreamed while gathering the herbs.

Long Claw Fearsome, claw and fang,
He gave his life for mine.
Then leaped so high he caught a star
And left this world behind.

Long Claw Mighty, pure and brave,
Now plays in Fields of Nip.
The sacrifice he freely gave,
Beloveds shall not forget.

Long live Long Claw! Long live he
Who gave his final breath,
Long live Long Claw! Hero he
His light shines even in death.

They covered the hole with dirt and lay on top to tamp it down. While Angel rested on Long Claw's grave, energy pulsed through her and she lowered her lids in a waking-dream. She saw the woman who caused so many deaths in the alley walking with her light and stick, poking in trash heaps for babies.

She was ugly. Her neck was stuck atop her spine at an angle, like the handle of a cane. On the end of that short neck was a knob of a face, round, flushed and fleshy, with short, steel-gray waves of hair lying close to her scalp. The face itself wasn't much, a pinched mouth, a bump for a nose and two small eye sockets, each holding a smaller, dull gray bead. The beads darted this way and that, always looking for little lives, vulnerable lives, lives different from hers who were easy to hurt. The beads saw little else, no color, no beauty, just as the nose smelled nothing sweet and the lips never tasted love.

Bound by judgment, the eyes hardened with age until nothing got through, no doubts, no troubling thoughts and certainly no wonder at the world. Anything not from *Authority* was rejected. New ideas were just a case of indigestion any good enforcer knew how to cure.

With passing years the eyes clouded over, and the outside reflected what was true within. Toward the end, *Authority's* commands blurred and other, more doddering ideas took hold. By then, the bones of those she had tortured were dust, their broken hearts long silent and their screams gone from the world. Only when she couldn't sleep and didn't know why, when ghostly whispers were almost heard, only then would the beads bleed tears and her ossified heart beat with a glimmer of remorse...for something...something they had made her do...what was it? How she would struggle for clarity. But it eluded her, as did redemption, for even as Death claimed her she wanted others to pay for her sins.

Starlight would tell Ghost the price of eating meat is not knowing past lives. Angel believed the price of cruelty is not knowing this one.

Angel tucked her babies beneath the rotting pallet. The journey back had been long and torturous. They were all exhausted, but Angel rested only a little before rousing herself to stand vigil by the gate.

The moon sailed high above the alleyway when the human finally came. Dropping her satchel near the dumpster, she began filling bowls with kibble, shoving them beneath the bin with her cane. It gave the ferals protection from the elements and from uprights, who were loathe to stick their hands into the filth to remove the food. Rolling her hair around her hand and tucking it up with a pin, the Provider squatted on the balls of her feet. Her long skirt brushed the pavement, so she pulled it up between her knees and tied a knot. She was filling bowls with water when Angel presented herself, Cloud dangling from her mouth. Padding cautiously toward the human, she placed her baby on the asphalt just outside her reach.

"Oh, Mommy!" the woman cried, opening her palm toward Cloud, exactly as she had in Angel's waking-dream. Angel sniffed it. Her son trembled but obeyed his mother's command to stay. The Provider cooed, stroking his back and narrow shoulders and soon the kit was arching the dome of his head against her palm, purring ferociously. With her other hand the Provider offered kibble and Cloud gobbled it up. *Great Mother's Tail, it's good!*

In slow motion, the human removed her jacket and spread it on the ground, placing the kit in the center of its folds. Angel appeared from behind the fence with her other boy, then fetched her precious girl. The Provider wondered what horrors the feral mother had endured. *Life must be tough to give your babies away,* she thought, noticing the dried bone tip protruding from her shortened tail.

"Good mommy, good mommy," she cooed, hastily preparing the last dishes for the local kin, whose eyes gleamed thankfully from their hiding places. The mewling kits tucked in her jacket, she tossed her food satchel over her shoulder and rose. Angel watched every move.

"I promise your children will be safe and happy. You are the best of mothers, an angel." The Provider turned and walked away, stopped and faced her again. "You can come too. There's room for you...and I don't have to touch you. Just come and be safe." The babies mewled and Angel knew she couldn't part from them. She followed the Provider out the alley. She never came back.

"Wow!" The kits trilled.

"So what about Rosie?" The little female asked.

"I'll get to that," Red answered. "But we've had a lot of story for one day. I'll tell the tall-ones we're hungry." He left the kitchen, returning with the female, who chirped to him while he wound figure-eights around her legs. She gave them all mush-meat, a prize the kits devoured.

After they ate and groomed, the kits collapsed in a heap in their basket. Red dozed nearby for a while, then rose. The orange tiger woke, mewling at him to stay, but Red ignored his pleas and easily jumped the mesh fence attached to the door that kept the kits in the kitchen.

Red returned the following morning and ate a large bowl of kibble. The kits waited for more story while he groomed. He licked his paws and cleaned his claws, biting between his toes. Then he licked his paws and dragged them over his ears and down his face. He cleaned his belly fur, the insides of his thighs and then his tail with long rasps of his tongue. With growing impatience, the tiger kit watched the silly old tom stick his face in his groin, hind legs in the air. He pounced, landing on Red's belly, where he was licked so hard it knocked him to the floor. Now, at last Red was finished and lay before their basket, contentment itself. The kits settled above him, a line of eager faces.

"Let's talk about Rosie." Red began, his voice as soft as a purr.

5 - LIFE IN THE GREEN

osie perched on the Guardian Stone watching leaves dance across the meadow. She yawned at a sliver of moon in the morning sky. Once it waxed full, the ceremony at Harmony Tree would mark the beginning of her life as a member of Hillside Pod. For Rosie, the Brightmoon of Falling Leaves was acceptance of a new life and severance from the old.

Other than Kyra's disdain and Browser's continued indifference, she was happy at the Green. She had no idea why Browser still avoided her. Surely he couldn't still be angry she encouraged Angel to trust the Provider. Grudges are silly and she didn't perceive Browser as silly, yet the easy friendship he began in the alley seemed to be over. Gone was the playful banter, the gentle nuzzling, the accidental brushing of pelts she'd secretly hoped would blossom into something more.

The black meanness leaped beside her and began to groom. Pulling her paws over her ears and down her face, she licked thoroughly between her fingers, extending long, sharp claws for Rosie to admire.

"Good morning, Kyra," Rosie meowed.

The dark queen sighed theatrically. "Good morning, your majesty. I'd stay and talk but I have to catch your afternoon meal." She leaped to the ground with a snooty flick of her tail. Rosie's eyes glowed like hot coals following Kyra as she strut down the hill, rolling her hips like a priss. *Catch my meals indeed! Ghost is teaching me to hunt and I'll be feeding you soon!*

Now Rosie followed Kyra down the hill, padding to the stump where she sharpened her claws to razor points, then crossed to the pool for a drink. It was a morning ritual, begun by sniffing up and down the water's edge, then kneading the earth at the perfect spot, another quick sniff and a final raising and placing of paws before she lowered her head to test the water. A little taste. If it pleased her, she drank. If not, the whole procedure began again. Today she drank.

"Rosie." All four of her paws left the ground. Browser stifled a chuckle. "Nee-ow, sorry I startled you. Ghost asked me to hunt with you this morning."

"Oh," she cooed, surprised again.

"Are you OK with that?"

"Yes." *Rabbit scat! He's going to see how pathetic I am.* They trotted across the meadow and into the western forest.

Suddenly Browser froze, a flick of his ear signaling her to do the same. He scented the air with an open mouth. "Longear," he murmured, and hunkered low.

She copied his movements. "Where?"

He pointed with his muzzle toward a clump of maidenhair fern where a plump longear nibbled on new shoots. "Will you try for it?"

"Yes!" she hissed, kneading the ground.

"Longear aren't easy. They feel every tremor in the earth and hear more. Get as close as you can before pouncing." Belly fur brushing the ground, Rosie slunk forward in quick, short spurts. The rabbit's musk filled her mouth and instinctively she uttered the kin's dry, throaty mimicry of feathertail wings, "eh-eh-eh-eh-eh." She instantly regretted it. The longear froze, one black eye staring, then fled full speed into the forest. Rosie crumpled. Browser shot past her, a blur in the trembling undergrowth. The creature squealed and Browser burst into the clearing, its limp body in his jaws. He dropped it before her.

"I shouldn't have given up," Rosie meowed. *Maybe Kyra's right. I am a spoiled princess who can't survive unless someone feeds me.*

Browser looked so sympathetic she thought he might lick her ears. "Don't worry. I lost my first longear too...more than one."

"Really?"

"Really." His eyes smiled at her for the first time since their visit with Angel and Rosie beamed. She moved closer to brush pelts but Browser stepped back, keeping distance between them.

Rosie spied some dreamweed, its clusters of fragrant white bells swaying above the bracken. "Oh, Browser, look! Let's dig the roots!" Her voice fluttered with delight, remembering how Ghost had treated her anxiety over Mee-am with a tuber to chew. It had calmed her and caused euphoric dreams. *How wonderful to loll about this paradise with Browser, daydreaming after our meal,* she thought. Browser sat scanning the undergrowth. "Wouldn't dreamweed root be a wonderful finish to this longear?"

"I need to bring my prey back to the cave. Others might be hungry," he answered, and Rosie felt admonished. Browser sensed her embarrassment and tried to soften his response. "Rosie, we should continue the hunt. Let's try for some fat mice," he trilled, pressing his cheek to her shoulder. "I'll show you where the biggest colony lives." Snapping up the longear, he ran deeper into the woods, leaving her no choice but to follow. They came to a small meadow graced with an offshoot of the stream and in the earth above its banks, nestling between clumps of tall grass were hundreds of mice burrows, which she would learn, were fertile with fat little rodents.

"Aren't those slither holes?" Rosie asked, afraid to come closer.

"Nah," Browser scoffed. "You can smell the difference. Listen to them scrabbling about." He crouched and sniffed, his ears at full alert. Rosie brought her face close to a hole then jerked back, amazed by the warm, earthy scent and pattering feet she heard below." Now you know," Browser trilled. With his coaching, Rosie soon caught more than she could eat and by sunhigh as many as they could carry. They climbed the gravelly slope to their den with aching jaws.

Kyra's eyes widened when they added their bounty to the preypile but she quickly recovered her sneer. "Hello, bowl-feeder. Good of you to help Browser carry his catch."

"Kyra," Buster chided, slapping his tail on the ground.

"Rosie's no longer a bowl-feeder," Browser said. "This is her catch." He neglected to mention the longear was his. Now it was Rosie's turn to groom her paws and gloat.

"Maybe you will fit in," the black queen muttered, eyes flickering with a grudging respect. She helped herself to a fat mouse. Rosie wanted to thank Browser, but he already sat in the alcove, offering Ghost the longear. Buster followed, hoping for a boon, so Rosie ate in silence with Kyra, content with a day well passed. She'd spent the morning with Browser and impressed the Queen of Scorn. Rosie groomed herself, then went to her cubbyhole where she curled like a snail in her nest. She dreamed.

🐾 🐾 🐾

The enormous cedar rose like a mountain against the night sky, a pale halo of energy surrounding its dark silhouette. From its high branches a white cat floated down, shimmering like a star come to Earth.

He settled on a branch above Rosie. "Hello, Princess. You've come far."

"Thank you for your help. I'm not in that dreadful alley anymore."

"My help? I did nothing."

Her whiskers twitched nervously. "I thought...I asked for help."

"Yes. The power of All That Is and All That Is *within you* answered," he said as if uttering a great truth, then tossed in as an aside, "...and other paws came into play."

"Other paws? What other paws?"

"Nothing is coincidence. Read the Prophecy." His pelt dripping gems of light with every breath, he rose and shook himself, sending galaxies into the air.

"Prophecy?" she asked, following the spiraling lights with her eyes.

"Ghost and Browser believe." He rose, paced to the end of the branch and back. "They didn't tell you about the Prophecy?" he asked, knowing they didn't and floating to a lower limb, perched directly above her to whisper like a conspirator. "A Queen discarded, saved by Clan, Will mate with King of her command, Will birth the future of the Green... something...something"

"What are you saying?" She mewled, her pelt rising down her spine like a crest.

"Isn't is obvious?...You're the Discarded Queen." Rosie's eyes narrowed and her tail began a tense, rhythmic thumping.

"You mean they brought me here to...those kits in my dream..." The more she thought, the more upset she became. Ears flat, she clawed the tree roots and growled. "They brought me here because they believe I'm...? No wonder Browser won't talk to me. He's ashamed because he lied to me!" The white cat seemed amused.

"Oh, he's dealing with more than guilt, Rosamonde. Listen to your heart."

"They tricked me."

"Did they?"

"They lied to me!"

"Had they told you the truth, would you have believed them...or thought them mad? They asked if you wished to leave the alley and you did."

"What do you mean 'Listen to my heart'?" The shimmering cat laughed outright. "Back to Browser, are we?" He settled his belly on the bough, his long, thick tail uncurling beneath him, waving like a hand.

"No evil committed, Princess, only an act of hope sprinkled with a little faith. Your path remains yours to choose. Read the Prophecy carved into this tree and you'll understand." He considered her in silence, at last adding: "Browser suffers because he holds you dear."

Rosie didn't reply. The meadow had been filling with mist and now she could see only dim lights above her, winking out as she backed away. She turned to leave, but fading into the darkness felt wrong. She would do what the white cat suggested. Fumbling back to the bole, she rose on hind limbs and pressed her body close. Rosie would see this Prophecy for herself. But she found only claws piercing the hard wood, hundreds of claws, some in groups of two or three, some with symbols scratched nearby, each a remembrance of a stolen life, all that was left of a loved one. Sad for the lost beloveds and those who grieved for them, she moved carefully along the trunk, but she found no Prophecy.

Discouraged, Rosie rubbed her forepaw across the rough bark in a farewell gesture and it was then her furry fingers slipped into a smooth scoop. She slid them to the right, slipping into another depression, then a third and a fourth. Pulling back the branch, the young queen saw a row of four indented circles identical to those above their den's entrance and the ones carved in Great Mother's altar. A row of four scoops, the sign for *Of the Earth*. Above that was the image: a row of four, below a row of three, two above the three, all capped by one: the three-sided symbol she had learned meant *All That Is*. Rosie knew the image was identical when flipped on any side, but somehow she couldn't shake the impression this one pointed up. She sank her claws into the bark and climbed, swiping a forepaw slowly back and forth and when she reached the second branching, it slipped into another groove.

Rosie tore at the ivy spreading along the trunk in all directions and found one word: QUEEN

She clawed away clusters of cedar needles and shredded vines of ivy. At last it shone, carved into the bark lifetimes ago, now encased by amber sap and surrounded by the softest green velvet moss:

> A Queen discarded, saved by Clan,
> Will mate with King of her command,
> Will birth the future of the Green.
> Then with Beloved, son, and Gray,
> Will find the one tossed her away.
>
> Earth for healing, Clouds to dream,
> Visions of fire, Oceans that bring
> Hearts of emotion, Four become One
> And black wings most beloved son
> Will guide the kin to All-Peace
> Where Love is Legion and All Is One.

Rosie sat paws together, tail curled primly before them. Deep in trance, she didn't move for a long while until another gleam of amber caught her gaze and farther down in the thickest part of the ivy, she found another poem.

> This is the way, the good: kind hearts shall heal and mend.
> Sweet Mother's love shall tend the children of the world.
> Rain shall not fall to bend a bough, nor break a clod of earth.
> And Fear at last diminished, Love shall know rebirth.

A blinding light burned it all away and Rosie woke thirsty and hungry, her bladder filled to bursting. The Prophecy was a beautiful dream, but the idea that she could be the Discarded Queen turned her inside out and by the time she leaped to the Guardian Stone, she'd convinced herself it wasn't her fate.

Rosie squinted into the sunlight. Something was wrong. The late afternoon sun was too bright and the angle of the light was off. Fear fluttered down her spine, but the needs of her body pressed, so she urinated behind some rocks, then headed for the pool, trying to place herself in the world.

Ghost hunkered near the reeds and they greeted each other with a dip of heads, then she remembered her dream and her belly clenched. The small shaman seemed so loving, but was he? Why did he and Browser lie?

"Browser hunts this morning," Ghost offered. Rosie looked up, confused.

"Morning?" Water drops on her whiskers gleamed in the sunlight. "It's morning?" *Don't sound surprised; don't show weakness. Is he lying?...It is morning!*

"We didn't want to disturb you, Rosie. We let you sleep through the night. Browser said you were tired from yesterday's hunt." Rosie's heart thudded. *How is it possible? How could I wander so long in another world?* Dizzy, she slumped.

"Are you all right?" The shaman's voice rang with concern.

"I dream," she murmured, searching his face. She remembered the white cat admitting Ghost and Browser had tricked her, yet it didn't bother him and now the little wizard was grooming her face. Had she misjudged him? "Can I trust you? Will you be honest with me?"

"By my heart, I hope *yes.*"

"Why did you bring me here?" Ghost met her gaze.

"A Queen discarded, saved by Clan, Will mate with King of her command, Will birth the future of the Green..."

Rosie averted her head and Ghost backed away, falling silent.

"You brought me here to fulfill a prophecy I've never heard, to have babies with someone I've never met." She glared at the silver wizard.

He whispered. "Rosie, please...This is the way, the good: kind hearts shall heal and mend..."

"...And fear diminished, love shall know rebirth." She finished.

His eyes widened in surprise. "You read the Prophecy in your dream." *She remembers her waking-dreams.*

Rosie nodded. "I understand it's a good cause, but you had no right to kidnap me..."

"We kidnapped you?"

She kneaded the ground with her claws. "Well, I wasn't told the truth."

"You would have believed the truth?" Rosie had no response. "You prefer the alley?" he pressed.

"Of course not, but why didn't you tell me about this prophecy?"

"You had enough trouble trusting us—"

"For good reason, it turns out."

"But you didn't know that."

"I sensed it!" she snapped and it was Ghost' turn to lack an answer.

His voice was almost a purr when he responded. "Rosie, if we'd told you we were following an ancient prophecy passed down elder to offspring for countless generations and you were the key who would unlock our salvation...You would have run and hid."

"Yes...maybe...well...OK, yes, but least I could have chosen a path based on the truth."

"A path based on your perception of the truth. We wanted to let you see the truth for yourself."

Rosie's angry tail thumped the ground. "You mean what you believe is the truth."

Ghost hunched. "Browser said you'd feel this way. He wanted so badly to tell you, but was afraid. You're not a prisoner. You may leave the Green whenever you wish." *We'll keep looking...But she feels like The One.*

"Where would I go? Back to the alley? Mee-am is gone!...I just wish you'd been honest with me. It might have taken longer, but it was the right thing to do."

"Browser thought so too. And you should know it was only Browser and myself who were following the Prophecy. Kyra and Buster didn't know."

"That makes sense," Rosie muttered, remembering Kyra's barbs.

Ghost looked miserable. "I swear by Great Mother, you're free to choose your own future."

Rosie stood and stepped back, eyes on fire. "And the children I'm to birth? Can I choose them?"

"Of course you can," he mewled. Head lowered in submission, he moved toward her, but Rosie hissed, raising an armed paw. "Don't you believe me?" he asked.

She turned her back to him and hunkered, paws beneath her. "I don't know...All right. I believe you," She said, refusing to even glance at him. Ghost cast her a cheerless look and walked away. Rosie called after him and he turned back, his tail raised with hope, but she only had a question.

"Ghost...why does Browser despise me?"

"He doesn't despise you, Rosie...He loves you." Another long silence.

"Thank you. You may go." The shaman trembled. He was a Wisdom Cat tending the needs of an honored clan in the Green, yet Rosie dismissed him the way a pod leader would order a kit to its snuggery.

Queen Rosamonde, he thought, entering the cave.

Rosie stayed by the pool, watching light play on the water. By sun-high her empty belly couldn't be ignored and remembering the glut of field mice by the stream, she padded toward the woods. Now that she'd established her independence, her pride wouldn't let her ask the Hillside Cats for food. Three of them stared down at her from the Guardian. Ghost wasn't among them. *Good. He's in his alcove atoning for his sins.* From the tree-line, she glanced back and saw Browser following her. Their eyes met and the misery in his told her Ghost had told him everything. He made no attempt to come closer while she hunted and ate her catch. Rosie stayed at the mouse warren until her hunger returned, knowing Browser wouldn't feed himself while guarding her. She ate a second meal with perverse satisfaction, letting him watch hungrily from a distance.

When Rosie returned to the pool, Browser trailing behind her, their shadows fell long before them. Rosie curled beneath a bush and slept until sunfall. Browser was gone, but a wonderful gift had been left: Mee-am's cloth, worn and dirty, but rich with her human's scent. Buster had brought it. She pulled the rag beneath her and the patchwork tux scooted playfully after its trailing threads. Rosie hissed and with a sad face Buster pulled his paws back. She regretted scolding him. Her eyes smiled, all the enticement he needed to roll on his side, eyes lit with joy while he wiggled toward her, pumping front and rear legs together like an inchworm. He rasped her cheek with his tongue.

"I love you, Rosie-Posie. Come home." With that, and a sweeping lick to her ear, he leaped to his paws and dashed up the hill. Undone by his sweetness and his eerie use of her special name, Rosie-Posie slept on the cloth, purring while she dreamed. She woke to a deep twilight, smelling fish. A bluegill. Its bright blue dorsal gleaming in the grass, a black whisker lay across its yellow belly. Rosie parted her lips and sniffed the bushes. Kyra was gone. *Is she telling me she's happy I've left the den?* Rosie wondered. *Oh, well, this is a great gift,* and she dug into her meal. Soon after, Browser, who'd been watching from the Guardian Stone, came down and settled nearby. Rosie curled beneath her boulder again and slept. She didn't stir until dawn.

"Are you hungry?" Browser meowed, stretching his paws before him. "Shall we hunt?"

"I'm starving and yes, we will hunt," Rosie answered, grooming her face. "But this doesn't make us friends again. You're a liar and a phony." Browser winced. Didn't she know he shredded ears for less? But without a word, he led her into the woods. Their hunt was quickly fruitful.

Rosie settled near the stream with her vole while Browser hunkered over his mouse. "You're not taking that to the den for Ghost?" she taunted. "He might be hungry." Browser pretended he didn't understand. "Now you eat with me," she muttered.

"What?" he asked. Rosie pretended she didn't hear. Browser raised his head. "I know you're angry, Rosie. I'm sorry for the way you were treated." Her eyes smoldered and her tail whipped wildly. "...The way I treated you," he corrected.

"First you trick me into coming here, then you treat me like I'm poisonous." *Why doesn't he care for me?*

"I should have told you the truth when we were in the alley, but I was afraid you wouldn't come." Browser looked down. *I wanted you to come.* "I've stayed away for my own reasons."

"I shouldn't have come," Rosie moaned. *And this was a mistake. Ghost and the white cat are wrong. He doesn't care for me. And worse, he'll see I care for him.* Her prey untouched, Rosie tucked her paws beneath her.

"I'm sorry," Browser murmured, ears low.

"Sorry for what, Browser?"

"Sorry you're not happy here. I want you to stay with us because you want to...Now that everything is revealed."

Everything is revealed? Then you truly don't care.

The pain on Rosie's face confused Browser and made him unhappy. He searched his heart for something to lift her spirit. "Rosie, it's almost brightmoon. I'd like to introduce you at Harmony Tree as a member of Hillside Pod. Of course it's your decision to stay or not."

"Where else would I go?" she moaned.

"Wherever you want. I saw you in the alley demanding Great Mother's help. Do you believe your prayer went unanswered?"

"You saw that?"

"Yes and I'll help you, whether you stay with us or not. I'll help you return to Mee-am if that's what you want."

"Mee-am's gone!" She yowled.

"Then we'll find her." Rosie stared into his eyes and knew he was right. Browser didn't give up. He had courage. *This is why he's a leader,* she thought, turned and faced the creek, ashamed of her weakness.

Browser nuzzled her shoulder while she drank. "Rosamonde, I want to clear everything up between us," he murmured, and suddenly she remembered with burning clarity why she was angry. Furious. Yes she was weak, but he'd wronged her. Pretending to have feelings for her, he'd lured her to the Green, then dumped her like last moon's longear.

"Now you want to clear everything up?" Browser knew not to answer. "...About my choices you've been quite plain." Browser lowered his tail. "Harmony Tree, you say? You'll have my answer soon." She left him at the water, then stopped, turned and faced him, quivering with rage. "One more thing to add to *everything*," she hissed, "If you ever lie to me again, I'll scratch your eyes from your head and feed them to the fish." With a lash of her tail, she was gone.

🐾　🐾　🐾

The first day of brightmoon arrived and the air was alive with change. It was the Brightmoon of Falling Leaves and each breath had a bite to it, a sense of new beginnings. Rosie, however, spent the day as she had the others, resting by the pool or in the meadow batting butterflies off milkweed stems while the pod cats took turns guarding her and bringing her meals.

At last the sun fell behind the treetops, and kin began the pilgrimage to the ancient cedar. Considered a sacred space, they would gather beneath its branches for the three nights of brightmoon. Rosie could feel its healing presence from where she sat. Tonight she too would swing on the great tree's limbs. *Will I see the white cat,* she wondered. *Probably not, unless I'm dreaming.*

Despite her frequent naps and butterfly obsession, Rosie had thought carefully about her future. Now the pod cats encircled her, awaiting her decree. "I will remain with you at Hillside Pod...If that is what you all still wish." she said.

"It is!" Browser blurted, his tail high, quivering with excitement. Ghost and Buster purred. Kyra dropped the fat longear she was bringing to the gathering on the ground. She yawned hugely, letting Rosie know whatever she said meant nothing to her. She was merely waiting for her podmates.

Rosie stifled a smile and continued. "I have no intention of fulfilling a Prophecy I don't believe in. I won't mate with your king or give birth to special kittens, so if your plans are to parade me before a row of candidates, forget it."

"We have no such plans," Ghost murmured.

"Well, good, because I refuse to—"

"Great Mother's Whiskers, this is ridiculous," Kyra interrupted. "The royal kiss-my-paw will join Hillside Pod. Let's go to the tree." She lifted the longear back into her mouth.

"Please, Kyra, let me finish." With an impatient flick of her tail, the black queen dropped her offering again and sat. Rosie continued. "I just want to say that after thinking about the Prophecy, I understand you did what you did with sincere hearts and while I don't necessarily agree with..." Kyra yawned rudely. "I don't believe you meant me any harm. In fact, you've helped me and I thank you." Despite her intentions to explain herself in detail, she'd given in to Kyra's demands and cut her speech short.

Kyra stood. "OK, good. Wonderful. Let's go." Everyone rose, but as Kyra, prey in mouth again, turned south toward the gathering, the others approached Rosie, welcoming her with purring head bunts. Browser was the last to greet her into their family.

"I couldn't be happier," he murmured, looking shy.

Forced to release the longear yet again, Kyra chuffed, "Great Mother's Teats, Browser, have you forgotten you're leading the ceremonies?"

"She's right," he whispered into Rosie's ear, gave it an affectionate lick, turned and trotted down the field. For a heartbeat Rosie stood stunned and flushed, watching her new friends retreat south. Then she remembered...she had to be there too.

6 – HARMONY TREE

armony Tree towered above its surroundings. Harmony tree, an ancient being so powerful even Kyra lost her snicker in its presence. Life-force emanating from every branch, each clump of needles and every knotted root; its trunk rose the height of four full-grown oaks and thirty kin standing nose-to-tail were needed to surround it. In human terms, the tree had a circumference of almost forty-five feet and a diameter of fourteen and a third.

Padding closer, Rosie felt herself pulled toward a vortex, her paws hardly touching the ground. "Sweet feathers!" she exclaimed. "This tree holds a powerful spirit!"

"That's what Ghost says," Buster trilled.

Approaching the tree, Rosie was surprised by the medley of kin. All sizes and colors hunkered, stretched, or tiptoed along the cedar's giant limbs. More cats rested or tussled in the grass. Agile cats with long legs and curved claws swayed in the highest branches, singing sweetly about the aerial nests of High Home in the northeastern forest. Ground-pounders from north and south enacted mock-battles between the tree's twisting roots. Older queens hunkered in prickly solitude, while young males strut before young females, hoping to impress. Ronin explored, whiskers spread and ears high. Some families slept in fur piles, keeping their younglings separate and safe. Some ate from preypiles where others shared their kill. Kyra proudly dropped her longear on one, then joined Rosie and Buster in front of the root-stage.

The moon rose above the tree line, golden-orange and radiant with promise. Browser settled in the talking seat, a bowl shape created by the branching of the trunk, while Ghost perched nearby as he'd done for many brightmoons. But tonight something was different. *He* was different, although he didn't understand how. Feeling curiously off-center, his breath came fast and shallow. Fear tightened his throat. He couldn't control it. The kin before him blurred, and worried he might faint, Ghost pressed himself against the bole.

He didn't faint. He sank into a waking-dream, into a state more relaxed than he'd ever known. Presence permeated his body, as if every cell had senses, and could see without eyes and hear without ears because eyes and ears were everywhere. Ghost surrendered. A popping sound like a bursting bubble, and he left his body and floated, a disembodied spirit. Fear swept through him. *Not now, not here,* he chided himself. Focusing his intent, he swam back toward his cat shape, but couldn't enter and again fear washed through him. *I spend too much of my life feeling afraid.*

Ghost calmed himself and faced what Great Mother wished him to see. It was beautiful: a blue mist rutilated throughout with filaments of golden light. The cloud sizzled and hummed. It surrounded the kin. No. It came from the kin, electric ropes arcing from one body into another, connecting them all as one. Ghost spied Rosie and the current sizzled from him to her and from her back into him. Ecstasy pulsed through his spirit. *We're all one thing,* he thought, surrendering to the One Great Life as it enveloped him in a harmony of nebulae and newborn suns.

The One Life danced with unearthly beauty while Ghost slipped through the mist, gorging himself on being alive. He knew its desire, its need to be born, to experience the worlds of form and matter. He knew attachment as the seed of sorrow. Because he was born, he would die. Everyone he loved would die. The One Life danced, creation and destruction, unworried by the fate of a single tendril of flame within its wildfire. It scorched him through, and a Shaman rose from the ashes. "Death is an illusion," said the One Life, "the delusion that You are separate from Me. Life is the All That Is. Death brings you sorrow because you don't understand the endless music. The One Life can never be destroyed." Ghost danced, ecstatic within the blue and golden cloud.

Gradually, Ghost merged with his body and lived through his limited senses again. But he was changed. Bliss had faded with the cloud and a coldness rose in the dark. He felt it watch him with hatred. His skin crawled with the premonition this evil would soon act. "Great Mother, he shuddered, "Tell me what to do." A breeze blew down from the north, parting the branches of the tree just enough for light from the sea of stars to crown the head of Princess Rosamonde. Their cyes met and the shaman knew: *It's Rosie and it's time. The Prophecy must be fulfilled.*

"Great Mother lift Her paw," Browser said, breaking Ghost' reverie.

"Great Mother bless us," echoed around them.

"We are Her beloved, Her pelted-ones, the Clan of Fang and Claw! Let the Brightmoon of Falling Leaves begin with news of birthings and the welcoming of new friends." The kin yowled, stomping their paws as a young, ginger queen climbed the root stage.

"I am Goldenpelt from Southbridge Pod. I have birthed three kits and will bring them for naming in two turns of the Moon." Goldenpelt melted into the crowd amid a hum of well-wishers, including Rosie. In the cattery where she was raised, the queens of high-bred families rarely applauded one another's offspring, but her mother, Victoria Silvertip, had been different. Gentle and kind, she'd shied away from gossip, and Rosie, who'd learned her values, warmed to the free-spirited kin of the Green.

An enormous tom strode to the roots. A dense, muscular male, his shaggy black pelt made him look even larger than he was. He surveyed the crowd with fierce golden eyes. Rosie shivered. Then he spoke. "I am Blackpaw, leader of the pod at Flattail Dam," he said with a voice so high and squeaky it was all Rosie could do to not laugh. "I announce the birth of two litters. Eight healthy kits for our clan!" His feathery tail swished with pleasure and he shuffled his paws in a happy dance. "Five lovely future queens and three warriors," he yowled. The kin thumped their tails with joy.

"You don't have to be male to be a warrior," called a cat from the rear. She was pure white, except for a gray head-jewel shaped like a crescent moon which flashed blue like her eyes.

"Of course, Sosay, you're right," Blackpaw called back, then left the stage.

Browser waited. "Anyone else? Another birthing?" he asked. No one answered. "OK then. Now we'll honor our beloveds." Several kin pattered to the front.

A male with a long gray pelt went first. He had a kind, owlish face with tufts of fur that burst from his slanted ears like feathers. "My name is Barney," he began, "I'm from Birch Grove Pod. Many of you remember my brother Threepaws, born with one leg nothing more than a stub." Barney lowered large, liquid eyes, so common to western kin. "Threepaws is gone." A compassionate trilling rose from the crowd. "He was the bravest cat I've ever known. He always did for himself, even hunted his own meals. But he grew frail and during last darkmoon his Fetch took him Beyond." Barney paused. "I saw it happen." The crowd gasped. "At first I thought I saw Threepaws coming to his nest, but he felt distant and strangely silent, as if all sound were sucked from the world. Then I saw that Threepaws was lying in his nest and it was his Fetch coming toward us. That's when the Fetch saw me. It stopped and stared and I confess my heart was banging in my chest so hard I thought it would explode. I figured the Fetch would take me too." Barney shuddered, staring at the invisible. "Then I saw how the trees and bushes shone right through it, as if it were water, but it was beautiful too, just like Threepaws, with a luminous heart and a kind face." Barney focused on the kin before him. "When it reached Threepaws, he woke. He looked into its face, his own face, bending over him and his eyes smiled. He wasn't scared, he was at peace. He turned and looked at me and with his heart said *goodbye brother,* and his Fetch melted into him and the light left his eyes." Barney's ears twitched. "I miss Threepaws, but I can be happy knowing he plays in Fields of Nip. He's Fourpaws now!" Much yowling and tail thumping as Barney stepped down.

A thin, gray-ocher crone was helped to the platform by two granddaughters. "I'm Graypaw from Bigmarsh Family. My mate WhiteFangs was leader for more turns of the Moon than I can remember." The old cat dropped her head to her breastbone for a moment of reflection, where it stayed...and stayed...and stayed until finally, one of her granddaughters hissed from beside the stage and Graypaw sprang back to life, then continued like nothing had happened. "He was old and slow...like me." Tittering from the audience. "Ghostdogs took him."Hisses and caterwauls. Graypaw padded to the trunk and sank a single claw. Twisting swiftly, she left it in that graveyard of memories, blood running between her toes and down the tree's knobby skin. Using her other paw she carved a long fang and leaning forward, nuzzled all that remained of her mate. Her girls helped her from the roots into the crooning crowd.

How brave she is, Rosie thought, watching the arthritic cat melt into the crowd. *No wonder she was mated to a leader.*

Tuxedo twins climbed the stage. "I'm Nit and she's Kit," the male began and they dipped identical black heads to their matching white shirtfronts. The catlings were in all ways but one perfect reflections of each other. "Yes, you can only tell us apart by peeking beneath our tails. Even our mother did it." The gathered kin purred with amusement, but the twins turned solemn. Nit sat, licking himself nervously.

Kit rose, fidgeting on her paws. "I regret we come with bad news," she said.

"Where are you from?" Sosay asked.

"We were born under two-legged dens southwest of the Green, but let us tell you why we're here." She looked over at Nit and something unbearably sad passed between them.

Kit plopped down, surrendering to her grief. Nit carried on. "White Trucks have been patrolling your western border for several turns of the Moon. You're mostly unaware because they don't come here, but in the alleys around you, entire families have been destroyed. We survived an attack like nothing we've ever seen. They don't just round up a sick cat or a dog who's causing trouble anymore. They come to wipe out a colony. My sister and I are the only ones left."

"How did you make it?" Goldenpelt asked.

"We crawled beneath one of the White Trucks and hid on top of a wheel. We were terrified. Two-leggeds with pain sticks and nets were everywhere. We hid until they woke their monster, then leaped off and ran. We were lucky."

"That's not the worst," Kit added. "What we witnessed..."

Her voice trembled so badly Nit again had to finish. "They killed the kin in the trucks, before they left. Our parents, our brothers..." A furious caterwauling rose from the crowd.

"No! It can't be!" an old mackerel tom hissed past his missing fangs.

"It's true," Nit said. "In their tall-walker tongue, they call us *feral*," he spat. "Feral means kin who don't trust uprights."

"With good reason!" the tom growled. Around him rose a cacophony of thumping tails and claws scraping the ground.

"They call us *feral*," Nit cried. "Because we run from their cruelty they *put us down*, even before we're taken to the kill-den. When the White Truck left, no cries..." Nit's voice faded away and he slumped.

Kit licked his ears. "It's all true! Nit and I have come to warn you... because next they're coming HERE." In the silence that followed you could hear a tail raise. "They plan to invade the Green...to cleanse it of *ferals*."

The meadow exploded. Browser was profoundly distressed, but sat tall, hoping his calm demeanor would calm others. "Anything else?" he asked through the bedlam, projecting more confidence than he felt. The twins shook their heads and Browser motioned with his tail for them to join the gathering.

"Wait!" a high voice called. Blackpaw padded forward. "Where are you living?" Nit and Kit stared blankly ahead. "Come with us. We'll make a place for two brave younglings." They loped to their benefactor and after a proper nosemeet were ushered toward Sosay. This diversion was short-lived, however, as the grumble of fear began again, gaining momentum until the meadow echoed with shrieks of terror.

The raspy voice of an old queen rose above the din. "I know whad'da do!" she wailed. "I know whad'da do." The kin parted like grass beneath her paws as she wobbled to the roots and turned her single milky eye on the crowd. The other had shriveled in its socket long ago and its lid hung closed. Her once-black pelt was now shades of gray, but her tail, little more than a skin-covered bone with random wisps of fur, still lashed on her command. This grand dame of the alleyways lived proudly in a world where a ratty pelt and a few broken fangs didn't matter. "I'm Diva and I know whad'da do," she rasped again. The caterwauling ceased. "I bin dancin' down them two-legged alleyways 'fore any-uh-yoo suckled at yer mama's bellies. My Fetch done worn his paw leathers off chasin' me. Now he's too tired ta take me!" Cackling at her own joke, her skeletal tail quivered. "There's one way, only one, ta keep them Leatherboots from pluckin' yoo outa yer skin. It's scarier'n uh pack'uh hungry snap-jaws, but it works."

"Well, tell us already!" Goldenpelt mewled.

"Ya gotta be took-n-uh feeder cage."

Gasps of astonishment rang out from branches in the tree and across the meadow. "What?...A what?...Taken? What's a feeder cage?" Voices rose and fell.

"She means a Provider, a two-legged who feeds kin."

"Oh, a Food Giver!" another yelped. "You're kidding! Let a Food Giver trap you?"

"I don' give-uh rat's whisker wha'choo calls it!" Diva yowled crossly. But she knew her words were crucial for their survival and lifting a mashy paw, cupped her ear from behind. The point was gone, they must see that. But the funnel was so ragged with mite bites, holes and scars, the fact that its top had been neatly sliced off seemed almost irrelevant. Diva didn't think so, however and paw up, continued her message. "I bin trapped, wuz uh young queen back then too and the one'r cetched me, fed me." She bristled happily. "She fed me good, many turns of the Moon. Wuz fat when she disappeared. Never knew what happened to-er. She jest stopped comin'." Then with a shudder, Diva roared. "I'm here cuz-uh her! Looky my right ear!" She leaned down, bending the shredded skin-flap forward for inspection and the crowd pressed close, Goldenpelt in front. The tidily-groomed mother cat wasn't thrilled by the essence-of-dumpster clinging to the crone's pelt, however, and after sniffing the ear, backed off as if grime were contagious.

"What else did this feeder do to you?" The ginger queen demanded.

"All good. She brung me to-uh place with uh upright healer. Wildborn, hundreds of us trapped in cages, all moanin' and pissin' in the dirt. But much'uz I could tell, no one wuz hurt or killed. It warn't no death-den, though some that was brung didn't leave, feral life bein' tough n-all." *Understand, prissy miss?* The milky eye gleamed, a silent reminder of Diva's strength. "Anyhoo, that healer giv'd me two-legg'd med'cine. I wuz sick, real sick. Neow...mouse pelts...I wuz dyin' and that healer and that feeder, they saved me."

Despite the old cat's stink, Goldenpelt came close again. "Well, that doesn't seem so bad," she offered.

"Not bad t'all. Course nev'r birthed another kit..." The new mother cringed and tail whipping, kneaded the grass with her claws. Diva glared at her. Being common had made life hard, not made her a fool, and she'd endured all the disapproval she cared to for one evening. She leaped forward and hunkered, yellow fangs and cataract-eye rudely close to the ginger face. "Yoo live...where?" Diva rasped, blasting ripe breath. "Here in the Green, all cozied up wit' lovies an' lotsa prey?" The young mother nodded. "Well, I ain't got that, never did. Yoo spoiled. Ain't no prey in two-legged town. Ain't no grass, no trees, nuttin' but cold stone and what the tall'uns throw away. Once the rats is gone, yoo starve. Yoo thinkin' that's good for kits? Ever watch yer babies' bellies suck up an' disappear? Ever seen 'em die? I seen a litter o'mine beat'n to death by two-legg'ds havin' their fun!" Goldenpelt gasped, her eyes wide with horror and Diva shuddered, still trying to shake off the pain. "I was thrilled I didn' bring more babies into that world," she whispered into Goldenpelt's ear.

The prissy queen rubbed her head along Diva's shoulder. "I'm so sorry," she murmured, but Diva no longer heard.

Again she lifted her paw to the mangled right ear, hoping the spoiled, foolish kin of the Green could accept her story and save themselves. "This here's the mark, the mark of kin what don't breed. Once yoo got it, them nasty Leatherboots won't touch yoo. But'cha gotta have the nuggets to be took'n by a feeder and yoo gotta have savvy what'sa feeder, *only* a feeder. They'rn the *only* two-legg'ds yoo can trust." She was done. She'd said everything she had and with Goldenpelt's help, tottered into the crowd that deluged her with requests to see the flat-cut ear.

Browser wasn't the only one upset by Diva's plan. Trapped by a tall-walker? Few kin had, as Diva put it, *the nuggets* to accept her solution. Ghost watched fear spread through the gathering like a disease. *Already it begins. They must be calmed, or they'll find a reason to be cruel.* Ghost turned to Browser, but the pod leader had lost his composure and shuffled in place, whipping an exploded tail. Finally he threw back his head and yowled. His roar rippled outward, silencing the kin, but only for a moment. Before he could speak their mutterings rippled back even louder.

Blackpaw raced to the roots. "Silence!" he screeched. "Our king will speak." A stunned quiet spread across the meadow, no one more surprised by the impromptu coronation than Browser. Not knowing what to do, he decided to ignore the remark.

"Clan of Fang and Claw, hear me! We must not succumb to fear. Let us expect the best, but prepare for anything. To those who live near upright dens: don't let them see you. Hunt at night when they sleep. Don't knock over their trash bins. Dive in; leap out. Leave no trace of yourselves and they won't think of you." The audience listened intently. "We need sentries to alert one another when a White Truck is seen." Browser paced in place. "Let us remain calm and work together." In his loudest voice, he cried, "We are Great Mother's beloveds. She will protect us." The encouragement seemed to work. Someone on a high branch began crooning the Song of Hope. Others joined in.

Ghost waited, but no one else approached the platform, so he leaped from his bough and scanned the crush before him. "Our pod has a lovely new fur-sister. We found her abandoned in an alley, deserving a better life. Please welcome Princess Rosamonde Whitewhiskers." Ghost waved his tail, bidding her to join him on the roots, but Rosie froze. Her eyes darted right then left, inwardly bemoaning there was nowhere to hide when Kyra came up behind and gently pushed her forward. Standing apart now with all eyes upon her, Rosie reluctantly climbed the platform and stood next to Ghost. The crowd welcomed her with tail-thumping glee.

But when the greeting faded a single voice lifted the fur from her spine. "Ghost. You found an abandoned princess and brought her to the Green? A young queen...perhaps...a Discarded Queen?" Sosay's long white pelt gleamed in the moonlight, the crescent moon of gray fur on her forehead glowing blue. An unearthly quiet fell over the crowd as she came from behind Blackpaw, wound her way to the front and with slow, deliberate movements sat before the little wizard and his new friend. The two shamans understood each other perfectly. Rosamonde also understood, and tapped Ghost' skin with an unsheathed claw.

Without lifting his gaze from Sosay, Ghost whispered, "I can't lie to a fellow Wisdom Cat."

"No, only to an urchin like me," Rosie hissed.

"Rosie, please...I will protect you."

Sosay's eyes narrowed on him. "Well, Ghost? Can't you answer? We're facing our greatest threat...the White Truck. Those Leatherboots want to kill us all and I would be encouraged to learn Great Mother has sent the Discarded Queen to stop the holocaust...or is Rosamonde just another princess who's lost her way." The night grew unusually quiet as she wrapped her tail over her unusually wide paws. No one moved. No one spoke. Crickets began their evensong.

"It's true," he said at last, his voice carried by the silence to the edge of the gathering. "She is the Discarded Queen." Sosay squealed with delight, Ghost squealed with pain when Rosie's claw sank into his flesh and Rosie squealed as she leaped into the crowd.

"It's not true! No one knows for certain, especially me!"

The kin were frenzied and didn't hear Rosie's denial. They let her pass, then trailed behind, trilling and bowing and reaching out, as if touching her pelt would bring fortune. Many cats already in the tree, more raced up the trunk to view her from above. Rosie was mortified, with no way to understand their behavior. She'd been raised in privilege, unaware of the short, brutal lives of the wildborn in the alleys. She knew nothing of desperation, of waiting for a savior. Her advent as the Discarded Queen would bring an end to the holocaust. The White Trucks would lose their wheels, their engines rust and freeze and the death dens crumble into dust...because she had arrived. All of the kin believed this, each somewhat differently, but all of them believed. They had nothing else.

Browser sprang from the talking seat to shoulder a path for her escape, but it was useless. When Ghost caught up, they'd managed only a sinuous tour to the other side of the trunk where they stood pressed against it.

Rosie glared at the silver-pelted wizard as he wiggled through the crush to stand with them. "This is the second time you've done something really terribly wrong...apprentice," she spat.

"Rosie, forgive me," Ghost murmured, looking miserable.

"Fight later," Browser chided. Kyra and Buster pushed through the crowd and began pacing back and forth, gleaning a space between the Hillside cats and those wishing to meet their Discarded Queen. A line of sorts formed, with Sosay first, her crescent moon still pulsing blue.

"My Queen," she began with deference, lowering her face to her wide paws. Rosie couldn't help but stare at them, having never before seen a six-toed cat.

"Queen?" someone caterwauled. "She's just a kid!" A snake pit of hissing disagreed.

"Please don't call me *Queen*," Rosie meowed. "I'm like anyone else. In fact, you might say I'm an alley cat."

Sosay purred. "Yes, we've been told...left in an alley...an abandoned female...a discarded queen." Sosay practically danced with joy while tail thumping shook the ground. Frustrated, Rosie clawed at the grass. "Your Majesty," the white Wisdom Cat crooned, "We have waited so long to meet you. You must know the southern clans will fight to fulfill the Prophecy." Behind her, Blackpaw and several females dipped their heads.

Rosie trembled. "By fight you mean *struggle*, right?" Head high, Sosay sat tall and said nothing, looking every claw and fang the warrior. Rosie was nonplussed. "You mean *fight*, fight? As in *really* fight?" She felt silly even saying the words.

"Evil does not relinquish power. It must be won and we are ready. Yes, we will *fight* fight, as you say, your Majesty."

"Uh-uh, no *Majesties,* please, Sosay. But getting back to it, *who* would you fight? You can't fight humans. So who?"

"There is a darkness, a cold descended into the hearts of kin. Not many understand yet, for only a few have felt it." Sosay glanced at Ghost whose eyes told her he understood.

"You have felt it?" Rosie prodded.

"Yes, my Queen. And I will challenge those who follow evil."

"Evil?"

"Evil is that which lies, is self-centered and selfish. It harms others by word or deed."

"The opposite of love," Sosay said.

"Yes, my Queen."

Rosamonde glanced at Ghost and Browser, both staring ahead like the good soldiers they were. She had a premonition then of what life here might become, and a chill lifted her scruff on its journey down her spine. She turned back to Sosay. "Call me Rosie, Sosay, so that I might feel close."

"As you wish, Queen Rosamonde," she said, and with a graceful motion, touched her head to her paws.

Rosie answered with a clumsy curtsy, and seeing many lowered heads, began to realize the futility of challenging Sosay's beliefs. More thunderous tail thumping as another group came forward to meet her. She stood, tail high to show her pleasure.

🐾 🐾 🐾

"My kit! Oh my baby, my baby!" All heads turned toward the frantic queen, then followed her eyes to the top of the cedar where a mewling kit hunkered on a branch.

"The fall will kill him!" Rosie cried, causing his mother to wail even louder. "Browser, do something!" Before the pod leader could move, something between a bat and a starving possum raced up the tree. It was the ugliest cat Rosie had ever seen and she couldn't help staring. Its legs and tail looked far too spindly to support its rumpled, scruffily-furred body, over-sized head, huge ears and long nose. And his front left leg appeared crippled, twisted so that the paw pointed inward. How could he even run!

The strange looking feline approached the hunkering kit. Stretching along a branch that barely held his weight, he reached out to scruff the baby, but it recoiled in fear, losing its balance. Now the kit hung upside down, yowling. The hero backed away, climbed down the trunk and crept out a sturdier limb. Crouching beneath the crazed yowler, his head swayed in rhythm with its swinging torso. Suddenly, the big cat leaped up, grabbed the baby's scruff and pulled him free. Baby in his jaws, he landed on his long back paws. For a heartbeat they made a triumphant silhouette against the moon, but the kitten still swung like a pendulum, and together they toppled into the tree. Branches shuddered and cracked, a thundering avalanche of needles and wood. Crash! Thud! Thump! Rosie turned away, horrified. Thud-thump! Thud-thump! Thud-thump! All the way down. Then nothing. Then, WHOOSH. A shower of leaf debris. Rosie crept over and forced herself to look. Branches! Only branches lay broken and splintered on the ground. Another rustle of leaves. Far above them, the big cat pulled himself to a sitting position again, still scruffing the kit. They'd fallen only a short distance and he'd taken the brunt. Blood trickled from a badly scratched shoulder, but the kit was unharmed. The kin went wild. Tails pounding the ground, they yowled with joy, and were still yowling when the misshapen hero deposited the runaway at his mother's paws. The kit dove beneath her belly with no plans to ever reappear.

The kitten was safe. The hero was thanked then ignored. Rosie watched him wander off unnoticed. He didn't expect anything else; this was what he'd always known. He padded to a thick-pelted tabby, and pressed his naked body against the other's fur. Even through dappled moonlight Rosie could see the shaggy cat's face was lit with love.

Ghost motioned them over. "Rosie, my mentor, Erasmus," he trilled.

The fatherly tom's eyes glowed with kindness. "Greetings, Rosie. I hope you enjoy your stay in the Green." The new Queen felt reassured. She liked this warm-hearted tabby, how his ears slanted away from feathery jowls. She liked the wisdom in his face, his dignity, and she liked how he didn't assume she'd live here forever. Erasmus leaned toward Ghost for a nose-kiss, then licked his ear.

Ghost quivered. "I'm sorry, you know I couldn't tell you...We brought her..."

The Elder Cat's whiskers twitched. "The grasses told me of her arrival and trees talk of little else." *What is Erasmus talking about,* Rosie wondered. Ghost nodded that he understood. But his body bobbed impatiently, and his eyes filled with questions, questions Erasmus didn't want to answer right now, so he soothed Ghost with a head bunt and more ear licking. "You'll be a fine Wisdom Cat" he purred, "with a future far greater than my own." The silver cat shuffled his paws, unaware of the quickly hidden jealousy that flit across Morsus' face. Erasmus turned to Rosie. "This is my other apprentice, Morsus," he said with pride.

"My Queen," the wrinkled bat-cat purred. Rosie met his gaze, black slits swimming in yellow, and searing pain tore through her heart. She gasped and turned away, quickly looking back to see a veil drop over his raw, naked soul. *That pain. What was it?* Confused and guilty, she murmured a reply, letting her gaze settle somewhere near his ears. *That lumpy, long-nosed snout. Poor Morsus. What insults has he endured...and now from me, staring at his many deformities.* She only hoped he'd leave soon. She got her wish.

Once Morsus and Erasmus had padded beyond hearing, she turned to Ghost. "I can't help it, Ghost, Morsus frightens me."

"He's not easy," Ghost said. "But he's not had it easy either."

"Tell me everything," Rosie demanded and after some badgering, Ghost whispered Morsus' story. He'd been born in a two-legged den to a normal mother who'd escaped while in heat. Her humans didn't understand she was pregnant when she returned. They weren't prepared for her birthing. And they certainly weren't prepared for Morsus. All his siblings were lovely, with lovely pelts, but their hearts were not as generous as their looks and they shunned their brother. Even his mother barely allowed him to suckle, leaving him small. Later, his siblings found homes, but no one wanted the ugly, scruffy cat with the sullen personality, so the humans took him to the Green and dumped him. Erasmus found him hiding in a tree hollow, emaciated and close to death, hissing at everyone to stay away. Erasmus didn't. He fed Morsus, protected him and taught him how to survive, giving him the only love he'd ever known. Now Erasmus was teaching Morsus the magical arts of the north, just like he'd taught Ghost.

"Ghost, I need you," Browser interrupted. "Rosie, I leave you Kyra." Rosie lowered her ears and tail wondering what unpleasantness the black sylph would bring. But Kyra was helpful, sitting before Rosie, keeping her eyes on the crowd. As the Queen continued meeting the kin, her thoughts returned often to Morsus' sad life. She imagined his hunger, his fear, hiding his rumpled, scruffy body in burrows and holes in trees. Her compassionate eyes sought him in the crowd and every time she found him he turned his gaze on her as if he'd heard her, and a heaviness would spread across her chest making it hard to breath. Finally, Rosie let him go.

As the moon sailed across the sky, Rosie learned much about her new home. Most of the kin wanted only to wish her well. A few came to have her settle disputes, but Browser explained they must still be aired on the root platform with pod leaders and Wisdom Cats as jury. Rosie was dismayed when one champion offered himself as a mate and more so when a mother dragged her young son by the scruff and dropped him before her, swearing amid protests from the crowd he'd be the best king the Green had ever known. Rosie was kind but firm, refusing the catling who slunk off with a grateful apology. Mostly the kin just wanted assurances they were safe. Here in the Green, they had enjoyed the best feral life had to offer, but now they too would live in fear of White Trucks and the Leatherboots who manned them.

Rosie did want to help these kin in whatever ways she could. By the time the moon fell behind the treeline she was exhausted, yet found herself unable to deny anyone the chance to speak. Kyra realized it would fall to her and with almost gleeful determination began stomping back and forth, flexing her bully muscles at those still waiting for an audience. "Enough, enough. Your Queen needs her rest," she snarled. Some of them snarled back, but no one dared cross the barrier of her claws. Until someone did. Kyra whirled, shoving her face into the face of a regretful young queen. "I said done! You want your Queen to Queen tomorrow, don't you?" Her white fangs glowed against her midnight fur.

"Yes...I...sorry," the transgressor mewed, slinking away from the dangerous Kyra.

"Wait," Rosie called after her and Kyra glared at both of them. "Kyra, please permit me this last audience." Rosie glided to the female, who felt as happy as the day she discovered fish in the pond near her den.

She was Rosie's last audience. The remaining petitioners melted into the night, muttering about the mean black cat. Rosie called after them encouraging their return, then nuzzled her protector and climbed the tree.

She napped, waking suddenly in the deep of the night. Stretching her legs before her with a delicious spread of her toes, she padded to the end of the branch and stared at the sky. The stars glowed like gemstones.

Rosie backed down the trunk to the ground. If the Prophecy existed in more than her dreams, she would find it here, carved into Harmony Tree. Standing on hind legs, she lifted her paws to the bark and inched her way around the bole, looking for resin, moss, any fragment of a mark. All she found was the graveyard of claws.

White cat, help me. If the Prophecy's true, it must be here. Droplets of blue light floated down and burst unnoticed against her pelt. *I must be crazy,* she told herself, lifting another leaf. Moonlight broke through the branches and Rosie's heart leaped. A row of carved circles, four of them! *The symbol for earth,* she remembered and rubbing her paw along the rough skin of the bole, found the three-sided image pointing up.

Silently, effortlessly, Rosie reached the first branching where Ghost and Browser slept. She climbed to the second and sat, staring through the branches at the moon. Paused at the edge of the world, it spilled a path of molten silver down the bough toward the bole. Rosie turned, knowing what she'd see: The Prophecy.

Rosamonde flooded with joy. She felt weightless. Were her claws not anchored to the tree, she'd have floated away, a mote in the air. *Am I truly the Discarded Queen?* More futures than her own hung upon that truth. *Can I help the kin?* Something inside her said she could. *Is this the path I should take?* Something deeper within said it was. Rosie breathed in the beauty of the world. Everything in her life had led to this moment. Even the Mate had played his part, abandoning her in the right place at the right time so that Browser would bring her to the Green. She forgave Browser. She forgave Ghost. She even forgave the Mate. Rosamonde breathed in the sweet night air. The Discarded Queen released it.

"Now you know." She whirled around. Ghost sat toward the end of the branch, haloed by the silver light. "I'm sorry, I didn't mean to startle you," he meowed, coming closer.

"No. I'm sorry...for everything." *Why did I doubt him?* she wondered.

"Me too," he said softly and licked her ear.

Rosie saw that he was beautiful, beautiful not as someone she coveted or needed, but beautiful unto himself, whole and living in his truth. *This is the Prophecy,* she realized, *this joyful understanding.* "Can we be friends?"

"We've never been anything else."

Rosie purred. She bathed his ears with her tongue, then pulled away, suddenly serious. "Ghost, I know now I *am* the Discarded Queen, but I don't know how to stop humans from killing kin."

"Great Mother will lead you."

Rosie remained tense. "They kill us without remorse, believing it's their right. We must show them they're wrong." Ghost said nothing. "Browser's right. What they do is evil and they must be stopped."

"What will you do?" he asked.

Rosie's eyes widened. "I don't know. I can't do anything...alone." He just looked at her saying nothing. Rosie shuffled her paws. She looked hunched and fearful. "It can't be wrong...the Prophecy...can it?" Nervously, she turned circles in place, then sat. "No, it's not wrong." Her scruff stood away from her body. "But if we don't fight back...Ghost, I don't want us to die because we didn't fight back!" Now her whole body trembled, struggling beneath the weight of the problem.

Ghost licked her face. "Fight how, Rosie? Our blessing is that we can't fight them. We have only the Prophecy, a key to unlock our hearts."

"How?"

"We change the humans by changing first. We heal ourselves with love. It's through the act of loving us they'll discover their humanity. They are immensely talented, Rosie. They will change the world once they've awakened."

"All of them?"

"Enough. Just as enough kin will grow and change."

"Enough to bring All-Peace," she affirmed. His eyes glowed.

The next evening, the brightest night of brightmoon, Rosie found Ghost resting on the massive roots of Harmony Tree, surrounded by litters of kits.

"Why are so many here tonight?" she asked, swishing her tail to entice them.

"To be named," Ghost answered.

"They don't have names?" she asked astounded.

"Yes, of course. They each have a lovename from their mother, and a playname from their littermates. But tonight they will receive their worldname from Great Mother so that they might face the world."

Rosie's tail froze mid-swipe. No one had chased it anyway. All the kittens seemed nervous. "Great Mother will be here?" she squealed, pelt on end.

Ghost was enjoying himself. "Great Mother is always here, Rosie. Tonight she will speak through the kits' mothers."

"Of course," Rosie murmured, licking a paw, trying to look like she'd always known that. She sat in thought. She herself had been given three names, but all at once, picked before she was born. At the cattery, names were long, and heavy with expectation, given by humans to delineate bloodlines. Rosie wondered if the wildborn weren't better served. At least their names were about themselves and not which prizes their ancestors had won.

Ghost smiled. "We're *all* the Clan of Fang and Claw, Great Mother's most beloved." His chest swelled with pride. "She names each catling Herself and tonight She'll test them as dreamers. They must hear their name when it's called."

"Has a kitten ever failed to hear its name?"

"Never." Ghost flicked his tail at an approaching kit. "How are you called, young one?" Both Ghost and Rosie were struck by his presence, an air of self awareness unusual in one so young.

"I am the dark tiger of my litter, and the first-born male, but I am called by my playname, Quick Paw." He turned to Ghost. "Today is special for names, isn't it, Master Wizard? Great Mother holds our worldnames and tonight they'll be spoken for the first time." He spoke with such relaxed conviction, Rosie couldn't stop herself from reaching out and licking his ear. Embarrassed, the catling examined his paws.

He's a warrior, she thought. "Each of us has a mission. It beats with our hearts, and yours beats strongly." He met her gaze. The resolve in his eyes was so focused, so fierce, it lifted her scruff.

"I follow the Four Become One," he said, turning to Ghost, and a shiver ran down the wizard's spine.

The chatter around them intensified, then faded as the naming ceremony began. Ghost nudged the kit's shoulder. "Go get the proud name you deserve." With a respectful nod, the youngling left. Moments later a dark-brown tom approached and whispered into the shaman's ear. "I'm needed," Ghost told Rosie, then followed the messenger to the far side of the tree and up into its branches.

Rosie watched the ceremony. She smiled inside when the kit Morsus had rescued reluctantly answered to Pumpkin. He slouched to his beaming mother, growling, "Call me Flash." Her heart missed a beat when young Quick Paw took his worldname: Kiliarcos, the name of a human general from long ago. When the last kit had answered to the last name, Rosie pressed against Browser's warmth in the safe embrace of Harmony tree.

Ghost, however, could find no rest and paced the giant roots. He climbed past his sleeping friends to the branch where Rosie had found the Prophecy the night before. Stars burned like jewels in the clear sky. The shaman crept to the end of the limb and sat lost in reverie, little blue suns drifting unnoticed past his half-closed lids.

🐾   🐾   🐾

Atop the massive dune, the sky was darker, the stars brighter than Ghost had ever seen. The night-dyed sand slipped like silk around his paws, but he was small and light and didn't sink far into the blue, meandering life. Surface crystals, caught by the wind, were were lifted in glittering spirals and dropped farther along the ridge. Thus the mountains marched to the sea. And Ghost marched with them. Down through shadowed valleys and up to moon-drenched peaks, until at last he stood, nostrils tangy with salt, embracing a wide, pale horizon.

The hill sloped down to a bay cradled by dunes stretching into the distance. Waves roared up to the shore and back to the sea, leaving necklaces of foam hissing into the sand. The power the little shaman felt here was beyond any understanding, and his attention shifted to a radiant point where ocean met sky. Instantly it flew across the water and floated below him, a crystalline eight-petaled lotus, the seeds in its core made of tiny suns. *I have been called to a Temple of the Elementals, a place of fire, water, earth and air.* Ghost lowered his belly to the sand, and tucked his paws beneath him. He dreamed within his dream.

It was then he felt the cold, the same dark venom that had hovered above the kin that first night of brightmoon. It pulled him from bliss. It attacked the crystal lotus. The little suns died, and the petals went dark.

On the horizon, gargantuan fangs curved into a splintered blackness, an immense maw sucking everything into itself. The whirlwind reached Ghost, yanked him into the air, and sent him spinning toward its starless gullet. "Nee-ooow!" he cried, hearing the screams of millions around him. Then silence. He floated alone in the dark.

7 – COLD MOONS, WARM HEARTS

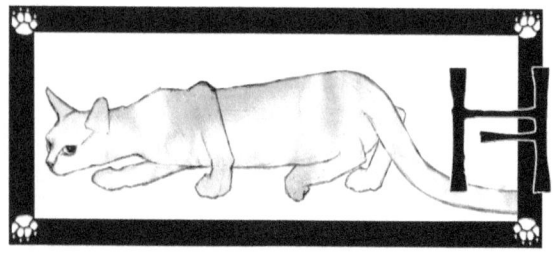 illside Pod trekked home with their new Queen. They slept late into the next day until hunger roused them and Ghost, Buster and Kyra left to hunt. Rosie curled in her nest, Mee-am's cloth beneath her. Watching her sniff and tenderly lick the fraying embroidery, Browser realized she'd part with her tail before losing her link to her human. He paced awkwardly before her.

"What is it?" she asked.

"Would you like to take a walk with me?"

Rosie studied him. "You mean a walk like the walks we took when I first got here?"

"Yes," he murmured, licking his paws to hide his embarrassment, but Rosie was agreeable to the idea. She rose and stretched her front and back legs thoroughly and they entered the big room where the scent of fresh mouse drew them to the prey pile. They ate and groomed and rested with Buster and Kyra before leaving the den together.

As the sun sank in the west, the waning moon floated above the eastern treeline, its soft light falling on two cats racing toward the woods. They cantered and pounced, clearing bushes and boulders with effortless leaps, rolling over and over in mock battle, Browser gnawing her neck and licking her fur, while Rosie rabbit-kicked his belly. Suddenly, he pulled away.

"No, Browser, don't be like that. Let's play."

"I'm sorry," he murmured, but remained apart, refusing to touch her.

"Come on," she teased, reaching for his ears. He ducked. She stretched her paw toward his. He tucked them under his chest and sat, limbs hidden and tail wrapped, looking like a furry loaf of bread.

Rosie chuffed. "Why'd you ask me to run with you?"

"I want to be near you...I just..." She glared.

"Tell me, truthfully, Browser, do you care for me?"

"I can't," he muttered.

"Can't care or can't tell me?" He didn't answer. "Browser, I'm tired of—"

"You're the Queen," he interrupted. "You must marry a king. I was born in an alley."

"I'd rather hoped you weren't born a fool."

His tail slapped the ground, raising a swirl of dust. "No, I was born under a dumpster, something you can't understand."

Rosie flurried his whiskers. "Hang the Prophecy!" she growled to his widening eyes. "How can it promise love and peace and create misery?"

"You need a king as your mate."

"Like a bird needs teats."

He stiffened. "Rosie—"

"No." Frustrated, she flurried the air. "Anyway, I've met the kin of the Green and I've yet to meet a king, or anyone remotely resembling a king. What royalty could you possibly be talking about?"

"You're wrong about meeting all the kin. We have families, old ones, who trace their lineage to pedigrees as strong as your own."

"Oh, cow feathers! Their grandfathers lived on the streets just like yours."

"No, Rosamonde," he replied. "They were born in a cattery like yours and brought to Ironstone Manor in the southwestern Green. They mated only with their own, those with long fur and an extra toe on their front paws. For a long time only one upright cared for them, letting them run freely through the manor. The old female seemed to live forever, but when she finally died no one came for the colony. They'd been forgotten. Their descendants live there still, and now they have an emperor. So you see, there *is* a line of royalty to choose from." His words had come in a rush, little shields building a wall between his heart and her questions. He felt tired.

Rosie was nonplussed. "Why didn't I meet them at Harmony Tree?"

"They don't mix with us rabble." She gasped. Guiltily, he looked away. *How can I push her toward this?* A heartbeat later, "When you're ready, I'll take you to meet them." His tone was flat, emotionless.

Rosie's eyes narrowed. *So he doesn't care about me. I'm just a tool to fulfill the Prophecy.* Still, tail low and ears to the side, she tried one more time. "Do you really believe bloodline means anything to me?"

Infuriated, Rosie attacked. She leaped on his back, sinking fangs and claws deep enough to sting. Larger and stronger, he could have thrown her off, but didn't, and they rolled across the meadow, Rosie a belly-kicking, neck-biting, screeching ball of fur wrapped around him while Browser tried only to defend himself. Finally they flew apart. Browser sat, looking sad and confused. Rosie paced before him. The slant of her ears and raised scruff told him she was still angry, angrier than he'd ever seen her and he honestly didn't know why. Then she lay on her side before him and began grooming herself.

"Great Mother's Tail, what was that!" he yowled, leaping to his paws.

Rosie panted, her little pink tongue sticking out of her mouth. "Answer my question," she said.

"What question?"

Her eyebrows formed a straight line. *Does he really not understand?*

"What question?" he repeated.

"Do you love me, or not?"

"I can't."

"At least tell me why."

"But I have," he meowed plaintively.

"So that I understand."

"I'm nothing more than the errand boy sent to escort the Discarded Queen to the Green. I've not a drop of royal blood. I can do your bidding, my Queen, but can never ask you to be mine."

He does care. "Browser," she cooed, "I come from that world of bloodlines and titles and guess what? I wasn't good enough. Despite my perfect heritage, I'm too pale. My ears aren't big enough and the furry points at their tips are too big – or was it the other way around – I forget. Anyway, my paws don't come to perfect points like they should." She paused, noting the incredulity on his face. "Awful, isn't it? Thank Great Mother She thinks enough of me to allow me life." She let that sink in. "The world of bloodlines and pedigrees is ugly and false. Don't be ruled by a lie."

"I'm a servant to the kin, Rosie. Therein lies my value."

"A gentler fallacy, Browser, but still not truth."

"Truth?"

"That you, I, every living being are perfect within ourselves as part of the All That Is and no one, *no one* has the authority to call us less than or treat us so. You are a king, Browser, a king for-the-kin, from-the-kin, the best kind of king, serving as a true king would."

"Rosie, you flatter me."

"No, I don't. You think I must flatter my choice of mate?"

She wants me as her mate? Browser's heart danced in his chest despite himself.

"Browser, you are my king. I will have you...or no one." Rosie rubbed her cheek on his, sharing her scent.

Browser didn't know what to do. He didn't move. When at last he met her gaze, his eyes were pools of devotion. "From the moment I first saw you, I loved you, but loving you and being your king are two things. Rosie, I was not born to be King of the Green."

Rosie heard nothing after *I loved you.* Nothing else mattered. Browser had said he loved her. Her throat filled with sweet crooning and her toes ached to dance. She wound her body around his, head low and tail high. *Everything is wonderful,* she sang to herself.

But not yet. Browser turned away, shoulders sagging, tail brushing the ground and for the first time Rosie saw his deeply wounded spirit. He believed himself unworthy, and she couldn't fix that, but must wait until he did. For now, they'd be friends. As friends they could roam the meadows, hunt at the warrens and perch in trees, pelts touching. As friends they could share secrets. As his friend, she would encourage him until he saw himself as she did, a noble, brave king.

🐾   🐾   🐾

It was the Moon of Sleeping Oak when Ghost noticed the smell. Not the physical smell, which was repulsive, but the spiritual odor, which was worse, so bad in fact, it traveled all the way from deep in the western forest to Hillside Den.

"A killer's spirit stinks more than his corpses," Erasmus had told him, "and psychic stink lingers until amends are made." Ghost recognized the reek immediately; he also knew the killers were gone. Murders were uncommon in the Green, so finding the crime scene was easy. Inspecting it was not.

South of the badger's sett, Ghost padded to the ravine they called

Boulderfalls and steeled himself to look down into the henge. Eons earlier huge slabs of stone had peeled off and slid into the valley, landing upright with artistic perfection. They formed the Ouroboros: the serpent eating its own tail, a symbol of infinity, of repeating birth and death. Offering sanctuary to anyone who asked, the henge became a locus of magical love energy, and a carpet of green grass flourished within the circle of whitening stones. Vines grew like rising smoke and bloomed with fragrant flowers. Of all places to commit murder, to do it here was a profound sacrilege.

Ghost stood on the overhang, looking down on a travesty. Those sacred megaliths now guarded carnage. Love and beauty had been replaced with hatred and fear. *Where were we when this happened,* he asked himself. *Such evil doesn't occur overnight. There had to have been a progression toward this denial of life. Why didn't we notice? Or were we cowardly in the face of it, denying to ourselves it existed.* Ghost mourned.

At last he climbed down and entered the henge, each step bringing more shame than the last. Bird bones, fragments of rats. A disemboweled possum, a headless skunk, a fox kit beaten into pulp. The younglings wrenched his heart the most: the baby raccoons whose limbs had been yanked from their bodies, a wingless, legless young raven; other defenseless children gnawed upon, not for hunger, but to enjoy their pain, their carcasses left to rot. *Only pure evil inflicts such pain...and on innocents.* Ghost staggered into the forest and retched.

The pod cats sprawled on the boulders above their den, fanning their tails beneath a wintry sun. Ghost had pulled Browser away from the others to tell him what he'd found at Boulderfalls. As he spoke, Browser's ears sank low to the sides of his head. The cruelty Ghost described was staggering.

Browser shuddered. "Two-leggeds did this?" Ghost stared at his paws. "What? You don't think they would?"

"We know they kill for food and pelts, but these killings weren't for either."

"Vengeance then? A clan war?"

"Against squawkbeaks, ravens, smelltails, ringtails? Doesn't make sense."

"So no kin were harmed."

Ghost gave him a sharp look, then said "No." They sat in silence for several heartbeats. "Do you know what I think?"

Browser thumped his tail. "I seldom know what you think, Ghost, but I'm always interested."

"I think kin committed the murders," the little shaman whispered.

"KIN? NEVER!" Heads turned. Rosie came closer until Browser signaled with his tail for her to stop.

"I don't mean kin like us, Browser. I mean something alien, stronger, larger and evil."

"That's crazy," the pod leader snarled.

"Moons ago, I would have agreed, but I've sensed things, terrible things and I believe evil is growing in our world, hidden among us."

Now Browser sat tall, ears high, eyes wide. "What do we do?"

"We stay alert, ready to do what's needed."

"The last time I did what you said was needed..." Ghost' eyes followed Browser's gaze to Rosie, sprawled in the sunlight, washing her graceful paws with her delicate pink tongue. "You don't know how that affected me."

"It gives you reason to be king."

Browser scowled. "Desire doesn't make a king."

"A king could muster guards to protect life in the forest."

"Yes! And were I king, I'd do that, but it's not my place."

"Browser, you could do so much good."

"I must do good as I am, as a clan cat."

"Will you do some good for our clan then?" The big tabby looked suspicious but nodded. "I'm troubled by the crimes at Boulderfalls and we must bury the remains of those poor creatures, but first, Browser, promise me you'll go and see for yourself." Ghost' scruff rose. "Boulderfalls, Browser. Understand me. Boulderfalls, our sacred woodland temple." He brought his face close. "Boulderfalls," he repeated, locking eyes, "has been violated. Our sanctuary is no longer safe."

Unable to ignore the warning or Ghost' pleading eyes, Browser nodded. "I promise," he said.

Browser kept his promises, even the tough ones, but this one...this one made him anxious. *What if Ghost is right? What if this evil is spreading, as he fears? Lizard Beaks! Is there no one else who can deal with the problem?*

He knew there wasn't. The purebreds didn't care about anyone but themselves and most wildborn returned the favor, seeing the Royals as self-important dullards who lacked the courage to lead. *And Rosie will choose one as her mate. I made sure of that!* He chuffed, his paws thudding angrily down the bank of the stream that ran through the western forest. He loped deeper into the thicket, passed the abandoned badger sett and crept down the hill called Boulderfalls to the stone Ouroboros, where he saw the corpses scattered just as Ghost had described.

Other than the work of beetles and maggots, the bodies lay strangely untouched by scavengers. Browser wondered on that. His heart recoiled from the crimes, but he was unaware of any sadistic vibration still clinging to the site. To Browser the crime was beyond understanding, but it was over and best forgotten with the burial of the victims. *No reason to anoint myself king.* Still, the carnage was so savage he stumbled into the woods, and just as Ghost had, he retched.

Browser had loped a ways from the crime scene before he realized he was being followed. And the stalker didn't feel friendly. Browser hunkered, slinking into the scrub beneath a twisted fir. A foul stench wafted to his slightly open mouth, and he took short, quick breaths to identify it. *What's this? Felidae?* It came from above. He looked up. Branches trembled and needles fell. A huge feline face rushed toward him. Pain! The cat behind the face was equally huge and twice as heavy and Browser lay crushed beneath him. The cat stood and Browser rolled away before its paw thundered down where his head had been. He was outmatched and knew it. Kicking his legs high behind him, his rear paws caught the slow-witted giant beneath the chin, knocking him back into the tree. Down he went. Browser sprinted away not stopping to look or even catch his breath until he burst into the meadow south of Hillside Den. Bruised, torn and winded, he limped home. *Ghost is right. Something is terribly wrong in the Green. I have to do something.*

🐾   🐾   🐾

In the cold beneath the Moon of Bare Branches Ghost fell ill. During Darkmoon Gathering of mentors and apprentices, he lay in his nest coughing into a leaf filled with shavings of buttercup root and sage. His podmates worried. Coldmoons was a bad time for a cough. If it spread to your lungs, you could die. Every night his dreams were haunted by the ghosts of Boulderfalls, and Ghost wondered if he wasn't about to join them.

Miserable and restless, he bolted from the cave to the boulders above, hoping the sound of water on the rocks would help him sleep. Turning the circles of past, future, and now, Ghost cooled his fever on the stones, paws tucked and tail wrapped. Finally, he dozed, but not well. He grew cold and heard himself coughing, felt his body shivering in waves. He grew weaker, the sickness pushing and pulling his will like flotsam in a frightful current. A dark shape loomed through hazy vision and a massive paw nudged his chest. Ghost moaned.

"Come on," Browser hissed in his ear, "Let's get you inside."

Ghost followed his rescuer back to the den, then collapsed. His dreams turned violent and chaotic with only scraps of sanity breaking through. Rosie's trill, Kyra's scent, water dripped into his burning mouth. A tender mouse brought to tempt him when he couldn't eat. Ghost fought, but the fever fought harder. He fought harder and the fever raged. By the third sunfall, he'd lost the war. *My body is broken,* he grieved, sad to leave the world. At the edge of his awareness blue skies cradled fragrant meadows and he felt the presence of the Great Mother Cat.

Ghost floated above his body. It looked twisted and small, his lower jaw jutting unnaturally forward. His eyes were glazed over and he felt cold, so cold. The warmth of that sun-drenched meadow was only a final breath away. He yearned for its radiance. His breathing slowed. The cave grew dimmer. It was then he saw his Fetch perched on the edge of his nest, smiling. *Forget your name,* it told him. *Just for now. Just for a moment. That's it, let go.* Ghost stopped breathing.

Rosie lay nearby, feeling every tremor of his death. "Nee-ow-ow-ow-ow-wah," she cried with such anguish Ghost' spirit felt his own heart rending. *Rosie must not suffer. Rosie must not suffer.* And his body drew a shallow, shaky breath. Browser's strength flowed into the strange other-place where Ghost was floating, grabbed him by the scruff and pulled him back toward life.

Ghost opened his eyes and stared into the faces of his friends. It was love that held him to this world.

"Thank you," the little wizard murmured, falling into cool, dark relief. He lay half-conscious several risings of the moon, emerging bone-thin and feeble, but alive. His illness had been as much of his spirit as his flesh and for the moments he wandered his inner world, he'd gone to the center where all life was one consciousness of light and joy. Along the path, however, he'd seen the enemy who would destroy the Green. A profound hunger, a vast fear. And while the shaman slept, it committed murder...wearing the body of a cat.

🐾   🐾   🐾

Brightmoon rose behind rain clouds, and the crowd at Harmony Tree was smaller than usual. Rainpelt, the new pod leader of Bigmarsh Family, led the ceremonies with the help of Darktail, Elder Cat of the West. Fortunately, the drizzling stopped after the opening ritual and announcements of birthings and passings, and the kin happily milled about, greeting old friends and making new ones. Rosie perched on the stage, ensuring the Discarded Queen was available to any who wished to engage her. Browser perched nearby.

A flurry at the edge of the gathering parted the crowd. Rising to her paws, Rosie strained to see, yelping with surprise when she did. Six large, long-haired cats, Chevalier Knights she would later learn, marched two abreast. They were followed by six Praetorian Guard, larger, more muscular cats who carried on their broad backs a makeshift litter upon which sprawled the largest cat of all: a Persian polydactyl, their Emperor Ozymandias. Six Chevalier came behind, ending the parade with sparkling symmetry.

All of them were strangely costumed. Rosie had never seen bits of frayed velvet, barren feathers and knotty strands of old sequins used as clothing on humans, much less kin. Glittering strings hung about the soldiers' ears and under their chins, or were woven into the matted dreadlocks of their jowls. Some wore sequined masks, strands wound above and below their eyes, the ends knotted around glint-and-sparkle treasures trailing in the dust. Much of what they wore was dirty and all of it was old. No matter. These odd Felidae marched as proudly as show horses.

The parade had almost reached the tree. Rosie and Browser watched the Emperor bobbing along on his settee, head high, staring into the distance, refusing to see the kin around him. His seat was the backrest and rear legs of a hardwood chair, upended across the shoulders of his Praetorian Guard. A pillow had been tucked into the slats for his comfort, but it was torn and its contents were slowly leaking away, its sham, once a lavish purple, now a gray-streaked mauve, its golden tassels nothing more than chewed fuzz.

Like the raggedly costumed soldiers who bore him, he seemed unaware of his threadbare bolster, resting on it like a god descended from the stars. This large-boned, overfed silver male, the Prince of the Procession, the Emperor of Ironstone Garden, was also the self-appointed King of the Green, and padding along at his side was Sylvestes Felaria, the Grand Vizier. He too was costumed. *Such an odd thing to do,* Rosie thought. *Ridiculously human.* Sylvestes limited himself, however, to a scrap of gray-brown velvet without the feathers, sequins, or pieces of waxy fruit, like the grapes and cherries she saw hanging from the ears of some Chevalier. *An attempt at dignity. Great Mother's Tail, he's ancient,* Rosie told herself, noticing his arthritic gait. Unlike the others, his pelt was short, more taupe than silver, his build too stolid to be a purebred Siamese and he lacked the polydactyl paws of the royals. He simply wasn't one of them, staring at the world through a wrinkled lilac face with a gaze neither friendly nor cruel. Sylvestes took everything in and gave little back, but Rosie was by nature a Wisdom Cat. She could feel what was hidden, hear what was unsaid.

She trembled violently, her breath catching in her throat while her heart thudded in her chest. The entire spectacle, the twelve Chevalier, six Praetorian Guard, their Emperor, his Grand Vizier, along with the fruits, nuts and baubles, the glittering strings of sequins, bony feathers and tattered scarves fluttering in the breeze like the flags of nations, were all headed straight for her. Sylvestes Felaria, his eyes dark like oceans and deep as the orbits of stars, had brought the King of the Green to claim her as his bride.

The Chevalier reached the roots, parting left and right, bringing the settee to the edge of the stage where the Praetorian dropped bellies to the ground in perfect unison and the huge silver cat disembarked. Ozymandias rose up on his hind legs and clothed as he was, Rosie almost expected him to walk on them, but he merely wanted to show her how tall and powerful he could be and to shake the trinkets in his velvet scarf, little bells announcing his arrival. He dropped to all fours and padded toward Rosie and Browser. Sylvestes leaped lightly as mist onto the platform, tiptoed to one side and sat watching.

Rosie wished she could hide behind Browser and let him greet this king in shabby splendor, but he stood before her, his vacant blue eyes locked on hers. Shaking his head, he tossed matted bangs and baubles up behind his right ear, then his mouth began to quiver. It took a moment before Rosie understood: Ozymandias was imitating a human smile. She struggled not to laugh. Great Mother's Fingers and Toes, she wanted to laugh! Had Browser's eyes even twinkled she would have, but the pod leader considered the emperor's visit a serious affair.

Failing to engage Rosie the way he wanted, Ozymandias turned to Browser. "Bumbler, right?...Boxer?" he asked, his ear twitching beneath the tickling curls of his fur. "No, don't tell me, starts with a B. I'm great with names. Never forget a name. Everyone says so." He grinned. "Of course that makes me popular with the females...you understand," he whispered slyly in the pod leader's ear.

Browser didn't understand, being an honorable warrior with a bashful respect for females until he chose a mate for life. He dipped his head. "I'm Browser, leader of Hillside Pod."

For a heartbeat, the emperor looked annoyed. "Browser...right. I was just about to say that." Another toss of the hair, and he turned back to Rosie.

He thinks that's appealing, she realized, tempted to laugh again.

"So, you're the Forgotten Female," he began.

"Discarded Queen," Browser corrected.

"Right. And I am Ozymandias...the 23rd Emperor of Ironstone Manor, rightful King of the Green, and everyone and everything in it." Closing his eyes, he extended a plump, six-toed paw for Rosie to sniff and lick.

"I guess that means me too," she said in a small voice and placing her dainty paw on his huge one, gently but firmly pushed it down to the roots. Ozymandias quivered. *Does she mock me?* He glanced at Sylvestes, but the vizier was himself flummoxed and only narrowed his eyes.

Ozymandias chuffed and withdrew his paw. Tossing his bangs again, he gave Rosie another crooked smile. "Yes, well, send your friend Blinkers here to the manor and my Chevalier will make the necessary arrangements for our union." *What union?* She screamed inside. *I never agreed to any union.* His smile grew brittle and Rosie sensed something sharper than fangs behind it. Now he placed his rejected paw on hers, pressing hard enough to cause discomfort, but not so hard it couldn't be accidental. "Understand, sweet girl, I am never denied," he whispered. Rosie shuddered nose to tail and seeing her fear, his face softened, then looking down with fake surprise, lifted his heavy paw. Rosie's foot throbbed, but she met his gaze like nothing was wrong. *I'll eat my own ears before I let him know he hurt me.*

He knew. "Yes, yes," he said. "We must make arrangements that suit the wildborn as well as we highborn." He glanced at Browser when mentioning wildborn. Rosie and Browser both flinched. "The kin will want to attend the ceremonies and meet their royals. We must *talk turkey* as they say." True to character, Ozymandias' self-congratulating mind went straight to a favorite indulgence. "Speaking of tasty meat, I always liked turkey. Actually, I've never had any. I like the idea of turkey. A story passed down through the family is that the first Ozymandias had turkey every day, given off the fingers of his human. They're all gone now...the humans...their turkey." Wistfully, he scanned the tree branches above them, as if the humans and their turkey slices had lived there. Another hair flip and he studied Rosie's face. *He wants me to fear him,* she realized. "Still own the house though," he went on, "and the grounds. You'll like it there." He leaned in, whispering like a conspirator. "Maybe we'll have turkey for our ceremony, or better yet...afterward." Rosie no longer wanted to laugh; she wanted to flee. Unsure how much power this monstrous king of the Green had, however, she hid her revulsion behind a placid face. Ozymandias wasn't thinking of her. The great-in-his-own-mind king turned and trundled back to his pillow ride. The Chevalier helped him unto his litter and his Praetorian Guard rose, bearing him on their shoulders.

Rosie stood, fearful and violated, and watched him disappear into the crowd. The last she saw of the king and his grand parade was Sylvestes fixing his uncanny eyes upon her before he too was swallowed by the crush.

She turned, bearing down on Browser like a tornado in a flat Kansas field. "You!" she screeched. "This is what you and your snake-hearted shaman had planned for me?" She flurried him against the tree, wailing loud enough to draw a crowd. "You sold me to that insane cretin, that *thing* who thinks he's a god, for your *Prophecy*?"

"No, Rosie, no! I had no idea he would come here." Browser moaned, deflating with every word. "Or that he was that bad. Anyway, he has no real power. It's all in his head." He hunkered, ears and eyes down.

Gradually, Rosie's scruff lay back against her skin and her breathing calmed. But it wasn't calm Browser felt when he met her gaze; it was her bruised heart. "I trusted you," she murmured, turned and padded into the crowd.

Brightmoon of Bare Branches was only the beginning of Browser's misery. Ozymandias' ridiculous demands had destroyed whatever trust he'd built with Rosie, and she was a master at shunning, much better than Browser had been. She wouldn't speak to him or look at him if he set himself on fire. And she certainly wouldn't let him explain that Ozymandias was delusional, that he'd never promised the crazy, self-anointed emperor anything, much less a life with his beloved Rosamonde. Yes, he'd brought her to the Green, putting her in his cross-hairs, but no promises had been made. It didn't matter. Rosie would never know.

Brightmoon of Bare Branches was also Ghost' first public outing since his illness. He found himself jostled to the back side of the tree, surrounded by Wisdom Cats. "Are you all right?" Darktail asked.

"Yes. Thank you."

"And Erasmus?"

The shaman's eyes widened. "I haven't seen him. Why?"

Sosay's crescent flashed. "Neither have we. No one from the north or the east came to Darkmoon Gathering." She stared at her paws, adding bleakly, "And my apprentice Reggie has been missing since then."

Now Ghost was worried. "You think Erasmus is missing? He's mentoring Morsus. What does Morsus say?"

Darktail and Sosay flicked their whiskers. "He's missing too," Sosay meowed.

Ghost thought of the garden of death, the murderous cat in his delirium and felt queasy. "I've not been well," he rasped, backing out of the circle. He was relieved when the others turned their attention from him to three approaching Wisdom Cats, Skyleaper and Starpaw, led by Nebula, the Elder of the East. The eastern cats were the largest and most muscular of all the kin, but Nebula, black as the abyss with startling silver eyes, was half again larger than his companions. They all had huge paws with webbed toes and long hind legs, their backs sloping slightly up toward their tails. It lent to their stride an easy grace, reminding Ghost of the legendary mountain cats with tails so long the ends dragged on the ground, enabling them to climb steep slopes with deer-sized prey in their jaws.

Tonight, the eastern kin looked angry, offering no greeting trill. Nebula sat back from the circle, letting Skyleaper and Starpaw take the lead. Skyleaper didn't sit at all, but rather paced in a circle within the circle, giving each of the gathered cats a hard stare. "Who last saw Indra?" he rasped, his tail swiping the air.

"Indra never came to Darkmoon Gathering," Sosay answered.

Skyleaper paused before her, bringing his face rudely close. "I can tell if you're lying."

Sosay scooted back with a hiss, her head jewel pulsing. "Why would I lie? Reggie's gone too! You eastern kin are so suspicious...and arrogant." Starpaw, black as Nebula but with a shower of white stars sprinkled up his front legs, dropped his speckled paw on Skyleaper's shoulder, and the big white male turned away.

"Skyleaper was her apprentice," Starpaw said to Sosay in an attempt to explain his friend's rude behavior. "Nebula heard her cry out...but she was already gone." A shudder passed through the gathering. "You can imagine the pain."

"I'll try," Sosay chuffed, thinking of Reggie.

"Have you..." The little wizard faltered, "Didn't you...haven't you tried to find her using your powers of mind?" Starpaw stared at the apprentice for a long heartbeat, unsure what to admit. He glanced at Nebula, whose eyes told him to speak.

"Yes," he murmured. An awkward silence, then Nebula rose and crossed to Ghost, eyes flashing.

"Her vanishing is shrouded from our minds."

Sosay's tail whipped, her face lit with emotion. "Nor can we augur what happened to Reggie!"

Darktail shuddered. "I feel nothing from the four who are missing."

"Four?" Starpaw asked, his gaze drifting from Darktail to the plush, chocolate-pelted Martileena, and the most beautiful eyes he'd ever seen. She returned his stare with a shy nod.

"It seems Erasmus and Morsus are missing too," Darktail meowed.

"Good riddance to the freak," someone whispered.

Ghost was offended for Morsus, but said nothing. He had to tell them about the grisly scene in the woods. "I have found something, something not good," he began. "A charnel yard in the forest, near the badger sett, but it wasn't the work of the badger. Creatures were killed there...for pleasure, not food." Shocked hisses all around.

"Any kin?" Nebula asked.

Ghost continued. "No. Nor do I know who did it, but—"

Darktail interrupted. "It sounds like the work of tall-walkers! Who else kills for sport?"

"Something evil," Sosay said, her voice trembling.

Ghost stood. "It wasn't uprights; there was no scent of them. It was kin who killed...like we did in the time of The Bloodlust." Horrified snarling followed by such intense staring he worried he'd need an alibi. "I've been ill. I've seen things in waking-dreams...murderous things," he paused, gathering courage for what he must say next, as he turned toward the majestic Elder Cat of the East. "I'm sorry, Nebula. Indra was murdered by kin."

Nebula sat quietly. "So say you. Indra is my mate. I would know if she died." Indra had been gone half a turn of the Moon and deep in his heart Nebula knew she no longer walked the Earth, but he couldn't yet face it.

🐾 🐾 🐾

Bittercold Moon was now upon them and a light snow covered the Green. Many creatures had gone to ground. Prey was scarce. In the dim glow before sunrise, the hunters met south of Harmony Tree. A joyless meeting, for no one had even a mouse to share after their all-night hunt.

"I don't remember being this hungry since before we came here," Buster rasped.

Ghost nuzzled his shoulder. "We'll eat today. I feel it."

Pelts dusted with frost, the three males crept to the peak of a knoll, and to their amazement, discovered two longear crouched against the tree-line, pulling at ice-stiffened stalks. But when the hunters rose above the whiteness of the hillock, the longear fled. *This hunt must succeed,* Browser determined, shivering despite his thick winter coat. He glanced at Ghost, whose fur wasn't nearly as thick, and leaned against his friend to warm him.

"What's that?" the little shaman whispered.

"Where?" Buster asked.

"There!" Ghost pointed with his muzzle, then belly to the ground, crept in short spurts toward a gray lump beneath a whitened juniper bush. Once close, instead of pouncing, he sniffed the bundle end to end and turned toward his podmates with a forlorn expression. Buster and Browser loped to him. A young tom lay unmoving in the snow.

"Is he dead?" Buster asked.

"Almost," Browser answered.

Through his damp fur, Ghost counted the tom's ribs. " He's starving."

"And freezing," Buster added. "And barely adult, without jowls or shoulder muscles."

Ghost sniffed him again. "We must help."

Buster swept a cloud of white sparkles into the air with his tail. "Help him? We have nothing to eat!"

"You don't see the good in this?" Ghost asked calmly. "Great Mother has given us someone to help. It means we'll find prey, lots of it."

Browser's eyes smiled as he lowered his belly to the ground. "Help me carry him to the den." Buster scruffed the gray cat and pulled him over Browser's back. The tom mewed weakly as the pod leader rose, just able to bear the weight, and with Buster beside him, headed home. Leaving the rescue in the females' care, they hurried back to the knoll, but Ghost, happy as a house cat, was already hunting. And he was right. Their preypile grew wide and tall.

🐾 🐾 🐾

Kyra chewed sweetgrass and buttercup root, pushing the cud into the gray cat's mouth with her own, then she and Rosie placed themselves along either side to keep him warm. Later, he wobbled to the stone basin for a drink and later still, ate a small mouse from the preypile. Shyly, he returned to the females, remaining between their warmth for three rises of the moon. Every day before sunrise he'd make nightsoil in the corner of the room. It smelled of sickness, but he buried it quickly and deep. No one scolded him, although they'd never permit themselves such a weakness. Patiently, they waited for his story and on the third day a much stronger cat turned to Kyra.

"What's your name?" he asked

"I'm Kyra." she trilled, half asleep.

"Thank you, Kyra." He looked at Rosie. "And yours?"

"Rosie."

"Thank you, Rosie. Who brought me here?"

At that moment, Browser entered and dropped a longear on the preypile. "We did. I'm Browser," he said. The others followed him inside with treasures of their own. "This is Buster...and Ghost," he added, pointing with his tail. "And you are?"

"I'm Robin, named for the red-breasted fliers who return when the sun warms and the trees bud." Everyone stared at the blush on his chest that interrupted an otherwise gray pelt.

"How did you survive Bittercold?" Rosie asked.

"I didn't," Robin answered, scanning their faces with grateful eyes.

"What brought you to the Green?" Browser asked.

Robin met his gaze. "I will tell you everything and by my good mother, I swear I mean no harm, but for now please permit me to rest." His head dropped to his chest and within a heartbeat he slept.

Each sunrise found Robin stronger than the day before and soon the day arrived when Rosie and Kyra led him from the den up the hill to the boulder near the falling water. The meadow stretched away an unbroken gleam of white silence broken only by the gurgling of the ice-choked stream, and the thud of snow piles hitting the ground. In the distance, a roundeye hooted three times.

"Can you tell us your story now?" Rosie asked.

"I have a debt to the others," Robin answered, "Especially to your mate, the King." Rosie stared in bewilderment.

"Browser is not my mate," she said.

Robin studied her. "Not yet?" Her whiskers burned. Later, when the three clambered down to the den, Robin sat between the queens on the Guardian Stone. "You are most fortunate to have the protection of a shelterveil."

"Oh," Rosie trilled, "You see the entrance?"

"I see it because you see it, Rosie. Like you, I am a natural empath."

"How could an alley cat know the rules of shelterveils," Kyra snarled with a swipe of her tail.

"I know they protect what Great Mother holds dear," Robin trilled, dipping his head like a courtier.

"Great Mother thinks I'm important?" she asked with wide eyes.

"By my tail, she does," he said, "And rightly so."

"Let's go inside," she cooed, swaying like a priss. Soon after, the males arrived, each with prey, and Robin, well enough to enjoy a meal with the pod, was also ready to tell his tale.

"I was birthed in an alley not far from the Green," he began, "where many are born sickly and don't survive. There's not enough food, not even rats. There aren't any feathertails because there aren't any trees. There aren't any longear because there's no grass. There's only the uprights' false stone. We live on scraps they throw away and too many fight for too little."

"Why do you stay?" Rosie asked.

"And go where? If you're born there that's your home, and more are always coming, dumped by tall-walkers who no longer wish to care for a pet. Some have been declawed and still they're dumped. Their humans move and leave them behind; some humans only want kits; some kin are dumped because they're birthing kits. There are many reasons for the abandonment, but only one end...slow, painful death."

Browser growled. "The life of a wildborn is hard...But to be raised inside and then abandoned...that's almost impossible to survive."

"...and without your claws..." Rosie added, shivering at the thought. Kyra's eyes grew round with horror.

"Tall-walkers pull our claws out?"

"Worse than that," Rosie said. "Their healers chop off the ends of our toes.

"They call butchers like that healers?" Kyra shrieked.

Rosie nodded. "When I lived with Mee-am, I met kin who'd been declawed because they scratched chairs or rugs. Vole-brained humans! They only needed to give their kin a scratching pole. Mee-am did." She shuddered, drawing her paws tightly beneath her, muttering, "Mee-am would never hurt me. Never."

"No. She let her mate dump you instead." Kyra chuffed meanly.

"She didn't know," Rosie hissed with a violent thump of her tail. Kyra looked away. It wasn't an argument she could win.

Robin continued. "I was birthed toward the end of coldmoons. Of six born, only four lived past three moon rises and only my sister and I survived the fleas and the worms in our bowels beyond two turns of the moon. After that, we had to feed ourselves, although our mother let us stay with her. Always heavy with kits or nursing, she was frail. I helped her as I could."

"Your father?" Rosie asked.

"Like all males, he wandered." Robin paused, remembering his father's wide face and sad eyes. "Always fighting...I was six turns of the moon when he told me to leave." Agitated, Robin kneaded the floor with his claws, then lowering his ears in submission, addressed Browser directly.

"I came here because kin say you are fair-minded and kind and I knew if you discovered me I wouldn't be killed, that the worst you'd do is make me leave. My sister found me and told me the White Truck had taken our mother, and our father had died from infected wounds. At least I had her...until a ghostdog..." His voice trailed off. "I've been living on your border for several brightmoons now. I found your scent-marker and ate your prey anyway. Then coldmoons came on so strongly and early and prey went to ground. When I fell in the snow, I didn't expect to rise." Robin tucked his paws and stared at the floor. He hoped he wouldn't be told to leave, but he'd told the truth and admitted theft. Some leaders would kill him for that. The moment stretched painfully on.

Browser approached and Robin hastily rose to his paws, head high, but tail low, unsure what would happen. Browser stared. Suddenly he rubbed his face on Robin's, bestowing the scent of Hillside Pod. Soft purring filled the den. "You may stay, but only here...with us. Does that suit you, Robin?" With a belly-deep rumble, Robin leaned in and licked his ears.

Everyone slept. Browser entered the alcove where Rosie had her nest. He sat in the dark listening to her breathe. The most beautiful queen he'd ever met, she had the most beautiful spirit. *Why hadn't that been enough for my bug-brain? She wanted me. Now she'll never forgive me for lying. First I trick her to get her here. Then Ozymandias. I don't blame her.*

But something kept him there with her. Hearing the cruelty of Robin's life, his suffering, the suffering of so many touched him. The extinction of wildborn by uprights, the sadistic murders at Boulderfalls, and finally, Nit and Kit's warning the White Truck was coming to the Green...Browser needed a friend, someone to be close, someone to trust with his heart. *I want to be with Rosie. I love her.* He wasn't sure what to do. Finally he rose to leave. Rosie lifted her head, meeting his gaze.

"Rosie...Ozymandias..." he began, wanting to tell her how much he'd changed, that he'd never let that flea-brained emperor be her mate. And most of all, whatever his birthright or birth-wrong, he understood now that he must lead.

"I know," she said.

He approached the nest. "I am yours to command, Rosie. Whatever Great Mother, whatever you ask of me, I will do it. If you'll still have me...I am your king." She made room for him on Mee-am's cloth.

Red settled near the sleeping kits and closed his eyes.

"Red?" the little girl whispered.

He was tired, but for her he raised himself. "Sleep, little one," he said with a lick to her ear.

"I miss my mother."

"You're a lucky kit. You've been saved."

"I know, Red." She yawned, then curled, tucking her face into her tummy. "But I still miss my mommy."

8 – Vision Quest

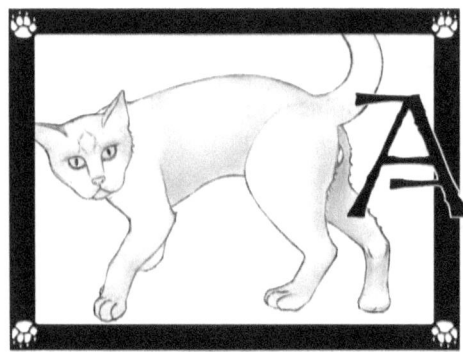

A fang of moon hung in the early-evening sky. Ghost padded south toward Harmony Tree. He'd spend three nights in its branches before returning home as a full-fledged Wisdom Cat. Reaching the Great Tree, he paused, offering a prayer before scrambling up the trunk. *If I fail, I must wait until Bittercold Moon comes 'round again...but I won't fail.*

As Ghost settled on a wide branch, pale blue lights floated down, melting into his fur. They gave him strength and energy. "Starlight!"

"Yes, I am," the Spirit Cat meowed, flitting down the branches of the tree, his quivering tail streaming galaxies behind him. "And here you are." He perched above the apprentice. "I trust you're familiar with the rules."

"I think so, but I'm worried."

Starlight rolled his ample whiskers forward and back as if clearing away a bother, then hunkered, staring into Ghost' eyes. Heartbeats passed in silence. "I'm waiting," he said at last.

"Oh, oh, sorry," Ghost ducked his head, embarrassed. "Um...Erasmus isn't in the Green and no one knows where he is."

"Yes...and?"

Ghost ducked his head again, more embarrassed. "Well, should I attempt my vision-quest? How can I receive the RA?"

Starlight's eyes smiled. "Do you know the stories of Rootheart, first Elder Cat of the North?" Ghost nodded. "How do you suppose he received the RA?"

"I never thought about it."

Starlight leaned down until their noses touched. "From me," he whispered.

"You? That was so long ago, almost from the time of the Bloodlust."

"Yes and as many moons will rise again before I forget this world." Starlight sat tall, swishing his star-laden tail back and forth below the branch. Galaxies spun through the air. "Or did you think Spirit Cat just means I have lots of waking-dreams?" Ghost felt foolish. He licked his chest fur repeatedly, avoiding eye contact. Starlight waited until his embarrassment passed. "Now, about the rules. One: you may not eat or sleep the duration of your quest. Waking-dreams are permitted, of course. Water is permitted, which you'll find pooled in needle clumps throughout the tree. Two: you may never tell anyone what happened during your vision-quest, not Browser, not Erasmus, not even me." Ghost nodded. "And three, and this is most important: you must remain in the tree or forfeit your right to receive the RA. Normally your mentor would come to you the morning after the third moonrise, but this time it will be me. Understand?" Starlight looked through the branches as if expecting someone, then turned back to Ghost. "You're alone. You know that, right?"

"Y-yes." Ghost seemed unsure.

"It's just that, well, normally there are several of you doing the quest. Not that you talk to each other, but I imagine it's a little less frightening that way."

"Frightening?"

Starlight fluffed his pelt like a preening bird, looking off so that Ghost wouldn't see the mischief in his eyes. "Oh, it's nothing, really. Just..."

"Just what?" Ghost asked, determined to keep the trembling from his voice.

The Spirit Cat waved his tail, shedding more stars into the night. "It's just that these are strange times, dangerous times." Now he was serious.

"I know," the little shaman replied. He was serious too.

"May She lift Her Paw," Starlight purred, disappearing in a shower of gems. Ghost sat quietly. Other than the chirping of crickets, occasional bird song, or the haunting call of an owl, the night stretched into a long expanse of sameness. The sliver of moon had arced far across the heavens before Ghost left his seat to explore, and though the creatures nesting in the cedar knew he wouldn't hunt, they still scampered or fluttered away when he approached. By morning his belly was painfully empty. *Why didn't I eat more before coming here,* he chided himself, filling up with water before tiptoeing to the end of a branch to watch the sunrise. He dreamed through short-shadows, woke and drank again, changed his perch and dreamed through long-shadows. As evening approached, Ghost began to fret, for the halfway mark of his vision quest was here and nothing unusual had happened. He hadn't been tested and no secrets of life had revealed themselves to him.

The starfield wheeled by overhead and Ghost grew uncomfortable. His muscles cramped, hunger knotted his belly and his burning eyes ached for sleep. He paced until exhausted, then lay on his belly, digging the claws of one paw into the other to stay awake. But despite his efforts, Ghost drifted into that space between wakefulness and dreams where thoughts and feelings flow freely past the *shoulds* and *don'ts* of living with others.

Swimming the sea of his subconscious, he felt buoyed in a state of grace until the powerful currents of fear swept him down into suffering. But he fought his way back, churning through choices made in deep, unknowable places of his soul. *Fear is delusion,* he told himself. *Great Mother is love. Life is joy.* Ghost burst into the beauty of the twilight sky, trees waving against its deepening blue. He heard rustling in the bushes. Overwhelmed by terror, he was the mouse, felt the talons sink into his body, and lift him off the ground. He lived its death, rested in the All That Is, then suckled at his new mother's teat. Ghost was Ghost again.

Fish or flower, beast or man,
We are one Life since Life began.
A Wisdom Cat in Harmony Tree
Purrs and cries but can't eat me.

Sang a nearby feathertail. A king snake beat percussion with its scales. "Good night all," it rasped, slipping into its hole at the roots of the tree. A battalion of ants marched down the trunk, passing a regiment tramping home. Twisting their antennae, the descending column saluted with a chant.

Fish or flower, beast or man,
We are one Life since Life began.
Down we patter beneath the weeds,
To find the food the family needs.

To which the climbing soldiers replied:

Fish or flower, beast or man,
We are one Life since Life began.
Up we clamber, doing our part,
Feeding the city beneath the bark.

"Neow," Ghost trilled, admiring their unity. As a Wisdom Cat, he'd been taught every living thing had consciousness, and to a degree he'd experienced it, but this was a watershed. Flooded with thoughts and feelings from the birds to the butterflies, he understood them all. Worms inched with purpose beneath the soil while spiders danced on silken strings and longear prayed over the ferns they nibbled. A mother fox nursed her kits, passing with every drop of milk and lick of her tongue her wisdom of the world. Every being, every thing, even stone, wind and cloud had a voice and Ghost had mastered their language.

Bathed in purple light, the meadow warbled and squeaked as daylight creatures retired to their nests and nocturnal hunters rose. A female smelltail wobbled toward Harmony Tree followed by two hopeful males. She lifted rocks and dug for grubs, paying little heed to their chittering until one pushed the other into her side and she released a small amount of scent. Ghost flew to the top of the cedar, where he stared through the branches at her vibrating life-force, the *All That Is* revealing itself as skunk. When the smelltails spoke to one another, their energy crackled, appearing to Ghost like ropes of electricity as bright as starlight, while his own energy encircled him in blue swirls like the aura of Harmony Tree.

The darkmoon rose. Milk Mother spilled her suns across the sky. *Tonight I will be tested,* Ghost told himself. He was far past tired, and hungry enough to eat dirt, but he filled his stomach with more water, and hunkered on a low branch. Crickets chirped, frogs croaked. The meadow tortured him with the reek of rodents and longear. The owl plucked another mouse from its hiding place, sending its family scurrying down their hole. The stars sank below the western horizon and light seeped into the eastern sky.

A faint mewl. *What was that?* Another faint mewl. *Am I crazy? A kit?* Another mewl and Ghost spied a lump of yellow fur exploring the roots of the tree. The wizard trilled. Up popped the kit's head, mostly eyes and ears. It opened its mouth and yowled. It dove into a bush, then climbed a too-small stalk that bent beneath its weight, depositing him on his back in the grass again. A male. Ghost chuckled and the kit dashed off. Ghost paced the bough, trying to keep an eye on his visitor.

He smelled the badger before he saw him, a low-slung bear trotting along the meadow's edge. The ill-tempered creature had left its sett near Boulderfalls, but the wizard was surprised to encounter it at Harmony Tree. Trundling toward the giant cedar, it stopped to snuffle and scoop, then lifting its wide, banded face, hissed with a flash of fangs. The kit had been seen. Badgers prefer to dig for their meals and don't consider kitten culinary delight, but how could it pass on the golden ninny tossing moss balls in the air.

"Come here," the shaman cried. The kit ignored him. Ghost slid down the trunk tail first, his claws digging furrows in its bark. "Come here!" The furball looked up and hissed. Ghost stretched, one paw hooked into the bole, the other extended. "Come on!" he yowled. "Danger!"

Now the feckless kit looked around and saw the badger. "Yeeeee- ow!" He turned sideways, lifted his pelt and arched his back. Hopping forward on tippytoes, he caterwauled and spit like some ferocious monster, a monster no larger than a good-sized cabbage, and almost as dangerous. The badger's long claws churned the turf with every stride.

"Get up here, bug brain! He'll kill you!" The kit froze. Ghost stretched farther, just missing his scruff. The stink of badger filled Ghost' nose. Frantic, the shaman flew over the roots and wrapping his tail around a twig, stretched as far as he could. He swiped at the youngling, who shuddered from his touch. His claws only combed the little one's fur. Ghost slipped. His forepaw slammed the ground. Definitely *out of the tree*, he sprung, just as the badger lunged. Ghost got there first, scruffed the golden punk and raced up into the branches, kit hanging from his jaws. The beast hissed meanly, but after a bit of grousing about the roots, digging holes and scratching the bark, he decided the cats weren't worth the effort and wandered off.

I didn't actually leave Harmony Tree, Ghost rationalized, *My hind paws were always on the roots.* But he knew he'd failed his quest. His paw hitting the ground echoed thunderously in his brain. *The kit's alive. That's more important,* he told himself, depositing his rescue on a wide branch. They hunkered face to face, sizing each other up.

"What's your name?" Ghost asked.

"Trouble."

"Trouble! That's no name for a kit."

"What's yours?"

"Ghost."

"Ghost? That's no name for a bony bag of fur."

The silver cat stared, dumbfounded. "You're right. Trouble's a great name."

"My mommy gave it to me," the little tiger asserted, then tilting his head back, yelped, "Ma-meeeee! Ma-meeeee," followed by whimpers and mewls that set Ghost' fangs on edge.

"Hush! You'll bring every predator in the Green upon us!" The kit fell silent and bending precariously over the branch, turned his head one way then the other. Feeling safe now, his body seemed to swell when he settled on his side, leaning against his hero as if they were the best and oldest of friends. Trouble cleaned his pelt with generous swipes of his tongue, each flourish expressing his rather large opinion of himself. After grooming, he began to explore, kicking Ghost in the face with a hind leg when he climbed past. He discovered he could loosen clumps of dead needles with his paws and delighting in the shimmer of falling debris, set off to clean every branch. He destroyed a feathertail nest and spilled two basins of water before Ghost reigned him in.

"Sit still!" the shaman admonished. "I need to waking-dream."

"Waking what?" the youngling asked, but his rescuer was in no mood to tell him.

"It's wrong to bother the nests of others. Didn't your mother teach you anything?"

"I miss my ma-meeeee. I want my ma-meeeee." Trouble's whiskers quivered and his mouth opened for another crescendo of wailing, but clamped shut when Ghost lowered a stern face to his.

"You'll have to wait." the shaman ordered. "I'll help you find her, but not yet."

"Why not?" the kit pouted.

"Because...Never mind, you wouldn't understand."

"Yes I would."

"No, you wouldn't."

"I would."

"No, you wouldn't. Now be quiet."

"Why, Ghost? Why won't you help me find my mommy?"

"You won't understand!"

"I will."

"Great Mother's Tail!" Ghost exploded, "You're never going to be quiet, are you?" Trouble lowered his ears and staring with bright, sullen eyes, slowly shook his head. "I can't go searching for your mother because I can't leave the tree. I'm on a vision-quest."

"I don't understand."

The wizard ignored him.

A few heartbeats later, "I'm hungry."

"*You're* hungry? Please, Trouble, please, I need peace." Wearily, Ghost lowered his belly to the branch and his head to his paws, but the furry nuisance didn't understand such an exhausted surrender and began tapping his face, one claw extended, one mewl per tap.

"Ghost," Tap. "Ghost," Tap. "Ghost," Tap. "Ghost, I'm hungry," Tap. "Hunt."

The youngling sat for a moment. "Ghost," Tap. "Ghost," Tap. "I don't know how..." Tap. Tap. Ghost opened the eye closest to his tormentor, who backed away and lowered the paw. "...to hunt." Ghost closed his eye. Tap. "Ghost," Tap. "Catch me some prey, won't you?" Tap. Tap. "Please, I'm so hungry!" Tap. Tap. But Ghost didn't move. The claw had failed. Trouble stomped to the end of the limb and with an overdone flourish and despairing mewl, threw himself down, legs hanging over either side of the branch, neck extended along it. He sighed loudly again. A moment later, an even louder sigh.

Oh, why not? Ghost thought. *I've already lost the RA. I might as well feed him.* He hauled himself to his paws and climbed to the highest branches of the cedar. A wave of guilt washed through him when he nabbed an unsuspecting tree rat, his empty stomach screaming when he laid it before the kit who sniffed and poked and sniffed the fresh kill like he didn't know what it was. His next prod knocked it off the bough. Dinner banged and thumped off every branch on its journey to the tree's roots.

Ghost couldn't stop grumbling as he maneuvered down the tree, angrily scooped the mangled prey back into his jaws, and re-delivered it to Trouble, whose intelligence he was beginning to question.

"I'm sorry," the catling mewed. "Now you know how I got my stupid name."

Ghost bunted Trouble's shoulder. "Don't worry. Everyone drops things." The kit brightened. The shaman slit the rat open with an expert swipe of claw and the youngling gorged himself. But the scent of the animal's flesh was torture, so Ghost climbed to a high branch and turned away, returning when Trouble had finished to flick the leftovers to the ground. Even its tail and feet smelled wonderful. *Only tonight,* he thought. *I've lost, but I'll stay to the end. Great Mother, I wish Erasmus could meet with me. Where is he?*

The day passed; twilight fell, and another fat rat was provided by a reluctant Ghost who now held no hope of receiving the RA, but still permitted himself no food or sleep this final night of his quest. He endured the kit's endless chatter with good humor until at last the youngling drifted off, snuggling his hero. Ghost didn't regret what he'd done, but he kept thinking that perhaps if he'd been stronger and smarter, he could have rescued the kit without leaving the tree. Seeking peace in the brightly shining stars, he watched a sliver of moon fade in a paling sky. By then Ghost believed he wasn't tested because he'd already failed, and when the sun rose behind a layer of clouds, and Starlight didn't come to counsel him, he felt sad. For the first time in his life, the little wizard believed not just that he'd failed, but that he was a failure.

Trouble woke and stretched. He looked at Ghost with surprising sincerity. "Thank you for saving me," he mewed, and they touched noses.

"Stay here until I return. I want to make sure it's safe, then we'll find your mother." Ghost did a quick lap around the meadow, but when he returned the kit was gone.

"Trouble," he called. No answer. Ghost sat on a low branch, anxiously twitching his tail. "Trouble!" Balls of light floated down and burst against his pelt. "Starlight, is that you?" More lights glittered around his head. Ghost searched the tree. Starlight wasn't revealing himself and Trouble was gone. Even his scent had faded. The wizard searched the meadow again, returning exhausted and hungry enough to eat his own tail. Hunkered on the roots, he called forlornly for the kit. Lights continued to fall about his head, and he fell asleep.

Ghost woke rested, feeling better about everything. *Surely the kit's all right,* he told himself, but called out one last time. No answer, only stars falling from the upper branches. Too impatient for Starlight's mischief, he headed home.

Hillside Pod proudly greeted their new Wisdom Cat, the preypile high, and the den fragrant with fresh herbs. Robin had replaced his bedding with new moss, putting nip and dreamweed where Ghost laid his head. But Ghost was withdrawn, lacking the courage to tell his friends he'd failed.

Days passed and he couldn't put Trouble's disappearance behind him. He worried the kit had been hurt...or worse. *Had a predator been lurking? One I didn't see? How could Trouble disappear without a trace?* the wizard fretted. Realizing he'd never know peace without the answer, Ghost bolted from the den and raced to Harmony Tree.

"Starlight?" The branches above him glowed blue and the Spirit Cat took form. "Starlight, I have a question."

"And I might have an answer," the shimmering felid smiled, shaking gems from his pelt.

"The kit I helped disappeared. I searched everywhere and couldn't find a whisker."

"Yes, you searched, but you didn't look."

"I did look for him, Starlight. What do you mean I didn't look?"

"O.K. You looked...but you didn't see."

Ghost growled. "Do you know what happened to him or not?"

The white cat stopped licking his paws and made eye contact. "I do."

"Well, are you going to tell me?"

"No." The little wizard slammed his tail and sank his claws into the bark. "Keep your pelt on. I did tell you...You don't understand."

"I don't understand."

"Exactly."

Sparring with Starlight was a waste of time. "Then tell me this. Is he safe?"

"Oh, yes, he's quite safe."

"Why can't you tell me where Trouble is in a way I will understand?"

Starlight chuckled, turned his back to Ghost and sat. He swung down and hung like a bat. "My little wizard, all truths lie within us, ever available. Stop believing you're unworthy and you'll know what happened." With a wink, the Spirit Cat swung back to the top, leaped into the air and landed facing his apprentice again.

"By Great Mother's Tail, Starlight, I can't do this!" Ghost' fierceness surprised even him and for once Starlight seemed more sympathetic than mischievous, an earnest expression on his face.

Then the Spirit Cat leaned close and whispered, "Have I told you the story of the cat who killed the rat?"

"Neow!!" Ghost yowled, thumping his tail on the branch.

Starlight continued. "Long ago, a wildborn queen made her home at the roots of my tree. She birthed and cared for her litter alone. One day she scented a rat's nest in my highest bough and braving the spindly branches, found a mother rat and all her babies dead. She was climbing down when one of the tiny creatures lifted its head and squeaked. Pitifully thin and dying, the baby kindled the queen's compassion. She brought it to her nest, where she nursed the tiny girl with her newborn kits, loving her as one of her own.

The kittens accepted their long-tailed sister and grew into catlings who would never think of rats as prey. The queen loved them all, but strange alliances are difficult and one evening while she hovered near her frolicking tribe, sister rat fell upon a brother and bit his neck. He died instantly. Wracked with guilt and despair, the queen slammed his killer against my trunk.

As she lay broken, rat sister called out. "Beloved mother, I am sorry. Let me tell you why I killed brother."

"I know why, beast. Despite the love I gave you, you are a heartless rat after all." The little girl died without another word, leaving the queen wondering forever if there had been something that justified brother's murder. She was never the same, believing she'd caused the death of her son as well as killing the little rat for whom she grieved with all her feline heart. Never birthing another litter, she punished herself, wandering the Green, wailing through the night until she died. Her children buried her beneath my roots, near their sister, for they believed little rat girl had a secret that explained her crime."

Ghost was curious despite himself. "Did she?"

"Oh, yes," Starlight answered, and once again began cleaning his paws. The shaman wanted to pounce him. "All right, I'll tell you...The adopted baby was not a rat, but Great Mother in rat form. She'd been watching the queen for many turns of the Moon, believing she would become a great Wisdom Cat...and so she must be tested."

"And she failed," Ghost said miserably, thinking of his own vision quest.

"No, she didn't." Ghost looked surprised. "Rat sister could see the future and knew her beloved brother would catch a plague from the sting of a bloodsucker. It would drive him mad, causing him to murder his whole family while they slept."

"Then the queen failed when she wouldn't listen to rat sister and judged her with prejudice."

"No." Again Ghost looked surprised. "What mother wouldn't punish a child who harmed its sibling? What cat wouldn't assume a rat is heartless; we've given them no reason to love us. As the Spirit of Great Mother, the little rat expected to die and gave herself willingly, erasing any sin from her murder."

Now Ghost looked truly confused. "Then why was the queen unhappy? Surely she'd seen many of her kits die; more than half of all wildborn kits don't see six turns of the moon."

Starlight waited until the shaman focused only on him. "She was unhappy because she blamed herself." His voice was low and calm, but his words traveled deeply into Ghost, lifting the weight of his guilt and fear, a burden he'd bound to himself every moment of his life. He stared into the Spirit Cat's eyes and saw how, like the mother cat long ago, he damaged himself. "Forgive yourself...always," Starlight murmured with love, and was gone. A shower of diamonds burst against the shaman's pelt as he dropped to the roots of the tree. It wasn't Ghost who padded slowly back to Hillside den; it was Ghost Awakened, blessed with peace and joy.

But old habits die hard, and as moons rose and fell, Ghost drifted back to sleep. A moment of illumination can't grow a seedling into a tree. And a life crippled by fear and self-reproach needs more than one urging from Spirit to free itself. *I failed my vision-quest* and *it's my fault Trouble is missing* became Ghost' mantra once more. When Bittercold Brightmoon lit the sky, he claimed a sour belly and begged off, even though Robin would be presented. His mood had been so dark of late, his podmates let him be.

9 – DREAMS

ewmoon of the White Moon Gathering also passed without Ghost, who spent the day and then the evening hunkered on Waterfall Boulder, staring into space. Robin seemed to be the only company he enjoyed and that, despite Robin's many talents, only in small doses. A pleasant companion, a great hunter, and the most melodic singer in their pod, everyone loved Robin. Even Kyra listened to him, and their friendship helped his own heart to heal.

Rosie's life was also changing. Joyfully she pranced the meadows, her belly rounding for a spring birth. But to Browser's dismay, she began sleeping outside, and to keep her safe, he had to keep her company. He groused every morning about his aching joints, but Rosie seemed oblivious to the cold. Warm in her winter pelt, she lay on her favorite stone near the falling water, entranced by the stars. Only when the sky lightened would she drift into sleep, and during those pre-dawn slumbers she began to dream.

Oh, how beautiful, she thought, awed by the kaleidoscope playing against her lids, giddily swirling her around and down into nothingness and then...a field of grass. A fish emerged. Its gulping gills sprouted wings and it flew away. A mouse floated up, waved his ears at her, transformed into a possum hanging by his tail from a branch, dropped to the earth and morphed into a smelltail, waddling off with a waving plume. A longear sat before her. She admired its sensuous profile while it chewed a dandelion, staring up with one huge eye. Starlight glinted off its wet, black surface. Drawing her in like a maelstrom, it filled her vision, the speck of light mutating into the white cat shedding streams of cerulean stars.

"Now you must tell me your name," Rosie trilled.

"I am Starlight."

"Made of stars?"

"We're all made of star-stuff, and children of the Earth. There's something you need to see," he said, shocking Rosie by erasing his body with every swish of his tail, leaving tiny stars tinkling and fading away. "Listen," meowed his disembodied voice, and Rosie heard the urgent mewling of newborns. She followed the cries to a burrow hidden in tall grass and crawled inside. Three kits quieted with the warmth of her belly, and began to nurse.

Rosie was dozing when Mee-am called. "Rosie, come home! I'm sorry! Please come back!" The new mother nosed her babies close together in the sweetgrass and leaped from the burrow.

It was Starlight, not Mee-am, who waited Rosie raced toward him and found herself in the urine-stained alley where she'd been dumped. She yowled.

Kyra came from behind and swatted her ears. "Quiet. They're coming," she hissed, leading Rosie to a rusted garbage can. They climbed through a hole in its side and burrowed to the bottom beneath the trash.

Wheels squealed. Engines stopped. White Trucks loomed at both ends of the alley. Uprights emerged with their nets and pain sticks, advancing with purpose. Rosie and Kyra pressed closer, bolstering each other's courage. The two-leggeds worked their way toward the center of the alley, poking with their poles, upending trash and scattering kin. But no one who bolted for freedom escaped.

A nursing queen and her babies were captured, locked in a cage marked for death. Would they be spared because they were new life? No. they were feral. They would die.

Rosie looked away, unable to watch. Kyra tensed, but stayed hidden. Fighting was suicide. A tall-one stopped before the bin, poked his stick through the hole and stirred. The little queens' hearts banged against their chests so hard the human had to hear them. Only he didn't. And he missed. He stared at them and didn't see, then retreated to his truck with the others. They drove away, the cries of their captives fading to nothing.

A young queen returned from a hunt and discovered her litter was missing. She stumbled down the alley trilling for her silent babies. One by one the few survivors crawled from their hiding places, dazed males and females searching for their mates, catlings calling for their friends.

Rosie sat in the middle of the alley, lifted her head and yowled. "Starlight, please! Why this cruelty?" A flash of light, and the dream burned away. She sat with Starlight in Harmony Tree. The evening air was warm though stars littered the cobalt sky.

"I don't know why humans kill wildborn, Discarded Queen. I know only that you must return to Mee-am to prevent it."

🐾　　🐾　　🐾

Ghost didn't attend Brightmoon of the White Moon at Harmony Tree. Thin and ragged, he hurt. Erasmus and Morsus were still missing. He knew they lived; he felt their presence. But Indra was dead, murdered. What was worse, dark magic bound the grasses and flowers of the Green to silence. And not just the grasses and flowers. The stream babbled nonsense as it bubbled over stones in its bed and the trees whispered riddles in the breeze. The wizard remained in his alcove, brooding.

Browser and Buster entered the den, jaws filled with prey. Buster crossed to a plump Kyra and Browser to a plumper Rosie, while Robin encouraged his glum mentor to sit with his friends and share a meal. Ghost was hungry today and the prey was quickly eaten.

Browser cleaned his face with swipes of his tongue, then licked Rosie's ears. "Walk with me," he trilled. "We don't walk together anymore."

"For good reason. My belly is lumpy with kits and the hill is steep."

"Shall we take a nap? I'll fetch some sweetgrass for you."

"Oh, don't smother," Rosie groused. "The Green awaits your rulings. Go be kingly in the woods." Even Kyra was taken back by Rosie's foul temper. Eyes and ears lowered, Browser leaped to the Guardian, and without a goodbye, bolted down the hill and under the hedge. He would not return. The air was clean, the leaves still dripping from early morning skywater. He breathed deeply, sloughing off his damaged pride. *So good to be outside.* The snow long since melted, late winter sun warmed his back. Browser drank at the pool, then trotted east on less traveled paths.

By short-shadows, he came to a small meadow west of the oak grove, home to a tribe of ravens. Several wheeled overhead squawking about his presence, but Browser ignored them. He was curious about the drainpipe protruding from the northern hillside above a landing of pebbly dirt. Wide enough for three kin to stand nose to tail, the pipe had been placed there long before he'd arrived in the Green, but he'd never known it to flow with water. Occasionally, skywater wet the soil that had blown onto its curved floor, producing a scraggly growth of weeds. A ficus had taken root, grown stem and leaves up one side, and sinking a second network of roots into the rocky dirt above. The wandering fig had mingled its vines with a prolific wild ivy and some creeping charlie, creating a thick, green curtain that hung across the pipe's entrance.

Browser faced the rise from a culvert buried in leaf debris. He opened his mouth and panted. The scent of barker filled his mouth, but Browser dismissed the thought as absurd. He knew every bush, tree and creature in his territory, and no dogs lived in the Green.

The landing was an easy climb, but as Browser approached the drainpipe, the absurd scent returned, stronger than before. Cautiously, he raised on his hind legs and poked his head through the leaves. A deep growl from a dark shape smelling exactly like dog rushed him, slamming his head with its own. He staggered back. Flailing paws grasped at the vines, but Browser fell, thunking his already battered bean against a stone. He slid down the hill. Growling biting, stinging biting, burning biting, throbbing biting. Growling...growling...fading away.

"Yip, yip, grrrrr, yip! Grrrrrrrrr!"

Browser leaped to his paws. A mistake. He plopped on his butt to watch the dancing stars. This time he rose slowly. Two fuzz balls with fangs dove at his legs again. Browser hissed and spit and slapped his paws in all directions, but they only rolled away, flipped around and rocketed back for more.

"Yip! Yap! Yip! Yip!" *What a joy to tease the cat. Tease the cat, tease the cat.*

"Come here at once," sang a voice of authority, and the fuzz balls rolled up the rise toward a larger puffball with bright blue eyes twinkling through a thatch of frizz. Her babies dancing around her, she stood on the landing, swaggering and grand and quite small. Browser would have laughed if her pups' fangs hadn't left his flesh full of fiery holes.

"Quiet," she scolded them, her eyes locked on the intruder. "Who are *you*?"

"What?" he chuffed indignantly. "Who are *you*?"

"I asked first," she countered, stomping tiny paws.

"Well I asked..." he swelled his chest, "as King of the Green. So, who *are* you?"

"Sugar Pie," she said flatly. "And you are...?"

116

"I told you, I'm King of..." he began irritably, then stopped, deciding not to educate her to his importance right now. "I'm Browser," he finally said. They stood staring. "What *are* you doing here, Sugar Pie?"

She jerked her head toward the water pipe. "I live here until my people return."

"What?"

Sugar Pie stomped her paws again. "Until they come back. I...we... have been...it's a...a vacation."

"What?" he asked again, trying to work out her craziness.

She eyed him nervously. "You must know, cat, what happens when humans take a vacation. Haven't yours ever gone away...for a while, just a while..." The more she talked, the more anxious her movements became and suddenly Browser understood: she'd been dumped, and it hurt so deeply she couldn't let herself know it was true.

Now he found her anguish difficult to watch. "It's okay, Sugar Pie. I'm sure they'll be back soon..." Then added, "from their vacation." He'd meant well but obviously didn't believe what he said, and Sugar Pie took offense.

Her body stiffened and her eyes examined him muzzle to tail tip and back again. "You're wildborn, aren't you? Never even had a home."

"As if I'd want one," Browser chuffed. Now she was really offended, stomping her paws twice as long. He couldn't resist teasing and stood on his toes, pelt puffed and ears back. "Yes, yes, that's me. Wild as they come. You're not afraid...little dog?"

Sugar Pie scoffed. "Should I be? You fell down the hill...mangy cat."

His claws shot out then retracted. "I admit you caught me off guard."

"While on guard," she snickered.

Browser looked serious. "Perhaps this wildborn is getting hungry. I might hunt down a meal...or two." Keeping his voice low and sinister, he lifted a paw to narrowed eyes and showed her his razors. A quiver of fear ran through her, and the pups dashed into the pipe.

Sugar Pie squared her shoulders. "I'd like to see you try."

Browser's whole demeanor relaxed. Purring loudly, he turned circles in the culvert and sat. "I would never hurt you or your babies," he said. "I just wanted to see what you're made of."

"I knew that," she insisted, but he heard the relief in her voice. "Are you like Miss Puddytat, Browser? I hope so."

117

"Miss Puddytat?" he asked, almost hoping she wouldn't answer.

"I grew up with her, so sweet and soft. She played with me from the time I was that big." Sugar Pie motioned toward her offspring, who had reappeared. "Miss Puddytat never used her claws," she added, as proudly as if she'd done it herself.

Browser watched the pups, wondering if a bowl of kibble was worth being called Miss Puddytat. *Not mine to judge,* he decided. "How'd you get here again?"

"I told you, Mister Browser. Must I tell you again?" Her attempts to sound confident convinced him even more she'd been dumped, probably because she birthed pups. *How could two-leggeds proclaim their love then leave her here to starve?* Anger welled within him. She wasn't much bigger than he was, just stouter and barrel chested. Her short legs, thick as branches, seemed stiff, and how could she see through the fur hanging in her eyes? How could she hunt? How would she feed her pups?

"Are you hungry?" He asked.

The mother dog lowered her head. "The food is gone," she mumbled, too embarrassed to meet his gaze.

"What have you been eating?"

"When they...when I was...my humans left food. I'm sure they meant to come back before it was gone..." Her voice faded, tinged with despair. "I'm worried something happened to them."

"Only if they return while I'm here," he muttered.

"What?"

Browser didn't answer. He climbed the incline, discovering a bag once filled with dog pellets, now shredded, its slick inner paper licked clean of the smallest crumb. His belly clinched with anger. Sugar Pie's humans had left her here, pretending she'd be safe, that something good would happen. In reality they'd left her to die. And still she loved them, protecting them with a loyalty they never deserved. "Do you have any food?" she asked shyly.

"I can get you something," Browser said, returning to the culvert. Sugar Pie did the tiny dog version of happy, her tail wagging so vigorously her rear-end slid over the dirt as if weightless. Browser watched with smiling eyes. "You eat dead food, right?"

Her tail wagging stopped mid-wag. "What?"

"The flesh you eat, is it burned with fire?"

She looked confused, then chuckled. "If you mean burgers and fries, yes, Mister Browser, I do eat food burned with fire." He turned away, not wanting her to see his distaste, and began his journey south. After all, many of the southern kin had developed a liking for seared meat, not unseemly, considering their element was fire. "I'll be here," she called after the receding cat who answered with a twitch of his ears. *Silly dog. Where else would she be? She'll never survive without me.* And his spirits rose. *I'm needed. My new friend needs my help.*

Sugar Pie and her pups were dozing when Browser returned, a bag hanging from his jaws. She laughed when he told her how he found it waiting for him on a bench near two tall-ones who sat with arms and faces entwined. They'd been most generous.

"Oh, french fries," she gushed, having unwrapped and devoured the two portions of bread and meat so rapidly Browser wondered if he'd have to find more.

"There's always a meal in the trash cans," he offered.

Shredding the sack with her claws, she nodded, not looking up until she'd inhaled every scrap. Then she sat beside him, nudging his shoulder with her head and thanking him again and again until he yearned for silence. Sugar Pie had been as lonely as she'd been hungry. Browser listened to the stories of her life, all about her pups, Jasper and Shorttail, and the uprights who abandoned her. Of course even now she didn't see it that way. He learned that barkers, like tall-walkers, named their offspring at birth. *Much simpler,* he had to admit. He wondered if Sugar Pie understood her desperate circumstances. She couldn't hunt. She couldn't even raid a trash can without tipping it over. Luckily, he'd found her soon after the food was gone.

Darkness fell and Sugar Pie shuffled into the tunnel to nurse her pups. Browser considered going home. He was pod leader and Rosie's mate. But he didn't move. Listening to the mother dog suckle, he felt good about himself, better than he'd felt for some time tending to the needs of Queen Rosamonde, who never seemed happy with his efforts anymore. Browser yawned contentedly, curled and slept.

When Browser didn't come back right away, Rosie understood. When he failed to return with prey for their evening meal, she felt his anger and answered with her own. It wasn't until she was lying on the rocks alone beneath the stars that Rosie felt remorse. She let her mind drift, tendrils of thought-feeling seeking her mate, and she found him with another. Browser wasn't alone. At first she was angry, then ashamed. *I drove him away because I feel guilty about missing Mee-am and dreaming of a white cat who commands me to find her. Browser hates humans! He'd be miserable if he knew how much I still love Mee-am...Well, he's miserable now. I made sure of it.* As light bloomed along the horizon, the young queen resolved to tell her mate the truth. She slept at last.

The glassy surface of the sea mirrored the star-laden sky. Rosie dipped her paw in the water, righting the world with a ripple, then followed the deserted shoreline south. Moments later she wasn't alone. A white speck raced toward her, blue mists trailing behind. Starlight. Rosie stood and waited, but he didn't slow down. *Starlight, don't you see me here?* He didn't answer and didn't slow. He passed through her like a ghost, sending an electric shock from her nose to the tip of her tail. "Wait," she called, but Starlight was gone. The glassy sea and starry sky were gone. Darkened by soot and smoke, the heavens glowed red with distant fires, and mazes of concrete sprawled in all directions. They crept across the earth, fed by ribbons of monster-choked asphalt, spreading over their mother's skin, dark veins spewing poisonous gas. Starlight filled Rosie's mind. *It's up to you, Discarded Queen. Fulfill the Prophecy and change the world.*

Finally the deathly vision released her, and her thoughts fled east to cliffs and canyons and spires of rainbow jewels. From there she went south where old-growth forests flourished through a maze of waterways and a secret, smoldering fire. She flew west and witnessed jungles of unearthly trees, jewel-like mosses and riotous flowers. Rosie finished her journey in in the north, feeling at home in the grassy meadows and woodland copses crowned by the shared polestar, Harmony Tree. Rosie didn't know, no one did, about the other one, the greatest and most powerful polestar of all. In an underground cavern waiting for the world to become wise, bubbled a pool of violet water that heals all wounds.

The lion-hued princess opened her eyes and padded down the hill.

Rosie watched Browser lope across the meadow toward their den. She had planned to tell him she regretted her hurtful behavior. Somehow, the closer he came, the more her "I'm sorry" morphed into "Where were you last night?" He scrambled up the hill with a fat longear in his mouth, pushed past her and dropped his prey on the pile. She followed him into the den.

"I love you, Rosie," he trilled, nuzzling her face. She pulled back with a hiss. Browser stank of valerian and Rosie was no fool. He hadn't spent the night lying in dreamweed; he was hiding something. And...she smelled his tongue on his pelt. So after his valerian roll he washed himself. Definitely hiding something.

"Where have you been," she snarled. Browser mumbled and padded off. Now they both kept secrets.

Rosie's second dream was more haunting than the first and clearly spelled out what she must do. It wasn't something she wanted. *I'll talk to Ghost,* she told herself, another challenge as they'd hardly spoken since Ozymandias. Browser she'd forgiven, believing he had nothing to do with the idiot king's appearance, but Ghost...

The sun fell beneath the edge of the earth and the little wizard climbed the hill to stargaze. Rosie waited a few moments, then followed. Ghost lay on his side, studying her with hooded eyes.

"I have questions," she said bluntly. "Why do we dream?"

"Tell me more," he said gently, happy Rosie was no longer angry and willing to forgive her slights.

Looking into his eyes, Rosie realized once again she'd judged him too harshly. *Guilt is not gentle or forgiving,* she thought and lowered her belly to the cool stone. "I'm sorry, Ghost. Again I've misjudged you."

"Tell me about your dreams."

"Sometimes they seem more real than when I'm awake. I dream of a white cat—"

"You've seen Starlight."

Rosie's eyes widened. "You *know* Starlight? Who *is* he?"

"It's a rare thing, Rosie, for someone who's not even an apprentice to see him. Whatever he's telling you, you must do what's asked. The vision isn't only for you, understand, but for the good of the pod, perhaps for all creatures of the Green."

Rosie groomed his silver fingers. "Who is Starlight?"

"He's our connection to Great Mother as the Spirit Cat of Harmony Tree, the Polestar of the North."

"There are other Spirit Cats?"

"Oh, yes. One for each of the four directions. And they are as different from one another as we kin."

"You mean like the giant cats from the east with their big ears, hind legs and paws, or those gorgeous western kin with huge, dreamy eyes."

Ghost chuckled softly. "There's a little more to it, but you've got the idea ."

"I've watched those eastern cats during brightmoon ceremonies. Can they really fly?"

"Well, not fly, but certainly leap very far."

Rosie trembled with excitement. "Tell me more."

"To the south are woodlands, sacred groves fed by meandering streams created by flattails. The southern kin respect them. They heed their advice, and their clans thrive with clean water and all the prey they need."

"Like Blackpaw's pod."

"Yes, but there's a problem with two-leggeds at Flattail Dam. Some tall-walkers don't like flattails any more than they like kin. They don't understand the purpose of flattails is to create streams and reservoirs that provide water in dry times. Given enough time, flattails turn deserts into meadows."

"I lived with uprights. They live in memories or dreams of the future. And they don't understand they're part of nature." She thought for a moment. "What polestar lies in the west?"

"Let's talk about Starlight," Ghost said, changing the subject. "Every Wisdom Cat senses change is coming. I sense Starlight has a message for you." He nudged her shoulder with his nose. "What is Starlight telling you?" Rosie fidgeted. She didn't want to answer, but couldn't lie.

"He's telling me to return to Mee-am. Oh Ghost, he showed me humans in White Trucks murdering kin! There's a darkness ravaging the world and somehow, my return to Mee-am will make it stop."

"The Prophecy says you will leave. A heart-bond ties you to Mee-am, Rosie," he paused, "but I never considered she might help us."

"Even if she will, I don't know where she is! A heart-bond ties me to Browser, and to you too, and my kits will birth this waning of the moon. I can't leave." Her tail lashed. Ghost waited until she calmed.

"You are by nature a Wisdom Cat. And you are the Discarded Queen.

You must do what you're asked, for the good of all."

Tenderly, Rosie licked his paws. "You can trust me." She rose and stretched, then lay next to him, gazing down at the tree-ringed meadow. The earthy scent of field mouse rose, clinging to her mouth, and for a moment she considered hunting. But she didn't really want to move. The starfield glittered like a carpet of gems. She pressed her warm belly against Ghost' ribs and when her kits moved, he sang them a lullaby.

"Never worry. Have faith." he murmured, releasing his spirit to drift by its silver tether. Rosie dropped her head to her paws, closed her eyes and followed.

🐾   🐾   🐾

Red headed for his dish. He didn't get far, however, before the male kits pawed his legs for attention. He batted them gently aside, but they flopped down in his path, making him stumble.

"So tell us, tell us! Have you seen Starlight?" The black tuxedo hooted, foolishly parked between Red and his morning meal. Red gave him a stern look and he scooted away, then wrapped his front paws around Red's ear and squealed down the funnel. "Well? Have you?"

"Neow!" Red yelped, shaking his head. The kit sailed into the air and only through some quick footwork and the inherited grace of being cat did his paws find the floor first. Red sniffed him, making sure he wasn't hurt, then tucked into his food.

"Tell us, Red. Tell us. Have you?" the little female persisted. Before he could answer, she warbled, "When I'm growed up, I will see Starlight... right after I meet Great Mother." Red guffawed kibble in all directions.

rowser had chewed his pelt raw with worry. He knew he'd have to tell his podmates about Sugar Pie and the pups but he didn't know how. Browser the proud clan leader, warrior with a chest full of battle scars...feeding stray dogs and playing with puppies? *How can I make them understand,* he wondered, loping toward the drainpipe. *Yes, Sugar Pie is a dog, but she has the heart of a lion, a great Felidae heart.*

"Mister Browser!" The frizzy mother roofed when she saw him coming, bags of food in his jaws. Her pups rushed him with yips of glee, fell into him and danced on his paws. "Kids!" Sugar Pie scolded and they scampered to their mother, smacking her face with waggy tails.

"Kitty's here! Kitty's here!" They chorused.

"Yes he is, now calm down." They obeyed by tumbling down the incline and rolling across the grass, where their play wouldn't disturb the adults. Browser climbed the outcropping and settled next to his friend, dropping the bags before her. She lowered herself to the ground, and using her paws, tore into them, devouring the first hamburger in two bites. The second bun she swallowed whole, followed by the lettuce, onion and tomato. Then came the meat which she decided to savor in little bites, the wrapping paper traveling toward her mouth by dental conveyor belt until Browser stopped its demise with his paw.

"I'm sorry you have to care for us," she mumbled through her food.

His eyes smiled. "Well, I just need to show you where the food-cans are and teach you how to knock them over." He remembered telling the kin not to do that, but Sugar Pie was so clumsy such a warning was useless. "I don't mind helping you."

"I know you don't. I just..." She looked up with wretched eyes. "I just...you should be told...I just...Ah, ticks and fleas, Mister Browser! My people aren't coming back for us. They never were. They left me here because I was heavy with pups." Dropping her head to the dirt, she crossed her paws over her snout, sorrowful black eyes peeking above them. Browser growled long and low, making Sugar Pie tremble until she realized it wasn't her but her tall-ones' cruelty that angered him.

"I'm so sorry," he whispered into her fur. "I promise that as long as I live, no harm will come to you or your children." He licked her kinky coat, regretting it immediately. Wiry hairs stuck to his tongue, but he didn't dare spit them out for fear of hurting her feelings.

Just then, Jasper and Shorttail dashed over, whimpering and nuzzling their mother. "I'm all right, babies, just sad," she murmured. They turned accusing eyes on Browser, who tensed despite himself. "No, Mister Browser is our friend. Go play," she ordered and they bounced back to their games. "We will always be your friends, Mister Browser. You saved our lives."

The little dog and the big cat lay quietly then beneath the winter sun, drifting down a slow river of kinder thoughts, until a white flash danced along his lashes and Browser stood, instantly alert. He found the source: sunlight bouncing off a mirror. *White Truck! White Truck in the Green!* It crossed the Northbridge and rolled to a stop on their side of the road, with only a tree-dappled meadow between the animals and the men who emerged.

Browser knew what was coming. "Sugar Pie, get the pups in the pipe!"

"Kids!" She roofed, "Up. Up. Into the nest now." They scrambled up the incline with pathetic whines, thinking only that their playtime had been cut short. Jasper turned to clamber back down the loose dirt, but his mother nipped his rear and he squealed like he'd been mortally wounded. The men turned toward the sound and Browser prayed the winter oaks had blocked their view.

"Move! Now!" he spat, flashing fangs in Jasper's face. Both pups bolted into the pipe. "No," he growled, "farther back where it's dark!" Jasper and his brother were afraid of the cat, but more afraid of the unexplored depths of the tunnel and stood quaking by their nest.

"Snakes and spiders live back there!" Shorttail whined, tossing his head toward the darkness.

Browser crept toward them like they were prey. "Death lives out there," he hissed, jerking his head toward the road. "And it's coming for you!" The pups dashed into the abyss where they found a discarded cardboard box. Everyone crowded behind it.

"Quiet," Browser warned. "And close your eyes. If the upright's little sun comes toward you, he'll see your eyeshine."

Bleggs and Wilson crossed the field heading straight for the drainpipe. Bleggs waited at the base of the rise while Wilson climbed to the opening. He pushed the vines aside and stood in the glare, a deadly silhouette. He flicked on his flashlight and aimed it down the tunnel. The hunted held their breath. The beam crisscrossed the bottom of the drainpipe and up its curved walls. It swept back and paused a long moment on the dog's bedding and Browser cursed himself for not dragging their nest behind the cardboard. If discovered, they were trapped.

"See anything?" Bleggs asked.

Wilson didn't answer. He just stood there thinking, his light burning against the rags. "No," he said at last. "Just some old junk. Someone's been living here, though." He stepped back on the landing and lifted the shredded dog food bag for Bleggs to see. "A bum with a dog," He kicked hamburger wrappers down the slope. "But they're gone." The thin man descended and Browser sighed deeply. Then to his horror Jasper bounced from behind the box with a squeal that echoed down the pipe.

"Hush!" the cat spit, but it was too late. Again pebbles crunched beneath boots, and again the light blazed, now against the flimsy cardboard wall and Jasper's haunches, which he hadn't managed to get behind the cardboard's protection. The pup ached to hide himself, but Browser's eyes told him not to move. Miraculously, he didn't. The beam played along the floor, the walls, then back to Jasper, always back to Jasper, scorching his flank for many thudding heartbeats. No one breathed. At last Wilson clicked off his flashlight and withdrew.

"What happened?" Bleggs asked.

"I thought I heard something. Guess not. Bum left some bedding behind." He descended the rise. "I'll call maintenance and have the pipe cleaned out."

"You do that." Bleggs ordered as they trekked toward the truck. Suddenly, the heavy man stopped and wheeled around, giving the pipe a hard stare. "I've been chasing these fool cats about as long as I care to."

Wilson looked surprised. "Cats? Excuse me, sir, but the rangers said stray dogs were living in that pipe." Bleggs removed his cap and wiped his sweaty forehead with the back of his hand.

"Wilson, I've been doin' this a lot longer than you've even thought about it. I have a nose for vermin, and I'm tellin' you, I don't care what the park authority says, I smell a rat."

"We're hunting rats now?"

"CATS, Wilson, CATS! A cat is a rat! Get it? Those filthy ferals are pests, Wilson, vicious vermin. And I want you to crawl down that pipe and trap 'em." Wilson stood motionless, his mouth hanging open, his own opinion of cats about as far from Bleggs' as Pluto is from Earth. And even though he'd never admit it to himself, he was as frightened of spiders and snakes as little Jasper.

"Boss, believe me, nobody and nothing's in there now!" Bleggs shook his head in disbelief. "And Boss, dogs and people, dogs, not cats, stayed there. I saw the paw prints!" The heavy man drew himself up and stood, grasping his pain stick with a clenched fist. Bleggs despised all strays and ferals, dogs or cats, but especially cats. For a long moment he did nothing. Then to Wilson's surprise, he collapsed inward on himself like a bag expelling trapped air, and head down, trundled back to their truck, cursing the new, stiff uniform that chaffed his thighs. Wilson, a giraffe of a man, loped after him, grateful Bleggs was too ungainly to climb the rise himself. Otherwise he would have seen what Wilson did: prints of a big cat alongside those of three dogs, one adult, two pups, and no humans. Other than the fact that they should be fixed and fed, he just couldn't see the harm in it. The men tossed their gear in the rear and drove away.

Browser's friends waited in the tunnel while he crept to the opening and peered out. The truck was gone. He motioned with his tail and Sugar Pie released her pups to their games in the grass, chirping at them not to worry. The gravity of what just happened seemed lost on her.

"Sugar Pie," the big cat commanded. They all turned. "The men will come back."

She stared at him as if frozen; even her tail didn't move. Finally, "We'll hide again. You'll help us."

"You must leave here, Sugar Pie. If you don't, you'll die." The mother dog dropped her belly to the ground, whimpering with fear.

Browser climbed the hill to his den in a dark mood, imagining his podmates' scorn if he brought them a family of barkers. Great Mother's Tail, it strained his own credulity. Just thinking about it was exhausting. He kept to himself, eating his evening meal in silence before curling into a ball and sleeping the through the night.

Rosie left the den for Waterfall Boulder. Easing her kitten-heavy belly to the stone, she gazed at the stars. Buster and Kyra arrived. The three lay together watching a slice of moon float to the top of the sky. Ghost glided up the hill, his silver coat blinking in and out of sight. He nuzzled Buster back enough to settle next to Rosie, then began grooming her neck.

After a solitary hunt, Robin joined them, bursting with song about the pool beneath the falling water and how the mist carried scents of flowers up the hill. He sang through the night. He sang about ferals in the alleys, about his mother and his family who were gone. Then he sang about his new family, how they saved him and how he loved them. The cats lay in fellowship until dawn, until the starfield faded in the rising light and their hunger demanded prey.

Rosie and Kyra retreated to the cave while the males climbed down the hill to hunt. They were almost to the rosemary hedge when Browser slipped into the low growth at the edge of the eastern woods, having never joined them. Now, without a word to anyone, he left.

"What's wrong with him?" Robin asked.

The silver wizard stood with his tail at half-mast, his ears back and down. "He has a troubling secret, one we'll know soon enough." They entered the meadow and caught the scent of prey.

A *perfect morning,* Rosie decided, having returned to her favorite boulders after morning meal. Beneath her drooping lids she spied movement along the eastern border of trees. She leaped to her toes. "Look! Look!" she alerted the others. The pod practically tumbled down the hill and stood wide-eyed and scruffs up, astounded to see Browser trotting across the meadow ahead of a small barker and two puffs of fur. The visitors reached the rosemary hedge, skidding to a halt before a gauntlet of fangs and claws.

"What's this?" Rosie demanded stepping out front.

The mother dog and her whimpering boys cringed, eyes glued to flexing claws. Browser made himself large. "These are my friends," he said. "They need a safe place to live." The pod cats were stunned. Pelts bristled, scimitars dug into the earth. Browser came toward her, ears down, his head tight to his shoulders as if expecting a blow.

Rosie didn't know what to do. "Yeow wow wow wow," she yowled. "Stop!" Browser sat. "What are you doing? You'd fight me? Your Rosie?"

He dropped his belly to the ground. "No, Rosie, I would never hurt you. I was afraid you'd charge them and I wanted to get close enough to beg for their lives." At last Rosie understood where he'd been going and why. Her dear Browser. Even his secrets served others.

Kyra lunged in a blur, and blood poured from Browser's muzzle. Shocked, he pushed himself up and leaped back, but despite her pregnant belly the she-cat pursued, frantic with rage and blindingly quick with deadly aim. Sugar Pie and the pups scattered.

"I will not tolerate a snap-jaw in my home!" the black queen wailed. Blood splattered everywhere, Browser's blood. Refusing to hurt Kyra, he only blocked her blows, and soon his face, shoulders and legs were a patchwork of wounds. Browser collapsed. Rosie screeched and Buster threw himself between his friend and the crazed Kyra, but it didn't slow her down. She sliced deeply into her mate's ear, notching out a corner, then punctured his neck, furrowed his chest and legs. His pelt tinged red; still the tuxedo stood firm. At last she realized it was Buster, not Browser, standing before her and eyes round as saucers, Kyra dropped her bloodied paws. Buster's muscular shoulder bunted her to the ground.

"How dare you!" She spit, too dismayed to rise. "Isn't it enough he let ghostdogs kill our kits!" She struggled to all fours and staggered up the hill into their den. Buster followed at a distance.

Rosie stared at Browser. "What is she talking about?" The pod leader said nothing.

Ghost, who was checking his wounds, finally said, "Browser didn't kill her litter. A tragedy, but not his fault." He turned back to his mauled friend. "You need cactus water on these and some need moss poultices."

Rosie stomped her paws. "Tell me what happened...now." The Wisdom Cat looked at Browser, who nodded.

Ghost began. "We were new to the Green and Browser had found us a den. The choice was a bad one, but no one knew. We hunted nightly, even

Kyra, who'd had kits coming on a turn of the moon earlier. That night, for a reason only Great Mother knows, she wanted to stay with them. He insisted she come with us, and she finally relented. It was good she did, or she'd be dead too. She couldn't have saved her babies."

"Ghostdogs?"

"Yes. Our nest was much farther south and east, in an old shed near the gulch. Tall-ones had things there, but seldom visited. We felt safe until that night. The hounds came up from the canyon, entered through a hole in the side...like us." He stared into the past. "All four gone."

Rosie lashed her tail. "Stop, please." She calmed herself. "Did it smell of ghostdog before that night?"

"No," Ghost replied.

"Were there tracks or any evidence of them?"

"None of us knew they raided the Green."

"Then tragic as it was, it's not Browser's fault." The pod leader lifted his gaze to hers, bathing in forgiveness he couldn't give himself. A long heartbeat of silence. "Browser, the barkers can't live with us. Kyra and I will birth kits within a turn of the moon. Besides," She looked at the short, jointless legs of the pups. "They can't manage the hill, or the Guardian Stone. And they could only come down by falling." She tittered at her own joke. Browser didn't share her humor, neither did anyone else and somehow that made it funnier. When her mate stood to speak, unaware a piece of his ear dangled like Chevalier jewelry, Rosie collapsed in a shuddering heap of mirth. Ghost clipped the shred away with his nibble teeth, spitting it into the bushes, and Rosie finally quieted.

Browser nuzzled her. "Would you like to meet Sugar Pie?"

What else? "Of course."

Motioning Jasper and Shorttail to stay behind, their mother trotted to the queen with small, prissy steps, then lowered her front in a well rehearsed curtsy. The effort wasn't wasted. Rosie sniffed the little dog's head, nodding with respect as she rose. Their eyes met and Sugar Pie beamed. That's when she lost control. Tail wagging wildly, her dainty paws slipped over the grass. "Oops, now I've done it," she chortled, knocking Browser down as she rushed the queen and stood on her rear legs, hoping to plop her paws on Rosie's shoulders and slather her face with kisses. But with a fluid motion, Rosie slipped aside and the mama dog's paws hit the ground. "Sorry, sorry," she muttered, eyes bright with embarrassment.

The pups considered her misstep an invitation to do better. Bolting past her, they knocked Browser down again and trampled the Queen. They were cuddly warm and sweet with mother's milk. Rosie couldn't resist rubbing her body along theirs, which set them to vibrating as if she'd released hidden springs.

She licked Shorttail and thick, wiry fur lodged in her mouth. "Blewh, blewh," she coughed. The pups settled at her paws, faces lit with adoration while they watched her choke.

"They have nowhere to go," Browser meowed, then he and Rosie, Ghost, Robin, Sugar Pie and the pups all looked up the hill. Kyra glowered from the Guardian Stone, spun around and leaped back into the cave. Yowling erupted and a moment later Buster staggered down the slope.

Rosie looked sadly at the pups. "Browser, the den is too small to add dogs."

"Leatherboots will take them if we leave them where they're living."

"White Truck!" she yelped, her pelt rising in a ridge along her spine.

"Rosamonde!" Browser cried, slamming his big tail on the ground with such vehemence the pups whimpered. "Surely you don't believe I would endanger our home."

Sugar Pie wiggled toward her. "We were careful, Princess Rosie Discarded Queen. We backtracked three times before we came here."

Browser's mate visibly relaxed. "Call me Rosie," she trilled.

The fuzzy mother's soft eyes blinked with gratitude. "We were careful, Misses Rosie Queen. I promise."

"We could make them a nest near the den," Robin said, as Buster approached the group, bruised and torn from Kyra's anger.

The usually jovial tux spoke in a hushed voice. "Let them rest for now. When they're ready, I'll take them south to find them a home with two-leggeds." That will solve their problem and appease Kyra.

Sugar Pie beamed at the thought of a home, a real home for herself and the pups, a home with kind tall-ones. "You can do that?"

"I can...I'm Buster," he added with a small nod and an involuntary glance up the hill.

"Mister Buster can do it!" the mother dog squealed, covering his face with kisses. Jasper and Shorttail knocked him over trying to plant more, even sloppier lip-loves, and despite his fear of Kyra's wrath, Buster's

131

heart was conquered. Robin and Ghost sniffed the fuzzy pups and their frizzy mother, who assumed a submissive posture for their examination. They accepted her as she lay on her back wiggling and whimpering, then jumping up to give one last kissy-kiss as they moved away.

"Let's dig a nest beneath the rosemary hedge," Ghost meowed.

"I'll help you," Robin offered.

"Me too," Buster said. Rosie's gaze traveled from Robin to her mate, to Ghost, to Buster, then back to Browser's pleading eyes.

"All right," she relented. "Only until Buster finds them a home with uprights." Kyra was on the Guardian Stone again, hissing and spitting with renewed rage.

"It's done," Buster snarled. "We will *all* honor this agreement." She slunk into the den, her tail angrily slicing the air.

The males found a spot in the rosemary hedge where the rock wall projected into the dense, perfumed needles, creating a natural shelter from the elements. Beneath the out-cropping, the dogs wouldn't be visible to anyone from any angle, and the only way to reach their nest was to enter where the hedge ended by the pool.

Sugar Pie helped the cats dig a deep and wide nest. She was more hindrance than help really, but no one complained. The cats gathered sweetgrass, moss and herbs to cushion the bottom, and delighted, mother and pups leaped into their hideaway. No longer confined to a dark, damp echo chamber, they had friends now too. Satisfied with their work, Browser and Ghost left to hunt, leaving Robin to protect Rosie, and Buster to deal with his mate. But Kyra refused to be comforted. Buster emerged from the den, and found his friends were almost to the woods. He loped down the hill and over the grass to catch them.

Rosie watched the hunters disappear into the thicket, Robin beside her, preferring her company to Kyra's hissing. They couldn't see the mother dog and her pups from their boulder, but they could hear and certainly smell them.

"Do you think this will work?" Robin asked.

Rosie seemed distracted. "It's only until they've rested and Buster can find them homes."

"Maybe they'll leave on their own."

"And go where?" she asked in a strained voice. Then she moaned, a deep, opulent, mating-call moan and began to purr loudly. She rubbed herself against Robin, purring and trilling sensually, then did it again. Surprised for a moment, the sweet, salty smell of blood told him Rosie's birthing had begun. He followed her as she crawled down the hill to the Guardian Stone, leaping into the den with a little cry. She crept to her nest and lay on her side, her head resting on Mee-am's cloth. Robin remained by the cave's entrance. Kyra, who dropped her anger when she realized the kits were being born, settled near Rosie's nest.

Panting and purring, Rosie tensed. She rolled on her belly and squatted. "Yeow!" A kitten appeared between her splayed legs. Rosie rolled back on her side, and licked the translucent sack from her deaf, blind baby, who immediately began rooting for a teat. A large newborn, he was his father's twin with a wide, dark head and back, a white undercarriage and a fat paddle tail ending in a point. "Umph." Again Rosie squatted and a second kit emerged, a girl with her mother's coloring. The third baby was a surprise, a deeply sorrel male. The fourth birth was painful, and the undersized male arrived with his rear leg bent unnaturally from his side. Licking him fervently, Rosie tried to ease the twisted limb to his body, but it couldn't bend. Her baby was crippled. At last she dropped her head on Mee-am's cloth and curled around her kits.

Robin left to fetch more sweetgrass while Kyra guarded their queen and her babies. The change from hysteria to compassion was dramatic, but Rosie had seen Kyra's true nature at Harmony Tree. Beneath her anger beat a brave and loyal heart. Both females dozed to the kits' hypnotic purr. When Rosie woke, Kyra was gone and Browser hovered above the snuggery, trilling with delight. The kits squealed when his cold nose met their skin, so he sat back, marveling at their small bodies, spindly legs and tails. Their eyes were sealed shut, and their ear flaps hugged enormous heads. They were the most beautiful cats he'd ever seen.

Later that night, Rosie tottered to the preypile, ate a huge meal and left the cave to relieve herself. She moved slowly over the boulders, reveling in the fresh breeze and sparkling night sky. A flurry near the rosemary hedge startled her. Sugar Pie roofed.

"I have something for you, Misses Rosie Queen. For your babies." With tail-wagging glee she bounced into the hedge, returning with a mouthful of white sage she dropped at Rosie's paws. "It cleans the air," she bubbled, dancing in place, then looked worried. "Not that your air needs cleaning. I didn't mean..."

"I know what you meant, Sugar Pie. Thank you." Rosie nuzzled the mama dog's neck and Sugar Pie began trembling with such emotion Rosie worried she might be trampled. Quickly, she gathered the sage stalks and climbed toward the den. Sugar Pie called after her.

"I love you, Misses Rosie Queen. Can I kiss your babies?"

"When they're bigger, Sugar Pie, and I love you too," Rosie trilled through woody stems. She meant it. When she returned to her nest, her runt lay stiffly on his side in the sweetgrass. Rosie pushed him to a teat, but he was too weak to latch on and had to be nudged to the nipple again and again before his tiny belly was full. Rosie closed her eyes and slipped into a waking-dream.

Floating to the ceiling, she looked down and saw herself connected to her body by an ethereal vine, her kits tucked into her belly. Browser slept nearby. She floated through the hillside and higher, past Robin on Waterfall Boulder, where he sat with Ghost, and both looked up as she drifted away. Pulled from cloud to cloud, Rosie came to a tall den of pale stone. Like phantoms escaping into the night, smoke curled from its chimney astride the peaked roof, and from the chimney's highest point rose a metal pole capped with a pewter cat running forever with the wind. Rosie had never been there, yet it all felt so familiar, then suddenly she was inside. Mee-am! Her beloved Mee-am!

Rosie called, but Mee-am stared right through her, speaking to the Mate who placed a box on her lap. He smiled as Mee-am lifted the cardboard flaps. Kittens! Five multi-colored babies wrapped in towels and huddled together, mewling for their mother. Their eyes had opened and their ear flaps had lifted. They could see and hear, and walked on trembling legs, which placed them at about three weeks. Not weaned, but given a good start on mother's milk, the ideal age to be rescued by humans. But when Mee-am picked up an orange tiger, his body stiffened and he squealed with fear. Immediately she scruffed him, holding him to her heart, cooing and stroking until he relaxed, then gently placed him back in the box.

"The litter we've been looking for," the Mate said.

"I can tell. I see Mommy and Daddy in their coloring and the shape of their faces." She rubbed their heads, leaned forward and kissed them. "Where were they? We looked everywhere."

"In the trunk of an abandoned car. The lid was jammed open and mom had made a nest in some old towels."

"Did she see you take her babies?"

"Yes," he said, sadly. "She watched, but what can we do? We have to socialize them or they'll just be another generation of ferals."

Mee-am nodded. "Let's catch her before next week's clinic. We can't let her breed again and she will, now that her kits are gone." Turning her attention back to the babies, she cooed, "We found you. We found you." She lifted the little orange tiger from the box again, and this time he purred. "We saved you. Yes we did," Mee-am chirped, rubbing her nose on his fat belly. She put him down and lifted a delicate female, examining the little girl's mite-infested ears. The hungry kits' eyes followed her lips when she spoke and her hands when they moved. Mee-am looked sad. "If people knew what happened to them, they'd never dump an animal." The Mate lowered his eyes, ashamed, but Mee-am was busied by a flea that scurried across the kitten's white belly. "Oh, bring me the flea stuff, will you please?" Mee-am rubbed the calico's distended stomach. "Worm belly," she murmured, gently placing the kitten back in the box.

The Mate returned with medications and each baby received two drops stinking like ammonia mixed with gasoline at the base of its neck between its shoulder blades. Rosie averted her face from the smell, but envied the kits their freedom from fleas. Next Mee-am squirted a dropper-full of milky fluid into each of their mouths. They grimaced and shuddered and the humans laughed.

"Worms-be-gone," their foster-mother trilled.

The Mate looked sheepish. "As am I...gone, that is. It's late." Mee-am nodded. But he didn't leave; he stood beside her chair, silently asking for something more.

Mee-am looked up and shook her head. "I think about her pain...and I can't forget or forgive you. Not yet. So if you're making these amends for me..."

The Mate slumped, then took a deep breath. "I'm so sorry, Miriam. I'm am sorry and at first, yes, I was doing this so you'd take me back. But I'm changing. I do it now to be a better person."

"Perhaps someday you'll do it for them."

The Mate deflated again. "I pray every day we'll find..." The words were too painful to finish.

"So do I." Mee-am's eyes filled with water and Rosie thought the Mate's did too, but suddenly she was outside, going home to Browser, her babies and her friends. Mee-am and the Mate hadn't just moved, they'd moved on, and Rosie wasn't part of their lives anymore. Mee-am had forgotten her.

The stony hillside rushed toward her, and someone waited on Waterfall Boulder. Starlight! "Now you understand," he meowed.

"Yes, I understand...Mee-am has a new family. She doesn't even remember me."

"You don't understand at all," the white cat admonished. "You are not forgotten. Everything they do is for you, about you, because of you. Your sacrifice changed everything for the better. Live in love, Rosie and you'll find your way home."

"I am home!" she snapped.

"No," Starlight whispered. "Not yet." Galaxies of blue stars smoldered to nothing and Rosie lay in her nest. She licked her kits, paying special attention to the runt, but he would no longer suckle. The sun rose, shooting pinpricks of light through the cubbyhole and for the briefest moment Rosie saw his twin, only whole, not crippled, cuddling beside him...his Fetch. The Fetch merged with his body and he passed into Beyond. Sadly Rosie nuzzled him, keeping him warm until Browser lifted him from the nest and buried him near the pool, marking his grave with a rosemary sprig.

Suns and moons would rise and fall, and the rosemary shoot would grow, dropping its blooms on those who passed beneath. They too would fall, nourishing the smallest lives, who fed the insects, who fed the birds, who fed the kin, who would fall again, the flesh forever morphing while Spirit turned the Great Wheel of Life.

11 – NEW LIVES

ews of a royal birthing travels quickly, so quickly that the following sunrise emissaries from neighboring pods sat in the meadow below Hillside Den. Each day thereafter kin arrived from farther afield. All brought gifts of precious herbs or exotic prey and sang songs conveying goodwill. Even a Chevalier from Ozymandias sat in the meadow one morning, a piece of worn plank-wood at his sequin-wrapped paws. Browser went down to meet him, assuring the Page of his Grace that the message was understood, the gift appreciated. All Rosie remembered was Ozymandias' threat to her person. *"Understand, sweet girl, I am never denied,"* rang in her head, along with the pain he'd inflicted on her paw. She was furious. "He's laughing at us, Browser. He gave us a splinter."

"Rosie, it's a piece of the fence that borders the palace grounds."

"So?"

"So what Ozymandias is saying is he's torn down the barrier between our clans and that Hillside Pod is welcome in his home."

"Or...here's a piece of wood like the one I'll use to bash your skulls in."

"Rosie, have some faith. This is good news, especially so soon after his ascension as Emperor of Ironstone Manor.

"Ironstone Manor? Browser, they think he's Emperor of the Green. They'd be funny if they weren't dangerous, a clan of crazies living in a fantasy world. I don't want us or our children anywhere near that place."

"You're right, it's a dream world. The grounds are overgrown with dreamweed, and all inhabitants imbibe, including Ozymandias."

"No wonder he's a pompous fool."

Browser stiffened, surprised by his young mate's intolerance. "Yes, Rosie, he's a fool, by birth as much as bad habits, but a fool who bears us no malice. In Ozymandias' odd view of the world, you were rightfully his, yet he holds neither our union nor our children against us."

"He wouldn't dare," Rosie cried.

Browser nuzzled her shoulder. "Don't underestimate his influence, Rosie. Many pledge him loyalty. He provides comfort to many kin in the Green as well as the surrounding alleys." She looked shocked. "In a world of few pleasures, a field of dreamweed is a balm to body and soul. For that reason alone no one bothers Ozymandias, or his clan, silly as they might be." Browser touched the plank with his paw. "Anyway, I don't think this came from him."

"What do you mean?"

"I mean, as you discovered, Ozymandias is a buffoon...but Sylvestes Felaria isn't. I believe this came from him, with the emperor's approval, of course, but I'm sure it was Felaria's idea. And considering the struggles we've been told are coming, we need allies. Ironstone Manor has many hiding places. This could be good."

"What's good, Browser, is that you're king of the Green."

🐾 🐾 🐾

Thirteen sunrises after the birth of Rosie's kits, exactly one day after their eyes opened, six venerated shaman, including Bent Whisker, Elder Cat of the South and the most venerated of the venerated shamans, waited in the meadow below the den. They had come to validate the offspring of the Discarded Queen and her consort. Would these kits save the Green? Bent Whisker would know.

As the sun washed the meadow in golden light, Ghost slipped down the hill to greet the kind-faced sage. "I've been expecting your arrival for two moons. Shall we meet the royal kits?" He looked to Browser who sat on the Guardian Stone.

"One moment," The pod leader meowed and disappeared inside.

"Has anyone divined what happened to Erasmus and Morsus?" The little wizard asked.

"Shouldn't you be telling us?" Sosay countered, the blue crescent on her forehead pulsing as she spoke. Ghost looked away, embarrassed. *Why is she always so combative?*

Browser loped down the hill. "Rosie is tired but welcomes you all. Please though, she dislikes any fracas about being the Discarded Queen."

"But she is the Discarded Queen!" Sosay moaned. Bent Whisker flicked his tail at her, nodding for Browser to continue.

"Rosie worries the kits won't be ours to raise, that others will interfere."

"I assure you, we're here only to witness their destinies. No one will interfere." Bent Whisker flashed a smile of missing fangs and honest eyes.

Browser consented with a nod. "Groups of two are welcome in the cubbyhole, but I invite you all to enter the den," he said with a flourish of his tail, then climbed the hill and vanished.

The shamans preferred to wait in the meadow, choosing who would go first. "I'll go last with my mentor," Sosay told the others, combing the fur on her cheeks with her wide paw. Darktail and Martileena, empaths from the west, sailed through the shelterveil, landing gracefully on the floor of the large room. Darktail sniffed the den with open mouth.

"Good herbs you've got stored, Ghost." Twenty plus turns of the Moon older than the little shaman, much larger and more muscular, he'd been protective of Ghost since they met.

"My apprentice helps me collect," the wizard answered. "We all take an interest in healing with herbs here, including our new mother who's quite gifted." The big tabby waved his tail, happy to learn his friend hadn't lost his modesty. At that moment, Robin came from the nursery. "This is my apprentice Robin," Ghost said with pride.

Martileena scanned the young acolyte with jewel-bright eyes while Darktail padded a circle around him. "You've chosen well," he said.

"In truth, he chose me."

"Even better," the tabby declared.

A glance from his mentor told Robin the visitors weren't ready. Once the Wisdom Cats were alone again, Ghost edged closer to Darktail, his demeanor almost furtive. "I'm glad you're here. I need to talk to someone who can understand. Something that's...it's heavy on me...I..." Still unable to speak of his botched vision-quest, his voice faded. Darktail nuzzled his friend and when Ghost pulled away, ashamed, the tabby's eyes welled with concern.

"Whatever you need to say, Ghost, I need to tell you something first. Something no one else has the heart to tell you, so I must." Ghost looked concerned. "At Darkmoon Gathering, it was decided the four missing cats are dead."

Ghost plopped on his haunches, stunned. "What do you mean *decided*? Bent Whisker augured this?"

"No," Darktail replied.

The wizard narrowed his sea-blue eyes. "Did Nebula find them dead in an astral travel?" Darktail lowered his head. Agitated, Ghost paced circles around both of his friends.

Martileena rose to walk with him, speaking softly into his ear. "No, Ghost, only Indra," she began, her voice like water lapping mossy stones. "No Wisdom Cat can find the other three."

"Starlight doesn't speak of it," he said.

Martileena nodded. "All the Spirit Cats are silent. Ripplemist also shows us nothing."

Darktail rose, tail low. "No one knows why the sight of Wisdom Cats is clouded...as if Great Mother..."

Martileena's pelt rose. "Don't speak it," She hissed. "Blasphemy!"

"Blasphemy or not, it's true. Great Mother no longer favors us with her secrets."

"We don't know that." Martileena snapped.

"We know we're blind, deaf and struck dumb."

"Everyone?" Ghost asked, secretly relieved it wasn't just him who couldn't decipher what happened to Erasmus, then felt guilty for thinking so selfishly.

"Not everyone and not in all things, but important things. Darkness surrounds Erasmus' and the others' disappearance. And other events trouble us. Reggie is not the only missing apprentice. Some have run off. Can you imagine? Run away!"

"Why?" Ghost tried to comprehend any kin fortunate enough to be mentored, abandoning the opportunity.

"We don't understand why. But it's beginning to feel like being a Wisdom Cat is no longer seen as an honor. At least by some catlings."

"Bug beaks," Martileena chuffed. "Catlings always rebel. Then they grow up."

The little wizard began pacing again, lashing his tail. *So, they're calling Erasmus, Morsus and Reggie dead. It's not true. It's disrespectful.* "You've buried what you don't understand," he said. Darktail and his second fell silent but Ghost could see their anger. "What you've done is wrong," he spit.

"Can't you understand why?" Darktail spit back, his tail also lashing as they paced opposite sides of a circle. The silver cat froze in place. Suddenly he *did* understand and every hair on his spine stood ninety degrees from his body. "Yes," the tabby said, "We need an Elder Cat of the North."

"It's you, Ghost," Martileena trilled with a lick to his forehead.

"No, please. That's not possible..."

"Of course it is," Darktail insisted with a thump of his appendage.

"No, really, it's not."

Martileena nuzzled his shoulder. "I understand it's hard for you to let go of Erasmus, but Ghost—"

"That's not it. It's not possible because...I failed my vision-quest."

The empaths stared wide-eyed.

"And you never told your podmates," Darktail whispered.

Ghost stared at his shuffling paws. "I couldn't. They were so happy for me, for our pod...I never meant...it just happened..."

"Ghost!" Darktail scolded.

The little wizard's head jerked up. "I didn't know it would turn into this. I thought—I didn't think," he yowled.

Martileena stepped between the males. She hushed Darktail with a flash of her eyes, then looked Ghost up and down as if it were the first time she'd ever seen him. "Well, you couldn't foresee Erasmus would disappear," she said, then licked his forehead. "Anyway, the past doesn't matter. But Ghost, you must tell no one you failed. No one. No one knows, right? No one but us?" Ghost stared into Martileena's fierce face. He thought of objecting, but her eyes burned so desperately into his, he couldn't open his mouth. "*No one* can be told," she repeated; Ghost turned to Darktail and found him as bullied into silence as he was. "Think about it," Martileena continued. "We can't have our status as Wisdom Cats questioned. Not now."

"I'm not questioning any Wisdom Cats," Ghost finally rasped. "But I can't be Elder Cat of the North when I failed my vision-quest."

Darktail seemed eager to agree with him, but somehow Martileena was in charge. Ghost thought it odd he'd never noticed that before. "You're needed," she said.

"But it's not truthful."

Martileena stomped her paws. "Something attacked us in the north,

141

Ghost. Anyway, no one really knows what the Truth is." He remembered saying something similar to Browser once and felt ashamed.

Darktail faced her. "Martileena, only Indra is dead for sure and she's an eastern Wisdom Cat."

The brindle chuffed. "And Reggie is a southern apprentice. But the north lost two Wisdom Cats and one of them was Elder Cat. They were taken from Flatstone Meeting Rock, also in the north. And Boulderfalls, so long a garden of northern delights, has been desecrated by the blood and pain of innocents. The evil lurked in the woods, waiting for the meeting at Flatstone and this evil is still in the Green. That much we can all feel. What if it intends to destroy us one element at a time? Where better to begin than the north? If we lose our healing arts we're doomed." She turned to Ghost. "You can't abandon us. You can't."

Ears and tail down, Ghost gave way to her fear and perhaps his own. "Nothing good comes from deceit. I'll do this...but just for now."

Martileena relaxed. After a moment of silence, "Well, perhaps we should visit the kits?" she chirped as if nothing unusual had happened.

As if by magic, Robin appeared again to lead them to the snuggery and Ghost wondered if he'd been listening. Then he realized he didn't mind if Robin knew everything. He knew how to keep a secret and it was good to have an ally. The guests followed the apprentice into Rosie's cubbyhole. As Darktail passed him, Ghost whispered, "Erasmus is *not* dead."

Rosie greeted her visitors with a drowsy purr. Their viewing of the kits was short and perfunctory as was the visit by Starpaw and Flyingtail that followed. They'd traveled far to offer best wishes and even Rosie, new to the Green and involved with her newborns, could see that life had changed much in the Aerie since Indra's murder. The eastern cats were grieving.

At last Sosay and her mentor climbed the slope. More fur than muscle, Bent Whisker didn't attempt a leap from the Guardian. He squeezed behind it and tumbled into the den, then needed to rest. Sosay waited beside him until he was strong enough to follow Robin to Rosie's snuggery.

"My queen, thank you for letting us visit," Sosay meowed. Rosie's eyes smiled at the beautifully groomed white Wisdom Cat, then lit upon the scruffy pelt behind her.

"And you are?" the new mother asked.

"I am nothing but old, my queen. My name is Bent Whisker." Rosie knew the name as the greatest seer who'd ever lived in the Green. She stared, trying to meet her fantasy of him with what sat before her. Feeling her eyes upon him, Bent Whisker believed he must bow, which he did with difficulty. But once down, he couldn't rise. He squeaked several times before Sosay, so thrilled to be in the queen's presence she didn't hear, realized he needed her help and placed her shoulders beneath his head, lifting him back to a sitting position. Muttering and wheezing, he spent several minutes regaining his dignity before he peered into the nest that smelled so sweetly of baby and milk. Three kits, each the size of a fat mouse, snuggled into Rosie's fur with rumbling purrs, their tiny splayed fingers pushing against her belly. The old seer's eyes were dark pools of love. *He's not the fool he appears to be,* Rosie thought. *How many have revealed secrets, thinking they dealt with dotage?* Bent Whisker chuckled.

"We use the gifts we're given," he rasped and she sucked in a startled breath, hoping she hadn't spoken out loud. Bent Whisker continued. "The sorrel kit will give you a lot of trouble, but don't despair. His heart is too strong and free to conform. In the end, his wildness will save you."

"Save me?" Rosie asked.

"Not just you, all of you...on the journey," the elder replied, staring now at the large kit who resembled Browser. "Ah, this one carries a heavy burden." Rosie sighed. "Don't be sad, mother. Your son has the soul of a giant. He will learn from his troubles as few ever do, and overcome." Bent Whisker closed his eyes, sitting so still Rosie wondered if he slept again. "No," he croaked. "I'm quite awake." The trembling queen looked to Sosay, who smiled. The seer continued. "I've lived long, but met no kits with the destiny of these. Within each of your sons beats the heart of a hero and both will be remembered, stories of their deeds passed down for generations."

"My little girl?" Rosie asked apprehensively. Bent Whisker paused.

"Don't worry. She'll be fine."

"That's it? *She'll be fine!*" Not at all reassured, Rosie raised herself to her paws the better to catch his gaze, but he wouldn't answer.

"I'm sorry," he finally murmured. "I'm afraid she's spoiled."

"Spoiled? Her eyes opened yesterday!" Rosie cried.

Bent Whisker responded by digging in his ear with his back foot, then held the toe before his face, examining what his claw had pulled free. Rosie would have laughed out loud had she not been put off by his crudeness. Moments passed while he decided what to do with his prize, then realizing all eyes were on him, sheepishly lowered the paw to the ground. "Forgive me. I must be mistaken," he crooned, but Rosie knew he didn't mean it.

"She's not spoiled...She's royal," she commanded.

Bent Whisker laughed so heartily even Rosie smiled. "Not to worry, madam. Your daughter will have the love of a truly pure heart. After some difficulty she brings on herself, she'll make a good life."

"But won't she do anything amazing?"

"It is amazing how we find our way through life, isn't it? Imagine her journey to the light." He closed his eyes again. "Yes. She will help." Rosie resented that his opinion meant so much to her, but it did, and with those words she found some relief. Bent Whisker turned to Browser and Robin, who'd entered the cubbyhole when they heard distress in Rosie's voice. "Ah, the Heart of the Queen," he wheezed, nodding to the pod leader. "And his friend the Gray." Sosay looked at Robin and realized it was true: to fulfill the Prophecy, Robin, Rosie and Browser, along with their sorrel son, would leave the Green. She almost blurted it out but Bent Whisker silenced her with a thump of his tail. He wouldn't demand more of his queen today. "We must go. I fear we've tired you."

"I'm fine," Rosie snapped, having decided which parts of his divination she'd believe.

The seer chuckled. "Like you, I'd rather be happy," he rasped. "Truth changes with one's viewpoint and like you, I trust what I see more than what I'm told. Wisdom, madam." He bowed sincerely, and Rosie felt vindicated. Robin led the Wisdom Cats to the cave entrance and Ghost accompanied them down the hill where they joined Darktail and Martileena. The eastern cats had left as soon as they finished their visit.

The old cat took measure of the silver shaman with his better eye. "You understand what's expected of you?" Ghost nodded. "You mustn't fret, son. I sense good will come of your efforts."

"I have many questions," Ghost meowed.

Bent Whisker chuckled. "Come south and augur with us. Come

quickly."

The little shaman stood lost in thought for many heartbeats, suddenly remembering his manners. "Would you eat from our preypile before your journey?"

"Thank you," Sosay said for all of them, her crescent moon pulsing blue with pleasure. Bent Whisker hunched over, rubbing his cheek along his thigh, rasping in discomfort. "Do you have Cat's Claw in your storehouse? My joints trouble me. And a little Willow Bark to ease pain."

Ghost dashed up the hill, reappearing moments later with herbs specially mixed for the seer. Bent Whisker thanked the wizard, then turned to Robin, who'd come down with jaws packed with longear and vole. "You'll do well," he said. "All that's needed and more."

Robin beamed, bouncing back up the hill to perch on the Guardian while the Wisdom Cats bantered below. After eating and grooming their pelts, they sauntered down the meadow as if they hadn't a care. Ghost could count many. He climbed the hill to sit with Robin. Sugar Pie released her pups, who'd been amazingly quiet, but were dying to play in the grass again.

"They must have smelled the barkers," Ghost murmured. "I wonder why no one said anything."

"They trust you." Robin meowed.

A ripple of contentment rolled down Ghost' spine. The kits were all they were supposed to be, Robin had been encouraged and he had been assured his secret served the highest good. Despite the unnamed foe lurking in the Green, for now Ghost felt all was well in his world.

🐾   🐾   🐾

The cry pierced her dreams and Rosie leaped to her paws. Browser behind her, she raced toward the sweet, metallic scent pouring from Kyra's snuggery, and found the birthing queen unconscious, her ebony pelt soaked with blood. Buster keened miserably with each head-bunt to her body. Kyra flinched, but didn't wake. Four babies lay between them, two of them still-born. They looked big next to their mother's slender body.

"Browser," Rosie whispered, careful to keep her voice calm, "Get some cactus water. Bring a big piece. There's a plant near the pool."

"All right," he meowed.

"And where are Ghost and Robin? Find Ghost and Robin."

"I will," Browser said and was off. Buster sat staring into space.

Rosie nuzzled his shoulder. "Don't worry, Buster, we won't let her die."

But Kyra was still bleeding. Rosie needed Ghost to tell her which herbs would help Kyra's wounds congeal. Where was he? She wanted to yowl for him, but didn't want Buster to know she was worried. "Buster, can you gather fresh sweetgrass for the nest? For Kyra and the babies."

"The kits?" He asked and they both looked at the newborns. The two who lived were wet, cold and rooting for milk against their unresponsive mother. They would also die if nothing was done to protect them.

"I'll care for them until she can." Rosie said, then scruffed the squirmers, licked them dry and tucked them beneath her. They wiggled to her teats and began to nurse and purr.

Robin entered the den, dropping a fat rat on the preypile as Ghost careened past him, the gray bark of a redberry bush in his jaws. He loped to Kyra's snuggery and began shredding the pliant husk with his claws, chewing the slivers into a pulp he pushed into Kyra's mouth. The juices from the redberry casing would mingle with her saliva and the bleeding would stop.

"Take the kits who passed and leave them near my baby's grave near the pool," Rosie told Buster. "Ghost will help you bury them later. Bring the sweetgrass." With sad eyes, Buster scruffed one of his stillborn children. The shaman nosed the other from Kyra's side, but Rosie stopped him with a paw on his back.

"Wait. Tell me what to do next."

"You've cleaned the wound. Browser told me you sent him for cactus water, but I also sent him for moss. Moss will also staunch the bleeding and its greenness will heal." Ghost licked Rosie with pride. "Later, she'll need buttercup root and furleaf to fight infection. Force the mixture into her mouth the way I did the crampbark." He glanced at Robin who'd been listening attentively, lifted the lifeless baby from the nest and left.

"Robin, there are buttercups behind the boulder where the stream enters the woods."

"Yes, I know them. Should I gather dreamweed? Huge patches bloom nearby." Rosie thought a moment.

"Better to use poppy seeds. She'll be in pain. Hurry. Kyra will awaken

146

soon."

Robin dashed from the den as Browser returned with the succulent and all the moss he could carry. Rosie tended to Kyra, then Buster returned, careening about in a state of hysteria, so she sent him to harvest more sweetgrass. By long-shadows, he'd filled every nest in the den.

Kyra lived. Or rather, a new and improved version of Kyra lived. She was changed. Much like Rosie, the new Kyra would sit alone on the hill, listening to the leaves, watching the moon and stars roll across the sky. No one knew where she dropped her temper or wicked tongue, but she never went to find them. Perhaps she realized a greater paw than any of theirs dealt life and death. Perhaps she just tired of her anger. Kyra never spoke of it. She simply grew more tender. Often she would lay where her kits were buried, leaving a sprig of lavender or sage. Sometimes the scent of the herbs followed her home and she would whisper to Rosie their children had come to visit.

Not long after her recovery, Kyra stumbled upon Jasper and Shorttail at the pool. She was backing away to let them drink when they saw her and fled to the safety of their mother who stood shuddering before the black queen.

"We're sorry to bother you, Misses Kyra," Sugar Pie's voice trembled. "We do hope you're doing well." The pups quivered behind her with lowered heads and tails, and Kyra, realizing how frightened they all were, felt ashamed.

"Sugar Pie, I'm the one who's sorry. Please believe I will never hurt you or your children. I'm sorry I've frightened you." The little dog tried to answer, but nothing come out of her mouth. She couldn't even wag her tail. "I'm sorry," Kyra kept whispering as she backed away from the pool without quenching her thirst. She could always return for a drink. She'd been given a second chance.

🐾　🐾　🐾

Ghost attended Brightmoon of Many Winds, but many of his magical brethren weren't there. Not a single Wisdom Cat from the east had come to celebrate. Neither Darktail nor Martileena were in attendance, and Sosay was nowhere to be found. His friends, he realized, were going through the same malaise of spirit he'd been experiencing. But not everyone was depressed.

He saw Monkey the moment she saw him. He'd known her since they were kits and she had always befuddled him with her charms, though Great Mother knew she never looked like much, with spindly legs and a protruding belly despite her underfed frame. Ghost could never figure out if her legs were too long or her carriage too high, but her tail was definitely too short. Her oddest feature though, was the coarse gray fur that grew in patches of different lengths in different directions around her neck. It had the texture of a cotton ball and framed her face in a way that ensured her name, a gift from some uprights who fed her a few turns of the Moon when she was a catling roaming alleyways near the Green.

She'd been spending cold nights in their monster-cave, and came through the window just after they'd put it to sleep. It was still warm when they crawled out of it, holding boxes of delicious smelling meats.

"Look at this kitten! She's wild, she's...and, oh my goodness...so hungry." The female held up slivers of meat and Monkey did the hand dance, coming close enough to snatch food, but too fast to be caught. "She's so hungry. Give her some of your burger, dear, please. She ate the rest of mine."

"What's that stuff around her neck?" The male asked, dropping tidbits along the window ledge. Monkey gobbled them up.

"It's fur. Listen to her purr. She's so grateful." The woman bent down and cooed, "Mommy will get you some real food. Would you like that? You with the pretty mane." Monkey purred even louder.

"She won't tame down, even with feedings, not a feral this old." the man said.

"I don't care. She's so homely, she's cute."

He chuckled, offering another bite. "With that fuzzy fluff ringing her face, she looks like a monkey."

"Well, she's my monkey and I love her." The name stuck.

Monkey did have one lovely physical attribute: big, brilliant eyes, green as new moss and bright as stars in a desert sky. Those eyes were pools of thoughtfulness, reflecting Monkey's strength. Self sufficient even as a catling, she had a knack of making the most of whatever life presented and regularly found tall-ones willing to feed her. They'd even leave blankets in boxes for her to sleep in. Monkey was smart and tough through and through, exuding an aura of resourcefulness tall-walkers

148

liked.

Ghost had always been drawn to her. As a monk, he dismissed the charms of most females, but Monkey touched his spirit. Now she sauntered toward him with a friendly meow, rubbing the length of her body against his.

"Monkey," he chirped, then licked his chest fur for no reason.

"Ghost, it's been forever." She purred and pressed against him again, leaving a bewitching scent. "I've missed you," she said with a throaty moan, and he lost all ability to process thought.

"Me too...missed you, not me, I mean," he stammered. "You can't miss yourself...Well, I guess you could if you—" She rubbed against him again and he fell silent, feeling dumber than tree bark. He spoke again, barely able to hear his voice above his thumping heart. "We have kits in the pod. Uh, not me, the new cat and Kyra. Rosie and Kyra had kits."

"Kits are good," Monkey cooed, resting her head on his shoulder. "Let me show you the nest I made."

"Really?" He warbled, rubbing his ear with a forepaw as if her words had made it itch. Lost in her green eyes, he let her lead him up the trunk of the great tree to a branch over the root stage. She'd found a hollow in the bole, softened it with cedar sprigs and claimed it with her scent. Impressed as always with Monkey's resourcefulness, Ghost settled on the greens, surprising himself with a contented sigh. This felt right, more than right. It felt wonderful.

They spent brightmoon together. Afterwards in the meadow, ready to say goodbye, Ghost pictured Monkey at Hillside Den. He was about to ask her to come with him when he remembered his promise to Bent Whisker. First he must travel south.

Monkey wasn't worried. He'd find her again soon and they would be together. She knew it. With a tender lick to his ear and a nose-kiss, she turned and bounded off. Ghost padded home alone.

12 – Bent Whisker's Hearth

host loped south through the western forest. He'd just passed Hillside pod's scent markers when skywater began to fall. Small, hard drops beat against his pelt, soaking him through and through. The Moon of Many Winds brought storms, fierce but brief, sweeping north ahead of the yearly flights of feathertails. This storm was fiercer than most.

The clouds burst open and the creek jumped its bank, washing away anything in its path. Forced up a fir tree at the edges of the Birch Grove, Ghost pressed himself to the bole while the storm gathered strength. Sleeping sporadically between lightning strikes and downpours, sometime during the long dark he woke to an arc of light that was monstrously huge and bright as the sun, and followed by a boom like a giant's fist slammed against the earth. Even the air smelled scorched. Ghost found he was no longer south of the Birch Grove clinging to the wet trunk of an old spruce, but rather at the edge of Harmony Tree's meadow, hunkered on the limb of a blackthorn. The tree felt weak beneath him. Many of its boughs had been severed and its red sap bled into the ground. Tucking his head into his shoulders, the shaman shut his eyes, willing the dream to disappear, but when he opened them again the vision was worse. He saw men, tall, broad men, swinging axes in their muscular arms, gouging and chopping the sacred tree.

"Stop that, murderers!" he cried. An awful stillness and the men backed away. The cedar groaned, and with the rending of a thousand giant splinters, the uppermost edge of the gash sagged into its bottom. A thunderous crack, and the sacred tree toppled forward.

Now the sky poured rivers that swept the cedar clean, pushing all life beneath raging currents. A spiral of blue light shuddered above the whirlwind then slumped into the torrent. Starlight was no more.

"Nee-oowww!" Ghost yowled, tumbling to the soggy earth. He ran toward the carnage but found himself in the Birch Grove again, skywater thudding on his back while rivulets threading through the grass tried to knock him off his paws and carry him away. Starlight dead! Harmony Tree destroyed! Was it true? If so, all was lost and nothing he could do would matter.

By morning the sky had cleared and the ground had begun to dry. Ghost rose and cleaned himself, trembling with every lick of his tongue. The dream had been so real. Was Starlight really dead? *Don't let it be true. Like Erasmus, Starlight lives, Like Erasmus, Starlight lives,* he repeated the hopeful mantra to himself.

He didn't know where Bent Whisker lived, only that his den was a hollow yew in the southern wilderness. Ghost needed Starlight's help. He closed his eyes and focused his thoughts until blue light shimmered against his lids. He saw Sosay and her mentor at a glowing pit of fire, cat shadows dancing on smooth walls of inner-bark. He opened his eyes. Starlight reveled before him in a patch of dreamweed.

"Starlight!"

The Spirit Cat looked up, little white flowers hanging from his lips. "What do you need?"

"You're alive!"

"And you're surprised."

"I need to find Bent Whisker's hearth. Can you help me?"

"Oh, yes, I'm able to do so," Starlight purred, licking his paws and cleaning his face with them, mischief twinkling in his eyes.

Normally, Ghost would be irritated, but today he was happy Starlight lived and Harmony Tree stood tall. "I realize you *can*, but *will* you please help me?"

"Oh, all right...only because you're my favorite." Ghost smiled, convinced the trickster said that to everyone. But he did help, beginning by padding deosil three times around Ghost to summon energy, leaving a trail of stardust in his prints. Then settling opposite Ghost on the edge of the galaxy he created, he took a deep breath and blew an icy mist into the air. Ghost could see into the dense wilderness beyond the Green's southern border. He stood on a peak of stony hills encircling a meadow, staring down at an ancient yew. Almost as wide as it was tall, eons had warped its fluted trunk into shapes of fanciful beasts.

Lightning struck and the tree burst into flames, burning the vision to nothingness. All that remained of Starlight were spinning stars bursting against foliage, opening every frond they touched and causing every stalk to bloom.

"Starlight," Ghost called, "Why the lightning? Is Bent Whisker in danger?" His answer was a tinkling blue shimmer.

The little wizard stalked the clearing, caught several mice, ate and groomed, then trotted south, reaching the tall-walkers' area by long shadows. Tired of battling undergrowth, he took to their path of false stone, then climbed a broad-branched oak and slept until sunfall.

Ghost clambered down and sharpened his claws in the crumbly bark. Gulping a mouse he snagged in the weeds, he set off, loping easily through patchy woods. As he approached the forests of the southern Green, the moon played hide and seek with the clouds, making the dark beneath the trees darker than ever. But it wasn't the darkness. He was a cat. He had night vision. No. The forest was unsettling because the threat couldn't be seen. Ghost shuddered, remembering the stories he'd been told about this wilderness. The local kin claimed it was haunted by wraiths, that many who entered came out no longer knowing who they were, if they came out at all. *Keep moving south,* he told himself, padding deeper in, regretting he traveled at night. But there was no turning back. *Keep moving south. Move quickly and you'll be safe.* A strangeness already pulled at his thoughts. *Keep moving south, keep moving south,* rang in his mind until the chant lost its meaning and his mind fell silent, and he heard only the thud of his paws. Thump, thump. Thump, thump. Hind legs, thump, thump. Front legs, thump, thump. Thump, thump. Thump, thump. Moving like a dream within a dream, he forgot so many things. Others screamed like fiery arrows straight to the heart. They followed at a distance where he couldn't see or hear, but he felt them and they were many. The mind-eaters. Part Felidae, part mist, they melted through boulders and trees, regaining their cat-ness at will. Evil shape-shifters.

A rustling above him sent a shudder down his spine. It leaped through the trees while he ran beneath, praying it wouldn't drop. Spider silk cast into the air. He felt it tangle beside him while he was running, running, running. Thud, then thump, thump, thump, thump, perfectly matching his gait. Thud. And a second creature ran along his other side. And then a third and a fourth, and then too many to count.

"Catch him 'fore he gets away," came a hiss from the dark.

"This one knows the magic," rasped another. "He's val-u-bul." Many snickers.

"Snag him, snag him," whispered a beast closer than the rest.

They ran a while in silence, then a voice crackled like fire burning through wood. "What's your worldname?" The question sent tremors through Ghost' body. He struggled to remember...and couldn't. *No, this you can't have. I won't give it to you.* And he ran faster. Under the trees, over the meadow, he leaped the stream and under the trees again. Faster, faster. Still, the voice at his ear demanded, "What's your worldname? Tell me your name." He was losing ground once lost he'd never recover. *How much longer can I hold them off? Will I make it to Bent Whisker's hearth?* In his mind, he saw the glow within the Yew, knelt before the seer and basked in Sosay's friendship. Yes, despite the barbs she was his friend. At last, up ahead...the edge of the forest, and he leaped forward with everything he was.

An audible sigh came from the trees and plants, the insects, birds and small animals, the dirt and stones, the currents in the air. Everything breathed out together. Ghost felt a surge through his body. And the wraiths were gone. He'd stumbled through a barrier he couldn't see, exiting their world, confused, exhausted and safe. *Or not,* he realized and froze, pregnant with expectation. Something huge was coming! Every hair of his pelt stood on end and tingling nose to tail, he dove beneath a nettle bush. A bolt of light and heat crashed down from heaven, lighting a nearby juniper like a torch. A heartbeat later only a smoking stump remained, the air around it scorched. Ghost crawled from his shelter trembling like a cornered mouse and stared at the valley below, Starlight's vision ringed by rocky hills.

He searched for the yew. Nothing. He searched again, and again found nothing. Kneading the damp earth, he lifted his head and yowled. It couldn't be wrong; it all looked right, but he couldn't find the heat-withered yew. *Great Mother's Tail! It's a shelterveil! The yew's a shelterveil, like Hillside Den and the Birch Grove.* Another brilliant sword cut through the sky and he saw them: a pride of ancient Felidae with paws the size of tree trunks and fangs curving almost to the ground. Muscular shoulders rising and falling with murderous grace, they crossed the plain unfazed by the thunder. They reached their destination and lay on their bellies in a circle, heads high, facing outward like rays of the sun. The Keepers of the Akashic Flame.

The vision faded, and where the Felidae had gathered, Ghost saw the yew, squat, with a tangle of needle-rich branches radiating from its crown. He was so relieved, he failed to notice when Sosay, Smokepelt and Tinypaw came up behind him, pelts bristling in the electrified air.

"Hello," Sosay purred, and Ghost jumped straight up, fur on end. He whipped around, embarrassed, but Sosay just gave him a nose-kiss. The heavens flashed and clapped, rain splashing off her shoulders into his face.

"Hello, Sosay," he meowed. "How'd you know I was here?"

"Well...you did yowl," she teased. Ghost lowered his gaze, embarrassed again.

"Don't worry, we expected you. Although I was surprised you traveled the forest at night. Very foolish."

"I didn't know those things were real, or I wouldn't have."

Sosay stared. "Things? What did you see?" She looked worried.

"I didn't *see* anything. It was more like I felt and heard."

She looked more worried. "You didn't talk to them, did you?"

"You mean did I tell them my worldname?" Now all three cats stared with tails lowered and ears back and down.

Sosay's claws dug the earth. "Did you? What *is* your name?"

"Sosay, you've known me forever."

"What's your name," she repeated, her intensity slapping his face like an unseen branch, and Ghost realized he wouldn't visit Bent Whisker's hearth without an answer that pleased her.

"I am Ghost of Hillside Pod." The southern cats visibly relaxed. Sosay's tail and ears shot up and she head-bunted him like the friends they were. He hadn't said a word to the wraiths and she knew that now. "What are they, anyway?"

Sosay avoided his question. "Let's get you to the prophet, shall we? This storm is gaining on us and the fire inside is warm."

"You didn't answer me."

"No, I didn't," she said, flicked her tail in his face, then padded down the slope toward the valley.

Ghost planted his paws wide, feeling petulant, then spied the smoke curling through the top branches of the yew. It smelled exquisitely of juniper, cedar, and rosemary. *Incredible.* "You have fire?" he yowled.

"You need to be quiet now," Sosay admonished. Seeing the stubbornness in his eyes, added, "I will explain everything. I promise." Ghost nodded and she led them into the dark, wet meadow of weeds and wild flowers, old oak and yew, their Sacred Yew by far the oldest and largest. The little apprentice Tinypaw padded alongside their guest while Smokepelt, a big gray and black Wisdom Cat, brought up the rear.

"Is there danger?" Ghost asked the small female.

She ignored him, but Sosay waved her tail impatiently. "I told you you'll know everything soon enough," she said, her words tinkling past him like bells in the wind. It should have been enough, but when she stopped before the yew Ghost came up beside her, unable to control his curiosity.

"What if I'd told them my worldname?" he asked.

"You'd be lost," Sosay whispered with such sadness in her eyes he didn't want to know how. Two cats came from the shadows and began clearing branches of natal plum, revealing a small door carved into the base of the tree. Marked with a single scoop for fire and the three-sided symbol of the polestars, it hung on protrusions from the midpoint of each vertical side. The bottom half swung inward when Sosay pushed her head against it, and Ghost saw a space wide enough for kin to travel two-abreast between the outer and inner bark of the yew. "I invite you into our home," Sosay meowed from the passageway. One by one they pushed the bottom of the door and entered. Inside the dim tunnel, the air was close and lumpy roots pushed up against their paws as they moved toward a softly lit outline, a second door, this one in the ceiling. Once beneath it, Smokepelt stood on his hind legs and pushed. The wooden lid slid off his shoulders to the side and they leaped up into the hollow tree. Smokepelt and Tinypaw knocked the cover back into its groove while Sosay called to Bent Whisker.

"I live like a badger," Ghost murmured, his gaze following a padway that spiraled up the walls to the top of the tree. The pale inner bark mirrored the convolutions of the outer with twisted pillars and fearsome shapes, features from imaginary beasts. The ceiling was thick with ivy. Vines had pierced the bark and woven themselves into hammocks, comfortable bedding for many kin. Boughs sprouted from the yew's crown densely enough to keep out any bad weather. Still, here and there, Ghost caught glimpses of the stars. But the most amazing thing was a circular pit dug into the hard dirt floor. Flat stones had been laid in ring patterns around a center where several logs burned like burnished gold. Ghost padded to the edge of the pit to warm his damp fur. He'd only seen fire from far away, thankful for the distance, but standing before such controlled use of it, he realized he understood nothing of the mysterious element and was in awe of the southern kin. "How do you do this? How does your clan accomplish these miracles?" he asked Sosay.

She chortled. "The flattails help us. They enjoy visiting their ancestors and divining the future as well as any kin."

Ghost stared wide-eyed. "That's amazing. This whole place is amazing, but I'm curious about the fire."

Sosay's ears twitched. "Ghost, you must realize I can't share secret lore that is given with the RA of the South."

"Of course," he said, dipping his head in apology. He'd forgotten. The cats of the north freely shared their herbal arts, but then their gifts demanded generosity. The kin wouldn't be well served if only a few Wisdom Cats could heal anyone.

Bent Whisker shuffled down the spiraling stairs. "What secret lore does the little wizard seek?" he wheezed. "It's safe to tell him anything. He is, after all, the Four Become One." This was the second time Ghost had been told he was the Four Become One, and he was as uncomfortable now as he'd been when young Kiliarcos mentioned it. Thankfully, Bent Whisker changed the topic. "How was your journey? Did you encounter any ghouls or wraiths?" he asked cheerily, as if the creatures Ghost fled from were mere nuisances.

"Ghouls and wraiths? What can you tell me about them?" Ghost asked, aching to know, but Bent Whisker's attention had moved on.

"Are the herbs prepared?" the old cat asked Sosay. She padded to some neatly stacked rows of dried herbs, picked up a folded leaf, and dropped it at Ghost' paws. It uncurled, revealing bits of petals, seeds and slivers of stems, all sprinkled with a layer of pollen that sparkled in the firelight. The spicy aromas of dreamweed, poppy seeds and other intoxicants wafted to his nose.

"A special brew to help you divine," she murmured.

Obediently Ghost ate the herbs, rolling his tongue over his lips with a grimace. *I wonder if she realizes I understand the properties of every twig and root growing in the forest.* She led him to a dip in the floor against the wall, carved from bark and collecting rain from the yew's upper leaves. After a long drink, he staggered away, the herbs proving stronger than he'd expected. Sosay guided him back to the pit where he dropped his belly to the floor and his head to his paws.

"Don't worry," Bent Whisker rasped. "The dizziness won't last." The room had begun to spin and Ghost wondered if he'd been enchanted as well as drugged, but he didn't feel threatened. He wondered casually, the way he sometimes wondered if Browser was still hunting or if the night would turn chill and after wondering about his wondering, he ceased to think at all. Smokepelt lowered his thick frame to Ghost' right side and Sosay settled on his left, neither too closely, while Tinypaw moved opposite Sosay and near Bent Whisker along the other side of the circle. The five cats faced the fire pit like points on a witch's star, paws forward, tails straight out behind them.

Deep in trance, through slitted eyes, Ghost watched the old seer push juniper and cedar twigs into the fire. White fingers of smoke twisted toward the top of the tree, and the veil between worlds grew thin. The spirit realm shimmered before him. He heard bells and leaves in the wind, and tall-one's laughter. Sharp talons swooped down with a raucous cry. Just as quickly they were gone.

Bent Whisker began. "Great Mother bless us. Solara, reveal yourself to this gathering of Fang and Claw."

The pyre grew, glowed brightly then died back, forming a ring of flaming tongues. Solara stood within. Her pelt was made of tens of thousands of slender, pointed flames that moved with her body like fur. Her eyes were crystalline. They reflected fire the way diamonds catch light. And when she threw back her head and howled, an inferno poured from her mouth.

Bent Whisker tossed dried sage about her paws and thick plumes of smoke rose around her. "Solara, with this offering we purify the fire within and ask that you guide us to the Sacred Akashic Flame." Again the Spirit Cat threw back her head and threw fire. This time it formed a flower of eight evenly spaced petals encircling a core of seeds, and from the seed pod rose a tongue of white light. Shapes wavered inside. The kin lost all sense of separation, becoming invisible participants to the vision.

☙ ☙ ☙

The dull-colored cat sat on the Flatstone, waiting. He couldn't be seen clearly. Waves of energy looking like heat waves rising off the desert floor obscured any details. No one could describe the cat. *The same dark magic hovers in the Green, distorting everything,* Ghost thought.

A mouse popped from its burrow and wandered close. The cat turned his head and looked. That's all. And the mouse couldn't move, held in place by his invisible paw. Growing ever more frantic, squeaking and scratching the dirt, it slid toward the feline, rose into the air and disappeared head-first into that perpetual smile. Crunch. The tail went limp.

The cat had nurtured his powers in secret, and catching that mouse gave him confidence. Ready to reveal himself, he waited for his victim beneath the moonless sky.

Indra lurked at the meadow's edge, her body language telling she knew and feared the cat on the Flatstone. Her black pelt merging with the night, she closed her silver eyes when his gaze raked the spot where she sat. He saw her anyway. Nothing to do but join him. She approached slowly, hoping others would arrive. They didn't.

"Great Mother bless you," Indra said, settling as far from the cat as possible.

"May She lift Her paw," came the equally formal response. "Hello, Indra. Welcome to our gathering."

"Where are the others?" she asked, cleaning her paws in an effort to appear relaxed.

His eyes glowed. "We're early."

"Just a little." Still cleaning her paws, her eyes searched the forest. *Why do I care if I seem polite? I feel danger. He must feel my fear.*

He moved closer and Indra flinched. "Do I make you nervous?"

"Of course not," she huffed, feigning indifference. He slunk closer still, crossing the barrier of her personal space, and Indra realized it wasn't offensive for her to move away; *he* was offensive. *He is mocking me. Me, mated queen to a great Wisdom Cat, the Elder Cat of the East and Shaman of the Crystal Aerie.*

Indra stood, keeping her head high. "I'd best go," she meowed without a glance in his direction.

But as she stepped off the Flatstone, something called to her, "Look back." She didn't want to. It felt wrong. But despite every shuddering nerve ending shouting "NO"...she looked back. And the Malkin caught her with his glowing eyes and an energy that drained her will.

"Nebula will worry if I don't commune with him soon." He placed his paws on her shoulders and pushed her down. "What are you doing? I can't move," she cried.

"Don't worry," the creature soothed. "This will be over soon. Nebula will be fine."

"Let me go. I love Nebula."

"Love," he mocked. "Love I don't need from you. But can you share, Indra?"

Her eyes widened. "You want the RA? You want the RA from me?" His whipping tail said he did. "But *stealing* the RA won't bestow power," she yowled, unable to turn her head away with his paw on her neck. "You'll hurt me."

"Yes," the Malkin said, bringing his face to hers, and prying her mouth open with his own. She whimpered when the pale blue light, her life-force, poured from her lips into him. Faster and faster it flowed, the monster growling and snorting, growing stronger as she faded away. When she was completely drained, he rose, leaving a stiff, sightless husk.

"Nebula! Nebula, I'm coming home," her soul cried, racing though the night sky.

Atop the Aerie, Nebula leaped to his paws. Alone with the crystalline pinnacles, he strained to hear his beloved's voice. "Indra!" He yowled. "Indra, I'm here!" Wind whipped through the spires.

🐾　　🐾　　🐾

The flaming flower wilted, releasing the Wisdom Cats back into their own world, but when they stood and shook their pelts the tongue of flame swelled, catching them again in its magic. They saw Erasmus padding toward the gathering, the meadow's frost-covered foliage calling out to him. *Danger. Danger.* He paused beneath a tree, slightly opening his jaws to let scent roll over the roof of his mouth. And he smelled kin, not the wildborn of the Green, but something foul without heart, something filled with rage. This awareness was fleeting, however, quickly replaced with a vision of Indra fearing for her life. Suddenly Erasmus knew she would be murdered, but before he could move, a raging mountain of muscle and filth slammed into his back. It flattened him to the ground and crushed the air from his lungs. Claws ripped his skin, fangs tore his throat and blood warmed the cold forest floor.

Meanwhile, the Malkin, drunk on Indra's power, and disdaining the body he'd so ruthlessly abused, slid her husk down the Flatstone with a nod. Then with a satisfied curl of blue-tinged lips, he strolled into the dark. His denchurls approached, orange eyes gleaming from coal-black pelts. Hissfurr and Snakeheart came first, Scratchblood behind, the Elder Cat of the North dangling from his jaws. "Caught this one sneakin' up, Master." Scratchblood rasped, dropping his booty in the grass.

"He wasn't sneaking up, Scratchblood, he was attempting to prevent Indra's misfortune." The words slipped down the thug's ear canals, past the mite nests into his stew pot brain, causing him to worry he'd done something wrong. He cringed ahead of the blow, but the Sorcerer only crooned, "Well done," and Scratchblood relaxed. "Does he live?" the Malkin asked, and Scratchblood felt danger again.

More cringing. "Wuz I suppos'd ta kill'im?" he whined.

"No. He's valuable alive."

"Good, cuz he's breathin'," the denchurl chuffed with relief.

Master rewarded each of his servants with a mouse, using only his mind to drag them from their holes and fling them into gaping mouths. Delighted by the magic even more than the snack, the brutes dipped their enormous heads in submission, believing their allegiance well placed. The Malkin was dizzy with pride. He'd stolen the RA of the East, and captured Erasmus, a wise and venerable Wisdom Cat. "Take him to the city. I'll join you later," he said with a glance at his prize. Scratchblood scruffed Erasmus again and stood waiting. With a whip of his tail, Master ordered Hissfurr to join his brother and Snakeheart to his own side. Another snap of the Malkin's tail and two posses disappeared into the night.

It took the yellow catling a while to stop trembling and gather enough courage to leave his hiding place. Warily, he tiptoed from the meadow's edge to the place where Indra had died. Her body was gone. Little flakes of dust were scattered over the Flatstone. Tomorrow, nothing would remain.

🐾　　🐾　　🐾

"Is that Reggie?" Sosay cried as the flaming flower wilted again.

"Great Mother's Tail," Ghost murmured, "I knew Erasmus was alive."

"We don't know if that's still true," Bent Whisker said.

"I know it is." Ghost replied. "And Indra knew her killer."

"Yes," Sosay meowed.

"Obviously it's one of us." Ghost' voice ached with shame.

"I don't believe that," Bent Whisker spat, ears back and tail whipping furiously.

Sosay's crescent pulsed blue. "Ghost is right. Who but a Wisdom Cat could manifest such dreadful, powerful magic?"

The old sage looked weary. "I can't believe it's someone from the Green."

"Where's your fellow apprentice in all this?" Smokepelt asked.

"Who?"

"Morsus."

Ghost leaped to his paws. "Not protecting Erasmus! Shameful! Erasmus has always protected him." He plopped on his rear, tail lashing.

Sosay spoke. "Ghost, I know Morsus look and acts strangely. It's hard to like him, but that doesn't make him a coward."

The little wizard chuffed. "Where was he the night Indra died and Erasmus disappeared?"

"Hasn't he disappeared too?" she asked. "Along with Reggie."

"Didn't we just see Reggie?" Ghost demanded.

"But where is he?" Sosay mewled.

Bent Whisker nuzzled her. "We'll find him, Sosay. I know it." He turned to Ghost. "Didn't you see the brutes who took Erasmus? Twice the size of most kin, even eastern kin. Big as bobcats they were...and their claws..." He shuddered. "They have to be city cats." He faced Sosay again. "Indra was an adept and she was no match for that Sorcerer. I'd rather eat my own heart than believe a Wisdom Cat would kill his own and I don't know anyone who can make mice fly. Great Mother's Tail, does anyone think one of us, or a mere apprentice, could pull that off?" Tinypaw and Ghost looked at each other. She crossed to him and they slumped together, staring into the fire.

"I'm still an apprentice," Ghost murmured. "Apparently I'll never be anything else."

Like a hawk focusing on a squeaking mouse, Bent Whisker turned to Ghost. "You haven't received the RA, but you're every hair a Wisdom Cat," he said.

Ghost lowered his head, embarrassed. "I didn't pass my vision-quest. I left the tree and I fed another cat from its branches."

"That's not true."

"But it is. And now I've broken the third rule by telling you."

"It's not true that you didn't pass," Bent Whisker chuckled. "You never wondered who Trouble was? Where he came from? How he suddenly disappeared?" Ghost stared at him like he'd burped up a rat tail, but the old seer just tossed a twig of white sage into the pit and within a swirl of fragrant smoke they were watchers again. This time, the scenes moved quickly, fading out while new ones faded in. They watched Ghost save the golden kit from the badger, then tend to his needs. They saw Ghost leave the cedar to inspect the meadow for predators while Trouble morphed into Starlight. The vision faded.

"Your heart was tested," Bent Whisker meowed. "You gave up the RA to save a life. You chose life, Ghost, life. Of course you passed." The little wizard didn't know if he was happy or humiliated. Maybe both. He remained in a crouch, unsure how to be this new Ghost, so publicly gullible, and a full blown Wisdom Cat. He watched Bent Whisker tend the fire, tossing an occasional twig with a swing of his head, keeping the flame low and practically smokeless. "Do you ever let it die?"

"No. An ember must always burn for Solara. She lives within the fire." The room was darker now, quieter. They were all drained by the death of their friend, feeling like they'd been there...horrifying. Smokepelt curled around Tinypaw. Comforting each other, they dozed.

Bent Whisker hunkered on the edge of the pit and closed his eyes. Ghost was too anxious to sleep. He scooted close to Sosay and whispered, "You promised you'd tell me about the ghouls."

Reluctantly, the white beauty left her dreaming. "Now?" His face pleaded. "All right," she groaned, raising herself to sit like a Sphinx. "They're the spirits of defeated and dead Malkins, some as old as First Kin. Those are wraiths."

Ghost cleaned the floor with his tail. "Wraiths? Wait. There's been more than one Malkin?"

Sosay looked sad. She stop talking and sat tall, calming herself by combing the fur on her cheeks with her claws. Finally, "This is a part of southern lore we don't like to share. It's our shame and our burden."

"Why yours?" he asked.

"Since First Kin there's always been a Malkin, a black-hearted master of the four elements and wielder of the darkest magic. Always, it rises in the south from our Wisdom Cats, hiding among us, corrupting and killing, spreading poisonous lies until at last it's defeated."

Ghost scooted closer and whispered, "Bent Whisker must know this. Why does he deny it?"

Sosay thumped her tail. "Could you admit your child is selfish or insane...a thief, a liar...a murderer? Plus, there hasn't been a Malkin for generations. No one, especially Elder Cat of the South, wants to believe another has risen."

Ghost trilled sympathetically. "When we greeted, you asked me my name. Why?"

"That's what the ghouls in the forest asked you, right?" He nodded. "They're walk-ins."

"Walk-ins?"

"Spirits who steal your body and eat your soul. You don't remember you. And when your body dies, the walk-in still uses it as a wraith, a half-dead, half-living parasite waiting beneath the trees for someone else to ensnare."

Ghost growled, slapping his tail on the floor. "Horrific."

"I had to see if you'd been taken. If you had, you wouldn't know your name. I know you're adept, Ghost, but you traveled the southern forest at night. It's full of ghouls and wraiths. Even you can be ambushed."

"This is too strange to be real."

"But it is real. You've seen it." Sosay paused to clean an already spotless paw, then spread her toes, all six of them, and stared. Finally she continued. "There will always be kin who lean toward darkness. Bullies. Thieves. Kin who kill not to eat, but because it excites them. Born among our proud hearts are those whose hearts are craven, who sell their brothers and sisters for power or the promise of a better life. Their self-serving energies align with the Malkin's, they seek him whether they know it or not. And when he finds them, he shares his power...or so they believe. Gradually, he replaces all their thoughts, their feelings, their will with his own; they become his slaves."

"Neow," Ghost murmured, staring past the dying embers. This was a corruption of the very nature of cat. "These wraiths, they serve the Malkin too?"

"They serve evil, and they serve themselves."

Ghost' pelt stood on end. "This is a nightmare, Sosay. Anyone could be in the clutches of a Malkin." He breathed deeply to calm himself. "Everything I know about this I've learned from you today," he added, softening his tone and nuzzling her shoulder with his cheek. "Still, I intuit you've got a few things wrong." Sosay's ears flicked to attention. "I don't believe generations passed without a Malkin. I believe they passed without the kin's awareness of a Malkin." She nodded. "And I don't believe the Malkins are only from the south. Doesn't make sense. Haven't you ever felt a strangeness elsewhere in the Green? I've felt things, bad things, in other places."

"Perhaps you're right, Ghost. It could be you've felt ghouls and wraiths elsewhere."

"Haven't you?"

Sosay's crescent flickered. "Yes...I've felt evil elsewhere. But that doesn't change the fact that all Malkins emerge in the south."

Ghost thought. "There's a reason for that. It has nothing to do with southern kin." He stood and a shiver raced down his spine. He whipped his tail. "I don't know what it is yet, but I will. I feel it." Sosay didn't move or speak. It would take more than a shudder and a premonition to change her mind. Now Ghost sat like a loaf of bread, silently watching the embers smolder. His companions were all dozing when he said, "I have visions of the four elements. I dream a huge maw on the horizon swallows the world." Smokepelt and Tinypaw opened their eyes. Bent Whisker dropped the twig in his jaws and clumsily kicked it into the pit. A pillar of flame shot up, then fell in a shower of fireballs.

Solara stood before them. "Give him the RA," she ordered, pointing a fiery paw at Ghost. Bent Whisker stared as her glittering eyes narrowed. "Give him the RA," she repeated and Bent Whisker lowered his head in a posture of submission. Solara erupted into sparks and was gone, but the log glowing in the pit growled. Ghost wanted to hide.

Smokepelt leaped to his paws, tossing off a mewling Tinypaw and stepping on Sosay's tail. "Rat pelts!" he yowled, "That's a message from Great Mother if ever I heard one."

"You will have the RA from the south, not the north," Bent Whisker said, "but Solara is right. You deserve to be a Wisdom Cat...officially, that is. Sit, son." Ghost sat tall, draping his tail over neatly placed paws, his heart thudding against his breastbone.

Stars smaller than grains of sand streamed from above into Bent Whisker's head jewel. They exited his paws, tracing pathways along the floor. He lifted a forepaw to Ghost' head and the current poured into the little wizard's crown. A cold fire lifted the pelt along his spine, igniting every nerve ending and his heart pounded. More stars exploded within him, surging through his body like electric ants. Ghost yowled. *It hurts! It hurts! It hurts! I am scorched to ash and blown into the void, my bones floating in space like asteroids orbiting a sun. I'm dead. The RA of the South has killed me... oh, Monkey, I'm sorry. I promised to come for you...*

A thought. He had a thought. But when he tried to take form, to find himself, he slipped away, a warm, buzzing light growing ever more distant, smaller, smaller, until it circled the cosmic drain, spinning down, down, down. Then nothing. And then he didn't know he was nothing, nothing for eternity.

Then he was. A thought with feeling, life yearning for itself. First cause. A tendril wrapped in joy, the brilliant unfurling of his soul and Great Mother lifted him into the world and flooded him with Her Grace. Her purr, his pulse were a love song. Re-born, he lived within Her and She through him, the *All That Is* now a small silver cat with eyes like green-blue seas.

Bent Whisker lowered his paw. "Do you swear to abide by the Code of the Children of Great Mother, honoring Her with all your actions, living a selfless life of service to the kin?"

"I do," Ghost said, his voice sounding hollow and faraway.

"Are you willing to share your hunt? Give help where there's need and live in peace?"

"I am," Ghost trilled. *Such an easy promise.*

"By Great Mother's Pelt, I declare you, Ghost of of Hillside Pod... Wisdom Cat of the South, Protector of the Akashic Flames." Ghost took a deep breath. Sosay gave him a congratulatory lick while Smokepelt and Tinypaw rubbed their heads against his shoulder. Tired but contented, Bent Whisker poked the embers with a cedar stick. Licks of yellow flame and a whirlwind of red sparks shot upward, casting soft cat-shapes against the walls. The room was like a womb, warm and deep in shadow and the cats soon dozed again, comforted by the crackle and pop of burning wood and the rhythm of their purrs. Ghost felt cleansed from the inside out, a respite from his visions of the dark force. Then he dreamed.

Daylight came to the valley, and Ghost and Monkey scrabbled in the dirt for grubs. They were hungry, clinging to life in a barren world. The roots of toppled trees rose from the sand like dried bones, while overhead a layer of cloud rolled tediously on with never a break to the blue above. No birds sang evensong when that gray sky darkened.

Monkey lay in the dust and lowered her head to bony paws. Ghost lay next to her, bringing his face close to hers. "We were cowards, waiting for others to do what was right. He ate the Heart of Great Mother," she whispered. "We should have stopped him. We should have kept Her safe. He ate Her Heart and now the world is gone." Monkey closed her eyes.

13 – TRUTH BE TOLD

Ghost and Sosay left Bent Whisker's hearth together, but he headed north to go home while Sosay went south, following a stream deeper into the forest. She was searching for Reggie in the wilderness where she'd first discovered him, a kitten so fearful he hid from gusts of wind. The monstrous two-legged who gave his mother a home had tied his siblings in a sack and thrown them in the river. Luck and hasty counting had saved Reggie, but his heart was in shreds. Sosay found him, enfolding his tiny, underfed body with her great soft roundness, comforting him with her tongue, even letting him suckle until he pulled milk into her glands. She fed him like her own child. He was the kit she'd never have and when he became a catling, he was her apprentice.

Reggie can't be dead! And just like that she knew where he was. A stream from the northwest poured into the creek and she followed the stronger, faster current southeast until she came to a place she remembered. Hopping from stone to stone, Sosay crossed to the western bank. *This is it*, she told herself, facing a lovely copse of Standing Folk. *This is where I found him.* Enchanted hazel, blessed sycamore, and hawthorn-the-heart-cleanser stood together, so strong no evil could live between them. Was it any wonder Reggie the kitten had found sanctuary here? Sosay waited, silently asking permission to enter, and when the moon silvered the sycamores she was answered and moved toward their welcoming arms.

Behind her a twig snapped. A scent sent shudders down her spine, and scruff on end, Sosay spun around. With only three tail lengths between them, she faced a young coyote, so proud of sneaking up on her he almost wagged his tail. She turned sideways, arched her back and exploded her pelt, doubling her size. "You must not attack on this hallowed ground," she moaned with an undulating voice, and for a heartbeat she thought he would honor the sanctuary of Standing Folk. Then he tensed to lunge. Sosay knew she couldn't outrun him, couldn't reach safety before his jaws closed around her neck. So she spit and caterwauled, hopping back and forth, always moving closer to the trees. The young hound stared stupidly, his every thought written on his face. *Attack now!* his eyes screamed and Sosay turned and bolted. Still too far from a low-branched sycamore, she yowled, "I'm not going to make it!"

And the earth opened up beneath her. A horned thing exploded from its hole. It streaked past her: a screeching face, four legs, claws and something like a tail, its entire body covered with dried mud, weeds, seeds, leaves, stalks, sticks, and pebbles, with a frosting of dandelion fluff. It stank of feces and mold. Finding the strange beast more frightening than the young coyote, Sosay raced up the tree.

She wasn't the creature's target. It ignored her, leaping instead on the gulchdog's rump, sharpening its claws in his hide. This was too much for the young coyote, who lurched about howling, dragging the monster behind him. Finally, he kicked both legs high up as one and rid himself of the spiked thing. Then whimpering with wounded pride, dashed away into the distance. The kicked creature had spun through the air legs tucked like a ball and landed on his paws on a branch of the sycamore where Sosay sought refuge.

Now it was Sosay's turn to be caught in the stare of the barbed thing. It stood below her poised for attack, whipping its prickly tail. She tensed, leaping over it with hummingbird speed. But the beast was adept. It also leaped, coming up beside her, sinking its fangs in her scruff. They landed on the ground beneath the tree, where it dragged her bucking and yowling into its fetid hole.

Sosay scrambled to her paws. She didn't remember falling asleep or where she was, but as her vision accepted the darkness around her, memory returned. She was confined to a short tunnel disappearing to her left and right in downward jogs. The beast lay against the wall opposite hers, its slow, regular breathing telling her it slept. It hadn't killed her, not yet anyway, and she wondered why. Sosay crept closer. "Neow," she cried, jumping back. Not only were the beast's eyes open, they followed her. Still it didn't attack, and staring into those eyes, the feeling she knew them settled into her mind, leaving her oddly comforted and upset at the same time. The eyes were lonely, distrustful, but they held an awareness of something else...of familiarity. Whatever it was between them, the beast felt it too. It was a bridge for Sosay, an implausible connection to this baffling creature. Now, as if to deny her access, it turned away, and lifting a paw, spread its muddy toes wide, cleaning between them with a specific tilt of its spiky head. A trademark move.

Sosay trembled violently. "Reggie? Is that you?"

The beast stopped grooming and rose. Fearful, Sosay scooted back until she felt the wall behind her, the creature creeping forward. Leaning menacingly over her cringing body, it snarled, "Never say this name. R... Rrr...don't know it, never heard it." It slunk back to its spot, turned circles in place and settled.

It is Reggie, every movement, every tilt of his head and lifting of his paw tells me its Reggie. Studying the monster's mud-caked face, Sosay called up Reggie's lovely contours and wasn't as frightened anymore. He'd always been more poet than paladin.

His eyes were still open. "What happened to you?" she asked, careful not to use his name.

The creature stared mutely for several long heartbeats. "She doesn't say this. No, no, she mustn't," he whined. Fear caught hold of his heart. "She'll bring the Life-Sucker! Oh, the Heart-Eater, Heart-Eater..." His eyes grew wild, his breathing ragged. "Run from the Heart-Eater. Run!" He yowled, leaped to his paws and scrabbled manically up a hole in the ceiling. Sosay sat alone in the dark, feeling her heart break.

Sosay woke feeling a little frightened and wondering how long she'd slept. In the constant, spectral light there was no rising or setting sun, no moon, and time was difficult to measure. As always, escape plans tumbled through her thoughts and were discarded. She yearned to be free of this muddy twilight, but she couldn't abandon Reggie-the-Beast.

It took a few heartbeats to remember the last place he'd brought her, for after that first outburst of terror over his worldname, he'd moved her every few days, or rather every few deep-sleep sessions. The maze was huge. She'd slept in both higher and deeper tunnels, some barely wide enough to travel, some large enough for a two-legged to traverse. Those usually ended in domed chambers with tree roots hanging from the ceiling, reaching for pools of the clearest, bio-luminescent water. These beautiful caverns were her favorites, but the beast doled them out as rewards in a game he played, a game whose rules he never explained and she never understood. Today's tunnel was average sized. She could move easily, even stand on her hind legs, but there wasn't much light and her drinking water was a small pool of muddy water.

Reggie-the-Beast appeared from a hole in the floor, tossed half a plump mole at her paws and backed away to watch her eat. Normally, she'd find a piece of mud-and-blood-splattered rodent repulsive, but in this rock-and-dirt canal it seemed an appropriate meal. Anyway, she was starving and gulped it gratefully. He seemed pleased. Eyes falling shut, his tail beat softly on the tunnel floor while a rhythmic purr rose in his throat. Once more, hope tugged at Sosay's heart that her gentle apprentice lived beneath the barbed coat of the crazed tunnel-rat. She would set him free. "How long have you been here?" she asked.

He stared at her, making her wait for an answer. "Turns of the Moon," he finally said.

"Alone?" She took him in. "No, not alone. He has the forest, the sky. Not always underground."

He approached, raised a tentative paw to her crescent, but lowered it without touching her, content to gaze into her eyes. "Yes, she is good He is happy to save her."

Sosay sucked in a deep breath. She knew she needed to comfort him, reassure him, coax him from this fear of whatever it was keeping him captive. But impatience won and she pushed instead. "*Who* is happy to save me?...Reggie? Does Reggie remember Sosay?" The moment she said their names, she realized she'd moved too quickly.

Reggie-the-Beast exploded. He rushed her, slamming claws against her neck, forcing her face against the floor. She squirmed, spitting dirt, but Reggie-the-Beast was strong, much stronger than Reggie her apprentice. Her blood oozing beneath his claws, his breath parted her fur as he lowered his fangs to her throat. Sosay made peace with Great Mother, forgiving her deranged friend. Then suddenly, he backed away, trembling with fear and remorse at his own behavior.

"She not say this name. R...r...rr...he is dead. If Life-Sucker hears her, we're dead too!" Reggie whirled and leaped upward into an unseen tunnel and was gone. Sosay cowered in the dark, unbearably sorry. She slept until hunger woke her, alone, with no scent or sound of her friend. She slept again and woke still alone and very hungry, but this time fresh prey had been left on the tunnel floor. She ate. It seemed Reggie no longer wished her company. Life became a lonely routine of sleep with long, dim interludes marked by gusts of damp air and gifts of muddy prey.

Sosay looked up. Crazed eyes gleamed from the ceiling, jaws loaded with rodent. The Beast dropped into the tunnel and faced her. She wondered how long it had been since she'd seen him and couldn't help but tense, but he was calm, having released his fever on the unfortunate mice. He left the battered prey at her paws and disappeared back up the tunnel. It pained Sosay to admit she feared him now, but she did. Reggie would give his life for Sosay, but Reggie-the-Beast's temper was fierce and out of control.

Glumly, she ate her food, remembering when she'd stayed with Reggie out of loyalty. Now she wondered if she could find her way out, having been led from tunnel to tunnel, up, back and down again until even her whiskers couldn't navigate the maze. And the worst of it was she'd made no headway returning him to reality. In fact, he'd gotten worse. Suddenly he stood before her, eyeing her so crazily she wondered why she'd ever believed she could save him. Sosay slumped, longing for a rising moon, starlight and a breeze through shadowy trees. Then he surprised her.

"Come. She must leave. He thinks it best she leave, best for her, best for him." Sosay rose to follow him to another subterranean chamber, and was startled by how stiff and weak she'd become. It frightened her. Not only had she lost all sense of where she was, she hadn't realized how long she'd been immobile. *I'll die here, wasting away, forgotten like Reggie in the dark.*

Feeling defeated, Sosay trudged along behind The Beast that had once been her beloved Reggie, only gradually realizing the tunnel angled up. Her hope grew with the light. Brighter, brighter, until her fear faded in a golden stream of healing warmth, an opening to the world. Heartbeats later Sosay lay beneath the fateful sycamore, stretching her body as long as it would go, claws sunk into the earth. The Beast slipped back into the underworld. Sosay didn't care. Woozy with freedom, she wondered if she'd see him again. At the moment it didn't matter. Later, after a nap, she examined herself, and was surprised at how dirty and gray her fur looked. But what surprised her more was how little she cared. Stretching herself even longer, she purred loudly, and with sunlight warming her body, she dozed.

Maybe she'd eaten a bad mouse, or breathed foul air...or perhaps lying against the earth staring at brightmoon rising in a vast expanse of sky was so overwhelming she couldn't cope. Whatever the cause, Sosay fell ill. She burned through the night, all the next day and the following night, living on slurps of water from the stream. By the second sunrise she lay healing. Her strength was returning and with it the understanding she couldn't leave her friend. Resting in a makeshift nest between two roots, Sosay combed her cheeks with a wide paw. As he had done several times during her fever, The Beast rose from a nearby hole to see if she was all right.

Sosay felt brave. "Do you know what I do?" He shook his head. "I save younglings," she meowed. "I find them in forests and save them."

The Beast's eyes widened with thought. "So kind. He knew she was so kind," he trilled with kitten-like joy before slipping down the tunnel. Sosay felt he'd given her a name: So-Kind. It resembled her real worldname. Did that mean he remembered?

She hunted through the night and the following morning when The Beast poked his head into the world he faced a preypile. His eyes lit with happiness while his mud-caked paw shot forward faster than a frog's tongue, pulling several fresh-kill down his hole. And he was gone. Sosay curled on the grass and waited.

The Beast returned during the long shadows of early evening and with a grateful chirp, helped himself to more prey. He was about to duck down his hole when Sosay cried, "Don't go. I'm lonely."

"So-Kind wants him to stay a little bit?"

"So-Kind would like that." He swiped another mouse from the pile with muddy paws. He couldn't be hungry because he'd just eaten two, but he wanted to stay so she didn't trouble him with questions while he pretended to eat. She inched closer, and had he not been so filthy, would have licked him. Instead she kneaded his shoulders with her paws. The Beast flinched, but quickly relaxed, leaning into her touch and giving her the slow blink of love. Sosay closed her eyes. He fidgeted, then his mud-stiffened pelt pressed against her. Their breathing slow and rhythmic, he was her kit again, and she his comfort and protection. They slept. Sometime during their dreaming, he slipped down the hole and was gone.

Again Sosay hunted through the night to replenish the preypile. The Beast popped up at sunrise, much of the mud gone from his face.

She could even see patches of ginger. "You look good," she meowed and his whiskers spread with pleasure. "Would you like to hear a story?" Snagging a feathertail from her offerings, he crunched its hollow bones. "Remember I told you I save younglings?" He nodded. "That's not all I do. I'm also a shaman who sees the past and future in fire and the most special catling I saved also has these powers." The Beast dropped his prey on the ground. "I found him in the forest when he was little." He shuddered. "I found him here," she continued. The Beast trembled again. "In fact it was over there," she meowed, pointing with her tail toward the stream. Ears to tail tip, he was heaving, trying to purge the unwanted thoughts her words called to his mind. But Sosay was too impressed with herself to notice. "He was hiding in a hole he'd dug beneath that very Hawthorn..." At last she saw him and fell silent. The muddy tunnel-rat's head hung on his chest, his ears pinned shut by his paws. Sosay was mortified. "Please," she whispered, carefully moving toward him as he slid down his hole. "I'm so sorry. I can help you. I've done it before." She looked down into the tunnel and he looked up at her, pinpricks of sunlight igniting the grief in his eyes. He backed into the darkness.

Headfirst, she fell after him, but it was too late; the scrape of his claws on pebbly dirt was fading away. She followed his scent, then her own intuition in ever deeper circles below the roots of the tree. Down, down and around, she traveled pathways off pathways, always deeper and darker, the tunnel growing smaller, then smaller still. Now lost, she crawled in total blackness, earth pressed tight around her until she was so constricted she couldn't inch backwards and couldn't turn around.

Sosay panicked. Every nerve ending jangled with fear, her breath catching in her throat, her cries for help muffled by the walls of her grave. Sosay pushed against the ceiling with all her strength, but the mountain above her didn't give way. More fear, a deeper panic. Her paws clawed the dirt and she dug. She dug and dug until suddenly she felt the ground give way. Down, down, down she dropped, a whirlwind of fur and dirt, flailing in a blue mist and shower of golden lights. She hit the water hard, and sank, swallowing huge cold gulps of water. She couldn't breathe. Then nothing.

Sosay woke unable to move. Everything hurt. Lying on her side, her line of sight led directly into the eyes of the Beast. Belly to the ground and freshly re-encased in his ultra-mud, he faced her, staring unkindly. Unable to turn her head, she stared back. She'd been lucky in her misfortune, having fallen through the roof of the very cavern where he hid. He'd dragged her unconscious body from the pool, and whether to punish her or just keep her from chasing him farther, he covered her with his natural concrete rife with bee wings and beetle legs, whirligigs and pinwheels, seeds, sticks, stalks and decomposing leaves. Pretty much all the debris from a forest floor that could migrate over time into a cavern. The Beast had built up quite a compost pile. His nest. So this was where he slept. And why not. It wasn't hot or cold or claustrophobic. The dome glowed with a natural luminescence, reflecting the water, in which, she would later learn, swam pale, blind fish. Food. Outside of fresh breezes, real trees, other animals, sunlight, moonlit skies, and the chance of finding companionship, he had everything here. A fugitive could survive. A fugitive who crouched across from her, glaring insanely, all her attempts to reach him undone.

Groaning with every movement, Sosay slowly sat then stood, her armor cracking at the joints, leaving her as barbed and horned as her crazy friend. With effort, she lifted her head and looked around. Yes, she'd fallen through the ceiling into a pool and now she realized how truly lucky she'd been. Staring at the hole she'd poked through the dome, Sosay realized it was Great Mother's mercy she hadn't been impaled. Spires rose from the floor, sharply pointed mineral blades reaching for their soulmates growing drip by drip from above.

A stream bubbled through the base of the northern wall. Flowing over crystal-encrusted quartz, it headed south down another tunnel carved by water and time. The water was magical. Tiny lights danced in its currents, over a carpet of gems.

The Beast followed her line of sight and agreed. "Water saved her," he muttered, then, "This is his home."

"Okay, but why *this*?" she asked, staring at her cocoon of mud. Like

The Beast, she was now a filthy horned thing.

He glowered. "She causes much trouble. *This* will hide her from Life-Sucker, before he kills her."

"How can mud keep this Life-Sucker from finding me? And why would he kill me?" Sosay rasped, as irritated as she was flummoxed by Reggie the Beast's mythology. Then her thoughts took a new direction. What if this Life-Sucker were real, some creature no one else had seen, something dangerous, and she shivered, almost grateful he'd disguised her.

His voice wavered with fear. "The Life-Sucker. It's earth. Not fire, not water, not air. It's from the earth..."

"But if earth is its element, won't earth serve it?"

"Life-Sucker betrayed Great Mother long ago. He kills Her children. He kills Her Wisdom Cats."

Sosay sucked in her breath and held it. Beneath a mountain of earth, her body encased in dried mud, staring into the face of her unhinged friend, Sosay had an epiphany: Reggie was the shadowy figure who'd hid at the edge of the clearing. He'd witnessed Indra's murder; he'd watched the Life-Sucker and his Denchurls melt into the night; he'd seen an unconscious Erasmus in Scratchblood's jaws. Not knowing what to do next, his mind distorted by pain and rage, Reggie fled south to the sanctuary of the Standing Folk where Sosay had found him as a kit, where she found him again. But something had happened before she arrived, something about the Life-Sucker, and Reggie was terrified.

This time she chose her words carefully, studying his response. "Did you see the Life-Sucker kill?" Reggie the Beast lowered his head, a shamed yes. "Was it Indra he killed?" His head dropped even lower. "Can you tell me...this thing...this Life-Sucker, does it have a worldname?" Jerking his head up, his eyes were slits. "Okay then. You said he's from the earth. Can you give me a clan name?" He hissed. Sosay licked some mud off his face. "Don't be afraid," she cooed, but his glare told her she should be.

"Come," The Beast muttered, slapping his tail on the ground, and he led her over a calcite bridge spanning the pool, bringing them to an opening in the eastern wall where they passed into another cavern. It was half as high as the one they left, and covered with druisy clusters glittering like stars. On its far end, the smaller cavern narrowed into a downward-slanting tunnel, and as they descended, the walls moved in until their bodies barely fit. Tufts of their pelts were scraped away by sharp rocks until the tunnel abruptly ended, dumping them on a wide ledge. Cold air slapped their faces. Rivers of mist flowed by, and Sosay clung to the wall, listening to the wild rushing of a river lost in darkness far below.

The Beast wasn't afraid. He paced, his head swinging side to side, searching. "There," he meowed at last, pointing left with his muzzle. The ledge they followed curved around to the left, narrowing until it ended in a natural stone arch that spanned the abyss. It hung like the crooked finger of an old arthritic witch, barely wide enough for a cat to cross, slowly, carefully, single-file, belly low to its center of gravity.

Sosay plopped on her rear. "I'm not crossing that," she announced.

The Beast scowled. "It's safe. He has crossed many times."

"Good for him."

He glowered at his mentor, who stared wistfully at the path already traveled. "He thought she would help."

"I will. I am, but everyone's afraid of something. This is my something."

"He fears the Life-Sucker, but So-Kind always says he shouldn't let that stop him. Right?"

He had her there. Pitifully, she pleaded, "I don't want to die."

"She won't die. She will learn."

"Learn what?"

"What is the Life-Sucker."

How could she refuse? Sosay stretched her neck and squinted at the far side of the chasm, reaffirming to herself the crumbling span of stone was the only way to reach it. She steadied herself with deep breaths and followed him, belly low to the stone, over the gorge. *Great Mother hold me up. Don't look down. Don't think about it. Don't think about it.* But she couldn't stop thinking about it or looking down or trembling and half way across dizziness overwhelmed her. She felt her innards tossed into the air with nothing to catch their fall. Sosay retched into the chasm, her claws gripping the sides of the limestone bridge. She wouldn't budge.

The Beast came back for her and was met with the otherworldly gaze and sonorous purr of a cat who knows it's dying. "She is safe," he urged, as little stones and powdery rock fell into nothing far below. Sosay yowled, her crescent pulsing a bright blue, then buried her face in her paws, ashamed of her fear. *In front of my apprentice, no less.* The Beast nudged her paw with his head.

"I'm sorry I'm so afraid," she murmured.

"Yes... but So-Kind came here because he is afraid. She came to help." Sosay's heart skipped a beat, hoping. "Now he came to help too. Both help. Both are the same." He groomed her paws and purred with her as if they had all the time in the world. It was the assurance Sosay needed and after a while she rose to a crouch and crept the final stretch of the arch. Once she'd reached the high-vaulted cavern on the other side, she expelled a long, ragged breath, drew in her neck and limbs like a tortoise and closed her eyes. The Beast let her rest.

Sosay woke feeling uneasy. So uneasy, she didn't want to continue, even if it meant re-crossing the crumbling bridge. She looked to The Beast to see if he shared her apprehension, but he only yawned and stretched, shaking clumps of dried mud from his pelt. *We're looking less like prickly beasts and more like dirty kin,* she thought.

With a raspy meow, the Beast told her it was time to move. Reluctantly, she followed him over a rise and down into a stalagmite forest where the ground was littered with sharp pebbles that embedded themselves between their toes. Painful and difficult to remove, the little rocks slowed their progress to a crawl, and the cats were starving when they reached the far wall. Sosay hadn't seen any prey scurry about. Thankfully, shallow pools of water held eyeless, eel-like fish. After a long drink the Beast snagged one, which they shared. Wanting to groom after her meal, Sosay raised her paw to comb the crumbling mud from her cheeks. He pushed it away, insisting they re-coat their pelts instead. "Must hide from Life-Sucker."

Sosay looked frightened. "It's here?"

The Beast shook his head. "Here, not here...always it sees." He jerked his chin toward the ceiling. From a dome as dark and distant as the river below, came the rustling of leathery wings. Sosay trembled. When The Beast scooped sludge from the bottom of a pool, rolled in it, then rubbed some on his face, she did the same. She followed him along the wall until he chose an opening, then followed him inside. The tunnel twisted deep into the earth, and the air reeked of mold, making it difficult to breathe. The walls closed in. Sharp stones drew pink lines through her fur. *Unbelievable,* she thought. *I miss the bridge.*

At last the tunnel curved sharply left and down, and they emerged. But this dark cavern felt wrong in every possible way, and the unease that had been building since she'd awakened became a heart-pounding dread.

"Don't move," The Beast hissed. Unnecessarily, because she couldn't, having landed on his back. Sosay struggled to find space on the floor for her own four paws, and as her eyes adjusted to a meager glow of greenish light, she was alarmed by the shapes surrounding them. Here were no graceful sweeps of petrified stone, no mineral drips or druisy domes, melted eggs or obelisks. Here stood an army created to eviscerate, limestone carved into razor-sharp edges, soldiers with blades at the ready. And so many of them, so close to one another, too close for an enemy to pass. Here were the methods and shapes of death.

"There is a way past," The Beast whispered. "Don't worry. She's safe with him." With a wave of his tail, he motioned her to follow his every move. She did. Slowly they crept between the limestone bayonets, but despite all caution, they soon bled from cuts along their sides, legs and paws. Sosay stumbled, shearing all the fur and every whisker off the right side of her face. It stung horribly, as if she'd scraped her skin with acid. Even worse, it would take turns of the moon to grow back. Sosay had always enjoyed her beauty, and this was an emotional blow. *At least I didn't cut my throat.* A real possibility, she realized.

She stumbled again, this time piercing her chest. It wasn't deep, but blood dripped continuously from the wound. Not wanting to slow their glacial advance even more, she said nothing. But the Beast smelled the iron and stopped as soon as he found a spot with room enough for both of them to sit. He turned, and found Sosay's bright red chest soaking wet. Suddenly she felt faint and lay on her side.

"She should have told him," he growled, parting her fur with his paw to see the gash.

"It's nothing. I just need the bleeding to stop. Maybe if I rest a bit."

"No."

Surprised by his lack of concern, but not wanting to appear weak, not again, not in front of Reggie-the-Beast, she snapped, "Okay, then." Then struggling to stand, found she couldn't.

The Beast looked at her with compassion after all. "She needs more. Rest, yes, but more."

"What then?"

"Belief."

"Wha-aat? I taught *you* about belief," Sosay rasped, belly to the ground, and slapping her tail behind her. "I taught you *what* to believe." She knew she was coming dangerously close to memories that triggered him, but what more could happen? They had already descended into Hell.

Beyond a few tremors down his spine, he didn't seem to care. He needed her to understand. "Listen," he growled with an equally hard slap of his tail. "She must listen." Subdued by his lowered ears and exposed fangs, and with her wound still oozing blood, she did. "This place, this hell beneath the earth, is strong in a bad way. Great Mother," he whispered the name, "Is the enemy here. Here there is no grace. Here no one believes. Hearts are dead. Thoughts are cold. Life is barren. Wounds... don't heal."

Wonder spread across her face. "Then why come to this hellish place? Was it because you knew I'd look for you, above in the hawthorn and sycamore grove?" *Where I found you the first time,* she left unsaid.

 Which was good because his body jerked with strong tremors before he pulled his limbs tight and sat like a loaf of bread, looking away to calm himself. "Mistake," he finally answered. They sat a while in silence.

He came closer and licked the bald side of Sosay's face, softening the burning pain. "So-Kind is good," he meowed. Her crescent pulsed blue, something it had done less and less since she was kidnapped. She hadn't thought about it, but now, centering her awareness on her life as part of the All That Is, emotions grew until her crescent shone as brightly as Starlight's stars. The bleeding stopped.

Sosay and The Beast continued through the forest of daggers. New forms of petrified stone surrounded them in shapes that hurt the heart. They crept past bent femurs and tortured humeri, crawled beneath splintered phalanges and domes of broken skulls. They leaped over pools of fluid beneath enormous eye sockets, empty and cracked. Had these dark puddles once wet the eyes of giant hominids, gargantuan reptiles or even alien species? The spirits haunting this hellscape said they did.

Sosay wished she'd never come. She wanted to run back over the crumbling bridge and through the tunnels to lie beneath the Sycamore and feed Reggie, a healthy, sane Reggie, from her preypile. She looked into his damaged eyes, his body hidden by mud, his aura riddled with terror, and knew she couldn't leave. She must help him, even if it took her life. Then seeing herself with half of her face shaved and scalded, her tattered ears and filthy fur, the crescent on her forehead, once a jewel lit by Spirit, now dark again, she realized it might.

Climbing an uneven terrain, they approached an enormous sheet of stone melting down from the darkness of the cavern's dome as it rose up from the floor. The Beast signaled with his tail and they sat. "Prepare yourself. This won't be easy," he said.

After resting, they worked their way to the front of the monolith.

Slightly above their heads, protruded a stone slab about four tails in width and two tails deep, a sacrificial altar with runnels down both sides. Much blood had flowed and dried, leaving dark fingers reaching for bones scattered across the floor. But most horrific was what lay upon this unholiness: the desiccated body of Indra with a hole in her chest where her heart had once beat. Sosay dropped to the ground. "How?" she asked at last, her voice wrapped in a crypt-like stillness. It came from a place of deep sorrow where even the air didn't move.

"He followed the Malkin and Denchurl who carried her here. She's an offering."

"To whom?" She asked, her voice cracking with fear. But before the Beast could answer, they heard the clicking of bone against bone. Behind Indra's body, A feline spine crossed the slab, its thoracic spikes longer than either of their tails, its skull and mandible rising on the left like the prow of a ship in hell. No limbs, only a spine curling down the altar's right side and across the floor. It was moving.

"Neow!" Sosay yelped, leaping back to avoid being knocked off her paws as the tail swept the floor. Tremors traveled downward as the monstrous skeletal head lifted off the altar and turned its eyeless sockets on the trespassing cats. It hissed.

Sosay screeched. Reggie-the-Beast pressed against her, nudging her chin up with his muzzle. "Look," he whispered. Above the altar, written upon the stone in dried blood was the the Dark Prophecy.

Who takes a life into his own
Grows strong of muscle, hard of bone.
And he who eats a beating heart
Will rule a kingdom, long and dark.

Behold! The greatest power comes
To he who eats the heart of one
Who is but spirit, body-free.
That heart bestows eternity.

And the finest heart to eat
Beats within the Mother Great.
A single bite of Her Sweet Flesh
And he can rule the Vast Expanse.

The Beast rubbed his face on Sosay's shoulders. "Now she must leave," he whispered. "Too dangerous."

Sosay pressed against him. "I can't believe you came back here, bringing me. I can't believe you came here at all," she murmured, staring at the horrors surrounding them. "Alone!"

"He had to know." Sosay's expression told him she didn't feel *knowing* was worth it. "She came here," he said accusingly.

"Yes, but not *here*," she said, emphasizing the dark chapel with a sweep of her tail. "I came to the sanctuary of standing folk to find you, to help you. I had a feeling you might be in the hawthorn grove, but I had no idea you'd—well, what you did to yourself."

The Beast moaned, "He followed the Malkin who murdered Indra, stole Erasmus then came here."

"The Malkin brought Erasmus here?"

"No, his monster cats took Erasmus north. But the Malkin came here with one monster to carry Indra. Great Mother's Prophecy is at Harmony Tree, and the kin gather strength and courage there. This is the Dark Prophecy, the Malkin's Prophecy, and he comes here to gather strength." They sat quietly. Then he whispered, "I remember now."

He'd said *I*, not *he*. Inwardly Sosay rejoiced and licked his ears. "What do you remember, R...r..." she said, stopping herself from using the worldname that had so frightened him earlier.

"I remember," he said, shaking his head as if loosening his thoughts, then met her gaze. "Who I am...who you are." Again with the *I* word.

"Who am I...Reggie?" He trembled when he heard his name, but kept eye contact.

"Sosay, the one who saved me. Who has saved me again. I owe you my life."

"We save each other."

"And now we must save Great Mother." Sosay twitched, startled by his unfolding courage. "This is the lair of the first Malkin, the Heart-Eater, King of the Suffering World," Reggie continued, and even beneath the layers of mud, their pelts stood on end. "His spirit enters body after body, devouring one corrupted heart after another. He seeks Great Mother's Heart to destroy our world."

"Great Mother is Spirit! He can't eat Her Heart!"

"There is a way, only one, and that path has been prepared."

Sosay's tail slapped the stone floor. "What do you know." It wasn't a question.

"Great Mother has been born as kin."

Her breath came in shaky gasps through an open mouth. "Kin?"

"In the Green."

Sosay leaped to her paws as if she would run, then plopped back on her haunches. She rose and sat again, her mind racing. Finally, "Who is She?" But Reggie either didn't know or wouldn't say. "Well then," Sosay meowed, "We must protect Her."

"Yes."

"You've seen the face of the Malkin. Tell me his name." Reggie looked miserable. "You needn't bear this alone. Give me his name. I'll help you."

His eyes round with fear, his mouth was moving soundlessly. But Sosay already knew the name; she knew the name a heartbeat before it passed Reggie's lips. She knew it because the Malkin's concealment magic was suddenly gone, and every tree, each blade of grass, and every bud, bloom and seedpod could speak his worldname. "Morsus," they all whispered. "Morsus is the Malkin."

Red eyes blinked open and leathery wings thrashed in the darkness above. Then it rained bats, chittering, clicking creatures with spiked thumbs, swooping over their backs with with sharp claws and fangs. Reggie and Sosay scurried away on their bellies, desperately seeking a place to hide. They scurried into a dead end. Pushing Reggie behind her,

Sosay whirled and rose on her back legs. She flurried wildly, but the bats were as large as she was and strong. They dove like birds of prey, ripping fur from her belly. Sosay screeched with pain and Reggie knocked her flat, trapping bats between them. Together they bit into dark bodies and shred filmy wings, but for every bat killed, ten more swarmed, until a bloody mass nipped and writhed about their paws and black clouds clamored above. Talons reached out lifting Reggie off the ground. Sosay caught his scruff and pulled with all her strength until he toppled on top of her. Again they ran, at last finding a crawlspace to squeeze beneath. Now the ghoulish creatures attacked one by one, and the cavern floor was littered again with broken bats flapping in their own blood.

Suddenly, survivors flew back to the dome.

"Even their blood is nasty," Sosay spit, licking drops off Reggie's ears. He licked her back and they cleaned each other's wounds, gathering strength while plotting a path from the hellish cavern.

Sosay was a mess, missing fur from half her face and now her belly. Her ears were tattered, her legs and shoulders veined rivers of red skin, scratches that throbbed with pain. She felt faint, curling her limbs beneath her. "Reggie, there's venom in the bat bites."

"It's not the bats." he said. "This is the Malkin attacking. You must be strong now."

But Sosay hardly heard him before the vision took her, tearing her from everything she knew, and she huddled, filthy, hungry, and sick to death against an alley wall. Alone, she waited for the end.

Heart-Eater, King of the Suffering World came toward her. Enormous and powerfully built, he extended a paw for her to lick. "Acknowledge your king and you'll have a home. The price is loyalty. Speak of my greatness in all things and the scraps from my hunt are yours."

Sosay looked into his selfish eyes, and saw the careless cruelty. His words meant nothing. "I won't," she said and he was gone, but she couldn't move. The bats returned. They lunged, hanging on her frail body, nipping open her flesh and lapping the blood. Once famous for the beauty of her white pelt, her crescent moon a beacon of inner strength, Sosay lay dying.

🐾   🐾   🐾

His nibble-teeth in her scruff, Reggie dragged her up the tunnel. *We must be close to the surface,* she thought, smelling green in the air. Past a side of ginger fur, she saw sycamore leaves, a patch of twilight sky. He pulled her into a bed a sweetgrass between the tree's roots. Sosay breathed deeply. Sleep covered her like a soft blanket.

Sosay had experienced the Malkin's powers of mind over heart and mind. Lies, fear, chaos were his weapons, but she had weapons too: truth, and the most powerful of all: love. *Evil flourishes in secrets and lies. We'll spread the truth and fulfill the Prophecy.* She lay on her belly, gazing at her brave apprentice. "The kin won't believe his lies forever. We'll defeat him."

Reggie blinked slowly, radiating affection. "I love you, Sosay."

Her crescent flashed bright blue. "Our greatest strength is our friendship. In that spirit, I love you too." Aware of the disappointment spreading across his face, she looked away. *I do love you, Reggie, but I can't tell you that, not yet, maybe never. It's true. I love you the way you love me.*

14 – The Naming Of Kits

"Big Kitty, Big Kitty, wake up!" Jasper roofed. Shorttail ricocheted from Big Kitty's head to the tip of his tail and back again. The large kitten lay on his back in the grass, arms thrown over his head, legs extended, a long tail unfurled between them. Big Kitty slept with abandon when and where he wanted and the pups' barking had no effect.

Bite 'im," Jasper demanded.

Shorttail sniffed one of Big Kitty's huge paws. "I'm not gettin' scratched. You bite 'im."

"You're closer."

"You're faster."

"Anybody bites me, you're both getting scratched," Big Kitty said without opening an eye. Startled, the pups jumped back.

"Big Kitty, get up, get up," they cried in unison.

The giant kit rolled over on his belly, shaking the sleep bunnies from his head. "What is it now?" he groused, pushing himself up to a lazy sit, his back hunched, front paws between his legs and close to his body, his gigantic feet flopping outward. Tilting his face to the sun, Big Kitty yawned. Jasper leaned forward and stared down his throat. His breath tickled and Big Kitty shuddered. "What is it now?" He repeated.

"It's your brother," the curious pup exclaimed. "He's doin' it again."

"What?"

"It's your brother—"

"I heard you...*what's* he doing?"

"As always," Shorttail snarled impatiently. "He's makin' ready to tease the skunk kits."

"Tell my mother," the over-sized kitten drawled, enjoying his sun bath too much to move.

"Auntie Rosie is hunting in the forest," Jasper began.

"Then tell Kyra."

"Auntie Kyra is sleeping," Shorttail finished.

"So was I." Big Kitty opened one eye to check the angle of the sun. Soon it would drop behind the treeline and the mother skunk would bring her brood-kits out to forage. Slowly he rose. He drifted to the pool where he took a profound drink, followed by a spine-limbering stretch up the stump. He turned briskly on the two pups "We'd best hurry," he meowed. And with that, he lead them down the meadow into Smallmarsh, into large clumps of pampas grass, where with a wave of his tail, he signaled for them to hide. They all sank to the ground.

The sorrel kit lay on his belly in weeds above the stream-bank, directly above the skunk den. Hovering on his flank was a scrap of black, Kyra's little girl. "Kyra will be furious," Big Kitty muttered. The swamp and stream-bank were dangerous places for kits to be, especially kits planning such mischief.

The sun dipped below the western treeline, and as promptly as if a clock had chimed, Mother Skunk stuck her head from her den and sniffed the air. Time to dig for beetles and grubs, time to teach her babies about the world. And out she came, kits behind her, heading for the stream. Bushy tails up, pointy faces down, little pink tongues eagerly slurped the water. Then their mother led them up the bank toward the grub-rich clumps of pampas grass. They marched single file, their black and white flags at attention behind the grandest flag of all, who still hadn't noticed the sorrel furball and his dark accomplice. *He rolled in dung to hide his scent*, Big Kitty concluded. *And he made Kyra's kit do it too. Shame!* Big Kitty leaped to his paws, determined to prevent disaster.

At that moment, Bad Kitty pounced the parade. The skunklings skidded to a halt. They stomped a warning, front paws together, tail twitching, slightly angling their rear ends toward the enemy. But they were seriously out-gunned. Bad Kitty raised on his hindquarters. Huge and confusingly stinky, he hissed and yowled, waving his paws in the air. Even in fading light, the skunklings could see the gleam of his claws and the length of his fangs. The little soldiers about-faced, chittering a retreat, but when they reached the fork in the paw-worn path that led to their den, a black panther leaped from the sedge. Screeching, the babies scattered. The sorrel tiger chased them. First one, then another, and another, until finally the runt of the litter cowered before him.

Mother skunk had had enough. Throwing herself between her baby and the bully, she launched into a paw-stomping, screeching tirade, then turned her back and twitched her plume. The brat leaped from harm's way, just as his little black accomplice ran up behind him. She took the hit. Eyes on fire, she screamed and crumpled, digging at her face with her paws. Mother Skunk and her baby fled into the reeds.

The sorrel brat was hysterical, echoing each of her squeals with one of his own. He danced around her, trying to lick the thiol from her face, but she recoiled from his touch, rendering his efforts useless.

Big Kitty thundered up, grabbed the kit by the scruff and leaped into the stream. He dunked her again and again, until the spray was diluted, then set her down on the bank. The sopping kit clawed a path up his chest and sat on his shoulder, shivering and sneezing into his ear.

The brat was sorry, truly, truly sorry. He knew it was his fault. But when her red, swollen eyes glared at him with resentment, he did what he always did when confronted. He lashed out. "What are you doing here!" he snapped at Big Kitty, his tail twitching furiously back and forth.

"Fixing your mess," his brother hissed. The punk growled, planting his paws for battle. But when his little friend growled back, he sat and lowered his head. He had a conscience after all. Jasper and Shorttail, who'd been barking and bouncing along the bank, suddenly fell silent. The reeds parted. Kyra towered above them all.

"Auntie Kyra, I'm sorry! I—" the perp wailed, cut off when she caught him by the scruff, and carried him home swinging from her jaws. Humiliation was complete. His partner, draped over Big Kitty's shoulders and stinking like skunk, stared at the world through sullen red eyes. She would pay for her misdeeds and his too with painfully vigorous tongue baths and endless soaks in the chilly stream. Everyone was angry with the sorrel kit. Everyone except his victim, who had forgiven him by morning. That's when Kyra found them sleeping, arms entwined.

Rosie fretted for her son. He burned with an inner fire no scruffing, scolding, or swatting could reach. His companion had barely recovered from their mischief with the skunks before he turned his callous heart toward a king snake living on the far side of the pool. The pod cats and the snake had an unspoken agreement. They didn't bother one another. This had worked for the good of all until the brat began sticking his paw down the snake's hole.

Rosie had caught her son tormenting the snake and smacked him all the way home, but it had no effect on his behavior. Whenever his mother wasn't watching, Bad Kitty, as everyone began to call him, would flurry Scaley's head. Only half awake, Old Scaley would rise from his hole and look around, but by then the perp had always dashed off and hid. Scaley would settle back down. As soon as he'd begin to dream: *scratch, scratch, scratch*...again came the claws on his head. Again he'd slither to the surface to find nothing. And again down he'd go only to be tormented once he fell asleep. Somehow the perp always knew when Scaley slept. The old snake grew irritable from lack of rest. His hunt was affected. He lost weight and his color faded.

Once again the bully lurked at Scaley's hole. He growled impatiently, hoping to find the snake before Rosie found him. Glancing furtively in all directions, he lowered an eye to the opening. Nothing. He groped inside with his paw. Still nothing. Bad Kitty sank his arm to the shoulder, so intent on finding the snake he failed to notice when Scaley slithered up behind him. And Scaley was furious. Before the punk-in-fur could turn around, the snake coiled itself around his torso and lifted him off the ground.

"Let me go!" The the youngling screeched, slicing the air with frantic paws.

Scaley tightened his grip. "Ssso you sssuffer me with your clawsss?" he hissed, tilting his head to show the scratches on his scales. The brat didn't feel remorse; he lashed out, but Scaley was faster, coiling his head away. "Ssstill you want Sssscaley sssuffer? I sssqueeze you dead."

Now Bad Kitty was scared. "I'm sorry!" he yowled. "I won't hurt you anymore! I promise!" Caught in Scaley's unforgiving grip, he writhed and wiggled as much as he could, but Scaley only tightened his hold. The youngling arched his torso, trying to rake his tormentor with his back feet. Scaley flopped this way and that, over the dirt and into the weeds, always squeezing tighter and tighter. At last the kit's struggles grew feeble. One last whimper, one last breath. He was still.

Rosie crashed through the reeds. "Drop him!" she yowled. Kyra leaped into view beside her. The females circled the snake, shuddering with rage, spitting and caterwauling.

He hissed back. "Sssscaley, sssay no! Your ssson...isss...sssupper."

Rosie gasped. The sorrel kit still hung in Scaley's coils, his mouth open, his tongue protruding past his lips. Her son. Her terrible, beautiful son. "I'll slit you end to end," she screeched, hurling herself at the serpent with the fury of a tornado.

Old Scaley decided a kitten dinner wasn't worth the vendetta he would face from this clan of felines, and spiraled into the reeds, leaving Bad Kitty face down in the dirt, a heartbroken Rosie staring at his unmoving body. She rolled him over and flurried his face. Nothing. She head-bunted his chest, nipped his ears and cheeks. Still nothing.

"Nee-owww wow wow wow," she wailed, licking him violently, then threw herself against him. He choked. He choked so quietly she thought it must be the last of his breath leaving his lungs, but she threw herself on him again, and again she heard the softest expelling of air. A wisp of breath entered his mouth. Spittle dribbled into the dirt. Now both mothers threw themselves on him and the kit spluttered, suddenly raising the upper half of his body off the ground. Holding himself up with his front legs, he stared wild-eyed with no understanding. He gulped air, then collapsed on his side, wheezing and choking. Slowly, his gaze found his mother's face. "I'm sorry," he coughed.

"You will be," Kyra scoffed.

Rosie hushed her friend with a wave of her tail, then comforted her son with her tongue. "Are you all right?" she asked.

"Yes, mother. I am," the catling wheezed, then remembering the serpent, attempted to sit tall, eyes darting left and right.

"He's gone," Rosie murmured and the kit sighed with relief. "You're sure you're all right?"

"I'm fine," he insisted, remaining upright despite his shortness of breath. The ordeal was over, the danger passed and his enormous pride was gathering in his awareness. After all, he'd battled a serpent and survived.

"You're sure you're all right?" Rosie asked a third time.

"Yes, mother," he meowed, an edge creeping into his voice.

"Good." Her paw landed hard across his snout, a single claw out to sting. The kit ducked the next swipe, leaped to his paws and bolted for the den. Rosie was right behind him, whacking the tender parts beneath his tail, Kyra chuffing approval with every squeal he made.

In the big room after evening meal, Rosie told Browser about Old Scaley and their son's reckless and cruel behavior.

"We thought he was dead," Kyra interrupted. "It almost destroyed Rosie."

Browser gave his son a long, withering look. Silently, the catling tucked his tail, and crept away. Kyra's little girl stood to follow him, but a cuff from her mother placed her butt back on the floor. He slept alone that night.

In the days that followed, everyone heard his story and despite the adults' disapproval, siblings whispered proudly of Bad Kitty's daring. Soon the ravens spread word to other pods how the Discarded Queen and her consort had produced a young warrior of note. So amazing was he, they said, he'd wrestled a snake twenty-tails in length, and won. Rosie's part was lost in the clamor about the Prophecy and the future of the Green. But to the ruddy kit's credit, he neither spread nor agreed with the claims. If asked what happened, he told the truth, that it was his mother who saved and revived him. He couldn't forget her suffering face. Suns rose and fell. The pups and kits played new games, ran new races, and the incident was forgotten. Anyway, this Brightmoon of Many Flowers the kits of Hillside Pod would receive their worldnames, gifts from Great Mother Herself.

🐾　🐾　🐾

The sorrel catling stretched as high as he could and sharpened his claws on the stump. Skywater had fallen during the night, and everything sparkled in the morning light. Leaves dampened his pelt as he passed beneath them on his way to the pool. He lowered his head to drink.

"Yee-ow-ow-ow," he shrieked, leaping back. Old Scaley's head rose from the water, glaring at him with cold eyes. "Ow-wow-wow-wow-wow," the catling moaned, back arched and pelt bristling as he hopped sideways before his foe. The snake didn't move. The catling straightened his back, and laid his fur flat against his body. The snake was dead. Definitely Old Scaley, the catling's claw-tips clearly embedded in the scales of its head. Now he saw Scaley's body had been jammed between stones in the mud, holding the corpse upright. The punk was stunned. *Who would kill the snake?* He asked himself, slowly realizing whoever did the killing, the death was on him. *Old Scaley never threatened anyone until I tormented him. I made the snake dangerous.*

Gazing into the mirror of water, wishing he could see something

190

other than his own cruel and thoughtless face, his father's floated nearby. The youngling mewled about the horror of finding Scaley's body, but Browser was already in the pool, pulling the corpse free and tossing it into the undergrowth, food for the worms. The young cat knew then who killed the snake and why. Browser's eyes held no anger, only disappointment. He padded off without a word. His son lowered his belly to the ground and stared into the pool. Born a carnivore, he would always kill his food, but for the rest of his long life, he never tortured another creature.

🐾 🐾 🐾

Kin came from all directions toward Harmony Tree. Coteries from the alleys, ronin from everywhere, even some of the local plate-lickers and bed-warmers wanted to celebrate the three night ritual. Brightmoon would soon rise and Great Mother would give the kits of Hillside Pod their worldnames. For days the little ones had hectored Rosie and Kyra to tell them what they were, but the queens didn't know. They knew only the lovenames whispered between heartbeats, hidden in the purr.

Browser led his pod south, including five nervous kits facing their first test as waking-dreamers. Only the sorrel male seemed calm. "Don't worry," he told his podmates, "You'll know when Great Mother names you. She talks to me every day." They entered the meadow surrounding Harmony Tree in a neat line, tripping to a halt and smashing face to tail before the polestar. "See, told you it's amazing," the chestnut kit whispered to his wide-eyed friends. He knew because every day he'd sneaked away to climb it.

The sky turned violet and Harmony Tree glowed, it's blue aura shimmering off every bough, each clump of needles, every root and twig. In its presence, kin became their best selves. Here they felt strong. Here they sang with hope. When they moved within the tree's cone of power, nothing seemed impossible and no fate too grim. Even the fiery marauder obeyed when ushered between its twisting roots. Browser climbed the bole, taking his seat in the Talking Perch while Ghost, Buster and Robin sat in nearby branches. Now the moon was directly overhead and kin in the highest boughs stopped their serenade.

Browser sat tall and lifted his chin. "Great Mother Be. All That Is the same as We."

"Great Mother Be. All That Is the same as We," the crowd repeated, followed by an ear-splitting caterwauling and tail thumping that only slowly died away. Then, quiet at last, kin climbed the root stage to share. For Rosie, that was a signal to climb up and sit next to Browser for the birthings and passings in other clans. She'd fallen in love with the kin of the Green, the honesty and strength with which they lived their lives. She loved their stories and never missed a word.

Not every cat hung on every word. Some busied themselves eating at the preypile, the best meals they'd know this turn of the moon. Others hunted, offering their bounty to Great Mother's children. Ghost spied Monkey pulling a feathertail from the pile and leaped from his perch to join her. They touched noses.

"I've missed you," she trilled. She'd waited for Ghost all of Skywater Brightmoon, but he never came.

He dropped his gaze, embarrassed. "I traveled south to visit Bent Whisker," he explained. Monkey's eyes widened. Respect flickered across her face and Ghost' chest swelled. He was thinking of details that might bring more admiration his way when a nervous, pacing Browser called him back to the tree.

"I have to go," the shaman whispered, giving Monkey a quick lick. No sooner had he begun his climb than a burly tom dropped from a branch and strutted toward her.

"Hello," he rumbled though his barrel chest.

Monkey looked bored, but the little wizard missed that, and sunk his claws into the bark with such force they stung. He scrabbled up to face Browser and snarled, "What."

"Your friends are asking for you," Browser meowed, leading Ghost down the far side of the tree and west across the meadow to the edge of the forest where a circle of Wisdom Cats had gathered apart from the crowd.

Skyleaper stomped about within the circle, his voice ringing with disgust. "Morsus calls himself 'Master'. His followers, mostly lowlifes from the alleys, are hostile toward kin of the Green, toward anyone who doesn't support and believe in their Master. They think *we think* we're smarter than they are and find ourselves special."

"We *are* smart and special," someone called from the darkness and the sound of purring filled the night air.

"Everyone is special," Ghost offered, finding a place to sit.

"Morsus is a...the Master? What is that?" Browser asked Ghost as he settled between him and Robin. "What does it mean?" He looked confused. "And how, by Great Mother's Tail, does that weird cat attract any followers?" Browser took in the crowd. He flinched, shocked by Sosay and Reggie's appearance. They looked like they'd been beaten, with Sosay taking the worst of it. One whole side of her face was swollen and furless. And she looked ill, like she'd been eating bad mice. He wanted to say something, but just then Skyleaper stopped before him.

"Why don't *you* tell us about Morsus," he hissed. "He's one of yours."

Browser stiffened, surprised by the aerie dweller's hostility. He knew nothing of Indra's murder or the disappearance of the three Wisdom Cats. Ghost had only told Robin. "I claim Erasmus and Robin. I never trusted Morsus," Browser said coldly.

Skyleaper lowered his ears and flexed his claws. "Erasmus trusted him."

"And I'm sure he's paying a hard price for his soft heart," Robin hissed, leaping to his paws. "If he's even still alive?"

Ghost lashed his tail through the dirt. "Of course he's still alive!"

"Indra never trusted Morsus," Nebula moaned, "She's paid the hardest price." He sank down, grumbling, lost in his own world of pain.

"It's all very unfair," Ghost said, nodding in his direction.

Browser sulked, his pride stung by Skyleaper's rudeness as well as Ghost seeming to notice only Nebula's discomfort. *Has he forgotten his loyalty to Hillside Pod? What hasn't he shared with me? What do Ghost and Robin know?*

Skyleaper, still pacing the circle, paused before the southern cats. "There is some good news. Sosay has found Reggie and brought him home. He has something amazing to share." All eyes settled on the white cat and her apprentice with a communal trilling. Both looked dreadful, their coats dusty and dull despite their efforts to clean themselves. They were covered with cuts and patches of missing fur exposing bruises and a few abscessing boils. Sosay was missing the fur and whiskers on one whole side of her face.

She dropped the paw that had been combing the fur on her other cheek and her crescent flashed with emotion. "Browser, I'm sorry, but you may not remain for this and please understand...nothing you've heard may be repeated...to anyone...including the way I look." She knew Browser would be offended, and had thrown in that last bit to be funny. It didn't work. The pod leader looked to Ghost, who nodded his support of Sosay's decision. Browser leaped to his paws, twitched his tail, and left without a word.

"That's going to be hard to fix," Robin told his mentor.

"Thank you for bringing Ghost to us," Sosay called after the retreating cat, but he was already clambering up Harmony Tree, angry as hornets. *Morsus has followers and I'm not told? Is war is coming to the Green? These secretive monks chatter back and forth as if they could defeat a real enemy! Great Mother's Tail, they play with herbs and cast spells. Pod leaders fight! Can they be so foolish!* Browser collapsed in the split of the trunk where Rosie waited. She tried to comfort him with ear baths, but he curled like a snail and closed his eyes to the world.

Meanwhile, at the gathering of Wisdom Cats, Reggie entered the circle. "I saw the Malkin murder Indra..." He glanced at Nebula who sat with slitted pupils, paws tucked, still muttering to himself. "I saw his denchurls take Erasmus. He lived." He glanced at Ghost who trembled with hope.

"What are denchurls?" Martileena asked.

Reggie waved his tail. "Big as young raccoons, black as moonless nights and meaner than hungry badgers. They kill for sport."

"And they're stupid," Sosay added.

Reggie's whiskers rolled forward, then back, nervously. "But the Malkin isn't. He's fox-smart and has powers beyond anything I've ever seen."

"Like what?" Darktail asked.

"He can move others against their will...with his mind. Even feed himself and his denchurls using only his mind."

"What? That's ridiculous."

"I've seen it. I saw the Life-Sucker pull a mouse from its hole. It slid across the ground toward him, running hard to get away, but it couldn't. He ate it." Horrified snarls from the Wisdom Cats. "And he fed his monstrous denchurls the same way, tossing mice into their open jaws using only his mind."

Skyleaper thumped his tail, rose and circled Reggie, anger pouring off his aura. "Why didn't this Life-Sucker see you? Why weren't *you* killed?"

The golden apprentice had asked himself that question a thousand times and the answer tormented him. "I came early that night and waited for Sosay in the woods. But I scented something evil. Once you've smelled a denchurl you'll know what I mean. Great Mother's Paws they stink!" Ghost nodded, remembering the smell at Boulderfalls. "There was something vicious about that smell and the aura hanging in the air. I hid, thinking I'd leap out if needed." He began to shake. "I couldn't."

Skyleaper faced Reggie, scruff raised, claws and fangs visible. "Coward," he spat.

"Not fair!" Sosay snarled, leaping to her paws. "You don't know what they're like. Or the Malkin. Reggie had the courage to face both!"

A cringing Reggie lifted his ears from the sides of his head. "Indra... the Malkin...I didn't understand what he was doing...and when I saw what he...I...Great Mother's Heart it was horrible!" He dropped his head on his paws. "Yes, I was cowardly," he said, feeling so miserable it took all his strength to continue. "With every passing moon I've regretted not trading my life for hers." He prostrated himself before Nebula. "I'm sorry."

"You couldn't have saved her," Ghost meowed. "The beast wouldn't have let you. He'd have snapped your neck with his mind before you knew what happened."

Reggie sat crestfallen. "I should have let him."

"No," Sosay said, licking Reggie's ears. She whispered for him to leave the circle and sit beside her again.

"Wait! I haven't told you the rest," he cried. "The Malkin had two of his denchurls take Erasmus north into the city where they'd find use for him later. I couldn't save him any more than I could save Indra." He stared at nothing. Finally, "Morsus went south with the other denchurl. I followed them into the karst caverns. Eventually, I found the Malkin's lair." The cats fidgeted, growling to themselves. "It's an unholy place," Reggie continued. "The origin of the Dark Prophecy. It's where I learned a terrible truth." His gaze swept the circle, resting on each of them, his tail low, swinging side to side.

Martileena slapped her tail on the ground, raising a cloud of dust. "Well, are you going to tell us or not?"

Reggie stood, plopped back on his haunches, then rose again. "First, you need to know that Great Mother lives in the Green." More restless movements from the cats, growling and raised scruffs. Reggie raised his voice. "There's more. She's taken feline form and she's in danger. The Malkin is hunting her." Tail lashing and claws ripping the grass. The growling got louder. "He plans to eat Her Heart." Shocked silence.

Darktail was the first to find his voice. "Great Mother can't be killed. Even if She dies, She doesn't.'"

"Yes, and even if we die, we don't, but that's not the point. It's the Dark Prophecy," Sosay cried, her crescent bright blue. "It tells how She *could die, really die*...forever. Then evil, real, cruel evil would rule the world. If the Malkin eats Her physical heart, he gains immeasurable power. Evil wins. We *all* die and the Green and everyone, everything descends into darkness."

Darktail rudely flicked his tail, telling her he refused to believe. Yet everyone had heard stories of Great Mother taking physical form. Sometimes as a great fish, sometimes as a bird of prey, or even a little rat, but the kin had always been her favorites. Why not be born a cat?

"Who has She become?" Martileena asked.

"No one knows," Reggie answered. "We know only that She lives in the Green."

"That's already too much information," Skyleaper snarled. "Her danger is ours."

"Which is why we must protect her," Sosay meowed.

"The Malkin stole the Eastern RA. Can you read his thoughts?" Martileena asked Starpaw, her eyes and voice much softer than usual.

"He's so dark, so closed, we can't," Starpaw answered, lowering a gaze filled with longing, hoping no one would see. But Ghost saw and so did Darktail.

"What does he want?" Robin asked. "Explain it again, please."

"He wants to rule the Green, and more," Sosay answered. "He wants to be worshiped and obeyed...forever."

"Rat feathers to that," Robin snarled to a chorus of hooting and tail thumping. "No one rules the Green."

"Well, we do have a king," Ghost meowed.

"And an emperor," Flyingtail added. Thinking of Ozymandias. everyone chuckled.

"The emperor's an idiot," Starpaw chuffed. "And Browser—"

"Browser's no idiot!" Sosay cried.

Starpaw nodded. "As I was about to say, Browser rules with good grace by always being of service."

"The *only* way to rule the kin," Nebula meowed.

"No one rules the kin." Darktail said.

Sosay growled. "Well, the Malkin is *not* Browser. Anyone who refuses *his* rule *will* die, and it won't take many deaths for the rest of us to kneel." Sosay's ears went down and back. "The Chapel of Horrors and the Dark Prophecy are real." She swept the circle with her strong, honest gaze. "We barely escaped with our lives." The others stared at her ragged pelt and battered body.

Remembering Boulderfalls, Ghost took a deep breath. "Browser and I have seen this darkness. It's already come to the Green."

"I can't believe there's a second Prophecy," Martileena moaned. "What should we do?"

Darktail leaped between her and Starpaw, letting his tail slap Starpaw's face. "Do? What's to do? I haven't seen any proof. Only a story of Morsus' vicious murder of Indra, and there's not even a body."

"But there is, Darktail. Go to that unholy temple and see for yourself!" Reggie chuffed.

"Look, Reggie, I'm sure you believe you saw what you say you saw, but...denchurls the size of raccoons fed with flying mice? A Dark Prophecy foretelling of hearts, real hearts, being eaten? Great Mother's Heart?" He faced Sosay. "I realize you're protective of your apprentice, Sosay, but tell me *you* understand this is a tender soul traumatized by some horrific deed." Martileena nodded anxiously, her eyes lit with fear. She too was desperate to preserve *normal.*

"I know what I saw," Reggie said.

"And I know what I experienced," Sosay added. "This is an ancient evil and if it succeeds, our world will die. The war has already begun." A long silence, then Sosay slapped her tail hard on the ground and stood. "We *must* warn the kin. It's only fair."

"They'll panic," Martileena yowled.

Sosay's crescent pulsed. "I know that in empaths fear runs deep, and I'm sorry you're afraid, *but we must warn everyone.* Imagine their outrage if the kin of the Green are ambushed by Morsus' minions, and we didn't warn them."

Martileena stood. "Yes and imagine how they'll react when they're told an army of muscled thugs is following an insane Wisdom Cat who can suck life-force from your body and float prey through the air with his thoughts. Oh, and Great Mother's just another cat who could be living in the next den, and the Malkin's hunting her, planning to eat Her Heart so that he can live forever." She looked to Darktail for support. "I've seen more than most and *I* don't want to believe that."

"As you never do," Ghost snapped, thinking of Erasmus.

"Martileena," Robin snarled, "Pod leaders spend their lives hunting for their clans and fighting to protect their borders. They deserve to know about serious threats."

Sosay nodded, as did Reggie, Ghost, and Flyingtail.

Martileena's tail slapped the ground hard. "At least for now, let's keep it to ourselves. Just for one turn of the moon." Now Skyleaper and Starpaw agreed.

"Waiting a short time does make sense," Nebula meowed.

Robin's scruff rose, his eyes large and dark. "Do we have one turn of the moon to ponder? My heart says tell *all* the kin, *no* exceptions, right now."

Flyingtail, who'd been sitting quietly, spoke up. "What if a Wisdom Cat tells their pod leader now and the pod leader tells the pod. Meanings are distorted with every tongue they pass through. And because no one is supposed to tell anyone, they'll keep it secret from us. Soon no one will know what anyone really thinks. This could get crazy fast."

"Good point," Robin said. "We need the support of every apprentice, every pod leader and their second. And sooner than we expect, we'll need an army. We should trust the kin. If we don't trust them, they won't trust us. And if they don't trust us, they might trust the Malkin."

"Flyingtail's right," Reggie yelped, "If we don't tell the kin the truth, the Malkin will fill their heads with lies."

"It's a chance we'll have to take," Martileena snapped. She softened her tone. "We need time to understand this. Please, tell no one. Just for one turn of the moon, that's all."

Ghost slapped his tail on the ground. "Understand, a mistake could be lethal." Silence while they all considered that reality.

"So, do we tell everyone or not?" Sosay asked, hoping the answer was yes.

"We're evenly split," Ghost said. "And both sides have a point. I suggest we hold our secret for half a turn of the moon, but not from other Wisdom Cats. We should inform those not here today. If nothing new has happened or been revealed by darkmoon, tell anyone who wants to know. This is harsh news, terrible to know. Don't force it on those who aren't ready."

"How will we know if they're ready?" Robin asked.

"They'll demand you tell them." He stared into each face. "Agreed?"

"Agreed," they answered as one. The cats began to leave. Ghost watched Starpaw follow Martileena with his eyes until she disappeared. *What chance do these two have?* He felt badly for them. Something tugged at his mind, something needing attention.

Browser's angry, he remembered. "Monkey!" Appearing from nowhere she pranced before him, rubbing her scent on his shoulder. Intoxicating.

"Ghost, you left me with that awful tom. I thought we'd spend another brightmoon together." She strutted ahead, the tip of her tail quivering with excitement. Over her shoulder she flashed brilliant green eyes. "You're the one I want," she cooed, slipping just beyond his reach. Ghost glanced back at Robin, all seriousness on his way to Browser. He'd try to smooth things over. Somehow. *I should be there,* he thought as he followed Monkey up the tree, and into her secret nest.

Ghost was right. Browser felt betrayed. Even Rosie couldn't soothe him. *How could Ghost and Robin keep such secrets? Don't they want me as pod leader or King of the Green?* Restless, he rose and turned the three circles, then settled again. *Do they plot against me? No, Ghost loves Rosie, he loves me. This I believe. But why would he hold such secrets?* Browser's scruff rose. *He doesn't trust me! All this time and all those words were simply to keep me calm at his side. He doesn't believe I can be king and maybe he's right. Rosie just refuses to see it, but Ghost knows. I can't be trusted with the truth.* He fidgeted, unable to sleep. *Forget me! What is happening to the Green! I must help the kin!*

Something else Browser didn't know because she hid it — was Rosie's discomfort. For almost a turn of the moon now she'd been in pain. Not always, but often enough a sudden, sharp pain would cut through her chest. She'd felt it again tonight and the best thing to do, she'd found, was to rest.

Ghost also rested in the tree, and next to him, purring in her sleep, was Monkey, her silly neck fur looking more beautiful than ever. For all the nights he'd gazed alone at the stars, nesting with Monkey in Harmony Tree made him happier than he'd ever been. His half-closed eyes caught flashes of blue in the branches above, proof his union was blessed. Curled blissfully around his beloved, Ghost listened to the kin in other nests on other branches trill in their sleep as falling stars landed on their pelts and melted, tiny explosions of blue and gold spreading warmth through their bodies and comfort into their hearts. Magic was afoot.

🐾   🐾   🐾

The pups and kits were up with the sun. "So, Big Kitty, still no name?" Jasper taunted.

"That happens tonight," the kit mewed sheepishly.

"Crazy! I gotta' watch you get it, or I'll never believe you really have one."

"That's for sure," Shorttail barked. "Anyway, we're gonna call you Big Kitty and Bad Kitty forever." Lowering his head and shoulders, he wagged a raised tail, inviting the over-sized kit to play tag. Browser's big son crashed down on the pup's head, mashing him into the grass with the usual whining, barking and 'grrrs' of an excited pup.

The sorrel kit finished a meal of field mouse. "I don't care what you call me," he said, fishing between his toes with his tongue, "You still can't watch. kin only." He held his paw up to Jasper's black nose.

"Eee-whew!" The pup groaned, pulling back in disgust.

"You're just lucky we feed you," the catling said, padding off with a flick of his tail that fairly shouted *FOOL*. Jasper ran after him. Bad Kitty whirled, stinging the pup's nose with one extended claw, and the chase was on.

Catling play was always good, and today more than ever. Tonight the kits would accept their spirit-given names, and they'd been fretting about it for a while. *What if I make a mistake and think Great Mother calls my worldname when she didn't? What if I don't answer when she does? How will I know it's my name? What if I don't like my worldname?* Only the sorrel kit swaggered about, his black shadow behind him, pretending to share his confidence.

The sun dropped beneath the edge of the world and at last it was time for the pilgrimage to Harmony Tree. Buster and Kyra gathered their two kits and Robin and Rosie gathered her three. Tails high and scruffs on edge, the kits were herded south toward their first rite of passage. Jasper and Shorttail watched with jealous eyes, for all their whining and paw stomping had failed to glean an invitation to the mysterious naming ceremony.

"I'm goin' anyway. Wanna come?" Jasper whispered, watching his playmates getting smaller in the distance.

"What?" Shorttail squealed.

"I'm goin'. I am."

"How?"

"Easy. Mama sleeps so hard we could pick her up and take her with us." They chased each other in circles, delighting in the mischief they planned.

🐾   🐾   🐾

A golden moon crested the eastern horizon as the troupe reached Harmony Tree. The polestar shimmered with a pale blue halo that invited the younglings to shelter between its roots.

Browser opened the ceremony, entreating the great round eye rising in the sky. "We thank You, Great Mother, for the roots and flowers that heal us, for the water we drink, the air we breath, and for the fire in the flesh of our prey." Rosie saw the edges of his fur radiating the same blue as Harmony Tree. She felt what coursed through him. It filled her too: oneness with All That Is. Browser finished the prayer. "And we thank You for our great clan. May Your bounty bless our hunt."

"The hunt yields prey," the chorus of gathered kin responded.

Then they fell silent, and the quiet stretched across the meadow so deeply and for so long the crickets began to bow. A feathertail answered with a cheerful flute.

A queen climbed the roots. It was Rosie. "Great Mother has given me a name." She paused. "Rosebud."

Her daughter erupted with joy. "That's me! Oh, I love my name, mama." She placed her paws on Rosie's shoulders and licked her face. Rosie licked her back, then ushered her to a spot between the roots.

A dark queen from the western forest stood. "I've been given a name: Zuba." And an ebony kit with a round belly and large, gentle eyes appeared behind her.

"I'm Zuba," he mewed shyly.

Kyra stood. "Great Mother Be, I have a name: Shadow." Kyra's little girl came forward, lifting her tiny black paws high like a prancing horse. The crowd cooed with delight.

"My name," she mewed proudly.

Browser's over-sized son was named Bigpaw. He marched up to Rosie on legs thick as branches ending in giant paws. Great Mother had named him perfectly. Buster's look-a-like son was now Patches. Then many kits from other clans were named. So many pods were present, each with several queens, each queen having at least one kit, most having two or more, and some had litters of five or six. Long moments might pass between names, but no one seemed impatient. The evening was warm, the sky luminous with stars. Finally, the only catling who hadn't been named was the chestnut brat from Hillside Pod. And for the first time since the naming ceremony approached, he was nervous.

🐾   🐾   🐾

Red stopped his telling here for the kits had fallen asleep. He tried to wake them with tongue baths, but they only curled into tighter balls, raised their paws over closed eyes and purred. Red left to find his humans.

The next morning, full of energy and twice as many questions, the younglings chased one another about. Red ignored them while he ate his breakfast and groomed, then sat tall, all seriousness. "I bring news." The kits formed a line before him. Drawing themselves up, they placed their forepaws together, wrapping their tails neatly across them. Never had they been honored with anything as important as news. "I know your worldnames," Red said.

"Noooooo..." the kits meowed in unison.

"I spent the night at the foot of the uprights' bed, pretending to sleep while they chose your names."

"But worldnames come from Great Mother," the little tiger said, his scruff rising.

"And who's to say these uprights don't hear Her. They saved you. They can't be all bad. Anyway, I have your worldnames if you'd like to hear them. The kits nodded. You," Red purred, touching the orange tabby's nose with his own, "are Tigertom." The kit beamed with pride. "You," he nuzzled the tuxedo, "are Starbright. You'll probably be called

Star."

"What about me?" the girl asked.

"You, my precious, are Petal, because you remind them of a flower they once loved."

She smiled, padded to Red and rubbed her face on his expansive chest. "Red? Will I stay here with you?"

The big tom averted his face. He'd helped his humans with dozens upon dozens of rescues, and they'd all moved on to forever homes, but the thought of Petal leaving was painful. "Sometimes kits stay," he lied, until she met his gaze and he couldn't. He sighed. "You'll be here for two turns of the Moon, maybe a little longer, but they'll find you a forever home." She looked miserable. "You'll be happy. I swear it." The boys were reassured, but Red felt the same sadness Petal did.

15 – FANGS IN THE DARK

asper and Shorttail had indeed slipped away from their sleeping mother to hide in the woods. Southwest of Harmony Tree, the doglets couldn't see everything, but they could see the root stage and occasionally someone from Hillside Pod popped into view. The copse sheltering them was dark, rarely pierced by moonlight, and they were having a party, dashing about, snuffling along the forest floor, tossing leaves into the air.

"What d'ya think Bad Kitty's gonna be named?" Jasper panted.

"Uhhh...Really Bad Kitty?" Shorttail squealed.

"Hah!" Jasper rolled on his back, laughing and shaking his Lilliputian legs in the air. "No, no wait!" he snorted, jumping up. "How about Thug-Tail!" They fell on each other with drunken glee and rolled in the fallen leaves. Suddenly Jasper froze. "Did you hear that?"

"What?" A twig snapped.

"That." Two heads swiveled as one toward the darkness. A shaft of moonlight caught in silvery fur, igniting yellow eyes, and a large, muscular ghostdog winked into their world. The shrieking fuzzballs fled deeper into the forest, discovering too late they'd camped on the edge of a ravine. Head over tail they tumbled to the bottom, jumped up, and dashed off in the wrong direction toward the dead end. Now they were trapped between two steep hillsides and a vertical wall, the ghostdog still creeping toward them. They whimpered, then a frenetic game of leapfrog, replete with snarling, snapping, and angry whining played out against the wall as each tried to be the last pup eaten.

The coyote froze in place. The little dogs stopped and stared, hoping for mercy, but the hound began again his slow creep forward, and they knew they would die. Shorttail plopped on his rear and sat trembling.

Jasper barked for both of them with all his might.

"Waow-waow-waow-waow-waow!" Claws gleaming in the moonlight, enormous paws flashed by, and a huge cat landed between the predator and his prey.

The ghostdog howled with pain. He jerked forward as if to lunge, but the sabers rose again and he backed away. "I'm not afraid of you," he lied, suddenly aware that the gully reeked of cat. "I ate your mother yesterday."

"But these you shall not touch," the bobcat snarled. Hissing erupted everywhere. Next to every bush and upon every boulder crouched the shadowy shape of a cat ready to strike. A muscular tom slipped to the bobcat's side and the gulchdog trembled with rage.

"You think you can take me, runt? I'll clean my teeth with your bones."

"You think you can eat me? I'll tear your throat to shreds and devour your belly from the inside," Browser hissed, planting his paws wide.

The ghostdog snorted and leaned in, his lips curling back from his fangs. "I'll bite you in half before your claws come out."

"But mine are already aimed," the bobcat said.

The coyote glared. The small cat was an annoyance, dangerous only if the others piled on, but a large, healthy bobcat was too strong to overpower without risk. *Those stringy dogs aren't worth it,* he told himself. "Take your pups then," he growled, "Probably tough as old crows." He glanced at them dismissively, pretending he didn't care although his belly was empty enough to hurt. And he was deeply wounded, the ruts carved into his muzzle swollen and pulsing with pain. He wouldn't hunt this brightmoon, no matter how hungry he was. Pawing the ground angrily, he shook his head, splattering blood in all directions, then lowered his face to Browser's. "This isn't over," he muttered, "I'll be back...and I won't be alone."

Browser didn't move. A sudden noise, a twitch of muscle could be lethal. Suddenly the ghostdog whirled and leaped into the forest, fading from sight like mists crossing the moon.

Browser turned to the bobcat. "Thank you."

"Ghostdogs are a problem for all of us," the big cat said. He had large, widely spaced eyes and a wide face with ruffs of fur that widened it more, giving him a gentle look. But he was a hunter, a warrior to the bone. He scanned the crowd, then turned his gaze back to Browser. "I admire your courage, cousin, and the way you help each other, but you should know the evil you face is profound."

Browser tensed, words from the Wisdom Cats' meeting ringing in his head. None of it had sounded good. "What do we face? And what should we do?" he asked.

The great cat paced, his ocher and black pelt glistening over taut muscles. "Your enemy plays upon your anger, spreading fear and lies, claiming to be the savior, while he himself carries evil. You must unite. You must trust one another. Don't keep secrets." Browser stared past the big cat at Ghost. He'd just been told to drop his anger and trust. Ghost had been told he mustn't keep secrets. *We're doomed.*

The bobcat levitated halfway up the gully in one bound, turned and looked directly at Rosie. "You must fulfill your part in the Prophecy or the Green will fall and the wildborn will die." Another leap and he was gone. Ghost watched Starlight dance along the ridge, fading into a mist of twinkling stars. Stunned, Rosie stared ahead, seeing nothing. A mated queen with a family she loved, she'd just been told she must leave them or everyone would die.

Browser fixed a stern eye on the pups cowering before him, a ghastly stink wafting from their behinds. "I hope you've learned from this," he scolded. Jasper whimpered a small yes. Shorttail couldn't even squeal. He just shook his head up and down.

"Hah!" Kyra scoffed, sauntering toward them, the tip of her raised tail swaying side to side with her hips. The pups had endangered *her* kits with their mischief and they wouldn't go unpunished. "They haven't learned anything. They'll face their mama, but first *me*." She lifted her paw, claws drawn to dispense justice, when Ghost slid between her and the cringing doglets.

"Kyra, it's possible the pups stopped the coyote from eating one of us. He could have picked off anyone at the edges of the gathering with no one the wiser."

Kyra scowled. "And if they hadn't been there stinkin' up the place, he wouldn't have come at all." The old, haughty Kyra wheeled around and sashayed up the hill, sneering over her shoulder, "Speaking of stench, nothing's worse than barker scat," and flicking her tail at all of them, she was gone. Jasper and Shorttail collapsed in a pile of relief.

Brightmoon celebrations were over. One night remained, but no one wanted to go back to the tree. When the pups had begun squealing, rivers of fur had popped off its branches, poured into the grass and flowed down the ravine. Now many of the cats sat glowering at Browser, asking themselves why everything was so strange. A ghostdog had attacked on hallowed ground, during a sacred ceremony. A bobcat had appeared from nowhere to protect them. Now both were gone, leaving the kin to wonder why barkers lived with the king and queen. Browser stared back at them. *And they don't even know about Sugar Pie,* he thought.

The instant he'd heard Jasper's cries, the sorrel kit had raced to the gulch. He'd crouched beside his mother, witnessing with her his father's selfless courage. Then it all made sense: who he was, why he'd been born with certain abilities, and what he would do with his life. He would be like his father, strong, fearless and honorable. But he knew, without any sense of superiority, he would be more. Because more would be needed. And then and there, without so much as a trill to call attention to himself, he discarded every cell and synapse of Bad Kitty, shrugging him off as a life too small for his larger Self. The sorrel brat had the soul of a hero after all.

Ghost also had an awakening, seeing himself through the bobcat's gaze. *I've let fear determine my actions. I, who crow that faith is to fear nothing, have been living in fear. I'll change. By Great Mother's Heart, I'll change. Beginning with this moment I'll do whatever is needed of me. Anything.* Following Browser, who ushered the pups up the hill, another wave of guilt washed over him; he'd treated his friend unfairly, keeping secrets from him, the leader and protector of their clan.

Monkey appeared from nowhere, rubbing her flank against his. Ghost nuzzled her tenderly, then feeling eyes upon them, turned to see Hillside Pod gathered around, looking stunned. "Everyone, this is Monkey," he said, a little unsure, then added with more confidence, "She's coming home with me and I pray she will stay." The queens trilled, showing Monkey she was welcome with flat pelts and happy purrs.

Browser accepted her. Ignoring Ghost, he touched his nose to hers and licked her ear, then turned to Buster. "Will you take the pod home? I need to check Harmony Tree for stragglers." Buster nodded.

Ghost padded after him. "Browser?" The pod leader stopped and met those sea-blue eyes. "We must speak."

"Yes, later," Browser answered tonelessly, then bounded toward the tree.

Buster led the pod home, Ghost at Monkey's side. They all carried an anxious energy, shuddering with every crunched leaf or scent on the breeze.

The humbled pups were delivered to Sugar Pie, along with the story of their escapade, her fangs growing more visible as the story unfolded. Jasper and Shorttail whined for mercy, dragging their stumpy-tailed butts along the ground. The cats heard them whimper when their mother marched them to the stream and icy water flowed over their dirty rear ends. The queens' eyes smiled, but they cuffed any kit who snickered. At last the pups' discipline ended and sounds of suckling rose from Sugar Pie's nest. The pod cats slept. Ghost slept with Monkey, limbs intertwined in the alcove they called Great Mother's altar.

At first light, Hillside Pod gathered in the meadow below the den. After last night, life must be different. Jasper and Shorttail lay like storm-beached flotsam, terrified they had condemned their mother and themselves to banishment. It wasn't true, but Browser let them worry.

He thumped his tail several times quickly. "Things have to change," he began, waving the great tail over his paws. The pups whimpered and buried their faces. This was the moment they'd be banished, forced to wander forever, alone and hungry.

Kyra narrowed her eyes, her cat smile clearly visible. "How?" she asked with a sideways glance at the mopey pups, clearly enjoying their distress.

"No more hunting at night. No more hunting alone. No more anything outside the den after sunfall." This surprised everyone and they groaned unhappily. Everyone except Jasper and Shorttail, who realized they'd been pardoned. They slobbered kisses on their mother, their tails whipping back and forth like hummingbird wings. "That also means no Harmony Tree until we know we're safe," Browser continued. More groaning. He looked into each of their faces, lingering on Ghost and Robin. *Surely they'll say something if the pod faces dangers we don't yet understand.* A shudder traveled his spine. "You can do whatever you want, but a price will be paid...and not just by you." He stared pointedly at the

Wisdom Cats. "The gulchdog is gathering his pack and they'll be stalking the woods by moonrise. If you're out on the meadows, you'll lead them here," he said, ending with a thump of the tail.

"They'll find us anyway. They won't quit until they do," Buster hissed.

"Don't say that," Robin hissed back. "You'll make it happen."

Buster leaned over the apprentice. "Keep dreaming, Mystic-Kitty, I'm just telling the truth."

Now Robin rose, bringing his face close. "So am I, Dead-Heart. Thoughts make things happen and words are stronger."

"I'll give you something strong." They stood facing each other, necks stretched forward with heads low, shoulders tensed. Their tails twitched irritably.

"This is *not* how we need to change," Browser said, padding between them, flicking his tail in each of their faces. The males looked guilty and backed down.

Rosie stood. "We're all worried, but anger won't help. Our family has grown and feeding us with limits on our hunting will be hard. We're scared." Now the males bristled at being told they were frightened, but she wasn't wrong.

"Faith is to fear nothing," Robin offered, parroting the words of his mentor.

Buster's whiskers twitched. "Oh sweet feathers and crunchy bones, another one?" Robin stiffened, about to take the bait when Sugar Pie stood.

"Mister and Misses and beautiful, kind cats, I know life would be easier for you if I took my pups and left..." Sugar Pie's sad voice faded.

"And go where?" Kyra asked, rubbing her sleek head against her friend's fuzzy shoulder. "You're family." The mother dog ogled her lovingly. "Don't get mushy on me," Kyra said. Sugar Pie licked her anyway. Deep in thought, Browser padded circles around the gathering, passing his ruddy kit, who pawed him for attention.

"Not now, son," he murmured, continuing to pace. "There will be no hunting at night. Agreed?" They nodded. "We must all return to the den before sunfall." Again all heads nodded, albeit not as quickly.

"You need sentries," Monkey offered.

"Yes," Kyra echoed. Again Browser passed his anxious son, who now stood on his hind legs and placed his paws on his father's shoulders.

"Not now, please," Browser rebuked, regaining his stride. "You're right," he said, nodding to Monkey. "Vigils of two."

Sugar Pie trembled excitedly. "I can bark, dear cats. It's what I do best."

"Yes, Fuzz Mutt," Kyra meowed, "But barking makes you dinner. They're called ghostdogs because they're practically invisible."

"Please don't bark," Buster cautioned.

"Even the fastest cat can't outrun a ghostdog," Rosie said. "And we're faster than you."

Browser paused before them. "The queens are right, Sugar Pie. We can't chance you or your boys getting hurt."

The mother dog trilled for her pups, who bounced to her side. "Then I shall tell you quietly, dear cats, when I smell one, for I can, long before I see it."

Ghost rose to his paws, waiting until all eyes rested on him. "Don't forget: we live in a shelterveil. Great Mother would never let a pack of hounds defile her home."

"Any more than she'd let a ghostdog desecrate brightmoon?" Buster scoffed, slapping his tail in the dirt. Ghost didn't answer, admitting to himself he had questions of his own about Great Mother.

"Waterfall Boulder!" Rosie cried. "We'll have enough warning."

Browser nodded as he paced. "Then it's settled. A moonrise shift in pairs, starting tonight. Rosie and I will go first." He paused before his sorrel kit.

"What's wrong, son?"

"Nothing, Father...except...Great Mother didn't give me a name."

Silently, the pod stared. That had never happened before.

🐾   🐾   🐾

"Browser." Rosie trilled. No answer. "Browser." Still no response. "Browser," she rasped, tapping his paw with hers, one claw extended.

"Neow!" He mewed with surprise, pulling himself more erect and his paws more tightly together. "I wasn't sleeping," he fibbed.

"I know," she fibbed back. "Browser, where would we go if we had to leave the Green?"

For several heartbeats he said nothing. Then, "Would you take our

210

kits to Mee-am, if I asked you?"

Rosie was stunned. She'd been happy with Browser, in some ways happier than living with tall-ones, although the loss of Mee-am still stung. His question left her reeling. "Leaving you would break my heart," she mewled.

He pushed his nose to her cheek. "I never wanted to be king, Rosie, I only wanted you. But when you crowned me and I accepted, I realized I want to be of service. I can't run now, not while the Green's in trouble. And I can't live in a tall-one's den, even Mee-am's. I've always been free. When the time comes, you must go with our children without me."

Rosie trembled, pressing close. "What do you mean 'when the time comes'? Has Ghost told you something?"

"Ghost!" Browser chuffed angrily. "I don't need Ghost to tell me about the two-legged invasion, or the threat of ghostdogs...much less anything about the Prophecy."

"Meet me tomorrow during short-shadows at Harmony Tree."

"What?"

"You heard." They snuggled in the predawn chill, returning to the den at first light where they found their sorrel son pacing the big room.

"Mom," he mewled, "I'm worried." Rosie licked his ear.

"We'll keep you safe from ghostdogs and tall-ones."

"No, mom, not that," he chuffed, dusting the floor with an impatient tail. "Did Great Mother not name me because I'm evil?"

"Lies! Who told you you're evil?" Rosie snarled.

"Oh, but he is," Rosebud whispered from a pile of tails and paws. She lay with Bigpaw and Patches, hoping Rosie couldn't tell who spoke.

But she could. "Naughty," she cried and nipped her daughter's flank. Rosebud squealed.

The sorrel persisted. "Mom, why wasn't I given a name?"

"Great Mother hasn't told me why, son, but I know She loves you. That she did tell me." His eyes told her he believed her. "When you were born, Bent Whisker the oracle said you were different, and that it was a good thing. Perhaps you'll earn your worldname...a special name for a special child of Great Mother." She held his face between her paws and felt his body relax with the caresses of her tongue.

"May I choose a name for now?"

"I think that's wise." Browser meowed. "We need to call you

something."

"Evil One," Rosebud snickered. Rosie leaned in to give another nip, but Browser tapped her shoulder with his tail and she let their daughter be.

"I'd like to be called Bravetail."

Browser chuckled. "So would I, but like your mother said, some names should be earned."

"Thug Tail," Rosebud blurted. "He's earned that."

"Devil Paw," her over-sized brother squealed. Their father looked unhappy. Bigpaw mewed an apology, but Rosebud just tucked her face into her legs, pretending to sleep.

"How about Scrapper? "Browser asked his son. "There's no doubt you're a young warrior."

"It's a good fit," Rosie agreed with a twitch of her ears. Their son looked pleased.

"Done," Browser said. Scrapper curled contentedly between his siblings and closed his eyes. Her ebony head resting on her mother's flank, little Shadow closed hers too.

🐾   🐾   🐾

Browser woke late in the morning to find Rosie gone, then remembered their appointment at Harmony Tree. Snatching a mouse from the preypile, he ate it in two gulps and left the den. The sky was blue, the earth fragrant and green. As he padded south beneath a sun that warmed his back, the threat of the White Truck, even the ghostdogs, seemed like fading dreams. Browser entered the meadow. Harmony Tree soared like a victory shout, and Browser sat, struck by its power. Then he saw Rosie waiting on the tangle of roots and loped toward her. When he was almost upon her, she moved to the side. And there he crouched, looking small, and so woebegone his silver pelt had tarnished. Ghost. Browser jerked to a stop. The king of the Green stared coldly at his queen. "Why have you done this?"

"Last night, when you talked about me leaving with our children, I thought of Ghost. Now he is mated. I don't want him to leave with Monkey and start their family elsewhere.

"I have Buster and Kyra," Browser chuffed.

Rosie's eyes grew dark with anger. "Whatever, fool." She dropped from the platform and stomped past him. But she suddenly stopped and whirled around. She stared at Browser.

"Rosie," he growled.

"Browser," she growled back. "You're a king. You can't do what you want. You must do what's good for the Green, and hostilities with your Wisdom Cat is *not that*. Whatever his trespasses, you need to forgive him." Head and tail high, she stomped off as best small paws could stomp through thick, tall grass. Browser turned and faced Ghost.

"It's not what you think," his friend offered, backing up when Browser leaped to the root stage and began pacing before him.

"How would you know what I think," Browser hissed.

Ghost hunkered, ears down and to the side. "And how could I explain what I didn't understand? I didn't understand anything until I visited Bent Whisker."

The pod leader towered over the Wisdom Cat. "Half a turn of the moon has passed."

"Not even a blink of Great Mother's eye. And so much has happened. And we needed to gather the Wisdom Cats first. You do realize I'm a Wisdom Cat." Ghost swelled his chest.

"Wisdom Cats!" Browser spat. "They keep secrets and tell lies!"

Ghost rolled his eyes, "I wish they were lies."

For an instant, Browser looked curious, but his rage prevailed, his claws clicking against the roots while he paced. Ghost leaped from the stage and sat in the grass. Browser leaped after him. And the grievances poured out in long, undulating yowls. "Haven't I been a good leader? Don't I fill your bellies? Make you safe? I would give my life to keep the pod safe. And how do you return my dedication?" Here Browser sat and slapped his tail on the ground. "Did you ever intend to tell me the truth? How can I protect us when I don't know what the danger is!"

Ghost wondered if Browser would ever trust him again. When his friend at last fell silent, he waited a moment before answering. "Browser, I'm a shaman, not a ruler. I never meant to deny your right to lead. What can I do to make this right between us?"

"You must tell me—no, tell all of us, the whole pod—everything. But tell me first. Now."

"I've taken a vow of secrecy," Ghost began. Browser's ears went down and back and a growl rumbled through his chest. Ghost scooted back. He'd never seen his friend this angry. "Let me finish, please. I have taken such a vow, but this brightmoon's meeting of Wisdom Cats showed me I can't keep it." Now he leaned forward, hoping Browser would feel the weight of his words. "I hold cruel secrets, Browser. Are you sure you want to know? Once I tell you, you'll be changed."

"Of course I want to know."

So two friends sat near the shimmering tree, beneath a warm sun and blue sky, wrapped in all that was good in their world, while one told the other the horrors of hell.

Later that day, Ghost sat in the meadow below their den, facing the cats and dogs of Hillside Pod. "I need to tell you what we Wisdom Cats discussed this last brightmoon. The fate of the Green affects more than us and although I encouraged the others to wait half a moon before telling their friends, Browser wants you to know now." Browser looked stern. "And I don't disagree," Ghost added. Wide eyes grew wider, but when he was finished, a thousand questions swam in those eyes, their hearts so shaken their lips couldn't form words.

"What should we do?" Rosie asked for them all, despite the sharp pains racking her chest again. No one knew what she was feeling, and no one seemed to know the answer to her question. "What should we do?" she asked again.

"Tell everyone you can," Ghost finally answered.

🐾   🐾   🐾

"Great Mother's Pelt!" The kits squealed in unison.

"What does it mean to not have a name?" Petal asked.

"Well, as Moons turned, a meaning revealed itself," Red said, turning his well-fed belly toward the fireplace. His eyes fell shut, and with a contented purr, he settled into his post-breakfast nap.

"Red! Red! You can't sleep now. Tell us more," the boys squeaked in his ears. He brushed them off with a swipe of his paw.

"How can you live without a name?" Tigertom meowed, climbing Red's back.

"Did Great Mother ever give the kit a name?" Brightstar asked.

"Later," Red whispered into his paws. "I was up all night catching mice."

Petal pranced before him and sweetly licked his face. "Uncle Red, why does Great Mother make bad animals like ghostdogs?"

"Or murderous cats like Morsus," Tigertom yowled.

"Doesn't Great Mother love us?" Petal wondered.

Red nuzzled her tenderly. "Of course She does, even when we're Morsus."

eneath a moonless sky, peeking from the bracken edging a path worn smooth by myriad small paws, the kin sat tall. Behind them rose a forest of ash, hickory and elm. Wisdom Cats of the South, little tongues of flame filled their eyes, licking at the darkness and reflecting stars. They had come through the mists of time to share their secrets with Ghost, and he tread lightly between their spectral bodies, absorbing all they had to give.

Approaching the woods he spied a silhouette moving toward him with a strange gait, a silver and blue pelt with enormous indigo eyes.

"Who are you?" he asked.

"I am Sylvan, water spirit of caves and forests. I bubble from the earth delicious enough to thwart hunger, pure enough to heal wounds." Her body rippled, became translucent, then solid again. "Ripplemist is waiting for you at the Scrying Pool," she purred.

She's a water elemental, he thought. *But I just came home.* Morning light poured into the nest he shared with Monkey and Ghost woke. Ghost woke. Since his return from Bent Whisker's, Monkey had been helping him adapt to the RA of the South. They'd spent time together, happy time. But now Monkey seemed angry, and sat outside their snuggery stirring dust with her tail. "You're leaving, aren't you? And you've barely been home."

"Monkey," Ghost wheedled, uneasy she knew his intentions almost before he knew them himself.

She tucked her paws beneath her and looked away. "I *might* be here when you get back."

Ghost nuzzled her neck, left the den, and joined Robin at the pool for a drink of water. Robin, sensing tension in Ghost' movements, touched his nose with his own.

"I'm going to the Sacred Scrying Pool. Monkey's..." He left the rest unsaid. Then pawing the ground with his left foot, he lowered the right side of his face to the water. Finally he drank.

"Shall I go and you stay here?"

But Ghost couldn't accept. "No Robin. You care for the pod while I'm gone. Tell everyone I've left."

Robin nodded yes, surprised Ghost would leave without telling them himself. With a quick nuzzle to Robin's cheek, Ghost headed for the western woods, traveling south through the underbrush, stopping at Harmony Tree to catch his breakfast and to pray Monkey would be home when he returned.

He came to Smallmarsh where he followed a sluggish stream west to the Sacred Birch Grove. He loved the grove with its slender trees, their pale limbs reaching skyward lifting whispering leaves to Great Mother. He loved how dabs of sunlight danced on the mossy earth so soft beneath his paws. He loved climbing the boulders between the trees, licking the healing sap he'd coax from the bark with a claw. It brought the most exotic dreams. Like Hillside Den, the copse was precious to First Feline, a treasured shelterveil.

Now Ghost sniffed along the edges of the grove, hoping to find the portal. He'd hardly paused before two birch grown so close nothing larger than a cat would fit between them, when he heard a whoosh and a pop and Martileena stood at his side. Her sudden appearance startled the little wizard, and he bounced straight up, fur on end and toes spread wide.

Martileena laughed, then nuzzled his side. "Oh, but you're too skinny," she meowed.

"I'm fine," he said, quickly sitting to avoid more poking. *She's not my mother, he thought.*

"But I'm a good friend," she said. He wasn't surprised she heard him.

Sosay and Reggie arrived from the south. Sosay was looking better. Her bruises had healed and the swelling was gone, but the fur on the left side of her face hadn't grown back, and her missing whiskers looked strange. Shortly thereafter, Starpaw raced toward them from the east, Flyingtail in tow. Then tails high, everyone began bunting heads and touching noses. Starpaw skidded to a stop and stood rigid, shocked and pained by Sosay's appearance. He bent his large body over her and slowly, tenderly licked her face and body. She let him, looking up at Martileena as if for permission. Martileena seemed pleased. Finally, they all sat facing the chocolate beauty.

"I'm taking you through our shelterveil to the Sacred Scrying Pool, but first you must swear by Great Mother you'll never reveal this portal to anyone," she said, then stood probing their faces. "Hearts as one."

"One mind, one heart," they answered in unison.

"By your oath, come." She turned, leaped between the trees and vanished. Starpaw leaped after her. Flyingtail followed. Sosay paused before the disturbance, sniffed, then leaped and was gone. Reggie stepped gingerly forward, raised on his hindquarters with a paw on each tree, then leaned halfway through. His head came back out and he stared at Ghost with wonder. A small leap and only Ghost remained outside the portal. He stood before it, the air subtly repulsing him. He jumped and found himself within the stand of silver trees. Everything looked as it always had. The difference was that he and the others were hidden from passersby, and most importantly, the shelterveil led to the Sacred Scrying Pool. It was the only way to get there.

With Starpaw beside her, Martileena led the Wisdom Cats west, following the stream bank at an easy pace. The farther they traveled, the cooler and moister the air became, and the grove morphed into a tall, dark forest of redwood and fern trees. Unseen creatures announced the kin's arrival with chitterings and squeaks, while small, large-eyed deer peeked from the ever denser thicket. Moss and fallen needles blanketed the ground, which seemed to glow as daylight dimmed. Tired and thirsty, the travelers stopped to rest. Martileena taught them to drink from tiny pools of blue water cradled by hillocks of lichen. It boosted their strength and filled their minds with visions of monstrous lizards who once trampled the earth; terrible lizards from long ago, whose bones now rested far beneath the travelers' paws. No one spoke while caught in these dreams, while still dreaming they rose and pushed farther west. The forest grew closer and darker still.

At last they reached a clearing before a stand of fern trees. Martileena sat and closed her eyes. The others did the same. They had reached the Sacred Scrying Pool. The trees encircled it like guardians, its waters painting their fronds with blue light while azure mists rose in the air. Ghost caught the scent of kin within the sanctum, along with an odd whiff of Valerian. *What's this,* he wondered.

The troupe padded to a parting of branches, the only opening to the pool, and Ghost saw for himself: the perfumed fool was his friend. *Darktail!* He glanced at Martileena whose posture was tense, her face drawn while from the far side of the waters, Darktail meowed a hearty hello, his tail waving with the happy abandon of a brightmoon celebration, not the solemnity of a scrying ceremony in search of truth.

"My apprentice, Annapurna Snowpelt," Darktail trumpeted, moving to reveal a female behind him. She padded to the water's edge and sat, welcoming the newcomers with a slow blink. Ghost burst into a loud purr for she was the most beautiful cat he'd ever seen. But just as abruptly he cut it short, embarrassed when thinking of Monkey.

It was hard not to worship Annapurna's beauty. Celestine eyes shone from her lilac face floating above a glistening cream pelt. Her long gloves, tall boots and graceful tail were also purple-gray, and like all western kin, she had large eyes and a well-proportioned body. She dazzled, and not just Ghost or Darktail. Reggie and Flyingtail stared as if frozen. Only Starpaw seemed immune. He had eyes for Martileena. Starpaw settled on her left. Thankfully, the scented suitor didn't complain.

Ghost wasn't sure what escaped his mouth, but he must have greeted Annapurna properly because he heard her silken voice answer, "May She lift Her Paw."

"And to you too," he stupidly added, then tried to hide his unease by looking for the spot to sit that felt like 'his'. Once everyone had found a place, then rose and turned the three circles of past, future and now, Darktail leaned over the waters, his face lit with an eerie blue glow. Silence fell upon the gathering.

Darktail spoke. "Ripplemist, Spirit of the West, Spirit of the Sacred Scrying Pool, see that we seek your truth. Show us, Heart of the Waters, what has passed into the void, and what will come from what is now."

Within moments, the water churned. A shadow spiraled from its depths toward the surface, exploding in a shower of froth, and a silver Spirit Cat burst free. Her body was long-limbed and slender, her face delicate, a sinuous tail coiling over her back. She was water, flowing, rippling water with eyes of liquid light. *Her heart's as naked as an exposed nerve,* Ghost realized. *She shimmers with every thought and feeling, gentle but strong, never recoiling from the intimacy her being engenders.* He thought of Starlight's trickster joking, Solara's aggressive intensity. *How different Spirit Cats are!* Lifting her elegant face to theirs, Ripplemist chimed, "Drink me," then slipped back into the pool.

Drink they did, and within heartbeats Ripplemist wakened within them, a siren singing in their hearts.

I am the changeling,
I wear mountains down to moonlight,
Polish pebbles in the stream.
I flow and fill a vessel's shape
To freeze and swell before it breaks.
I am the cleanser of the world.
I am mist beneath the morning sun.
I am many, I am one.

An indigo current spread across the surface of the pool, forming a vision of gentle hills and verdant valley. With their minds and hearts, the watchers had the sensation of being one with Ripplemist as they saw themselves race up a slope and into a forest. It grew darker and the cats slowed. Ahead in a clearing in the dimming light, a pale shape crouched over a fallen feline. *Was it helping?* they wondered, smelling blood on the downed cat's throat. The attacker lowered his mouth to hers. She was a young, malnourished wildborn, her lifeless eyes staring forward. The watchers' breath caught in their throats as her life-force was sucked into the open jaws of her murderer. His furless belly bulged with indulgences, while across his shoulders and down his back hung the pelt of another, a recent kill whose blood dripped down his sides.

Ghost yowled and the Malkin looked up, arched his long neck and screeched victory, the last wisp of the wildborn drifting into the air. The clearing lay littered with corpses and skeletal remains. A killing field.

Ripplemist released them.

Annapurna stood, radiating fear, her tender heart unable to process such a cruel world. Darktail whispered into her ear, and she obediently sat, but with lowered ears and trembling body, looking desperate.

"The Malkin's afraid," Darktail yowled, as much to Snowpelt as anyone else.

"*He's* afraid!" she warbled.

"Afraid or not, we must stop this demon," Sosay cried fiercely. Others growled agreement, thumping their tails on the ground.

"Those weren't Wisdom Cats he sucked the life from. They weren't even healthy," Flyingtail spat, flashing long, scimitar-sharp claws. "Coward!"

Starpaw sat tall. "None of them possessed the RA, but Morsus stole their life-force anyway. Why? It can only be to add their energy to his own, to make himself stronger. Yes, he's afraid of us."

"So how do we defeat him?" Ghost growled, "I'm sure as fish-feathers not going to suck the life from innocents."

Darktail stomped his paws. "He surprised Indra. I can't imagine she expected such violence. We'll never know for sure, but I do know he's afraid. I feel it." More paw stomping, and this time others joined in.

"I feel it too," Martileena meowed. She sought Snowpelt's gaze to see if she agreed, but Snowpelt just sat there, ears drooping, looking confused and frightened. Martileena shot Darktail a withering look. "I think Starpaw's right. The Malkin gathers strength from his victims." Her gaze traveled the circle. "He'll come for each of us when he's ready."

Sosay stood, the crescent on her forehead pulsing bright blue with emotion. "Ghost, we've told only our apprentices of Morsus' treachery while he has an army of liars spreading lies. Kin are turning against us. They're not protecting themselves. At Flattail Dam ronin are everywhere, prancing before uprights, begging food. Now Blackpaw's catlings are doing it. He warns them not to, but the liars are winning with their lies."

"Windclaw's been acting strange of late," Starpaw murmured to Flyingtail, then addressed the gathering. "Remember, Morsus stole the RA of the East. He can invade our minds and use our dreams against us."

"You mean really be here? Inside us?" Annapurna asked, shuddering nose-tip to tail.

"I don't understand the question," Starpaw meowed. "Are you asking if the realm of mind is real?"

Annapurna didn't seem to hear him. Her wide eyes searched others' faces. "Maybe he's here, inside one of us right now," she whispered to no one in particular. They hunkered in silence, tucking their paws and tails close to their bodies.

"Stop that!" Ghost yowled, breaking the spell. "Fear is exactly what he wants us to feel." Some stood and shook themselves while others licked their pelts as if washing off a contagion.

The pool churned. Ripplemist rose, fixing her liquid eyes on Darktail. "Give him the RA," she commanded, pointing a shimmering paw at Ghost.

Darktail bristled with surprise. "Give him the RA of the West," she repeated, then sank into the pool. Its surface now calm, tendrils of blue mist rose into the light of the evening's first stars.

Ghost padded away from the group. He wished he could keep going, just vanish into the forest alone. If only he and Monkey could sneak off somewhere, start over where no one knew them or expected. But he couldn't, and he plopped on his rear in the pathway and lifted his eyes to Milk Mother's Spill. Had he been human, he would've cried.

Sosay came up behind him. "What's wrong?" she asked, gently nuzzling his shoulder. No answer. "Ghost?" The little wizard met her gaze, then looked away, ashamed.

Anyone could see he lacked a hero's essentials. Small, thin, a hermit by nature, left to his own he'd withdraw from everyone but Monkey and a few friends. The mission was big, huge even, and he wasn't strong or brave or capable. "My life is so strange," he murmured. "I thought I was an apprentice and would never be anything else. Then I'm a Wisdom Cat of the North with the RA of the South and now...the West too?" He looked as lost as Snowpelt. "Why me?"

Darktail ambled over. "Because Great Mother knows you can carry the power of all four RAs without becoming cruel."

Ghost trembled. "Surely not."

"Of course!" Sosay trilled. "Bent Whisker called you the Four Become One." And she danced a circle around them, her bushy white tail quivering with joy.

Darktail bunted Ghost' shoulder. "To defeat Morsus you must be given the four RAs. Don't fear them. The Malkin craves them and steals them, but theft perverts their power."

"I don't want that power," Ghost whispered, ears low to the sides of his head.

"And that's why Great Mother trusts you with it." Darktail meowed, licking one of those folded ears.

Waiting on the Guardian Stone, Monkey watched Ghost trot north across the meadow. Behind him loped the ginger apprentice called Reggie. Sosay had sent him north to learn to heal kin with leaves, roots and flowers. He seemed a shy catling, even making Ghost appear alpha.

Monkey decided she wouldn't be jealous of her beloved's attention, but be generous with her love. Ghost saw her then and Joy flooded his face. And Monkey began to understand what he already knew: he couldn't do any of this without her

Moons rose and fell and Monkey understood something else: Reggie was a blessing. He showed such talent with recognizing and preparing herbs, he could have been born in the north. Robin, who did most of the teaching, grew quite fond of him. Everyone liked humble, honest Reggie, whose friendly head bunts and shoulder nuzzles were as healing as any herbs.

Ghost spent all his time with Monkey. She'd helped him assimilate the powers of the South and was helping him again. The empathy of the west had left him throbbing like a bruise, and he needed to blend his new powers of intuition and heightened feelings with his ability to see secrets of the past. He often wondered what creature would have emerged without the tempering presence of her love.

Monkey never left his side, but even with her gentling influence, Ghost became an unnerving presence. He knew what his podmates would do before they did. He knew what they felt, what they wanted, and being northern kin, he knew what they needed for their mental and physical health. Secluding himself with Monkey was best, at least for a while. Then, Starlight told him to leave.

"I will visit the Eastern Wisdom Cats at their Crystal Aerie," Ghost told his podmates, sharing a morning meal on the grass. Monkey's face lit with somber pride. "Robin, I need you to come; the Malkin will oppose this and I'll need your help." He turned to the golden apprentice. "And you'll be our Wisdom Cat while we're gone," he said, ceremoniously tapping each of Reggie's shoulders with a paw. Reggie stammered an honored 'yes'.

The next day, Ghost and Monkey rose before the sun and went hunting. After a meal and a nap with his mate, Ghost found Robin, and they rubbed their paws in a mash of bearberries in cactus water meant to toughen their leathers. Once they left the softness of the forest floor they'd be walking on sand littered with cactus spines, pebbles and grit.

The travelers said their goodbyes by the pool, Monkey at Ghost' side, the pups dancing around them. Browser, who would accompany them a short distance, led them off at a comfortable trot, ears and tails high, but once the trail twisted behind the hill, Ghost lowered his head and slung his shoulders into a steadily increasing pace that even Browser struggled to keep.

When they reached the drainpipe, the wizard stopped and sat facing his friend. "Browser, Great Mother willing, this will be the third RA I'm given."

Browser seemed confused. "Third? You've already done three..."

Ghost looked guilty. "Yes, well, one was...a misfire...I'll tell you more when I return." Browser nodded, accepting without understanding. Ghost nuzzled his shoulder. "Do you forgive me?"

"Forgive what? There's nothing to forgive."

"Good, because I have to ask you a favor." Robin's eyes widened with apprehension. Browser only nodded. "You must promise me, that if I change, if I become like the Malkin..."

Now he understood. "No! And no and no and no! I couldn't...no, Ghost, never!"

"Browser, it wouldn't be me. It wouldn't be your friend, but something different, more powerful than the Malkin, and more dangerous." Browser stared at the trees, the sky, the ground, anything but those sea-blue eyes. "Promise me you'll protect the Green," the shaman meowed.

"I promise." Browser finally whispered, never meeting his friend's gaze. Ghost nuzzled his shoulder, turned and led Robin into the woods. Browser watched them disappear. He sat a long while before slowly padding home.

Twilight deepened. The waning moon rose. Bathed by the starlight that slipped through the latticework of tree limbs, Ghost and Robin pushed on, determined to reach Snake Tongue Gulch by sunrise.

When the sky lightened, the earth had dried beneath their paws. Hawthorn, elm and poplar gave way to oak, old gnarled oak with flaky bark and large, lobed leaves. Ravens circled noisily in the cloudless sky. The travelers' bellies responded with cries of their own and they left off their trek to hunt. The grove reeked of small prey, along with chamomile, dreamweed and long creepers of catmint growing plush in the shade of twisted trunks. After a meal of vole and mouse, the cats discovered a wide swath of the heady mint and settled in its opulence.

"We mustn't eat any though," Ghost warned as they rolled on their backs, the intoxicating scent seeping through their fur. Robin couldn't resist. Tilting his head back, he let some leaves fall into his open mouth. Then he saw Ghost was watching and spit them out.

"It was an accident," he said, rolling on his stomach and looking stern.

"Robin, we're in ghostdog territory. We'd be idiots not to keep our wits. And Morsus has spies," Ghost scolded. The apprentice ate no more. But after a sleepless night their full bellies warmed them, and they dozed the morning hours away dreaming of a sun-dappled meadow and the flutter of wings.

"Kronk! Kronk!" Frightened, the cats jumped to their paws. A raven step-step-skipped along a low branch, staring at them with one bead-bright eye. Spooked, the cats moved on, but the bird followed them to the next oak where it was joined by a second raven, then a third. Ghost and Robin quickened their pace. Another, then another and another bird added itself to a maelstrom growing above while a flapping black mass filled the branches of the nearest tree. And still more birds came. One dove down and pecked Robin's head.

"Nee-ow," he cried, scurrying off, belly scraping the ground. Ghost was close behind. More birds dove, pecking, grabbing at the cats with their talons, trying to lift them off the ground, forcing them south toward the edge of a deep gulch.

A bone-shattering "Kronk." The felines froze flat to the earth then looked up at the biggest raven they'd ever seen. Its ebony chest wider than an adult tomcat's, its wingspan was wider than a large human male was tall. The massive bird cocked its huge head sideways, staring with one golden eye. "Roak roak kronk kronk roak," it commanded its aerial armada, which landed with a whoosh and flutter in nearby trees.

The cats tensed to flee. "We mean you no harm," Ghost meowed. "We're only passing through."

"Kronk. Kronk. Yes, it's good you visit Nebula," the raven answered, bobbing his head and fluffing a mane of feathers around his neck.

"You know where we're going?" Ghost asked.

"Kronk kronk roak. My children heard you tell your podmates. They watched you leave your home." The cats' eyes widened. "Rak-ak-ak-ak-

ak. I'm Nightbeak, father and shaman for my tribe, a tribe some call a *conspiracy* or even an *unkindness*, but these words are neither accurate nor kind."

"How would you like to be called? Ghost asked.

"We are a coven. I am a warlock, my mate a witch, and all our children learn the magical arts." He leaned down, fixing them both with his glittering eye. "*White magic*, even if our wings and bodies are like a moonless night. Rak-ak-ak-ak-ak." His soft, rolling clucks sounded almost like purring.

Ghost realized he and Robin weren't understanding Nightbeak through Commonspeak, the sharing of body language, scent and intuition, but through the white magic the raven spoke of, a magic that enabled the tribe to commune with all of Great Mother's children. *Ravenspeak*, Ghost decided to call it. "You have powerful alchemy, Nightbeak."

"As do you, Ghost and Robin." Despite those warm words, Robin nervously licked his chest fur. Nightbeak leaned down toward the gray cat, bringing his golden eye close. "What troubles you apprentice?"

Robin squirmed. "My mother said your kind were bad omens, that terrible things would happen whenever you spoke to us."

Looking a bit cross, Nightbeak pulled back. He smoothed a long quill with his hooked beak. "Kronk, kronk. Your Mother is wrong."

"Was," Robin mewed with drooping ears.

"Rak-ak-ak-ak," Nightbeak purred. "As messengers we're often blamed for the bad news we bring." He fluffed then flattened his neck feathers.

"Can you see the future?" Ghost asked.

"No."

Robin was still thinking about his mother. "Can you talk to those who've passed?"

"Kronk kronk kronk. If they have a message for the living, we meet in the blackness of Beyond." He closed his eyes, tilting his head back and to one side as if he were doing just that right then. After a moment he said, "Your mother is proud of you, Robin, and happy you run with good friends, as are your sisters, father and brothers. No one suffers now." Robin gave Nightbeak a slow blink of gratitude.

"Can you hear Erasmus?" Ghost blurted, his tail lashing with excitement. Try as he might, he hadn't been able to contact his mentor, not even in waking-dreams.

Nightbeak pulled his feathers close to his body, his body close to his perch, shutting out the world, closing his eyes. At last, "I have a message for you, Ghost, but not from Erasmus. It's from Indra." A shiver ran down the cats' spines as Nightbeak swayed back and forth, his voice once more a rolling, clucking purr. "Rak-ak-ak-ak-ak-ak-ak. Beware the beast. Ghost, you can defeat him only by defeating the Malkin within you." The cats stared in silence. "He is not the evil you imagine."

"What!" They cried as one.

The raven stretched and folded his wings. "Kronk. Kronk. Just as you've been chosen, so has Morsus. Like you, he has a mission. A terrible, fearful one. Imagine the courage it took to be born so ugly, so despicable, having stones thrown at you, being starved by your own mother. Wouldn't you be angry? Wouldn't you fear and hate? Wouldn't you want to destroy the world?" Their tails swept the ground anxiously. "Morsus doesn't yet understand how he feeds the Malkin within. He's the greed, anger and foolishness that permeates the world, and if you are more of the same, how can you stop him?" The cats were stunned, but Nightbeak seemed unaffected by the spiritual bomb he'd dropped in their paws and danced along the branch with the step-step-skip of a happy raven.

"Nightbeak," Ghost called.

Eyes glowing with purpose, the raven sauntered back. "Here, I have a gift for you," he said, digging into his wing and pulling loose a long, perfect feather he let flutter down to their paws. "Use this to call my tribe and we will come. It's a flight feather to guide you on your path." The raven chief stretched to his full height and lifted his wings from his body. He faced the other ravens, who swirled above with no interest in the cats.

"Wait!" Ghost cried, still unwilling to end their meeting. "How?"

Nightbeak looked back and blinked. "We'll meet again," was all he said, and with a downward plunge of his enormous wings, glided into the pale sky. A heartbeat later he was a dot against the blue.

Robin turned to Ghost. "So, how *do* we use this feather?"

"No idea," Ghost meowed, running a paw over it. They jumped back, surprised when small glimmers of energy played over its surface.

"Nee-ow," Robin cried.

Wings rustled. Suddenly ravens were bending the branches above them, kronking and roaking and bobbing their heads.

"Thanks, we're all right," Ghost told them and just as quickly they flew away.

"We'll take turns carrying it," Robin said. "I wonder if this means the birds will follow us." But when he lifted the feather into his mouth, no energy flitted over its surface and no ravens returned.

"Like all good magic, it knows your intent," Ghost chuffed happily, then pointed with his tail toward the edge of the cliff. "We're almost to Snake Tongue Gulch."

They continued south, soon finding a path winding down into the flat expanse of hot sand. Its walls shimmered in the heat, and were much farther away than they appeared. The floor of the gulch burned the cats' paw leathers, but they'd entered where a stream flowed down from the north to join another flowing west to east, and the sand and air were cooler near the water. They picked their way through sage and succulent and primrose, then stopped to drink. No mice grew fat on forest berries here, no gophers were feeding on wild onion roots. But once they learned not to pounce on their detachable tails, the cats caught a few of the many lizards scurrying about doing push-ups on hot stones. More scales than meat, they were tough and bitter, but empty bellies are grateful.

"We mustn't linger," Ghost said. "There are no trees to climb and this is the only water." Waving his tail from one side of the gulch to the other, he added, "Ghostdogs live in those boulders." Robin finished drinking, lifted the feather from beneath his paw, and they pushed eastward. The walls of the gulch grew steeper and the creek evaporated to a trickle in a wasteland of heat and dust. Now only an occasional succulent poked above the sand, and there were no more primroses. Rounding a curve to the north-east, Ghost and Robin stared forlornly. The runnel that had made their travels bearable ended in a shallow pool. The two cats in fur coats must now bear the searing sun with nothing to drink. Without a word, they drank all they could, then pressed on, keeping thoughts of thirst to themselves. But their pace slowed as the sun rolled toward the cliff tops. By long shadows they were barely creeping forward. The canyon curved to the southeast, throwing shadows across the ground. Ghost and Robin entered the cooler shade.

"Eeeeeeeeeeeeee! Eeeeeeeeeeeeee!" A hawk shrieked. The cats jerked to a stop and looked up. "Eeeeeeeeeeeeee! Eeeeeeeeeeeeee!" the bird screeched again from atop the canyon wall.

A blue glow erupted along the edge of Nightbeak's feather. Robin dropped it with a "Neow," before catching it beneath his paw. "It stung me," he cried. "What did he say?" he asked as the hawk flew away.

"He warned us not to continue," Ghost replied.

"Maybe he's right. Maybe we shouldn't."

"You're free to go home, Robin. I mean that. Truly. But I can't." Now the canyon curved sharply eastward, and they stopped mid-stride, eyes wide and fur on end. Robin dropped the feather again.

Before them rose a labyrinth of enormous cairns, tall towers of huge stones balanced on tiny ones, carved through eons of wind and sand.

"We'll never get through this," Robin said, wiping grit from his eye with his free paw.

"We'll be fine," Ghost answered resolutely, then fished the quill from Robin's grasp. But he'd taken only a few steps before his apprentice fished it back. *Wherever you go, I follow,* Robin's eyes told his mentor. They marched forward and the stone towers closed around them. Everything changed. Sand blurred their vision and deadened smells. Distant sounds rang close by while their own voices echoed as if far away. The RA of the West whispered in Ghost' heart, telling him that he and Robin were the only living creatures in the gorge, yet they were not alone. He shuddered.

The sun dropped behind the canyon wall, bathing the world in purple light. Hungry eyes burned from the shadows, eyes like those in the southern forest. Wraiths. Spirits as old and as cruel as First Felidae, jealous of the flesh they no longer wore. *What terrors will emerge when the labyrinth is lit by moon and stars?* he wondered but said nothing to Robin, who was also quiet, his ears swiveling toward each disembodied whisper. Nightbeak's feather glowed like the sun along both edges, making it painful to hold.

Finally he dropped it, protecting it with a paw. "Tell me you hear that." he growled.

"Yes," Ghost answered. "And I know what they are. Don't tell them your name...or mine. Upon our lives, do not say our names."

Robin's eyes widened with fear. "What are they?"

"Ghouls, wraiths. I encountered some traveling south to Bent Whisker's and they begged me for my worldname. Sosay told me it's how they steal your body." Robin's scruff stood on end.

The cats moved forward in silence, doing their best to ignore the whispered pleas. Heads down, eyes focused on their path, they arrived for the third time in the same clearing. Exhausted and frightened, they tried to remember which twisting trail had led them back to the clearing again. Darkness closed around them and the whispering grew louder. Ghost feared that if they failed to exit the maze before morning, they would never get out.

Robin took the feather and padded left. It dulled. He padded right and it glowed, giving his lips a sting. He dropped it with a grunt. "You see that?"

"I did." Ghost grasped it and padded left. It went dark again. "We'll do what it says," he meowed and they re-entered hoodoo city, taking turns holding the feather. It glowed to warn them off and went dark to lead them on. The wraiths still tortured them with taunts and pleas for their names. Time slowed to the forever now. Fear grew in their hearts, slowly like the stone towers around them, and like the towers it leaned in, crushing them, suffocating hope, until at last they stumbled from the haunted, starless dome into an immense flat canyon, its wide sky lit by a backbone of stars. The travelers sank to the ground, breathing deeply. Nightbeak's feather had saved their lives. They rested only a moment before pushing on, however, for a breeze carried the scent of water, and they were very thirsty.

A little ahead the stream re-surfaced from a cleft in the wall, tumbling over rocks to feed a pool in an underground cave. The water glowed blue, sending waves of light dancing along the cave walls. But Ghost and Robin were too tired to climb down. They simply lay across the wet boulder, and lapped and lapped and lapped.

Robin took the quill and on they trekked, until at last they saw the spire rise in the distance. The Aerie soared above the narrowed gulch, glittering in the starlight. The cats sat and stared. They stared at the Aerie, the twinkling sky, the shadowy canyon walls, the undulating sand, and the Aerie again. Side by side they sat, like comfy porch dogs who'd finished their chores.

Finally, Robin grew restless. "Something's wrong."

"Neow," Ghost purred. Still, his friend's words gave him a vague feeling he should move. His thoughts drifted. He floated up and saw himself and Robin: little dots on the canyon floor waiting for nothing.

"It's a shelterveil," they said together.

The same magic that saved Hillside Den was protecting the Aerie. The kin were blessed with many shelterveils. Otherwise humans would swarm over their treasures, steal the Aerie's gemstones, cut down Harmony Tree, pollute the Scrying Pool with empty bottles and plastic straws, douse the Akashic Flame as dangerous, then chop down the Sacred Yew and scorch all life from the land to build their concrete hovels.

Now that Ghost and Robin acknowledged the magic, they were able to move forward toward the huge, square boulder atop a stone blade. The surrounding canyon walls were terraced and dotted with caves. Padways led from the canyon floor to the mesa above.

"Kin live here," Robin meowed, sniffing the air.

"Don't move," boomed a voice from the northern wall. "Please," it added softly. Ghost and Robin looked up. A slender dark gray male emerged from the shadows. He had the long hindquarters of eastern kin and an amazingly thick plume.

"Flyingtail," the wizard called, "It's us, Ghost and Robin."

The sentry leaped. He floated to the canyon floor and crept warily toward the visitors. "So it is," he meowed, flicking his tail for emphasis. "We're careful since..." he let his voice fade, unwilling to speak of Indra's murder. Ghost and Robin looked down. Flyingtail looked past them. "You came through the canyons?" he asked nervously, his eyes narrowing with suspicion while Ghost and Robin considered what might be good to admit and what might not. Finally, in a friendlier tone, Flyingtail added, "You're really brave, you know that? And lucky."

Ghost relaxed but Robin squirmed. "You don't go through the hoodoos?" That was not good to admit, and Flyingtail's eyes narrowed again. "We had help," Robin added quickly, trying to ease the tension by bringing up the magic feather.

"Help? Did anything touch you? Tell me your clan names now."

Ghost knew the drill. "I'm Ghost of Hillside Pod."

"I'm Ghost' apprentice, Robin of Hillside Pod, and this is our help." He touched the quill beneath his paw with his nose.

Flyingtail looked down and jerked back, surprised. "A squawkbeak feather?"

Gingerly, Robin pushed it toward the eastern cat. "It was a gift."

Flyingtail sniffed it end to end. The hunting skills of northern cats were legend, and he could easily imagine Ghost or Robin snagging such a bird, even though eastern clans wouldn't dream of preying on Great Mother's Messengers. "A gift?"

"From Nightbeak, their shaman. Its magic showed us a way through the hoodoos," Robin purred.

Flyingtail sat in thought, staring at them for another long moment. "Don't know about that feather," he said at last, "but I do believe you're untouched," He rose, lifted and extended his rear legs one after the other in a spine-limbering stretch, his eyes glowing with pleasure. Even his thin black lips seemed to smile as he spread his toes as far apart as possible. His trills were infectious. Ghost and Robin both yawned hugely. "Well, bug juice and lizard ears! Let's go to the Aerie," the sentry chortled.

"Lizards don't have ears," Robin whispered to Ghost, who shushed him with a twitch of his own.

Flyingtail led them up a crumbling trail in the northern wall to the mesa above, where a sea of tall grass swayed beneath the stars, and a full moon cut a path of silver light into the distance. The smell of wild hare tickled their noses and their pelts fluffed with pleasure. "Why *didn't* we come this way?" Robin again whispered.

"Brightmoon ceremonies are beautiful," Flyingtail called over his shoulder, heading for a twisted pine whose tortured branches grew out over the gorge. He tiptoed to the end of one, then leaped for the spire, landing as lightly as a floating seedpod on a path winding to the top. "Nebula just told me he waits in the capstone," he said swinging his great tail. Robin wondered. He didn't hear anything, then realized: *these are the mental kin.*

Ghost followed Flyingtail along the branch and through the air, landing on the narrow path with a thud. Robin came next with a powerful leap, but only his front paws caught in the pebbly dirt. "Nee...ow!" he yelped, releasing Nightbeak's feather to the wind. His mournful eyes watched it sail into the dark, his claws scraping for a paw-hold, hind legs kicking the air. Ghost grabbed him by the scruff and pulled him to safety.

Without a word Flyingtail leaped over them both, raced back along the bough and down the trail into the gully where the raven's totem skipped in the night breeze. He caught it beneath a paw, then with a proud shake of his head, lifted the quill into his mouth. A spark flashed against his fangs and he shot off the ground, a ball of electrified fur with splayed toes, his tail straight as a frying pan handle.

"He believes in the feather now," Robin said, licking his paw.

Leaning against the spire wall, the ground-pounders followed Flyingtail up the path to the capstone. Even glancing at the canyon floor made their stomachs jump, and they were relieved when at last they stood on the widened path at the top. The capstone had one open end. It faced east, so all who sat within were privy to the beauty of rising suns, setting moons, shining stars and planets almost bright enough to cast shadows. Tonight was brightmoon.

Ghost and Robin stood at the entrance, their bodies haloed by moonlight, while Flyingtail joined his clan in a semi-circle before them. Nebula crowned its center. He was enormous, half again as large as any of the other Wisdom Cats, and they were all large. Despite a sprinkling of white stars on his chest, throat, and muzzle, he was black, genuinely blue-black, not the black that turns deep brick red beneath the summer sun, the black that upon close inspection has dark-gray tabby stripes. No. Nebula was blackness itself, the bottomless pit, the vacuum of space. He was the void with a splattering of stars and two golden eyes. *He looks like Milk Mother's Spill,* Ghost thought. *But dangerous.*

The visitors lowered their heads hello but Nebula didn't respond, making the clan cats nervous. Flyingtail rose in greeting until an angry thump of Nebula's tail sat him back down. The massive cat continued to stare at the intruders, finally growling, "Why are you here?"

"How can you not know why!" Robin hissed through the quill, tail lashing.

"I hear your thoughts on it, fledgling." The eastern cat spat with a show of fangs. "Answer my question."

Robin dropped the feather, trapping it beneath a paw, and was about to launch into a screed on Nebula's lack of manners when Ghost said: "We bring a message from Indra."

A tremor rolled down Nebula's spine, raising a ridge of his coal-black fur. "How dare you," he spat, rising with a panther's grace. Ears pinned, he crept toward his visitors as if stalking prey. "You know nothing, northern cat. You have no psychic abilities, fraud."

"But I have this," Ghost said calmly. He glanced at Robin, who pushed the feather between himself and the panther, who looked down and froze. When those golden eyes met Ghost' again, they were filled with wonder. He understood what Flyingtail hadn't: Ghost had the trust of the Father of Ravens, Great Mother's messenger. *He is entrusted? How?* "Indra waits for you patiently," the little shaman said. "She said she loves you more than ever, but you're not to hurry to her, for you have much to do." The panther dropped his belly to the floor and stared at his paws. Ghost sat before him. "I can help you. Tell me your dreams."

"Neow, neow dreams, dreams...neow," echoed through the chamber.

Nebula growled petulantly. "Even with a raven feather, what does a forager of berries and twigs know about dreams?" He lashed his tail, anger flashing through his slitted eyes. Never the friendliest kin, Nebula had always guarded his emotions, even with so much at stake. His heart was raw with pain, and screaming for relief. At least part of him didn't believe sinking into darkness was the answer, and that part of him, that glimmer of hope knew Ghost had come to help. But it was still just a glimmer.

Intuition told Ghost Nebula was slipping into the Malkin's grip. He couldn't let that happen. He sat tall. "I *am* a healer with berries and twigs, and Great Mother has blessed me with the RA of the South and the RA of the West as well. Despite my foolishness and weakness, She's given me the task of defeating the Malkin." Nebula's clan mates were won over, but the panther still wavered. Ghost felt a secret, something Nebula believed was his shame, and hiding it kept him isolated. "Know this," the little wizard continued, grandly swelling his chest and sweeping his tail, "I am Ghost of the North and I *will* defeat the Malkin. If I must poison my flesh and lay it at his paws to devour, I will destroy him." He met Nebula's stare with equally fierce eyes. "I will heal you, and you will help me."

"You *can't* heal me," the black cat hissed, then looked down. "Can you?" he asked, embarrassed he still held a sliver of hope.

"Yes. Nebula, Great Mother sees us as we are, and She finds no fault."

Nebula dropped his burden with such intensity, the air was palpable with relief. He seemed even larger, and he definitely looked stronger. His eyes opened, his pupils wide and clear as he began his confession."...I can't dream. Imagine that." Feeling humbled, he hung his head. "The Elder Cat of the East can't dream. That is, again and again I dream only this: I watch my beloved Indra die, nothing else. Again and again I watch Indra die...and I'm the one who killed her."

"No. The Malkin killed Indra."

The panther's face contorted with pain. "I'm the one who sent her to her death. Indra went to Darkmoon Gathering in my place. I remained at the Aerie."

"That doesn't matter. The Malkin killed Indra," Ghost repeated. "He uses this cruel lie to weaken you."

Nebula lowered his head even more. "I'm so tired."

Warmth rose in Ghost' belly. It rolled like waves through his body, and out his paws. He'd never felt anything like it before, but ollowing his inner voice, he pressed his forehead to Nebula's shoulder, and healing warmth surged into the black cat. Eyes shut, Ghost discovered he could 'feel-see' the landscape of Nebula's spirit, and found a knot wrapped like a black serpent around the panther's heart. Ghost sent the warm, healing energy to Nebula's strangled heart, and the snake withered. The instant it was gone, Nebula pulled back, and for the first time since he'd lost Indra, he felt grief without shame. At last he could mourn.

To those gathered around the two cats, Ghost and their leader seemed to merge within a warm light. When it was over, Nebula touched his nose to the wizard's. "I've heard it said northern cats are kind and wondered if you weren't just weak. I see now you are *not* weak and you *are* kind." He and his clan mates stepped to the side. Moonlight revealed a high-desert feast. They had everything from lizards to black beetles to hairy spiders that lived beneath the sand. There were some crunchy brown birds, a few rodents, even a few stringy longear with over-sized ears and feet. Gourds filled with the magical blue water stood in the corners. Ravenous, the northern cats fell upon the prey, tasting even the most exotic desert delights. Soon their bellies were full, and they realized they were exhausted. Nebula had already curled on his side, his head tucked into his legs. Others followed. Ghost settled at the opening, mesmerized by the brilliant desert stars. *Great Mother, I am so small beneath your sea of lights, and so blessed to be one of them.* Closing his eyes, he ran through forests in the Green.

"Wake up!" Ghost opened his eyes; his muscles felt stiff and his head was pounding. Flyingtail stood over him. The travelers had been given only a short nap, hardly enough to heal from their journey. He looked around for Robin and found him tucking Nightbeak's feather beneath a stone. The apprentice met his gaze, limped toward him on swollen paws, shook dust from his pelt and sat, spreading his toes to clean out the dried blood.

Nebula stood at the chamber's open end. "Come, we shall meet Cloudrunner," he meowed, then led the visitors up a narrow path to the top of the capstone. A breeze greeted them as they crested the Aerie. The moon had set and the dome of sky was at its blackest, so black it seemed tinged with red, and teeming with stars, more stars, brighter stars than they'd ever imagined, shining from different depths in the heavens. Some smaller and closer, some larger, brighter, and farther away. Hundreds of thousands of lights in the sky. It was dizzying, and Ghost and Robin were grateful when Nebula motioned them to sit at his side.

From the quartz-rich floor along the eastern brink rose six pinnacles, each with minute, faceted gemstones covering a crystalline core, each one a different size and color. The most northern was no taller than a cat tail, its pink quartz core adorned with rubies. The second spire was twice as high, covered with imperial topaz, and glittered orange. The third peak was half-a-tail higher than the second and smothered in citrine. The fourth pinnacle, twice as tall as the third, sparkled with emeralds, the fifth and sixth descending respectively, the fifth flashing pure aquamarine, the most southern glimmering with gemstone quality amethysts. The visitors sat transfixed, only gradually aware of the hum between the towers and crystal spheres resting in channels between the peaks.

An eastern cat settled before each sphere. Nebula nodded to Flyingtail, who placed his paws on the red-orange sphere and rolled it between the red and orange obelisks. The humming morphed into a single note and a cloud formed above them. *They call Cloudrunner with sound,* the shaman realized.

Starpaw's new apprentice, a white female named Windsong, pushed her orange-yellow sphere between the second and third crystal columns and a higher note harmonized with the first. The cloud darkened.

Skyleaper nosed his yellow-green ball into the notch between the yellow and green towers and a third note merged with the first two, creating an intensely satisfying tone. The dark cloud formed a funnel in the center of the Aerie and the black-and-silver shape of Cloudrunner was visible within. Lightning raced along his spine and down his limbs, sparking off his paws. The electricity in the air lifted pelts and caused hearts to thump. Cloudrunner was weather itself, powerful, unpredictable, and dangerous. Ghost marveled at the magic of the eastern kin.

Nebula's new apprentice, Windpaw, deftly rolled her green-blue sphere into the slot between the fourth and fifth towers and the first note repeated an octave higher. The funnel grew less dense and the eyes of the sky-god, wielder of thunder and lightning, bored into Ghost'. Now Nebula's second acolyte, Windpaw's twin brother Windclaw, would roll the final sphere into its notch, creating the sound that would free Cloudrunner...but it wasn't to be.

A terrible purpose flashed in his eyes as he leaped from his sphere, and pushed a smaller stone into the empty slot. The harmony of the towers became a screeching caterwaul. The noise was unbearable, especially to eastern kin, whose big ears were so sensitive they could count the mice scrabbling behind canyon walls. They collapsed on the floor of the Aerie, folding their ears down with trembling paws. Ghost and Robin weren't as badly affected, but they grew nauseous and found it difficult to move. They both retched. Cloudrunner clawed at the walls of his prison, lightning streaking down his back and off his tail.

Windclaw wasn't affected at all. He turned toward Ghost and glared. *He means to kill me.* Ghost unsheathed his claws, and arched his back. But Windclaw was a step ahead, and leaped across the aerie, landing on Ghost' back. The shaman lurched forward and back, his legs bending under the weight, and with a sickening crunch, he collapsed. Robin yowled.

Windclaw whipped around and crawled up Ghost' spine like a venomous spider, sinking his claws to the bone. Blood rose through the silver pelt and pooled on the aerie floor.

"He can't die! Great Mother, please, he can't die," Robin shrieked, careening toward his mentor by the force of his will. Windclaw parted the fur on Ghost' neck with his fangs. He could see the artery pulse. In a heartbeat, it would be over.

But Ghost didn't accept that. Through the cacophony, the weight and the pain, he filled his lungs with air, and roaring like a king of beasts, he

237

rolled and pinned his startled enemy beneath him. Windclaw was strong and they rolled again. On his back now, Ghost bit and clawed and pummeled Windclaw's belly until he kicked him off. They both stood. They circled, heads down, then flew at each other, slamming together and spinning across the blood-splattered floor in a snarling mass of knives and fur. Heaving and frothing, they pulled apart. Ghost had the worst of it. His back to the Aerie's edge, Windclaw prowled back and forth before him. With undulating cries, the warriors measured each others' strength, looking for a heartbeat of weakness, the opening to attack. Windclaw was younger, stronger, an athlete. Ghost was losing blood.

Suddenly, it was on. Windclaw crashed into him, pushing, scratching, biting, pushing, until all that kept the shaman from tumbling into the gulch were his prayers to stand against the pain, and the long, curved claws of his hind feet digging into the Aerie's edge. *Great Mother, I must defeat Morsus. I know you won't take me now.* Ghost' body flooded with strength and he pushed himself and Windclaw from the brink, but he couldn't get around him, and readied himself for the final strike.

Windclaw lunged. For Ghost, time distended and the world slowed. He had an eon to move aside as Windclaw sailed past and out into the void. He didn't want to kill Windclaw anymore than he wanted to die, so he twisted around, snagged Windclaw's flanks, swung him back unto the Aerie, and collapsed on top of him. They lay in a breathless heap.

It was over. Ghost had won, but when they rose and separated, he saw no justice in Windclaw's eyes. No mercy would be returned for mercy given. *It's a battle to the death and saving Windclaw has taken the last of my strength. The death will be mine after all.*

To others lying incapacitated about the aerie, Windclaw launched in a blur, but for Ghost the world slowed again. The blaring towers faded into a single dull and faraway note while his killer floated toward him, claws gleaming in the rising light of dawn. Baring his fangs, he yowled, leaving a wake of sudsy red bubbles in the air. Acceptance wrapped Ghost like a sun-warmed pelt. His remorse was for those who would suffer because he failed to defeat the Malkin. *I didn't keep my promise to Nebula. I tried. I did my best.* He thought of Monkey and grieved. *I promised to come home, but I'll never see her again. But she'll be proud of me, and Hillside Pod will care for her...and the kits.* In that moment Ghost knew about the coming kits. Standing in the cold morning air, blood flowing from his wounds, trembling and too weak to fight, he grieved for what he'd left undone. The killer was almost upon him.

Big and gray, it flew in from the side. It knocked Windclaw flat. Robin! Robin straddled the assassin's back, poised to end his treachery. Then he saw the moss in Windclaw's ears, and with jerks of his nibble teeth, pulled it free. Like other eastern cats, Windclaw buckled beneath the screaming towers. Robin crept to the last channel, rolled the offending stone into the abyss and the correct one into its notch.

A pleasant harmony filled the air, and the eastern cats staggered to their paws, Nebula first. He leaped on Windclaw, pinned him with a paw and flurried him with the other. Windclaw lay on his back, defeated. "This is not the time to call forth our Spirit Cat," Nebula told his kin, and they each rolled their sphere back to its original position. Cloudrunner faded, and the quiet hum between the gemstone spires returned. "Why?" the Elder Cat asked, returning his attention to the traitor.

Windclaw rolled on his side and cowered. "Master told me he'd kill my sister if I didn't murder the silver cat." He glanced at Ghost, ashamed.

"Master!" Nebula spit. "Who is this master?"

Windclaw squirmed. "Morsus," he whispered.

"You're a bigger fool than I realized." Nebula chuffed, turning from Windclaw in disgust. "Thank Great Mother your sister doesn't share your stupidity." He looked expectantly at Windpaw who sat with paws demurely before her, staring sadly at her brother. At that moment the sun crested the eastern mountains and the spires caught fire, flashing gemstone lights across the aerie floor. Windclaw used the momentary distraction to leap to the top of the emerald spire. He stared into the gully. The Malkin had demanded he throw himself down after killing Ghost, but he had failed, and he didn't want to die. His mind churned. The ugly hairless cat, for all his threats and dangerous spies, didn't feel so powerful here. He gave his sister a slow blink of love, pushed with his long hind legs, and leaped toward the northern mesa.

"Don't leave me!" she yowled, beneath his sailing body.

Landing safely, Windclaw turned and faced her. "I've no home now. I can't be trusted."

"That's not true!"

"Yes, it is," Nebula said flatly and Windpaw lowered her gaze, heartbroken. Her brother raced away.

"He'll redeem himself," she said. "He's not evil. He will."

"No. The Malkin will have him killed. That's the price of failure," Nebula meowed.

For a heartbeat, Windpaw looked upset, then a beatific smile spread over her face. "Not for him," she murmured.

Ghost needed to sit, then collapsed, his wounds on fire. He laid his head on crimson paws. *So much blood,* he thought, feeling it ooze away. He floated on it, bright and metallic, unable to stop it from leaving his body. *So much blood.* Robin bent over him. Robin's kind, worried eyes, haloed with bursts of light. "Robin, help me," he called feeling as if someone lifted him, brought him to the sea and dropped him on the water. "Robin," he cried, waves crashing over his sinking body. "Robin, tell Monkey I tried to come home." His voice sounded thick through billows of salty red. Waves of blood crashing...receding...crashing. Deeper and deeper he sank. Into the abyss where the world was dark and quiet, and the waves now pounded far away on the surface, where light had many colors. "Robin, tell Monkey I love her..." and the world blinked out.

🐾   🐾   🐾

Scrapper waited in the grass near the drainpipe, leaping to his paws when a very different Ghost and a very different Robin burst through the undergrowth. Robin was larger, more muscular, and walked with the self-aware bearing of a Wisdom Cat. Ghost was smaller than ever, with a pinched face and skeletal ribs. Patches of his body had no fur where abscesses had burst, leaving oozing holes that continually scabbed over, broke open and scabbed again. Robin worried Ghost' Fetch had followed him home, and Scrapper felt it too.

Later that night, the travelers gathered with the pod around their prey pile, feasting and sharing stories. They all had so many questions, but Ghost lacked the strength to answer. He left Robin to explain, retiring with Monkey to their snuggery. She'd made a fuss about their nest, freshening the moss, mixing furleaf, chamomile, and rue into the lichen. They groomed each other, Ghost with a drowsy purr, Monkey licking his wounds meticulously clean, then rubbing them against cactus water. Ghost relaxed, rolling on his back, stretching his neck for her touch. He told her how he'd slept for half a turn of the moon while Robin nursed him back from near-death. He described the Aerie and its Crystal towers, how the eastern cats called Cloudrunner, how the RA ceremony had been held at night beneath an orgy of stars. He told her about his bond with Nebula and when he finished, she told him about the kittens. He pretended to be surprised and she pretended not to know he was pretending.

Ghost healed slowly, struggling to balance the RAs of air, fire, and water, each wanting dominion of his heart and mind. The only RA for which he'd been trained, earth, was the one he'd been denied. Erasmus was still missing.

But Monkey was a diligent helpmate, always cleaning his wounds, protecting them with cactus water, and he was healing. Until one night, missing her mate's warmth, she woke and found him pacing in the big room. "What's wrong?" she cried.

Ghost turned toward her voice, his eyes as sightless as faraway suns. "He tells lies with fair faces."

"What? Who?" Monkey padded to him and licked his ears.

The licking had always calmed him, but not tonight. Tonight Ghost sat looking through her, speaking to spirits she couldn't see. "The good do nothing. They do nothing until their own...and the White Truck...the White Truck..." he whispered, now looking into her eyes, sending a shudder down her spine. She heard a scuffle and turned. The kin of Hillside Pod had crowded into the room.

Browser padded to them. "What's wrong?" he asked.

"It's the RAs," Monkey rasped. "They're too much for him."

Robin's scruff rose. "Did he say so?"

"Yes," Monkey cried. "But did you listen? All those energies pulling him apart!" *Guess it suits you, letting him fulfill the Prophecy while you live your lives. At least you, Robin, tried...you care, with your sideways ears and tucked tail.* She knew she was being unfair, but she couldn't help herself.

Robin was stunned. Not by the tongue lashing, but because he heard Monkey's thoughts as clearly as her words. *This is the RA of the East, the power of mind, a power foreign to me...as it was to Ghost...Ghost the healer, now a seer and an empath who hears thoughts. He hears me.*

Ghost rolled his eyes upward toward his second, and bared his fangs. Monkey hissed, fearing the poison in his wounds had reached his brain, but Robin heard his cries. *It hurts! It hurts!* Ghost careened to the Guardian, tumbled off the far side and rolled down the hill into the rosemary hedge. Yowling, Monkey ran after him. Browser leaped from the stone to the hedge in a single bound. He bent down to scruff Ghost and carry him home.

"Stop!" Robin cried. Browser looked back and the wizard slipped beneath the bush. Browser followed and again Robin yowled, "Let him go. He knows what he's doing." Now they all loped down the hill and into the meadow, where they saw it: the sphere of lights, millions of minuscule suns rotating and orbiting, crackling toward them. Ghost staggered forward and threw himself into the light furnace, a small cry of relief escaping his lips. Within this mass of exploding galaxies, for a heartbeat the pod cats saw something else: a white cat shedding blue-hot stars. Then Starlight merged with Ghost and both disappeared in a blinding flash. Rosie shrieked and Monkey caterwauled. Had Robin not grabbed her scruff, she would have followed Ghost into oblivion. Heartbroken, she hung from Robin's jaws as the stars spread apart and spiraled outward from an empty center where Ghost and Starlight had fused as one. The spinning lights engulfed the kin, supernovas flashing into existence and dissolving before their eyes.

Then the lights were gone. Starlight was gone. Ghost lay on his side in the grass next to the rosemary hedge, his chest heaving gently up and down. His pelt as silky as a kit's, his wounds were healed, his mind was calmed. Robin released Monkey who threw herself on Ghost. "Now you are truly the Four Become One," Robin said. The shaman looked up and smiled.

17 – HEARTBREAK

Bent Whisker pushed a small log into the flames. He'd augured from darkness til dawn, growing increasingly agitated. "If anything happens to me, Sosay is to take my place," he muttered, not for the first time that night.

The two Wisdom Cats sitting to either side regarded him sadly. "Stop talking about that," Tinypaw mewled, stretching her paws before her and fanning her tiny toes. "It's morbid."

Bent Whisker stared at the flames. "The time comes for each of us to speak of such things. Mine is now." He turned gentle eyes to the handsome, dark-swirl tabby. "Smokepelt, tell Sosay that Reggie is ready to receive the RA. She will know, but tell her that is also my wish." Smokepelt rose to his paws and stared worriedly at his Elder.

"Bent Whisker, Reggie's been with northern kin since Darkmoon of the Green Moon, and Sosay's with Blackpaw's clan, helping queens with their birthings."

"I know where Reggie and Sosay are, Smokepelt. I'm tired, not crazy." Then regretting his harsh tone, whispered, "What I have augured this night, is too terrible to believe. But again and again Solara shows me..." His ears and tail drooped.

Trying to comfort him, Smokepelt pressed his muscular flank against Bent Whisker's gaunt frame. "Let me help you to your nest, Elder. Perhaps after sleeping the flames will speak more kindly."

"Perhaps," his mentor said, and trembling with exhaustion, permitted himself to be guided to the rise encircling the inside of the hollow tree. Night had given way and dabs of pale light peeked through the vines above them. *Bent Whisker has never looked so ragged and frail,* Smokepelt worried, nudging him upward. The Elder Cat slowed, then stopped, leaning over his companion to stare at the apprentice by the fire.

"Tinypaw, you must go to Sosay and bring her here. She's tending the pod at Flattail Dam."

"Now?"

"Now! Now!" Bent Whisker rasped, chest heaving with emotion. "She's not safe!" Turning frightened eyes to Smokepelt, he whimpered, "We cannot lose her!"

"What's wrong? What's happening?"

"Sosay is to take my place. You will be her second." The dark cat nodded.

Bent Whisker sagged to the ramp, lifting his face to the dome of ivy, his sight focused far away. "The White Truck...run...run," he cried, then, "Great Mother, they will all die!" He slumped. Smokepelt bent over him, cradling the wizened face between his paws. The seer was gone. The dark cat yowled. Tinypaw froze, unsure what to do.

"Go, like he said, Tinypaw! Go now! Run!" Leaving the door in the floor ajar, she dove into the tunnel and shot from the tree trunk, galloping north as fast as her little paws could move. She would be too late.

The light of a sun soon rising crept down the tunnel and Blackpaw opened his eyes. As always, he was first to rise. Shaking leaf debris from his pelt, he padded to his second's mossy nest.

"What?" Whitewhiskers asked, stretching his gleaming white paws before him.

"A good morning is coming," the pod leader answered. "And it's time to hunt."

The tuxedo's huge whiskers curved downward with his yawn and he rose, lifting his rear legs and spreading his toes in a stretch. "Should we take Sosay?" They glanced at her, curled like a snail and deep in sleep.

"No. She's worn from tending to the queens and their newborns." Feeling energy directed her way, with closed eyes Sosay licked her shoulder, then fell back into her dreams, comforted as they all were by the smell of milk, the purring of kits, and the trills of loving mothers.

Their burrow was a perfect sanctuary. Abandoned long ago by flattails, it had slowly dried out as poplars and willows sprung up along the bank where it rested, anchoring it with their roots. For countless turns of the moon, the sluggish current had reinforced its walls with dead branches and when the kin at last re-purposed it for their den, it seemed impregnable. It even had a bolt hole, once underwater, now emptying into reedy mud at the pond's edge. And it wasn't the only discarded den the pod was using. There were half a dozen or so, but Blackpaw's was the largest and home to the clan's nursing queens. The only males permitted inside were Blackpaw and his second, Whitewhiskers, who had as yet not found a mate and boasted no offspring. He was young, only eighteen moons, but intelligent, strong, and loyal, and Blackpaw trusted him completely.

Flattail Dam Pod had been blessed with four new litters, two of them the previous sunrise. Blackpaw gazed affectionately at his dozing mate, Pebblepaw. He licked her forehead, gave their kits a nosing, then crawled along the tunnel toward the opening, Whitewhiskers behind him. The pod leader paused before stepping into the light. "Something's wrong," he whispered, flicking his tail.

"What is it?" Frozen in a crouch, they craned their necks and rolled their ears forward.

"Too quiet." Not one feathertail chirped in the trees. Blackpaw and Whitewhiskers waited, jaws slightly parted, using scent glands in the the roofs of their mouths. Nothing came to them but the stench of human. Not uncommon as some were always on the bridge. "Man scent is strong today, unusually strong," Blackpaw said.

"Should we go?" Whitewhiskers asked.

Blackpaw glanced back at the nests full of life. The queens must be fed. Yet he waited. *What would King Browser do? Browser would be brave and hunt for his family.* They padded from the tunnel.

Whoomph! Down came the nets.

"Yeeoooww! Waaahhh Owaaahh ow wow wow ow yeaow!" Whisking his net into the air, the tall-walker slammed Blackpaw's spine into the ropes. He twisted, bucked, jerked, bit, clawed, hissed and spit, but the braided nylon cut deeper into his pelt. It caught painfully in his mouth, and he tasted blood. Squeezing an arm through the net, he clawed frenziedly at the upright who held him. His claws scraped furrows in the man's leather gloves, nothing more. The White Truck loomed closer with every step of his leather-booted captor. Blackpaw wailed miserably. Thrown face down in a cage, the ropes were yanked from his body. The lock clanged behind him. He would die here. Soon.

His cell was so cramped he could barely turn his head, but to his left he saw Whitewhiskers, unconscious. *Perhaps it's better to not know,* Blackpaw told himself, straining to see more. Row after row of cages were stacked floor to ceiling and Blackpaw had seen three trucks. The Leatherboots were filling them with friends and family he'd known since birth. Kin moaned with injuries; some pissed in fear on the unfortunates beneath them. Some didn't care they were pissed on, crouched in a furious silence they would take to their death. Blackpaw trembled with rage.

"Run! Everybody run! White Truck!" he howled before the door swung shut and his cries fell only on the captured.

"That black cat was a monster! Did you see how big he was?" the two-legged gulped, drawing his arms far apart to show the size of his courage as well as the cat's enormity. "Scary big!"

"Yeah and I bet there's more just like him in that burrow," Bleggs sneered. "You almost missed it, so close to the water. Go clean it out." The Leatherboot tramped back to the den.

Tinypaw crouched on a high branch, unable to tear her eyes from the carnage below. Countless uprights armed with nets and lightning-sticks surrounded the lake, trampling the grass beneath their boots, splattering mud with the wheels of their trucks. Kin leaped from their nests in futile attempts to escape: old toms and crones, young bucks, queens, and catlings barely old enough to leave the nursery, all scooped up and tossed into cages where not one would be acquitted. Their crime was being homeless, and the punishment was always death.

The little female drew deep, ragged breaths searching in vain for Sosay, blaming herself for not arriving soon enough to warn her or the southern pod. Leaves rustled behind her. She shook so hard she almost fell as she whipped around, fangs and claws ready. Pelts on end and frozen with fear, Nit and Kit hunkered on the branch.

Blackpaw screamed. Sosay leaped to her paws, awake and ready to race from the den to help him, but his cries were a warning, so she dropped her belly to the dirt and crept toward the entrance. A Leatherboot stood a mouse-tail from her nose, preventing their one chance at freedom. The clan's world had fallen. Leatherboots armed with nets and pain-sticks guarded the entrances and exits of the burrows she could see. She assumed from the stench of terror and chaos in the air, they had the rest as well. Sosay backed down the tunnel to the trembling queens. She couldn't speak. So many newborns to carry to safety. And where was that?

The new mothers surmised from Sosay's drooping ears and tail whatever she'd seen wasn't encouraging. Suddenly Graytail scruffed her largest kit and bolted toward the entrance. "No, stop!" Sosay yowled, but the new mother had panicked. The Leatherboot turned, a net swept down and a stunned Graytail and her baby were gone. The queens set up a miserable clamor.

"Silence!" Sosay snarled. Pushing down her fear and grief, she scruffed Graytail's two remaining kits and placed them one by one in Pebblepaw's snuggery. "We'll escape out the rear," she said, crawling over the nests and squeezing into the narrow tunnel. She was halfway to the exit when a pain stick flashed in the sun. Sosay froze. The tunnel was so narrow she had to back out rear-first, graceless and defeated, but she put her best face on. "We'll save that way for later," she lied. "They'll think poor Graytail was the only one and go away." the queens knew it wasn't true. They also knew they could trust Sosay. She'd do anything to save them. Muffling their cries, they settled into their snuggeries while Sosay hunkered in the front.

The morning wore on while desperate kin dashed for freedom. Only a few escaped. Gradually, fewer and fewer bolted from the dens. Mostly older cats, in pain or infirm with age, were forced out of hiding by poles and men who stomped and yelled. Frightened, they crawled out on their bellies and collapsed in the grass, waiting for the end.

Bleggs swaggered to Wilson, who hung about the entrance of Blackpaw's burrow, glum-faced and head down. "Anything else come out of here?" he demanded.

"No," Wilson answered flatly.

Bleggs' small eyes darted across Wilson's face. "Well then, we've got to force them out. Do something."

"I think the burrow's empty."

Bleggs gave him a hard look and stomped off. "Anything come outta here?" He grunted at the guard standing before the rear entrance.

"Nothin'."

Bleggs lifted his cap and wiped his forehead. "Wilson, climb on the roof and check if something's inside."

"The roof? Seriously?"

"We've caught over thirty ferals and only one was a nursing queen. Guess where she came from," Bleggs said, sweeping his beefy hand toward the den.

Wilson hated what Bleggs was doing. He hated everything about this day. He'd dreaded it since he'd heard the plans, and it didn't disappoint. Every moment had been hell. But now at the end, being told to lure young mothers and their newborns to their deaths was more than he could bear. He stared at his soul-dead boss without moving. "Do what I tell you," Bleggs ordered.

Slowly the tall man turned and faced the mound, grasping his net pole to balance his climb. The den quivered, dirt and leaves falling away with every step.

"There's no opening," he said, walking the roof.

"Use your flashlight," Bleggs commanded and Wilson dropped to his hands and knees. Pressing his face to the branches, he aimed the light down. Half a dozen queens recoiled, making themselves wide and flat to hide their babies. Wilson and Sosay stared into each other's eyes, both their hearts pounding hard enough to burst. Wilson pulled away. "Nothing in here, boss. Empty, just like I thought." He stood and began his descent. The lodge shook. A branch splintered. Wilson lifted his foot, dropping it on a branch too flimsy for his weight. "Arghh!" he screamed as his leg crashed through the roof to his thigh. He tried to free himself with his other leg and it crashed through too. He twisted and flailed about, seeking a handhold to keep him from sliding inside. At that crucial moment his intent to help the wildborn welled up within. *I can't help them stuck inside their den,* he told himself and calmed his mind. Pulling himself free became a simple task, and he soon crouched on what remained of the roof. Despite Sosay's warnings, the mother cats wailed throughout the ordeal, but not as loudly as Wilson. He made sure of it. Once they quieted, he began to climb down the shuddering den.

Bleggs thought he should help. "This way," he yelled, lumbering toward Wilson, his arms open and up. He tripped on a rock and fell forward, his mighty chest and belly landing like a battering ram against the den. The shuddering knocked Wilson off balance and he took a bottom-first ride to the ground in an avalanche of splinters and mud. He scrambled to his feet and began pulling debris from what had been the entrance, while Bleggs dusted off his uniform and his pride.

Grabbing Wilson by the shoulder, he pulled him away. "Stop. It's dangerous."

The tall man stared at the wreckage. "But...but..." he said, choking on the horror of it.

"But, but..." Bleggs taunted, "It's empty. You said so." A mean smile flit over his face while Wilson slumped, unable to dodge a clap on the back. "Good job," Bleggs snickered, lifted a whistle to his lips and blew. The Leatherboots gathered their gear, got in their trucks and drove away. Bleggs sat in his truck finishing paperwork. Wilson stood outside leaning against it, staring at the desolation they left behind. The silence was deafening.

Miraculously, Sosay and the queens survived both cave-ins and thanks to Wilson, the roof had an opening through which they could breath and might possibly escape. The mothers licked and nursed their kits, grateful none of them had been injured. *Now to the business of getting out,* Sosay thought. Both ends were sealed and the hole was too far above them to leap out. Only a tangle of twigs hung down, nothing strong or safe enough for a mother scruffing kits. *It's hopeless,* she fretted, and the queens began to wail again. This time she let them. But soon their little patch of sky filled with another miracle, and Tinypaw, Nit and Kit peered down into the dark, and cried for survivors.

"We're here," Sosay meowed, "but we can't get out."

"Help me," Tinypaw said to the twins and the three of them wrapped their jaws around a branch and pulled it loose, but stopped when the surrounding ones only sank into a more dangerous maze and a dirt cloud filled the air.

"No use, no use," Sosay coughed. "You'll kill us."

Tinypaw thought. "Can you pass the kits up?" The queens nodded they could.

"Feed them," Sosay cautioned. "This might take a while."

Pebblepaw's face furrowed with worry. "They'll get free though, right?"

"Pebblepaw, Great Mother is with us even when it storms," Sosay purred, licking her friend's ear.

"Blackpaw?" the mother cat whispered shakily. Sosay looked down.

Pebblepaw's body jerked in a reflex of pain, then she drew herself up and returned to the mound of dirt to nurse Blackpaw's three kittens plus the two from Graytail she would raise as her own.

Nit and Kit maneuvered their small bodies down tenuous twigs into the den. Once a baby was passed by its mother safely into Kit's jaws, she would lift it to Nit, who would pass it up to Tinypaw. Tinypaw remained outside near the opening in the roof. She'd managed to make a depression in which to place the babies, covering them with her body while waiting for the next. Thus one by one the kits were scruffed up the line, but the terror of the morning had taken a toll. The cats' movements were were slow and shaken. They'd extracted only eight kits by sunfall, with almost as many to go. The mothers were edgy, as frightened for the kits above ground with no one to nurse them as they were for the newborns still trapped. And they were the lucky ones, the survivors of the massacre. A few toms had escaped into the forest, but the queens didn't know who they were or where they'd gone.

Darkness fell and two more kits were freed. Fortune arrived with Goldenpelt who'd come to visit her sister Pebblepaw's new litter. She'd followed the stream south to its dumping point, and there she stood in a state of shock. Reeds and grass had been trampled to muddy pulps by the Leatherboots and their heavy trucks. The whole area reeked of murder. To those with awakened souls, this was a place of heinous thievery. Lives had been stolen. Goldenpelt rushed to Tinypaw's side. "What happened? Where are my relations? Where is Pebblepaw?"

"I'm here," Pebblepaw called up. Goldenpelt leaned over the opening and trilled at her sister. "Will you help Tinypaw? She has no milk." Goldenpelt examined the newborns Tinypaw had kept warm while freeing others. She nuzzled the little brindle her thanks then loped to the edge of the woods where she quickly scooped out a hole in some bushes beside a boulder, and filled it with grass and moss. Scruffing the babies one by one, she carried them to her snuggery and fed them. They were so hungry! The queens, Nit, Kit and Tinypaw worked on.

A monster roared. Its lights bounced over the mud and reeds until it came to rest in the ruts left by a murderous White Truck. It fell silent. But its lights blazed against Blackpaw's den and the little brindle perched on its ruined roof.

"Nit, Kit! Get out of there!" Tinypaw yowled. They bolted from the hole.

"What's wrong?" Sosay cried.

"Pray to Great Mother it's not the White Truck come back to kill the rest of us!" Tinypaw raced with the twins to the forest. Sosay and the queens cowered together over the remaining kits, praying for Great Mother's protection.

The door of the truck opened and a black boot hit the ground. Out stepped Wilson, shovel in hand. He strode to the battered den and plunged the blade into what had been its entrance, tossing branches and soil as if they were weightless. He dug furiously. He dug until the mothers could stroll from their prison, babies safely in their jaws. They didn't. They hunkered together, too traumatized to move.

Wilson backed away. No one came out. He backed farther away and still no one left the den. The truck's grill pressing against his back, a queen finally showed herself. She was beautiful, with long white fur. He remembered her piercing blue eyes. He'd met them when he shined his flashlight into their shelter. He remembered the distinctive mark on her forehead. "It's a crescent moon" he whispered to himself, amazed by its perfect shape. She stared at him for a long moment, and he looked away in shame. Earlier that day, he'd come with murderers.

"I'm sorry," he murmured, mostly to himself.

Fix this, came the answer, as clearly as the crescent on her forehead flashed blue.

A current of fear zapped Wilson's spine, and trembling head to toe, he scrambled into his truck. *That's impossible. She talked.*

I did, Sosay answered. *And if you listen, I can tell you many secrets.* Wilson stared at her from the safety of his vehicle. Sosay stared back. She turned toward the wreck of a den and three queens appeared behind her, all scruffing babies. On her signal, they loped to the woods. Sosay remained at the wreckage while the mothers returned and left and returned again until all the newborns were safe with Goldenpelt.

Now Sosay strolled toward the man, levitated to the hood of his truck and sat. *Ye-yes, I'll listen and I'll make amends,* he promised. *Tonight is only the beginning.*

We'll meet again. I have much to tell you and you will have much to share. She rose and stepped to the edge of the hood, ready to leap down.

"What if I can't?" he blurted.

But you can. She assured him, floating to the ground. She looked back. *Don't doubt that. You've been chosen to help, just like me.* And she padded to the woods.

Wilson gathered his courage. Lifting a can from the flatbed, he walked the grounds, confirming each den was empty before dousing it with gasoline. He walked the grounds a second time holding a flaming branch, lighting each den with a tongue of fire.

The cat with the crescent moon watched the burning from beneath the trees. She watched Wilson cover the ashes with dirt. *Cats must never return here,* he told her. *You'll never be safe this close to the lake, near humans, near Bleggs.*

Yes, she answered. Then she was gone.

Wilson wiped his tears with dirty hands. He'd never heard of Great Mother, but that night as the spirits of those murdered at Flattail Dam ran from their blazing homes, Wilson begged Her forgiveness.

Ghost keened. It was a long, bitter wail that sent Monkey scrambling for help, Reggie and Robin rushing from their nests. "Leatherboots have destroyed Flattail Dam," the shaman cried. "Bent Whisker is dead."

Reggie felt like the air had been kicked from his body. "Killed at Flattail Dam?"

"He died at his hearth. I saw Smokepelt with him." Ghost stopped, not wanting to cause more pain, but Reggie wasn't having it. He moved closer and lowered his face to the shaman's.

"You must tell me everything," he said.

"Bent Whisker augured through the night. What he saw was too much for his heart."

"What did he see, Ghost?"

"White Trucks. The dead are too many to name." Reggie dropped to the floor, beyond miserable. Ghost licked his face. "Sosay is alive. So is Tinypaw, Nit, Kit, most of the nursing queens and their babies."

"That's all?" Monkey cried. Ghost said nothing.

"Blackpaw? Whitewhiskers?" Reggie asked. The shaman looked down.

"Are you sure, Ghost?" It was Browser, who was awakened by the noise and stood at the cubbyhole's entrance.

"The messengers will arrive first light."

I let this happen, Browser told himself. *I'm responsible for every death, a king who can't protect his kin.* He left, heading for the Guardian Stone, where he spent the night moaning over the deaths of innocents, worried this was only the beginning of violence in the Green.

At first light Ember and Firetail loped north across the meadow. Browser went down to meet them.

🐾 🐾 🐾

After Wilson's departure, Goldenpelt had run home, returning with enough kin to carry the kits to safety. They followed the stream north to Southbridge, to a well-disguised hollow where a dense canopy of Cape Honeysuckle grew between two stone outcroppings on the gully's western slope. Similar to the now defunct dens farther south, pebbles, dirt and leaf debris filled the holes between branches, creating a weather-proof ceiling. The vine's twisting trunks gave them a kin-sized entrance between the stone outcroppings, while the gully walls curved in such a way to provide room for many.

The refugees were fed and given nests to rest and suckle their kits, after which everyone gathered and Sosay described the massacre. A moment of silence, then all eyes turned to Broadface, the leader of Southbridge Pod. He'd listened carefully, resting on his side, fanning his sizable belly with a shaggy tail.

When Sosay finished, Broadface sat tall, looking thoughtfully at each of his guests. "Did anyone else survive?"

"Tinypaw said a few escaped into the woods," Sosay murmured, "but I couldn't say who."

Ember rose and paced, anxiously swishing his tail. "We're next." Goldenpelt's kits stopped their tumbling play and scurried to their mother.

Broadface focused on Sosay. "Do you agree?"

"Perhaps not," she meowed, "Flattail Dam Pod was always too trusting of the tall-walkers, letting themselves be seen, and though Blackpaw strictly forbade it, many younglings took food from them."

"Ugh," Ember sneered.

Goldenpelt rose to her paws. "Yes," she rasped, remembering her encounter with Diva and what she'd heard about the alleys. "They're all dangerous. Can't trust them..." Echoes rang through the den.

"Except—" Sosay interrupted. "Before your queens carried our kits here, an upright saved us." Goldenpelt licked her shoulder, embarrassed at being corrected. Tinypaw stared at Sosay, hurt her strenuous efforts to save them weren't mentioned.

Pebblepaw stood. "It's true. Tinypaw and the twins worked all day to get us out of the collapsed den, but it was the tall-one who dug us free." Her tail waving behind her, she looked down at her paws. "Then he burned our homes and left," She stood there, looking as confused as everyone else.

"Pebblepaw, he burned it so that no one can return, so that no one else is murdered," Sosay said.

"I don't think he'd murder us," Pebblepaw began, still confused.

Ember slunk to her, ears back, bringing his face rudely close to hers. "You're saying we should trust uprights because one of them helped you after killing everyone else in your clan?" Pebblepaw sank to the floor. Blackpaw was gone, as was their home, leaving her with newborn kits, dependent on the mercy of Southbridge kin.

Sosay pushed herself between her friend and the churlish male. "No, she's not saying that, Fur-For-Brains, but we can't deny what happened. We don't know why he saved us, only that he did."

Broadface rose. "Where are your manners!" he spat, glowering at Ember and stomping his wide paws, paws like Sosay's, with tufts of long fur between six toes. "In this den, we are respectful, especially to those who need our help." He paused before the queens. "You are welcome here," he said, then swung his large head back to his flame-striped second. "And we honor the good deed of the two-legged who helped you. Yes, they are foul and dangerous, but this one we honor." The chocolate-pelted leader motioned to all the males with a sweep of his tail. "Come. We need sentries around our camp." And he left, the toms behind him.

"We'll be back," Sosay told Pebblepaw, then she, her brindle apprentice, and Blackpaw's adopted twins also left the den, heading north along the gully. The rising sun laced the clouds in the east with rose and gold. They came to a place where smooth, white boulders sloped down to the water's edge. There they sat staring at the stream and now Sosay keened, grieving openly for her murdered friends and for Blackpaw. He'd once been an ardent suitor and she'd returned that love until she chose the solitary life of a spiritual warrior. Elder Cats have no time to raise kittens. Sosay never regretted her decision to follow Bent Whisker, but there had been moments when she thought about what a life with Blackpaw would have been. This was such a moment, and losing him was a knife in her heart.

Tinypaw waited before speaking. "Sosay, I must tell you something, a charge given me by Bent Whisker, who...Sosay, Bent Whisker is gone."

"I know. I felt it happen."

"He wants you to take his place as Elder Cat of the South. Smokepelt is waiting to welcome you and Reggie is to receive the RA." Sosay licked the little tortie's ear.

"You've done well. I've no doubt you'll soon receive the RA yourself." Tinypaw gazed at her paws, embarrassed by the praise. Sosay turned to the twins. "Nit, Kit, where will you live?"

They eyed each other, then Nit began cleaning himself as if he didn't care, but Sosay knew the loss of his mentor hurt him deeply. Nit seldom exposed his feelings. Kit, his double in so many ways, bared her heart to everyone. "I want to stay with Pebblepaw," she mewed. "She's alone now with Blackpaw's kits. In this way, I can honor Blackpaw's kindness."

"I could do that," Nit said.

Sosay swished her tail, happy the catlings would remain together and that Pebblepaw would have their support. Eyes smiling, she turned to her apprentice. "You're coming south with me, right?"

"Yes, but I miss Reggie. Will he come home soon?"

"He'll come home, but not soon," Sosay answered. Tinypaw's ears and tail fell. Sosay nuzzled her mottled cheek. "I miss him too, Tinypaw, but these are hard times with more to come. Gather your strength."

They all sat quietly then, absorbing the new day, a day they'd never forget.

🐾　🐾　🐾

Wisdom Cats, apprentices and pod leaders gathered at Harmony Tree on the first night of brightmoon, the first brightmoon since the massacre at Flattail Dam. This wasn't a celebration with all kin welcome, but a meeting of hearts and minds committed to fight the darkness.

Browser came with Rosie, Ghost with Robin and Reggie. Sosay had arrived early with Smokepelt and Tinypaw. The brindle apprentice ran joyfully to Reggie, and they head-bunted and rubbed, both purring loudly, until Sosay separated them, custom requiring Reggie sit with his northern hosts.

From the east came Nebula, Starpaw and Flyingtail. Sandpelt, leader of Windcave Clan, arrived with his second, Edgerunner and Edgerunner's son, Stone-Fly, a young taupe male who raised dust devils scaling vertical cliffs faster than most kin could run on flat ground.

Broadface and Ember represented Southbridge Pod, while Mistypaw, pod leader of Cattail Island, came with her trusted mate Rushpaw.

From the west came Silverpelt, leader of Birch Grove Pod and Rainpelt of Bigmarsh Family.

Even Topbranch and his mate Leafturn arrived from High Home, far north in the forest of firs. The shy warriors with thick, brown pelts skipped along the uppermost branches. Their eyes were large and dark, their faces long and slender like their torsos, legs and tails, their long, strong toes baring scimitar-like claws. Looking like fearsome warriors, they held violence in disdain, and were thoughtful kin preferring a hermit-like existence in the trees. They preyed upon bark beetles, slugs, spiders, caterpillars and moths, their diet staples so low on the food chain, they were as close to vegetarian as any Felidae could come, and kept the fir trees healthier.

Darktail and Martileena arrived with the Elder Cat's apprentice, Annapurna Snowpelt, the center of his world. Darktail fussed over her so much, Martileena was no longer perceived as his guaranteed successor though Snowpelt possessed no talent. She was beautiful, even more beautiful than Sosay who was considered the most beautiful female in the Green. Snowpelt had a sweet, forthcoming nature, but she couldn't feel fear coming from a forest fire, and she knew it. Humbled by her shortcomings, she was shy and withdrawn while Darktail hovered, pretending all was well. It wasn't Snowpelt who had pretensions, Ghost realized. It was Darktail. For her part in the love triangle, Martileena stole longing glances at Starpaw, glances he returned when she looked away, glances Darktail never missed and deeply resented. But all this was a distraction. How to curb Morsus' pursuit of power was the reason for this gathering.

When the moon reached its zenith, Ghost rose. "Great Mother bless this gathering."

"Great Mother Be, the same as we," they answered.

"Let us honor the passings at Flat-Tail Dam. I am particularly grieved to lose Blackpaw, as I'm sure each of you has someone special to remember." Everyone fell silent, tails unmoving and tucked close. After a few moments, Ghost continued. "Let us also honor Bent Whisker from far south guarding the Sacred Flame. He has left this world, but he will never leave our hearts."

"Great Mother lift Her Paw," the chorus rang.

Tinypaw stood. "Bent Whisker wanted Sosay to take his place as Elder Cat."

Tail thumping seconded the motion and Sosay rose. "I will protect the Sacred Flame and serve the kin with my life." She looked at Ghost. "Let me begin with another passing...Erasmus. He disappeared with the death of Indra."

"We have no proof he died," Ghost meowed, his tail quivering with emotion.

"And none he lives," Martileena offered.

"And no Elder Cat of the North," Sosay added.

Ghost was struggling for the right words when Martileena cried out, "I propose Ghost as Elder Cat of the North." She thumped her tail like a drum and others joined in.

Ghost knew he had no choice. He stood. "I accept until Erasmus returns. My heart tells me he lives," adding under his breath to quizzical glances, "and so did Nightbeak."

"There is another matter between north and south tonight," Sosay trilled. "Reggie. He is ready to receive the RA, but should it come from the south, where he began his training, or the north, where he finished it? I've been told he's as adept as any northern kin with herbs and grasses."

Tails thumped in support of Reggie, who looked surprised. "You don't want me to come home, mentor?" he bleated. "More than anything, I want to be with you, avenging the murder of my friends."

"And how would you avenge them, Reggie? Uprights killed our kin. Will you attack the sun and moon as well? Violence won't bring Blackpaw or Whitewhiskers or a single innocent back to us. Revenge is not part of a Wisdom Cat's life." The ginger looked down, grief stricken. "Reggie," she cooed, "Great Mother's Prophecy promises an end to this holocaust. We'll win by following Her teachings." A stir in the gathering and a nervous Rainpelt stood.

"You're wrong, Sosay. Forgiveness is weakness disguised as hope." A charged silence hung over the gathering. This wasn't just bad manners. Interrupting a Wisdom Cat teaching an apprentice was profane, and Sosay would be within her rights to drive Rainpelt from the group.

"Why would you think that?" Sosay asked, her scruff, ears and tail relaxed.

This was not the response Rainpelt expected and his body jerked with surprise, but he continued, "I know you don't understand. Wisdom Cats have been running things forever and it just gets worse and worse. The wisdom of the Wisdom Cats *must* be wrong."

"Wrong?"

"Despite all your divinations, mind-readings, heart-feelings, healing herbs and trances, none of you understand the Prophecy." An audible shock-wave rippled through the circle.

"Blasphemy!" Martileena snapped, slapping a cloud of dirt into the air with her tail. Before Ghost could calm her, Darktail was dancing on his toes, flashing his fangs.

"*You* cry blasphemy, *you,* with your secret lust for Starpaw?" The fur on Martileena's back exploded and she leaped at her tormentor, slammed her forehead to his, and began pushing him from the circle. Once outside those gathered, they hissed and spit and danced the Dance of Flying Fur. Starpaw and Annapurna watched, paralyzed with embarrassment, Starpaw making himself as small as possible to avoid Nebula's stare. Annapurna bolted into the night. Darktail's head swiveled from Martileena to Snowpelt's receding rump and he plopped on his, staring after her. He leaped to his paws and ran after her, crying, "Anna! Anna!"

As his wailing faded away, all wide eyes turned to Martileena. Like Annapurna, she'd had enough of the pretense and hypocrisy, and with every fiber of her being blazing with defiant dignity, she walked to Starpaw and sat. He nuzzled and licked her like she was catmint, then they both turned to their audience and stared. No one twitched a whisker.

Rainpelt's rebellion was frozen in an irrelevant universe until Sosay turned back to the pod leader. "Tell me again. How are we wrong, Rainpelt?" Nervous titters from the crowd.

Rainpelt's body jerked again. He'd been assured the Wisdom Cats would be hostile and Sosay's openness confused him. His eyes grew furtive and his tail sank. "It's just...well, we pod leaders hear things..." Sosay's gaze wasn't angry, it was direct. "It's wrong, don't you see?" he continued, "A ghostdog attacks during a Naming Ceremony and then we discover Hillside Pod, home of the King and Queen and Elder Cat of the North, harbors barkers! Since the attack we've been too frightened to gather. We were told the Leatherboots had plans inside the Green and what was done? Nothing. Now an entire clan has been massacred. Even you must see that's wrong."

Edgerunner stood, ears back and fangs bared. "Kin shouldn't wait, hoping everything will sort itself out. We're hunters, warriors, the Clan of Fang and Claw. Isn't that what you..." and he hurled the title like a curse, "...*Wisdom Cats* say?"

Heads turned, surprised. Sosay had never met a Wisdom Cat who wouldn't give its blood and bones to help the kin and Rainpelt's and Edgerunner's remarks hurt terribly, but still she remained calm. "What is it you believe we should do?" she asked.

Mistypaw leaped to her paws, then up on her hind legs. "Fight!" she cried, and flurried the air viciously. Pelt on end, she was twice her normal size, and looked frighteningly fierce.

Sosay waited a moment. "Is that how you'll fight the uprights?"

Mistypaw stared blankly, dropped her arms to her sides but remaining on her toes. Now she looked ridiculous. "Well, we must be strong!" she snapped, and dropped to all fours, trying to salvage her pride.

"Of course, but strong to fight tall-walkers...or each other?" Almost everyone chuffed with amusement at Mistypaw's silly ideas.

Ears pinned back in anger, she slapped the ground with her tail. "What you're doing doesn't work, Sosay. We need to be ready. We can't survive co-operating with and tolerating two-leggeds the way you prissy northern cats..." Her fiery nature sweeping her along, ideas burst forth like seeds from an overripe pod. But they were strange ideas based on false information and would yield no good fruit. The longer Mistypaw spoke the more she exposed herself. "Everyone knows there's too much posing before Great Mother and too little action," She stared with open disdain at Martileena and the very different-looking Starpaw. "...And too much mingling of clans. Mixing the different elements weakens us." She flexed her claws in the dirt and hissed. "It makes us impure." Martileena jumped up with a growl, but Starpaw leaned a shoulder against her chest and she sat back down. A flicker of fear crossed Mistypaw's face, then she swelled with anger. "When Master rules, this will stop," she spat, looking more demon than cat. Her meaning slithered into the gathering's awareness and silently lines were drawn, sides were chosen. Most of the cats were repulsed, but a few agreed.

Rushpaw stood. "What Mistypaw can't explain, I will. No, we can't fight uprights, but we can and we *must* fight the pervasive softness, this tolerance of humans that flows down from the north and poisons the Green. Two-leggeds plan to destroy us, all of us. We can't reason with them. We run. They're dangerous and we must teach our children they're dangerous, not to believe in miracles."

Browser sat looking glum, the harsh words from other pod leaders almost more than he could bear. As a pod leader working with Ghost, he was guilty of that tolerance they found so toxic. He'd been proud of it, and it *didn't* extend to humans. That was a lie. Their hatred of Wisdom Cats offended him, but for now he kept silent. *They're right to fear uprights,* he told himself. And then there was the guilt, his guilt, his failure. *I was king when Flattail Dam Pod was massacred. Nothing can change that.*

Ghost stood. "So, Rushpaw, you believe these ideas of tolerance and change from within are poisonous?"

Rushpaw centered himself. "I believe it's foolish to pretend the tall-ones aren't dangerous. That we can somehow defeat them by following this Prophecy no one understands. In other words, by doing nothing."

"And what would you do?"

"Fight."

"How would you fight uprights, Rushpaw?" The southern cat didn't respond. "In truth, wouldn't it be kin vs. kin? Would you fight kin of the Green to see your beliefs followed by all?" Ghost knew the answer. He wanted others to see.

Rushpaw dug his claws into the dirt, his lowered tail swishing nervously behind him. Finally, "If there were no other way, I'd fight kin." He looked around, his gaze resting on Browser. "It's not my first choice"

"What *is* your first choice?" Martileena chuffed.

"He can't tell us," Starpaw growled. "That would expose him as a tool of the Malkin,"

Both Rushpaw and Mistypaw tensed, their scruffs at full alert. Rushpaw scratched angrily in the dirt. "All right. You want the truth? You're weak, all of you! You sleep while tall-ones surround you, just like Flat-tail Dam. Who will we fight? We'll fight YOU if we have to, fight our way free of your lies to save ourselves!" He stepped away from Mistypaw into the center of the circle where he faced Ghost. Lowering his front end, Rushpaw pinned his ears back and thumped his tail wildly. Ghost braced himself, certain Rushpaw would attack. But he didn't because of Browser's low, undulating growl, and how he mirrored Rushpaw's fighting stance. So did Robin and Nebula and Starpaw, Broadface and Ember, Topbranch, Leafturn, Smokepelt, Sosay and Tinypaw, basically everyone. Even Edgerunner and Rainpelt drew back, refusing to support Rushpaw's violence. The big male realized he was defeated. His ideas were defeated. He and Mistypaw sank to the ground in submission, ears sideways and down, tails curled around their bodies.

Sosay had questions. "Where do you and your mate get these ideas, Mistypaw?" The eyes lifted to the white queen showed little desire to answer.

"She asked you a question," Ghost meowed.

Mistypaw threw him a daggered look. Finally, "The Council of Great Mother. Its members are everywhere for us believers...and nowhere for..." She paused, unsure about using the words she wanted, but finally she couldn't resist. "For those doomed to Beyond, who will never enter Fields of Nip."

"Believers and heretics, huh?" Ghost mocked. "Of course you and Rushpaw are with the saved."

Mistypaw took the bait. "You must perform a service to prove yourself worthy, but after your trials and initiation you eat better, you're safe and so are your kits."

"What kind of service?"

"It's our beliefs and I'd rather not say." Mistypaw chuffed.

"You will say," Ghost replied.

She rolled her whiskers in a smirk. "I'll say this. We have protectors in the forests. Monsters black as midnight, bigger than Nebula and they can't be beaten." she scoffed, glaring in his direction. "They protect only us, the Council's servants and our children. You didn't know that, did you?" She bragged.

Sosay wondered if Mistypaw would spout such nonsense with cuffed ears, but she controlled her anger. "We *do* know about the denchurls, Mistypaw. What you don't know is these beasts your Master sends are to keep *you* in line. Disobey him and you'll need protecting all right...from them."

Mistypaw stomped her paws. "That's a lie!"

"Is it?"

"Sosay tells the truth," Reggie cried. "I saw the Malkin murder Indra, and on his orders his denchurls beat Erasmus then dragged him off. We don't know where or why. Your Master said he'd be of use later. I heard it and I saw it!"

Despite her armor of dogma, Mistypaw was shaken. "The Master murdered Indra?" she whispered bleakly. This changed everything, or it should. It almost did, but the pod leader had swallowed so many lies, some comforting, some bitter, but so many. Now she couldn't find her way home. And Mistypaw was stubborn. "Master tells us not to believe what we see and hear. We're to believe HIM, and all I know is that it's an honor to be a Guardian of Great Mother, a privilege to seek Her Heart."

"You've always been an intelligent cat," Ghost said. The praise caught her by surprise, and Mistypaw's fur fluffed-up a little despite herself. He went on. "Sometimes I've tested my ideas against your view of our world. You watch, you listen, and you weigh the evidence. I've seen you go against your own inclinations to speak truth. How could this... Master, as you call him, take that from you?" Mistypaw said nothing and stared at the night sky.

Sosay interrupted. "I have a question. Has the illustrious Council of Great Mother told you what they want with Her Heart?" Back on Earth, Mistypaw snorted derisively, but Sosay held her gaze.

The pod leader faltered. "What are you saying? Seeking Her Heart means you submit to Her wishes."

"No. They seek the actual Beating Heart of Great Mother."

"That's impossible," Rushpaw snarled.

Mistypaw glanced anxiously at her mate then looked down, somewhat subdued. "But Great Mother is a Spirit Cat," she murmured, "She's not one of us."

"Oh, but She is," Ghost meowed. "Once again She has incarnated as a living being, this lifetime as a cat, and She's living in the Green. That's why the Malkin and his minions are here."

Despite her bad judgment, and the disillusionment she'd let cloud her thinking, Mistypaw, as Ghost had pointed out, was once a courageous seeker of truth. Now she began to see how her anger had let bad ideas seem like good ones. *Have I been misled,* she asked herself. "Are you saying they want Her real Heart? Her Beating Heart?" The truth biting at her heels like a mischievous kit, she stood trembling tip to tail.

"Yes," Ghost answered.

Reality crashed around Mistypaw like pines in a burning forest.

"Why?" she asked, but she already knew.

Nebula shuddered with rage. "They will feed it to Morsus, that avatar of evil you call Master, and it will make him immortal...Those black monsters you think protect you? They're just bugs who do his bidding, nothing more. If he ordered it, they'd happily eat your kits rather than guard them. Your leader, Mistypaw, is a killer without a shred of conscience."

Remorse poured from Mistypaw as palpable energy. She scooted closer to Rushpaw, who was also beginning to understand, and they sat, paws and tail tucked, calculating their crimes.

Nebula turned to Rainpelt and Edgerunner. "What about you two?" he rasped. "Seen Windclaw lately? I imagine not. If Morsus hasn't sucked him dry, he's hiding, for that's his fate once he failed his mission to kill Ghost." Rainpelt and Edgerunner exchanged anxious looks. Nebula chuffed and faced the group. "We came to tell you that ronin cats wander our mesas spreading the Malkin's lies. He has followers in the east, members of his sham Council." He glanced contemptuously at Rainpelt and Edgerunner. "Anyone smellin' the nightsoil that group is sellin' is dumb as the dirt that covers it."

Starpaw rose. "Morsus' followers gather near our shelterveil. Windclaw must have told them about the Crystal Aerie. We've beaten them back but more will return." Gasps all around.

"I feel the Malkin," Martileena whispered. "He'll sacrifice anyone to enter our shelterveils, but he still fears our strength. For now he lies and misleads, gathering kin to his side." She glared at the rebellious pod leaders. "Perhaps Edgerunner can tell us more."

The sand-colored male stood, tail low and paws shuffling, hardly the rebel they'd met earlier. "I knew nothing of this and nothing of Morsus," he began defensively.

Mistypaw couldn't help bragging again. "Of course he didn't. New initiates don't know about Master," she said with a dismissive glance at Edgerunner. "That comes later, when you're trusted. Few know anything about Master and even fewer see him..." She angled her face toward Sosay. *Am I redeeming myself,* her eyes asked. Sosay's eyes told her to continue. "I heard things...that he'd always looked strange, that his power makes him stranger still. And then he...well, he..."

"You've seen him!" Nebula hissed, and Mistypaw trembled.

Sosay intervened. "I know this is hard for you, Nebula, but let her unburden herself."

With that, Mistypaw abandoned all pretenses. She collapsed and stretched her paws toward Sosay, almost weeping her story. "I'm sorry. I was so stupid and I knew it was wrong but we were all so frightened and the Wisdom Cats...well, we didn't think you cared. They told us you didn't care even if our babies were lost and some of them did disappear and you didn't come. But now I wonder if you even knew. Did they steal our kits and keep it secret? Great Mother's Tail! Sosay, would they really..." She couldn't finish the thought. Eyes wide, she stared down the abyss, her claws raking furrows in the earth.

Sosay's crescent glowed brightly. She cooed, "Mistypaw, I care very much. Let me help you help others. Tell us what you saw."

"Saw?" she asked, dazed and faraway. But gradually the traumatized pod leader returned from the horrors haunting her mind. "I saw him... only once...and only for a heartbeat when those closest to him knelt. Few are allowed in his presence and we're told to keep our eyes down, but everyone sneaks a peak. I was told he was born small, but he's enormous, bigger than his denchurls, bigger than Nebula."

"Because he grows with every life he sucks dry," Nebula growled, slapping his tail in the dirt. A groan traveled the circle.

"Al-Allright," Mistypaw mewed. "What I saw...I couldn't believe, didn't want to believe..."

"What did you see, Mistypaw," Sosay coaxed.

"I was told he was born without fur, but he was covered with fur. Then I realized it wasn't his. He covers himself...arghh...the smell. He drapes pelts...the pelts of his victims over his back. When you're finally allowed to see him...you can't show it bothers you that he's...that he's...I can't say it." Her eyes pleaded with Sosay for a pass.

"Say it."

Mistypaw took a deep breath and stared into the abyss again. "...So many small, pitiful paws dangling above his enormous ones, dried heads ringing his neck..." Chaos erupted.

Nebula lunged at Mistypaw with a murderous growl. He would have killed her had Starpaw and Flyingtail not leaped before him, shoulders against his expansive chest, forcing him to back down. Everyone caterwauled an opinion with no one listening to anyone else until Ghost bellowed, "Silence!" Surprisingly, they all shut-up and sat.

Rosie, between Browser and Ghost along the northern curve of the circle, had flinched with pain when Sosay declared Morsus sought the Heart of Great Mother and again more violently when Nebula said the Malkin would eat it. Pain shot through her chest so strongly now she would have fallen had she not already been sitting belly to the ground. Browser felt her tremble and not wanting to worry him, she whispered something about a bad mouse. Quietly, he rose and left. And as the truth began to sink in, Rosie was grateful he was gone.

Listening to Mistypaw's confessions, she remembered the day she met Morsus, how repulsed she'd been, how Ghost had helped her feel compassion. *Were we wrong? He seeks the Heart of Great Mother.* Again her chest throbbed painfully. She turned toward Ghost and met his gaze and everything became clear. *I am the Discarded Queen and I am Great Mother embodied in flesh. I am Her, incarnate as cat. The Malkin is my mortal enemy. Ghost knows.* Rosie looked at Sosay who turned from Mistypaw and met her gaze. *Sosay knows.* Reggie's anxious stare told her he also knew. *But Browser must never know.*

"I will protect you," Ghost whispered. "This horror will never come to pass." And Rosie understood now why she must leave the Green. Ghost was right. *It's time to find Mee-am.*

Browser returned, his jaws filled with chamomile which he dropped at her paws. "Eat. Your belly will feel better." *It's not my belly, it's my Heart,* Rosie thought, but she couldn't tell him that, not ever. So she nuzzled his cheek and lowered her nose to the delicate daisy-like flowers.

Ghost stood. "We're in the greatest struggle of our lives. We're fighting for our souls, for the soul of the Green. Who will we be? Will we fear and be cruel to those who are different? Or will we open our hearts, living lives of kindness and mercy? The choice is ours. I'm sorry we've kept secrets, leaving our pod leaders feeling abandoned. From this night forward Wisdom Cats will share all we know about the Malkin with you. Together we'll defeat this evil." He gave Mistypaw a wary look. "Your spirit is strong, Mistypaw, but you must tend to your heart." He pointed with his tail to Martileena and Starpaw. "No kin is less than another and differences are not defects." Tail lashing side to side, his eyes burned with emotion. "I believe someone other than yourself and Rushpaw should serve Cattail Island until your hearts have healed." He stared at them.

Finally, "But this is a decision to be made by members of your pod, not by me. I expect you'll be telling us about changes next brightmoon, and I look forward to it." Now his gaze caressed Mistypaw and she could feel him counting all that was good in her. "Thank you for your honesty about the Guardian Council and the Malkin. I know that was hard for you."

"What should pod leaders do to help?" Rainpelt asked, hoping he wouldn't be replaced while *his* heart healed.

"Trust your Wisdom Cats enough to tell them what you know. Tell others who the Malkin really is, how his world will have no kindness, no remorse, and no honor." Sosay answered.

Ghost scanned the gathered cats. They looked as if they'd awakened on the edge of an abyss. They had. Even Darktail, who waited with Snowpelt beyond the circle, looked worried.

With the moon-greeting howl of a ghostdog, the kin rose, readying for their journey home.

"I can't leave with you," Martileena whispered to Starpaw.

He rubbed his cheek on hers. "I know," he meowed. "Someday."

"Yes." With that, she joined Darktail and his love, Snowpelt. Martileena licked his ears, then rubbed her flank against Snowpelt in a gesture of acceptance, for Anna would no longer apprentice. Darktail had set her free. They left three abreast and friends.

Starpaw followed Martileena with his eyes, only faintly aware of Nebula's call to leave. She'd almost faded from sight when his heart touched hers. She turned and met his gaze. They stared each other, then turned away, the thread between them unfurling as they moved apart.

Browser and Rosie remained with Ghost and Robin to witness Reggie receiving the RA. The RA of the South, for it was Sosay, Reggie's mentor, who bestowed it with love and pride, her first deed as Elder Cat. His vision-quest had been his struggles in the tunnels beneath the sycamore. Moonlight silvered the tips of his fur as he emerged as Wisdom Cat, a healer with roots and flowers burning with the passion of the south.

19 - TRIAL BY GHOSTDOG

The kin lay along the banks of the stream in the shade of willow trees, trying to beat the heat. Eyes closed, bodies stretched out long and flat, the cats hardly moved. Bees buzzed through the primrose and feathertails twittered in the branches, mostly about how hot they were. At last the sun moved off its searing pinnacle, and the air cooled. Kyra led Shadow downstream to the pool below Big Falls to fish for dinner. Lured by a dragonfly, a good-sized finback rose to the surface and the catling struck. Kyra trilled with pleasure when the sweet sailed past her and flopped on dry ground. Shadow sank her fangs into its brain.

"Good catch," the queen meowed. "You don't need my help anymore."

"No, mama, but I love being with you." With a gentle head-bunt, Shadow offered her mother the prey, and Kyra carried it to the meadow below their den to share with the pod.

Scrapper didn't like water. He stalked the woods for longear. Bigpaw tagged along, crunching leaves, stumbling over sticks and stones, scaring off their prey. A frustrated Scrapper held his tongue because his mother had told him to, and since the night of the bobcat he'd done his best to be worthy - in the way his father was worthy. Anyway, no one felt worse about his clumsiness than Bigpaw. He knew he needed help and Scrapper always tried.

Rosie had spent the day sleeping on the stream bank, Rosebud at her side. They'd hunted at first light, retreating beneath the willows when the sun grew hot. Rosie doted on Rosebud, with her fawn pelt and graceful legs, longer and more graceful than her own. And she had Rosie's beautiful face.

A fang of moon rose in the early evening sky, a sign for hunters to come home. Patches and Robin trotted from the eastern wood, a plump longear hanging from Patches' jaws. He wanted to trade it for a nose-kiss from Rosebud, but she got it from him for nothing. Hopelessly smitten, Patches' heart took whatever crumbs she offered, hoping for the day she'd return his love. But as Bent Whisker had predicted, Rosie's daughter was spoiled, and like all spoiled princesses, she confused love easily given with weakness. *Patches is too soft for his own good,* she told herself, taking another bite of his rabbit.

Ghost and Monkey remained in the den before Great Mother's altar. Water dripped from the petrified wall, cooling the air, plunking into the stone basin like music. It settled Ghost' spirit. He had as yet only nominal control of his eastern and western abilities. The feelings of others flooded his heart and their thoughts wandered his mind as easily as the kin climbed Harmony Tree. Sometimes Morsus invaded Ghost' mind, forcing him to watch him feed off wildborn he ambushed in alleyways outside the Green. Ghost abhorred this dark world where fear was currency, and relationships were measured by dominance. Surrounded by his bestial bodyguards, the Malkin had grown larger than any of them, yet he never felt safe. More than one sycophant had paid with his life for Morsus' paranoia.

The twilight deepened and the pod retired to their den, everyone but the guards standing watch on Waterfall Boulder, and Browser who scoured the western treeline. Scrapper and Bigpaw still weren't home. Browser paced small, nervous circles on the Guardian Stone. He felt anxious, a familiar feeling since the massacre. Every step he took was dogged by the ghosts of Flattail Dam, the faces of friends who were no more. *It's my fault,* he told himself. *I should have prevented it.* But what he should have done and how he could have prevented it went unanswered in the foggy pit of his guilt. In truth, there was nothing he could have done.

"They come," Buster cried, shaking Browser from his brooding. He looked up and saw his sons racing north across the meadow.

"Father!" Scrapper howled. "Buster! Patches! Ghost! Robin! The coyotes are coming!" More than one heart caught in a throat, then Hillside Pod poured down the slope into the field.

"What happened?" Browser demanded, staring at Bigpaw.

"We...the...the...g...ghostdogs..."he answered, out of breath from the long run. Browser nuzzled his shoulder and turned to Scrapper.

"We...were...hunting," the catling wheezed, "along the crest...of the gulch...behind Harmony Tree." He paused. "They were in the gully, headed for the cliff where the big one trapped Jasper and Shorttail." The pups whimpered, with Jasper prostrating himself before Browser, licking his paws. Browser hardly noticed. "We hid," his son gasped.

Kyra's pelt stood on end, her ears back and down. "Did they follow you?" A shudder passed through them all like an ill wind.

Scrapper stiffened. "Would I be standing here if they did?"

"How can you be so sure?"

"Because we followed them home." Everyone sucked in a hard breath.

"Scrapper!" Rosie cried, then turned to Bigpaw, her eyes full of questions.

"I don't know how I kept up, mom. I just did...and I didn't get us caught."

Proud of him despite her fears, Rosie whispered, "Foolish boy."

Scrapper's tail flayed the air. "The trip back we waded upstream to hide our scent."

"Good boys," Kyra said. "We've taught you well."

"You're sure they're ghostdogs?" Browser asked.

"Father, I've seen a coyote before." He'd never forget Browser hunkered beside the bobcat, facing down the gulchdog.

"How many were there?"

"Seven. Four adults and three younger ones. The biggest male has scars across his face."

Browser remembered those malicious yellow eyes, smelled the beast's fetid breath, the blood on its fangs. He rose to his full height, meeting each member of his pod with studied calm. "We all know what to do," he proclaimed, then marched up the hill into the den. Actually, no one had any idea what to do. They were cats, not uprights with nets and pain-sticks. How could a few kin, half of them younglings, and three little barkers stand against a pack of blood-hungering ghostdogs? Shelterveil or not, they were terrified.

Buster and Kyra endured a tense vigil of gulchhounds howling until dawn. The following evening Browser and Rosie stood watch and again the coyotes bayed with every kill while the kin trembled in their cave. The following morning Browser called a meeting on the grass.

"The ghostdogs will come farther north." he said, pacing a circle around the pod. Whiskers and ears twitched in agreement. "They can't discover us in our shelterveil. You know that, right?"

Rosie faced him. "Browser, do you not feel the fear we do? Even if the dogs can't find us, we're captives in our den. What if they lay siege because our scent is thick here? And what of Sugar Pie and her pups with nothing but a rosemary hedge to protect them?"

"Yes!" Buster cried, worried for his friends.

"Mister Buster," the mother dog roofed, "Didn't you say you would find us a home with tall-ones?"

"I did. I can," he meowed, "But such things take time." Sugar Pie cocked her head, baffled. Many turns of the moon had passed since she arrived and he had made that promise. Buster looked guilty. "Truth is..." he mumbled into his chest fur, "I sorta got used to you being here."

Sugar Pie smiled but Rosie looked sad. "Fuzz Mutt, there's something else. If we do that, we'll need to find three homes, one for you, and one for each pup."

"What?" Sugar Pie trembled.

"Two-leggeds seldom take more than one dog. You'll have to part from your babies and they from each other."

"But you could try," Kyra growled at her mate.

Browser passed between them, keeping the peace. "We need more than that. We need a plan that saves everyone. Anyway, we're not dumping Sugar Pie on the first upright who says yes. We need to follow up on her new home...break her out if they lied." Sugar Pie wiggled forward and tried to lick his leg, but Browser was so pleased with himself for reminding them all that two-leggeds lie, he didn't notice.

Rosie took offense. "Browser, I know you believe if a tall-walker isn't silent he's lying, but that isn't always true. Some are honorable."

Browser looked smug. "You mean the Mate?"

Rosie exploded. "Of course not. I mean Mee-am."

"Who let the Mate dump you."

"She would never! She didn't know!"

Browser grew stern. "Rosie, before we talk about Mee-am and what she did or didn't know we must protect our clan."

"You brought it up."

Browser saw that she still suffered over Mee-am and relented. In a softer tone he said, "You're right. I'm sorry, Rosamonde." He rubbed his shoulder against Sugar Pie. "If the ghostdogs reach our meadow, you'll have to live in the den." The dogs whimpered, wondering how they'd manage the hill and the Guardian.

"Perhaps we should leave before the gulchdogs find us?" Reggie asked.

"And give up our home?" Buster yowled.

"Wouldn't be the first time," Kyra muttered.

"But where would we go? To the alleys, where we live on filthy asphalt, and eat from dumpsters?" His eyes fiery slits, Buster's tail pounded the ground.

"How about another part of the Green?" Robin asked.

"The Green is full," Browser said. "Kin live everywhere the living's good."

"I know places that aren't so terrible," Monkey offered. "Not in the Green, but they'll do in a pinch." The others stared at her as if she came from another world. She did. "You don't need to twitch your noses at me," Monkey spat. "I survived as well as any of you." Ghost licked her ears.

"Tomorrow I will take Sugar Pie and the pups to the south end. We'll look for tall-ones who would give them a home," Buster said, nuzzling Fuzz Mutt.

Browser turned to Reggie. "Will you protect our queens?"

"With my life," he answered without asking when, for how long, or even drawing a breath.

Browser dipped his head in thanks then stomped his paws for attention. "Buster, tomorrow, you and your son Patches, with Ghost and Robin, and my sons," he said, pointing his tail at Scrapper and Bigpaw, "are coming with me. I have an idea."

"No!" Rosie cried. "Our sons are too young!"

Browser wheeled around and they stood muzzle to muzzle, tails flitting tensely, but he kept his voice calm. "They must come, Rosamonde. You must trust me."

Neither moved nor spoke until at last Rosie relented. "This is their first quest, Browser. Be careful with our boys." He whispered that he would.

"Browser," Kyra meowed, "Patches is my only boy."

"Don't worry, Kyra. Buster will be there."

"I'm ready for this," Patches said. Then to his embarrassment, his mother cupped his face between her front paws and began licking it. Patches pulled away, glaring at her between furtive glances at Rosebud, who he needn't have worried about. She was plumping her coat with her tongue, paying attention only to herself.

"Listen," Browser commanded, then told them his plan. For the first time since the threat began, the pod felt confident.

In the predawn light, three young males sharpened their claws on the tree stump near the pool. Ears pricked, tails high, they bristled with excitement. They weren't frightened; they had the immortality of youth, each secretly wishing for glory in glorious battle. But to the elders they showed cautious yet willing faces, and followed them into the stream, stifling the urge to whimper when the cold soaked through their fur.

The cats reached Smallmarsh where Scrapper had teased the skunks. Remembering his sins, he lowered his head and tucked his tail, hoping to slip by unnoticed. But the sun hadn't crested the horizon. Mother Smelltail and her brood were still rooting along the creek bank for a breakfast of crayfish, and when she spied the cats coming, she trilled for her kits to enjoy the spectacle. The felines trooped by with soaked, spiky fur and miserable faces, the skunks' once-terrifying foe slipping into the water with almost every step. Now he was so small, so wet and so unhappy it wasn't even fun to tease him.

"At least he's clean," Mother Skunk chittered and her babies giggled, their short front legs dancing on the sand.

The kin arrived at the waterfall. They sat on stones, gathering courage for the plummet. Browser went first. Slipping off his perch, he floated toward the precipice, whirling eddies jerking him this way, then that, then over the edge. Splash! Into the pool.

"Rat tails! That wasn't half bad!" Browser called up. Buster followed, then Ghost, who did it differently. He hopped from rock to rock to the edge, then climbed down the boulders jutting outside the plunge. Spray buffeted him, slippery moss tried to toss him off, but his body was agile.

Just above the basin, he leaped into the water, then paddled to Browser and Buster waiting in the shallows downstream. Patches' turn. Copying his father, he slipped over the cascade, swimming easily to the shallows. Scrapper mimicked Ghost, climbing down the slippery stones and diving into the reservoir.

Bigpaw followed his brother, placing his front paws on the first boulder below the plunge then slowly easing his rear-half down. Success. Again he descended front-end-first to the rock below. His paw slipped but he froze and regained his balance. Now that all four of his over-sized feet crowded the mossy ledge, he slowly faced the stone wall and lowered a hind leg. Accomplished, until his second paw kicked away the first one and his toehold was lost. He had only the hold of his forepaws unless he could calm himself and quiet those flailing hind legs. Bigpaw concentrated. At last they dangled together as-one, and as-one, they touched the stone beneath them...at exactly the moment his front paws, as-one, decided they'd done enough. They scraped through their stone's moss blanket, tearing it free, and Bigpaw's body floated backward into open air, limbs reaching for the wall as if he'd been pushed away by mischievous spirits. For one delicious heartbeat he defied gravity. He hung in space, his face shuffling though a series of emotions: surprise, fear, then absolute panic, his limbs gyrating wildly as if he were space-walking back to the ledge. No such luck. Bigpaw's body tilted forward and he plummeted head-first into the pool. Down he went, breaching the surface with thrashing paws. Down he went again and up he came, gasping for air. Scrapper reached his side. A frenzied Bigpaw mounted his back and down they both went, Bigpaw gulping water like a fish. Up they came.

"Calm down!" Scrapper howled. The exhausted Bigpaw gave up, and his face bobbed above the drink. "See? We float." They paddled to the shallows, where Bigpaw collapsed before his father. Browser licked his humiliated son head to tail.

"I should have known I can't do what Scrapper does," the catling mewled.

"No. You can do other things," Browser said, nuzzling his ear.

Robin was the last to brave the falls. Like Browser and Buster, he relaxed and let the current drop him into the pool. Then he swam to his friends. A short trek south brought them to Northbridge, where they rested on a slender stretch of rocky dirt beneath its wooden planks. Farther south, the creek added a tributary flowing down from the northwest and they came to Bigmarsh with its bullfrogs, snapping turtles and venomous snakes.

The troupe reached Marshbridge, a layered-stone construction running east-west through the center of the bog. Water flowed beneath the arch, but the elevated ground beside the stone walls built to the edge of the swamp was rich with willow trees, climbing roses, pampas grass and blooming wild violets. The travelers lunched there on little fish and mice until a green jeep belonging to park rangers and two White Trucks rolled overhead, heading west.

"Something's happening," Browser whispered from their hiding place.

"The gulchdogs are eating puppies and house-kin," Ghost meowed.

"They have no self control," Robin snarled. The younglings stared in fear after the White Trucks while Buster hissed and flurried the air. Soon the troupe was wading through swamp water, keeping a sharp eye for slithering ripples. At last the marshland narrowed into a stream. They came to Southbridge, and again were forced into hiding when more White Trucks rolled overhead, also heading west toward the Ranger station.

"What in the fur-fly is happening?" Buster exclaimed.

"I'm not sure," Browser meowed, "but I'm thankful we're witnessing it from safety."

"Are they looking for us, Father?" A very wet Scrapper asked through chattering teeth.

"I don't think so. They wouldn't need all those monsters just for us."

"Ghost is right," Bigpaw meowed. "I heard they're after ghostdogs."

Browser looked at his other shivering son. "What do you mean *you* heard?"

Studying his paws, Bigpaw whispered, "From the ravens."

"From the ravens?" Browser yowled.

Now the center of attention, Bigpaw hunkered, his ears twitching nervously. "Don't you listen to them?" He glanced furtively at Browser, knowing the answer. No one did...just him.

Browser's eyes smiled. "That's wonderful, son." Bigpaw visibly relaxed, relieved that for once he didn't need to hide who he was. "Do you speak to them?"

"No, father, but I understand them. I don't know why." *I do know why; I love them.* But he didn't say that. The kin hunted feathertails. Maybe not the big black ones, but sometimes their smaller cousins, the squawkbeaks. Moons ago, Scrapper's eyes had smiled with warmth when Bigpaw confessed he couldn't see ravens as prey.

Scrapper never laughed at him. The other catlings did though, often. Every brightmoon he proved to them how clumsy and odd he was. They seldom noticed the tender heart behind his blundering paws, so Bigpaw learned to keep his tail down and his muzzle shut.

"Son I..." Browser began in a warm voice, then stopped. He rose, his gaze fixed on something behind them. All heads turned. On the sandy bank sat a large brown male with fierce golden eyes.

Broadface thumped his tail. "You bring warriors to the door of my den, Browser? Northern prey is not enough?"

Before his father could answer, Scrapper swaggered toward the southern pod leader. "I don't see a den," he chuffed, his pelt puffed and chest thrust forward. Browser growled a warning and Scrapper plopped on his butt.

A young flame-pelted male sauntered past Broadface, the glint of battle in his eyes. "And if you can't see it, it's not there, neow...kit?"

Scrapper knew Ember from the games at Harmony Tree and had never liked him. Now he clawed the dirt, aching to rush the insolent punk and throw him down, but Browser slapped his face with an angry tail. Realizing Scrapper was beneath his father's paw, the ill-mannered Ember taunted him, walking a slow circle around him, barely brushing him with the bushy tail his clan was known for. He strutted over to his den, and marked the entrance, staring at Scrapper the whole time. Scrapper lost it. A wavering war cry escaped his throat, and had Browser not cuffed him across the muzzle with enough force to bring his shoulders down, there would have been a dust-up on Southbridge turf.

"This is not the way to behave," Browser hissed in his son's ear, his paw on Scrapper's neck. Scrapper blew the dust from his nose and wiggled his hindquarters, but couldn't throw off his father's domination. "How would you feel if their warriors camped beside our rosemary hedge." With that Browser relented, permitting his humiliated son to sit. Broadface's golden eyes mellowed and he snarled at the smirking Ember to go inside. Ember didn't move until the large chocolate-pelted leader rose and faced him with a hiss. Wide-eyed and tail tucked, he scurried out of sight. "I'm sorry, Broadface. We didn't know this was your den. We'll be on our way."

"But you haven't told me why you're here." Broadface demanded.

"May I?" Browser meowed, gesturing with his tail he wished to cross the distance between them. Broadface met him half way. A gentlemanly nose-greet and Browser told his story, beginning with the ghostdog attacking Jasper and Shorttail and the miraculous appearance of the bobcat. It was a story Broadface had heard from kin who'd been there, but not the coyote's promise to destroy Hillside Pod, and of course, Browser's plan to save them. Listening intently, the southern leader's eyes were alternately kind, worried and stern and when Browser finished, the two alphas sat silently appraising each other.

Finally Broadface spoke. "I understand you are Consort to the Queen, but this is still my territory. You must promise something before I give consent to use it."

"What do you need?"

"Give me your word that your plan will not lead ghostdogs to our den."

The King of the Green hesitated, asking himself how to fulfill this request and his own pod's need. "Our plan was to return north up the meadow, evenly between woods and creek," he said.

Broadface shook his head. "No, Browser, you must travel away from the stream, close to the trees until you've passed Southbridge."

Browser searched his heart. Perhaps their plan wouldn't work as well, perhaps it wouldn't work at all, but Broadface was right. He couldn't be responsible for ghostdogs slaughtering more kin. "I give my word," he said, and the leaders sealed the agreement with a nose-meet.

Goldenpelt appeared, followed by four fuzz balls with wide, fluffy tails, their pelts swirling brushstrokes of gold, brown and black. She rubbed her cheek against Broadface and he licked her ear. "Are you hungry?" she asked the northern cats. They'd eaten nothing but a few tiny fish and skinny mice since dawn and they were starving, but they stared at their paws like all good soldiers, letting Browser answer.

"Thank you, Goldenpelt, but we won't impose." Wrong answer. The younglings fought the urge to moan.

Goldenpelt was motherly and smart. "Nonsense," she purred and loped into the shelter, returning with a longear and several fat rats. Browser and his troupe ate, then lay in the sun, watching her kittens play. Once their pelts were dry and the food and rest had strengthened them, Browser signaled it was time to leave. "You and yours are always welcome at our preypile," he said to Broadface. "A worthy leader sees beyond his clan. Thank you for helping us and for helping the queens and kits from Flattail Dam."

"I trust you," Broadface answered. Browser dipped his head, then led his charges back into the stream.

A short distance south, Buster and Ghost came up beside him. "The plan won't work now, will it?" Buster asked.

"Do your best," the pod leader answered, but they both caught the worry in his eyes.

The sun crossed the sky. Southbridge was lost behind curves in the stream and the graceful ups and downs of the southern terrain as the troupe moved steadily toward Flattail Dam, not sure what they'd find. Rangers had destroyed the dams countless times, but what humans demolished by day, beavers rebuilt by night. Finally, their constructs were far enough into the wild that the men let them be. The lake had flourished, drawing frogs and water fowl, turtles, fish and raccoons. Humans built a foot-bridge to span the water, hanging lanterns from high poles along the railings, perfect for romantic couples to stroll the bridge beneath their soft, warm lights and those of the stars.

Then kin arrived, sheltering in the abandoned flattail dams. Whole new levels of energy and patterns of life emerged as the feline settlers grew plump on rats and finbacks. The colony was thriving when Bleggs destroyed it.

Now the pond lay just beyond a gentle crest whose far side sloped down to the water. Snaking a trail between sheaves of grass that dipped and rose in the breeze like whispering waves, the travelers reached the top of the hillock. They looked down on the lake and shuddered. *What force destroys beauty*, Browser asked himself. Before them lay charred branches and pits of ash. Broken reeds trampled by muddied boots, crisscrossed by death-trucks, and christened with terror-scat. The den where Blackpaw and Whitewhiskers had guarded nursing queens was shattered and burned and the rubble had floated away. Many dens had tumbled over the falls, or sunk below the surface, becoming part of the dam. Branches rose from the water, spidery fingers reaching from the grave.

If you didn't know what happened here, if your memory didn't hold the screams of the dying, if you didn't speak Earth and couldn't hear Her pleas for help...there had been men and trucks and frightened kin and a fire and now it was calm. *Life flows in a circle that cannot be destroyed,* Ghost thought. *The pond will repair itself, the boot prints dissolve and the reeds again stand tall. Ashes will enrich the earth and most of Great Mother's children will never hear about this brutal theft of lives.* The shaman couldn't tell if this tore his heart or healed it, maybe both, and he prayed for his beliefs. Surely Blackpaw and the others now played in Fields of Nip. Nightbeak had assured him it was so, and he did believe, for to think that Great Mother would give them a spark of awareness only to snuff it into oblivion, was too barren an idea to endure. And then Ghost felt Her embrace and when he opened his eyes he no longer saw desolation, but change. The murders were despicable acts, but the deaths were not tales of suffering at the last. *Death is a transition, not a finality to be feared. Life cannot be destroyed.*

Ghost watched the stream flow in from the north, feeding the lake whose waters toppled over the dam. Tall grasses grew along the shoreline, and duck families swam quacking to hidden nests, while ripples of jeweled light followed a swan couple headed for the bridge. The sun warmed his back. The breeze was soft, tickling his fur, and all was well with the world.

In silence, with deference for the dead, the troupe approached the water. They waded single file through the shallows, climbed the dam and leaped down the falls into the stream. Here they turned west, crossing through forest, then north, trotting in groups of two or as loners, hiding when tall-walkers passed nearby. Through open doors they heard young men laughing while they bounced a ball, the rubber skins on their feet squeaking against the shiny floor. Some splashed in a pond of blue water while others cooked prey or ate at nearby tables. The unwanted-food bins reeked of burgers and fries, but today no one would bring Mama Frizz and her pups the leftovers. Today they were saving the entire clan. The warriors gathered north of the snack bar, ready to begin their trek up the meadow.

"Stop!" Browser called. "We can't leave our scent trail here." The faces of most were confused; only Ghost and Buster knew the truth. Buster looked cynical, Ghost was stoic. "I promised Broadface," Browser said.

Scrapper slapped his tail on the dirt then leaped to his paws. "What! After all that water!"

"We'll work near the woods until we pass Southbridge."

"We have no guarantee the ghostdogs will snuffle near the woods!" Now his tail cut the air as if delivering blows. He seemed dangerously close to forgetting the lesson learned at Southbridge.

"I promised," Browser replied.

Ghost approached father and son. "We've only ever had a fool's chance anyway...no matter where we leave our scat. But I guarantee that if the king breaks his oath to a clan leader, any hope that others will support our cause is gone. Don't worry. Great Mother will protect the kin." Watching the anger fade from Scrapper's eyes, Ghost turned to Buster for his customary heckling, but the big tux's eyes were as sincere as his tail was high.

Browser led them to the edge of the woods. "We'll do our work here, close to the trees, until we're past Broadface's den." The troupe nodded in agreement but Browser saw the doubt in some of their eyes and couldn't blame them. "This will work," he meowed with more confidence than he felt and with that the males of Hillside Pod began their scent trail. They rubbed their cheeks on every trunk, marked every bush with urine, leaving unburied scat on the ground. This was radical. Only a confident alpha cat left his scat where others could find it. Exactly the message they wished to give the ghostdogs. *Do you see? Do you smell? I live here. I have always lived here without worries, without enemies.*

When they were far enough north of Southbridge to ensure that pod's safety, they padded to the center of the meadow, marking copiously until they were almost to Harmony Tree. Browser caught a longear which they ate right there in the center of the meadow, leaving leftovers for the ghostdogs to find. The troupe traveled to the stream for a drink, then returned to the spoils before backtracking south, arriving at the tall-walkers' area before sunfall. Here they left more scent. With Great Mother's help, the coyotes would be caught by the rangers and given to the murderous White Trucks. Now the cats reversed their path, leaving scent until they crossed the southern forest, climbed the short falls and waded once more around the lake in the opposite direction.

"I don't know how the kin of Flattail Dam endured it here, so close to the uprights," Buster muttered nervously and a shudder crawled down their spines. The pod bunched together at the northern end of the lake, eyeing the stream's rippling current, all of them cold and wet again. Even Browser hunkered with tucked paws watching the sun fall. The air had chilled and the young males were gripped by a painful weariness. They all knew the trip home would be harder, but were buoyed by the hope their plan would work.

"It's late," Ghost said, seeing the sun crouch low on the treetops.

"Yes," Browser meowed, easing into the cold water, forcing a grin from a grimace. The others followed, slogging along with quiet determination until they reached Southbridge. No traffic rolled above their heads, which was a relief, but Broadface and Goldenpelt must have gone on a hunt, for the only kin who peeked from the den was a gold and white female they didn't know. And seeing them shelter beneath the planks, she nervously withdrew. The younglings' ears twinged with disappointment. No longear or field mouse to sturdy their stride home. Not one of them complained, however, not one, and their rock hopping skills had so improved even Bigpaw's pelt had dry patches.

Just before Bigmarsh, Browser slowed his pace. Ahead the stones of Marshbridge glowed purple beneath the setting sun. The Bigmarsh could be dangerous, especially at twilight, but once they'd made it through, home wasn't far after that. All they had to do was keep moving, and they'd soon be safe and warm and fed. Browser froze in place, stopping the others with a jerk of his tail while lowering his belly to the streambed. Water flowing past his haunches, he stared ahead like a stone. Seven ghostdogs splashed into the stream and crossed to the western bank. Miraculously, they didn't notice the trembling cats. Bigpaw, Ghost and Robin sank so deeply only their heads broke the current, but Buster and his son Patches, closer to the bank, were caught on clumps of watergrass. Scrapper crouched behind them. The sun sank and the sky quickly darkened. The breeze turned even chillier. The water was biting-cold, but the dogs, instead of moving on, sniffed along the reedy bank so closely the cats could hear their growlspeak.

"Grimfang!" a young female called out to their large, gnarled leader.

"What!" he raised his head and the cats could see the bobcat's work:

four pink furrows that began a hair's breadth below his left eye and ran down his snout, the flesh scooped away so deeply fur would never grow back. "Keep your voice down," he muttered as she trotted to his side. They sniffed along the bank together.

In the water, the kin shivered miserably. Why didn't the hounds move on? Now the female sat, back to the stream while Grimfang continued to sniff and pace. "Are we gonna' look for them mangy pelts tonight?" she gruffed, "The flyin' spies say they're on the move."

"You can understand ravens?" Grimfang asked, pulling his nose from the grass.

Redears, so named because the fur from her neck up had a ruddy cast, shook her shoulders with pride. "Nah. A lil' rat told me...once I promised to spare his life."

"Did you?"

"Of course not, but I did let 'im tell me everything he knew before I ate 'im," she grinned, proud of her betrayal. Grimfang wasn't, but he was fully aware of Redears' value to the pack, her gift of speaking to different kinds of animals. Beyond the common-speak used with big cats and birds of prey, not many gulchdogs could do that, himself included. He forced himself to grin back.

"So," she asked again, "Are we lookin' for them whiskery bug-eaters or not?"

"Dog Father willing, we'll catch them tonight."

She ran her tongue over her lips. "I bet they're tasty." Raising her ruddy head, she shook it as if her jaws held prey, and howled. The other five ghostdogs, who'd been snuffling the ground without purpose, yipped at her antics and broke into a game of nip-your-paw.

"I said be quiet," Grimfang snarled, then stared into space. "Something's strange." He sniffed the air. Wind blew across the cats' damp pelts and the ghostdog's nostrils flared. "There's nothing on the grass...but I smell...cat." His gaze focused on the reeds. Patches shuddered, causing the reeds to tremble and Grimfang leaned in, parting stalks with his face. Lips curled back, fangs exposed, his yellow eyes narrowed on the terrified catling. "What's this? Oh, I see...a snack for my pups." Patches urinated with a heart-rending yowl, shaking so violently he began to slide from his tuft of rivergrass into the water. Grimfang opened wide to snap the catling's neck.

"Eeeeeee-ow-ow-ow-ow-ow!" Scrapper slammed into his face.

Grimfang howled and staggered backward, his big paws flailing at the thing sharpening its claws in his flesh. Scrapper rotated his body, head facing down, and bit deeply into Grimfang's throat. Then he yanked, spitting blood-soaked fur, turned and vaulted up and over Grimfang's head. The coyote gurgled and choked between howls, careening from the stream, trying desperately to shake loose the beast now on his shoulders. Puffed-up to twice his size, Scrapper swung around and hunkered, his tail whipping the air. Grimfang bucked wildly and for a heartbeat the little cat lost his hold. Floating as if weightless between the dog's ears, his short past and questionable future hung beneath a rising moon and stars. An ear flapped close by and Scrapper sank his fangs again. The hound bellowed as he soared, plunged and soared, and the small sorrel jockey, his claws firmly planted again in his victim's flesh, released the ear. A piece of it sailed away like a tossed scrap, landing at the she-dog's paws. Her eyes rolled back in her head, and she fled whining up the creek into the marsh.

At last the pack dogs gathered to their leader, snapping at the little cat. Scrapper whipped around, clawed his way down Grimfang's back, and leaped to safety. Jaws snapped shut where he'd streaked by a heartbeat earlier. Angered, the gulchdogs yapped ever more wildly, one of them biting down on the bloody remains of Grimfang's ear. Beside himself with pain, Grimfang lunged at his tormentor, while his soldiers, yelping like demented banshees, dove crazily at one another's legs. Scrapper rocketed away. Suddenly the hounds froze, realizing the truth: the cat who'd committed unspeakable crimes was a blur receding into darkness. And they did what Scrapper wanted. They ran after him.

Scrapper ran for his life. With shorter legs and only a few heartbeats' head start, he pushed from his mind what he'd been taught his whole life: cats can't outrun coyotes. Scrapper ran, believing with every pump of his blood he would survive. Legs firing like pistons, he ran and ran and ran. He ran so fast his pelt seemed to stream behind him and a calmness filled his heart as he floated above his body, a serene, disembodied spirit watching himself succeed. Effortless, in slow motion, running became everything, and he knew with utter certainty he would outrun the dogs.

The uprights' food area loomed ahead and Scrapper veered right, the seven coyotes yelping behind him. Grimfang reached his flank and lunged, his fangs missing their mark by a hair, but his bloody snarls touched Scrapper's quiet place and the catling slammed back into his body, zigzagging away from the hideous hound.

The ranger station came into view. Scrapper streaked toward the forest the oblong of asphalt and resting monsters. The cacophony of coyotes caused humans to pour from the station, some running, shouting and waving their arms, some holding pain-sticks. Some had poles with loops of rope at the end to encircle the ghostdogs' necks. One succeeded, but the dog was moving so fast it ripped the pole from the human's hands, dragging it behind until he was downed by a dart. A loud thwack, another feather lodged in a haunch. Redears collapsed while running and tumbled head over tail, sliding over the asphalt until she lay unconscious, momentum spent. A dart whizzed through the air, a yelp and a third coyote hit the pavement. A net slammed on the ground. Scrapper leaped over it, running even faster, dodging trucks, two-leggeds, darts and falling ghostdogs. Now only Grimfang remained behind him, the safety of the trees looming ahead. Fueled by rage, Grimfang stretched his bloodied neck and snapped. Searing pain lit Scrapper's haunch. He flew toward the forest, his pounding heart feeling like it would burst. Gasping for air, he slammed into a fir tree. Thunk! A dart pierced its bark so close to his body the impact stung his paw. Yowling, Scrapper shot upward and flattened himself to the first branch. He trembled violently. Bouncing off the trunk Grimfang leaped as high as he could, but Scrapper whipped his tail away and the coyote's fangs cut air.

The catling scrambled higher, then higher, always crouching against the trunk. Another whizzing dart bought a pitiful whine. Peering down through the needles, he saw Grimfang lying on the ground. The barb in his haunch had pierced him sideways, so the hound bent over and pulled it free. Ribbons of flesh oozed blood while he lay whimpering, too traumatized to run. But the uprights with their nets and tranquilizer guns never stopped, so the battered ghostdog stood, glaring upward. Scrapper saw he'd just missed the blood-pulse in Grimfang's neck and knew then if the hound hadn't been weakened, he wouldn't have survived. The bite was serious, as wide and deep as his open jaws and should a piece of tooth remain to abscess and explode, the wound would grow deeper yet, probably fatal.

Another dart hit the tree and Grimfang leaped into the forest, gone like smoke on the wind. Bleggs and Wilson reached the spot where he'd lain.

"Coyote's wounds will make him dangerous," Wilson said, touching the blood-stained earth. Bleggs grunted, pulling darts from the trunk and when Wilson handed him the bloodied, bent one Grimfang had yanked through his flesh, the fat man just stared at it absently.

"Where the devil did that cat go?" He grumbled, shining a light into the pine's upper branches. Scrapper pressed himself to the bole, closing his eyes as the beam approached.

"Cat go?" Wilson asked, not even trying to control his tone. Since the slaughter of the southern ferals he'd realized Bleggs operated from his own book of laws, fulfilling his own vendetta, and gentle-hearted Wilson was determined such a massacre would never happen again. He cleared his throat. "We're *only* here for the coyotes."

Bleggs shot him a baleful glance. "Just tell the rangers about the wounded dog. 'K?" He shuffled toward their truck, tossing the bent dart into a recycle bin. "I'll get 'em one way or another...with or without you," he muttered to himself just loud enough for Wilson to hear.

Beneath the glare of floodlights, the rangers loaded the tranquilized coyotes into the rear of their trucks. They'd captured all but the biggest, who was injured. Wilson showed them the bent dart he'd fished from the recycling. Some thought the coyote couldn't survive his wounds untreated. "We must find him," one said, "give him medical care and release him with the others in the wilderness."

"Or put him down humanely...if he needs it," said another.

"As a last resort," offered the female among them. Everyone nodded.

But Scrapper knew they wouldn't find Grimfang and that he wouldn't die. Not without revenge, no matter how ill he became. He'd seen the hatred in Grimfang's eyes. With a sigh, the catling dropped his head to his paws. Exhaustion spread with every heartbeat, paralyzing his limbs. Cold and dizzy, he faded in and out while the waxing orb rose in the east, and Milk Mother spilled Her stars across the sky. *What was that?* A pale flash in the boughs above shed pale blue lights that melted into his fur. Warmth spread through his cold body.

"Starligh', 'zhat yew?" he slurred, dizzy and silly, thinking he saw Ghost' faerie tales. *Spirit Cats, my big furry jewels.* More lights merged with his pelt, and he crashed into a deep, snoring sleep. Nothing else happened for Scrapper that night. For him, no rangers stalked the forests shining lights into the bushes. No trucks rolled over the meadows catching the rumps of fleeing deer or the eyeshine of midnight bandits. He never heard his name called, Browser and his podmates searching wet and exhausted until the sky paled. He didn't hear his mother wail with grief, or his sister Rosebud and auntie Kyra keen. He didn't see Shadow collapse with a strangled moan, his death too dreadful for her to bear. And he didn't hear Grimfang, alone in the canyon, lamenting to the moon.

20 – THE ROAD HOME

Scrapper woke with the sun, feeling wonderful. A luxurious stretch and he scurried down the pine, caught a mouse scuttling through the leaf clutter, gulped it down and caught another. After his meal, he licked his sore paws, discovering they tasted as much of ghostdog as rodent, and sitting back on his rump, inspected them carefully. His claws were caked with blood and shreds of Grimfang's flesh. Several from his left forepaw were missing altogether. *I left my claws in the gulchdog's pelt,* he gloated, remembering with deep satisfaction the rush of dancing up its face and down its back. *That'll teach him to attack Patches!* Yawning huge, Scrapper arched his spine, spreading his swollen toes in the mulch. His belly full, the youngling clambered back up the tree and napped. By short shadows he was ready to go home. The slight limp in his left forepaw and the abrasion along his hindquarter only made him proud. *If that's the worst I fared against seven ghostdogs, I am one lucky furball.*

Scrapper crept close to the trees while passing the ranger station, relieved when no one challenged him. Crossing the uprights food area, he hid in bushes watching them eat what they caught at the kiosk. The scent of cooked meat was intoxicating. At just the right moment he sprang to a tabletop, liberating a meat patty with a swing of his head. The human who hadn't been watching his food howled and rushed him a heartbeat too late. Another leap and Scrapper hit the pavement running, gulping meat with every stride.

"That damn cat stole my burger!" the man screamed, as the damn cat dodged a cup of ice and soda with a perfectly timed vault into the air. He headed south, then east across the ball courts, the hard ground painful to his bruised paw leathers. But Scrapper refused to stray from the path his father laid out. Grimfang was now the only ghostdog threatening Hillside Pod, but the last one Scrapper would lead to their den. Climbing the dam at the lake's southern end, he waded through the water to the stream's dumping point and headed north, waving his tail at a surprised Broadface when he passed beneath Southbridge.

Beyond a soaked pelt and the fearsome climb up the stones bordering the waterfall, the journey back to the den was uneventful. He did stop once, however, in Smallmarsh near their home. It was early evening and Mother Skunk stood on the stream bank lapping up cool water. As the sorrel trouble-maker approached, she signaled her brood with her feathery tail and they scurried behind her chittering with fear.

Mother Smelltail stared warily as Scrapper plopped on a stone in the stream. "I'm sorry," he mewed.

"I'm sorry," she repeated.

Scrapper sighed. "No, no, I'm sorry."

"I'm Daisy," she smiled, flourishing her plume while dancing on petite black paws.

Scrapper's tail whipped across the water, sending a flurry of drops toward her and her skunklings. "Oh," he cried. "I didn't mean to do that."

Daisy had dodged the drops. She giggled, the faces of her kits peeking through the fronds of her tail. "How is black kitty?" she asked, suddenly serious.

"Shadow? She's fine...now..." Scrapper said, dropping his gaze. "I'm sorry about that too. Daisy, I don't want to be Bad Kitty anymore." He looked up, happy to see her skunklings feeling safe enough to wander from mom's protection.

"Scrapper, you're not Bad Kitty anymore. You're Hero, Big Hero...We thought ghostdogs ate you. Mama Tail is happy you're alive," she chittered, flashing a toothy smile.

"You are? Me? A hero?"

"The ravens told everyone the dogs are gone...all but Claw Face, but he's hurt. Maybe he'll die."

"Ravens?" Daisy threw her tail to the side, arching the center and dipping its end, flapping it twice in such a perfect imitation of a wing, Scrapper couldn't help but laugh.

"Black beaks. You know," she chittered. "They tell everything."

"I know who they are, Daisy. But...they're talking about me?" She nodded. Urgency crashed through Scrapper's brain. His parents and podmates, his beloved Shadow, all believed he was dead! He leaped to his paws.

"It's been a pleasure, Daisy, but I must go home."

"Pleasure," she mimicked as Scrapper loped north. She cooed to her babies, who skittered to their mommy, trilling their love.

🐾   🐾   🐾

Rosebud stood on the Guardian Stone, about to enter the den when she saw her brother racing up the meadow. Alerted by her yowl, everyone stopped whatever they were doing and bounded toward him. The pups knocked him off his paws, smothering his face with slobbery kisses. Scrapper pulled himself up but Rosie knocked him over again, running her raspy tongue over his body.

"Mom!" Scrapper squealed, limbs in the air.

"What?" she mewled, lifting her head from his belly.

His father's eyes loomed above her. *Until a moment ago, your mother thought you were dead.*

"I love you, Mom," he answered. Shadow's face hovered briefly, then Ghost' and Robin's and Reggie's kind eyes, Monkey's sweetness and strength, Buster and Kyra's smiling, Bigpaw and Rosebud, faces lit with love, Patches filled with wonder and finally Jasper and Shorttail, and Sugar Pie, hearts of pure joy. Standing at last, Scrapper wobbled toward the den, followed by an army of beloveds. Gently, he head-bunted his pup buddies. "I promise I'll tell you everything, but now I'm tired and hungry." Jasper licked his forehead and the pups bounced away to wait with their mother. The cats followed Scrapper into the cave, where he fed heartily, then told his story. Silence and awe filled the den. Scrapper had saved them from the ghostdogs!

Buster licked his ears. "Thank you for saving my son." Patches was also grateful, but embarrassed. He glanced furtively at Rosebud, hoping she'd never hear he'd wet himself.

Scrapper jumped to his paws. "Patches was too close. Grimfang had him by the throat before he could do anything. Luckily, I had room to jump that sack of crow food." He looked directly at his wide-eyed sister. "Patches would have done the same for me." Her eyes, rapt with admiration, settled on Patches. Scrapper's work was done.

"With six of them gone, it's over!" Buster cried, waving his tail.

"Not yet," Scrapper meowed, "Grimfang waits in the canyon."

289

Turning to his father, he whispered, "He hates me," and Browser nodded, remembering the gamy breath and yellow fangs once pressed against his face. But his son's return and the demise of the other coyotes made him happy. He didn't want to dwell on Grimfang.

"You have earned your name...Bravetail," he said. As if for the first time, Scrapper counted the scars ringing his father's thick neck and broad chest, and admired his battle-torn ears. To earn the respect of this warrior meant the world.

"Bravetail!" Shadow chanted and everyone joined in. "Bravetail! Bravetail! Bravetail!" Happiness beat his heart. *What's left,* he asked himself. *What can be better than this?*

Shadow glided to him and tenderly licked his face. "I love you, Bravetail," she whispered. "I will always love you."

Caught in the mystery of her clear eyes, the scent of her silky fur, for the second time in his life he knew the truth. "I love you too," Bravetail whispered. "I always have."

At first Bravetail enjoyed his fame. The Green buzzed with stories of his courage and kin everywhere showered him with praise. But after a while the fawning dragged on his heart. He wasn't who they imagined him to be. The story grew with every telling and not truthfully. Now he'd barely finished his milk-feeding before he bounced off the snouts of a dozen coyotes, biting and clawing them into submission, felling them with bolts of lightning from his nostrils, leaving only charred remains for the Rangers to sweep away. *Let the kin recount it however they please,* he decided. He was the only one who knew the truth and he'd never tell anyone, not even Shadow. The moment his father tensed to pounce, Great Mother told him Browser wouldn't survive his second encounter with Grimfang. Scrapper attacked to save his father's life.

🐾 🐾 🐾

Surprises came with the Brightmoon of Warm Rivers, not all of them good. At the celebration at Harmony Tree, Southern kin took to the root stage, claiming the scent trail left by Hillside Pod brought danger to their dens in the forest.

Broadface knew this wasn't true. "How could it be," he defended, "when the gulchdogs were rounded up at the Ranger Station the very day Hillside Pod made the trail." It didn't help. Factions were forming. Before

290

that brightmoon, Ghost had never seen the cats who were complaining, but he knew what they were: ronin, well-fed and meticulously groomed, with no loyalty to the Green. Grifters. Servants of the Malkin, payed for their services with promises of protection, promises he'd keep only as long as it suited him. Beguiling followers with half-truths and outright lies, Morsus had become a master of using fear of *the other* to divide brother from brother, then claim himself a savior bringing peace. All successes were his and all failures stuck to the Wisdom Cats. He even claimed he made it safe to celebrate brightmoon again. Nothing could be farther from the truth, but the Malkin didn't care about truth. He cared about power.

All but a few pod leaders rejected his Council of Great Mother as a self-serving sham, *but even one fooled is one too many*, Ghost thought. The Malkin knew a lie told often enough, is believed by too many. Coupled with his claims of protecting his followers, they became sleep-walkers defending his every sin, and his sins became too horrific to describe.

Everyone forgot the wounded coyote in the canyon, Grimfang, alone and lonely, cleaning his wounds with acid spittle. Weakened, but refusing to die, he lay in the shadows, lifting his face to the moon. His haunch had healed and he had four good legs. More than that, his heart blazed with desire. He must revenge his honor, his family's honor. He lusted for it, was consumed by it. Had he only three legs, he would hop into battle. Had he but two, he would drag himself to a place of ambush. And if he had no legs...well, then he would lie in wait until Bravetail crossed his path, even if it took forever.

21 – The Moon Of Painted Leaves

Darkmoon brings change. Everyone knows this. Apprentices and Wisdom Cats take their clan's dreams to the gathering stone, stir them with the light of stars, then embrace the new pathways rising with the dawn.

The fate of Hillside Pod changed much that gray morning after darkmoon when a slender black cat found a path through the forest to the rosemary hedge below the hill. At closer look, the cat wasn't slender, but painfully thin, and half of his tail was missing. He no longer groomed himself, and his coat, ragged and dull, showed that his Fetch had found him. He sat and stared up at the Guardian. Most would see a weedy hill terraced with boulders, and in the center half way to the top, a large stone egg buried sideways in the dirt. It was so unusual, anyone would notice it, but few would understand its power. The black cat did. He knew it was a Guardian, and that it guarded Hillside Pod's shelterveil, the cave that kept them safe.

After a few twitches of his ragged ears and thumps of his mangled half-tail, he called out, "I must speak to Ghost."

No answer. Sugar Pie lifted her head and peered through the rosemary, hushing her pups with an obey-your-mother stare.

"I must speak to Ghost," the cat repeated.

Monkey leaped to the stone. "And you are?" she asked, looking regal despite her kit-swollen belly and frizzy ruff of neck fur. She would have pitied the creature on the grass had his soul not carried a secret that swallowed more light than his pelt.

"Tell him Black Max is here," he cried as Monkey dropped into the den. She stared worriedly at Ghost, who with Robin, peeked around the boulder.

"It *is* Max," Ghost whispered. "A friend from the alleys." He took another peek. "He hunted with Browser and me." Ghost stared into his past. "I'm surprised he's still alive."

"Just barely," Robin said.

"Max wasn't a bully or a thief. Great Mother's Pelt, he's had a hard time of it!" Something else about his friend worried him though. Ghost sat with eyes closed, releasing his spirit-body. He settled next to his visitor, both staring up the hill.

"What are you doing? Max asked.

"Also my question," Ghost replied, lifting a paw to Max's shoulder. Tinkling like little bells in a breeze, the shoulder dissolved beneath his touch. Max continued to talk as if nothing had happened, while Ghost stared into the hole he'd made. On the spiritual plane, Max was an empty shell. Again Ghost raised his paw and swiped. Half of Max's body disappeared.

Max didn't seem to know. "What's wrong, Ghost? You seem unwell." The wizard reached for his face.

"Ghost. Ghost!" Monkey cried. Disoriented from his waking-dream, he couldn't speak, but she saw recognition in his eyes. "You're all right," she murmured, licking his ears. And he was.

"Monkey, I understand who he is."

"Who?" They all asked.

Ghost shivered. "Whoever – whatever – is sitting in our meadow, it's not Black Max; it's not even a cat." His friends stared blankly. "I mean, yes, it's a cat, physically it's a cat, and it's Max, Great Mother help him, but he's missing his thoughts and feelings." The others chuffed angrily. "That thing's a shell of Max. Whoever, whatever is guiding his paws...it's not Max."

"If that's not Max, who is it?" Monkey whispered, unable to grasp something so dark, so wrong...

"It's a trap, is what it is!" Robin snarled.

Monkey leaped back on the Guardian. "Black Max," she commanded, "What is your business with Ghost?"

Max paced, eyes shining like polished gems. "Erasmus sent me. He needs help."

Monkey jumped back into the den. "Don't talk to him! Robin's right. It's a trap," she mewed, trembling with fear.

"But Monkey, what if I can find Erasmus?" And before his mate or his friend could stop him, Ghost leaped into view. "Hello, Max."

"Good to see you, old friend," Max called up.

"I'd say it's good to see you too, if I knew who you were."

Nervously, Max quivered his half-tail. "A strange thing to say."

"A strange thing you are. I feel no heart in you, Max, and hear no thoughts. And you have no scent, which is very strange." They stared at each other over the rosemary hedge and gravelly hill.

Max looked away. "Erasmus needs your help. Will you help him?" A lie. Ghost knew then for certain Max was Morsus' creature, that Morsus moved his mouth and lifted his paws. The Malkin had drained Max of his identity as surely as he'd drained Indra of her life. Then, with a flash of insight he knew Erasmus was no longer a prisoner. Why his mentor hadn't returned remained a mystery, but the Malkin no longer held him, and was desperate for the RA of the North. He needed the Power of Healing.

"How can I help Erasmus?" Ghost asked, hiding his excitement.

"Come with me."

"So...Erasmus lives."

"Of course he lives. He sent me to fetch you to him." Another lie.

Ghost slipped down the hill and under the rosemary. Straining forward on his tiptoes, he leaned into Max, a growl rising from deep in his chest. "Fetch. An appropriate word. Tell me. Do you still have yours or did Master take it when he took your heart, your mind, and your will?"

Max stared at his paws. "I don't know what you mean."

"I know when you're lying, Max, and I'm relieved to see you can still feel some shame when you do it." Max met his gaze, and for the first time his eyes were lit with a glimmer of emotion. His short tail swished in the grass. Ghost leaned closer and rasped, "I know you're here to deliver me to Morsus." Max froze. "And I know if you fail you'll be killed." Ghost stared at the shell of Max, remembering their friendship. "I'll go with you."

Max hung his head, his ears low to the sides of his face, openly shamed. "No...no, Spook, you mustn't," he barely whispered. It was a name Ghost hadn't heard since they were starving catlings, sweeping the streets for scraps of food. Max dropped his belly to the ground. "I've betrayed you," he moaned, staring up at Ghost. He rolled on his back and let his legs fall away, exposing himself to attack. "My life is worthless,

Spook, my soul rotten. Just kill me."

Ghost didn't kill his old friend. He closed his eyes and fell into trance. He saw many like Max, an army of starved and tortured warriors, drained of life-force, forced to submit to the Malkin's commands. He saw Max's Fetch circling the prone cat, unable to enter because of an unnatural spell. Max had been caught, starved and beaten, then sent forth to trick Ghost, who would face the same. But Max still had a glimmer of conscience burning in his battered heart and wanted to tell the truth. The wizard opened his eyes.

"The Master is not what he seems," Max said. "He befriends those he can use, but deals only death to kin he no longer needs. He murders many, but leaves more in a fugue, not strong enough to live by their own will nor weak enough to die. I am such a slave, a soldier in his army of expendables. He feeds us a mixture of herbs to make us abnormally strong when he needs us. We can work without sleep, hunt for hours with no appetite for our kill. Afterward, we're exhausted, our minds confused. We're an army, Spook, an army of slaves led by corrupted kin who support him."

"Why?"

"He's turning the hungry against you, telling them Wisdom Cats are to blame for their suffering. And once we're strong enough, he'll attack. He plans to kill all Wisdom Cats and all pod leaders who oppose him."

Ghost slumped back on his haunches, his worst fears confirmed. What he'd dreamed and heard of the Malkin's ambition was dwarfed by the awful truth torn from his friend. He left Max and returned to the den.

Browser padded from the shadows. "I've heard enough. Ghost, tell me you don't believe that wretched thing." Ghost said nothing. Browser slapped his tail in the dirt. "Tell me you don't believe him."

Ghost met his gaze. "I do believe him and I have to go," he said, turning toward a miserable Monkey.

"I forbid you to go, you hear me? As pod leader, I forbid it."

Ghost gave him a quizzical look. "But you must leave too, Browser, or has the Queen not told you?" *Don't you see, Browser, that like me, your mind is also not in charge? Like me, you must answer your heart, the call of your destiny.*

Browser gave him a hard look, then stared at Rosie, who kept her gaze on Ghost. "It's a trick, Ghost. Max is a traitor."

"That may be, but Great Mother has told me I must go with him." Monkey sank to the floor at his paws.

"I pray She doesn't tell me I must live without you," she whimpered.

"This will end well," Ghost whispered into her ear, then turned to Robin. "Tell Max I'm coming," and he padded to the altar to prepare for his journey.

🐾　🐾　🐾

The following dawn, and for a dozen dawns thereafter, a gloomy Browser sprawled across the Guardian Stone, believing he'd never see his friend again. The morning of the first night of brightmoon, Rosie and Kyra sat by Monkey, who crouched in her snuggery purring through her birthing pain. By sunhigh she'd pushed out two daughters and a son, replicas of their silver father but large like their mom. Tired but happy, Monkey lay with her babies tucked into her belly, purrs large and small spreading contentment through the den.

Browser entered the big room and lay near Rosie, who was resting. They dozed and together they dreamed of a northern hill in the Green. At its very top, a twisted, wind-torn pine grew from cracks in the stone, and balancing on its uppermost branch was the Father of Ravens. It was his three-hundredth darkmoon in the tree, and as always, he waited for a sign.

Just before dawn fingers of fog crept from the woods into the meadow. Countless times he'd seen the night-smoke rise and dissipate. It always did. But this time the vapor flowed like sap up the trees and along the branches, dripping globules into itself below. The raven purred. Now the brume shot snaky vines into the air, separated down the center of the field, and shapes emerged.

To the east rose the head of a wolf howling silently at the stars. To the west a long tail unfurled. A puma quivered to attack, her hiss as muted as the hound's cry. Dog Father, the Great Wolf, bared his fangs. The raven hardly breathed. If Dog Father and Great Mother battled, an age of war would follow and the world would drown in its own blood. Fenrir and Freya must not fight. They stalked each other in ever smaller circles while the Father of Ravens prayed.

Suddenly, the great feline halted, lifted her face to distant suns, then bowed to the nebulous wolf. His shoulders dropped to the ground, head between his paws in a posture of submission.

Swooping with joy, the great raven flew off to spread the word. Dog Father and Great Mother would work together for the greater good. The world would have peace.

Rosie leaped to her paws with a moan. "Mee-am? Am I dreaming?" She stared at the Guardian Stone. Ghostly wisps of her tall-one formed. Mee-am knelt, arms extended before her placing bowls of food on the ground. She morphed into a dark shape, and her arms became wings. She spread them.

"Kronk. Roak. Ka ka ka ka ka." the raven screamed. "*Leave,*" he told Rosie. "*Leave now. Leave for home, for Mee-am.*" Just as suddenly, it was gone, taking with it Rosie's future at Hillside Pod. She felt as if the earth were yanked from beneath her paws, forcing her to obey or fall into the abyss.

Her children were catlings and no longer needed her attentions. In fact, Rosebud chafed against her control. Unbelievably, Ghost was gone. Browser would always serve the highest good, and the raven had told them plainly what that was.

The massacre at Flattail Dam had killed more than cats. It had murdered the comforting belief that kin in the Green were entitled to thrive, murdered it with a finality that haunted all survivors everywhere. The White Trucks left with the coyotes, but the kin worried the quiet was only a lull. The holocaust would continue until the Prophecy was fulfilled.

Browser stretched out a paw. "Rosie? Was I dreaming? Was that really Mee-am?"

"Yes...no, but the message is real, Browser. It's time to leave the Green." They nose-kissed.

"The children?"

Rosie swished her tail. "Rosebud and Bravetail will come. Bigpaw should stay here. The journey could prove too dangerous for him." Browser agreed, but was sad to leave his son. "And we'll take Robin," she added. "We'll need a Wisdom Cat. Reggie can tend to the pod." Again Browser agreed.

The news traveled downhill before they did, and Sugar Pie was inconsolable. "Mister Browser! Misses Rosie! No! Don't go," she whined, smothering them with wet kisses. All attempts to comfort her were useless.

Disheartened, the royal couple returned to their den, and were greeted by an angry Rosebud. "We're leaving?" she cried, fear scent spilling off her pelt.

"Yes." Rosie trilled, and tried to nuzzle her daughter, but Rosebud backed away.

"Why?"

"Can I come?" Patches asked, eyes glued to his beloved Rosebud.

"I won't leave my home," the youngling spat, pacing and snarling at the air.

Browser leaned over her. "You will do what you're told," he said quietly, his voice a stone wall. Rosebud froze. For a heartbeat she seemed unsure, then her eyes pulsed angrily at each of her parents and with a leap to the Guardian, she bounded down the hill, yowling furiously. Patches scrambled after her, calling her name.

"You see that?" Browser said. "He'll watch over her whether she wants it on not."

Rosie dropped to the ground, feeling miserable. She looked at Bigpaw eating from the preypile, indifferent to family drama. Only he wasn't. And feeling his mother's eyes on him, he licked his paws and cleaned his face, then padded to her. Rosie lay on her side, opening her arms, but today wasn't a day to snuggle.

You're leaving me here," he said.

Rosie quickly sat. "Bigpaw," she cooed, reaching for him as he scooted away.

"I know why...I'm Bumblepaw."

"No!" Rosie and Browser cried together.

"I know I seem the fool. I'm not Bravetail." Bravetail rose in protest, but Bigpaw turned his back to him. "It's all right. I've decided not to go... for my own reasons."

"No one but Bravetail...is Bravetail," Rosie murmured. "You must never doubt we love you just as you are."

Now he accepted his mother's tongue-bath. "I know what's wrong with me."

"You do?" Rosie, Browser and Bravetail all exclaimed.

"I thought I was...what everyone thinks...clumsy...but it's not true...I can't see," Bigpaw yowled proudly. Stunned silence, not the response he expected. "Don't worry. I can see, just not like the rest of you. Anyway,

I'm teaching myself to get around. I'm fine." Rosie had loved him as clumsy, silly and shy, easily frightened and too gentle for his own good. Browser had too. Now they saw Bigpaw's courage and determination.

"I'm amazed by you," Browser meowed, and his son's eyes shone with joy. Shortly after that Bigpaw left for a hunt in the woods, assuring them he could managed on his own. The truth was he didn't want to answer anymore questions. Telling his parents his world was dim was difficult enough. How could he tell them it was going black?

All day Bravetail had sought Shadow's warmth. She curled like a snail before Great Mother's altar, and wouldn't speak to him, her spirit fading from his grasp like the light of their last day together. Bravetail buried his face in her fur. "I'll come back for you. I promise." To which Shadow stifled a moan, her body stiff and unyielding. Heartbroken, Bravetail pulled away.

Bigpaw returned to the den at dusk with a longear for the preypile. After eating, the elders delighted the catlings with stories of their exploits when they were catlings too. Though she'd heard them all, Rosie listened intently until brightmoon rose and she climbed to Waterfall Boulder one last time. Singing cats and thumping tails beckoned from Harmony Tree, but Rosie enjoyed the moon and stars, then returned to the den. The room was warm and comforting, bathed in the scent of friendship, and more than anything Rosie wanted to lie in a fur-pile with her podmates, but Browser padded to the Guardian Stone. It was time to leave. His gaze traveled from face to face, resting on Buster.

"I entrust Hillside Pod into your capable paws," he meowed. Buster approached and they rubbed noses, cheeks and shoulders.

Bravetail slipped into the alcove where he knelt beside Shadow for a last goodbye. She sat on her paws, looking miserable and refusing to speak. He placed himself before her and she closed her eyes. Sadly and tenderly, Bravetail licked her ears and left. When he passed his parents' cubbyhole, he was startled to see Mee-am's cloth crumpled in their nest. PRW, once in golden threads on shining white cotton, was now a stringy darkness on a stained rag, but it still held the faintest scent of Mee-am, so Bravetail pulled it free and brought it to his grateful mother.

The travelers slid beneath the rosemary hedge into the meadow where Sugar Pie waited in the grass, her face twisted with grief. Browser flinched when he saw her. Had it been possible, he would have brought her along, and Sugar Pie knew this, but the parting was still unbearable. For all her days to come, Browser would remain her most beloved friend.

"I love you, Sugar Pie," he whispered, licking her fuzzy head. Fuzz Mutt only whimpered, kissing his face again and again.

"Goodbye, Bad Kitty," Jasper teased. Bravetail swiped his ears.

Browser motioned with his tail and his troupe started for the western woods. They were almost there when Jasper leaped from his mother's side, and dashed across the meadow. "Bravetail," he howled. The catling turned and raced toward him, yowling all the way. They met in the middle, and Jasper threw his legs on Bravetail's shoulders, slathering his face with kisses. Purring loudly, the catling rubbed all the love he could make into Jasper's body. Nose to nose they hung, until with a heart-rending whine, the pup broke away and dashed back to Sugar Pie.

Bravetail rejoined his family at the edge of the trees. Robin turned and faded into the woods. Bravetail followed. Rosie and Browser still faced the hill, their small shapes silvered by moonlight.

Kyra sat on the Guardian Stone. She'd been quiet all day. Once she'd believed Browser and Rosie caused her pain; now she felt the pain of their departure. She loved them. And lifting her face to the moon, she filled the world with a single cry that told her story of love and fear and love again.

And love buoyed them. With tsunami force it cleansed any doubt clinging to their hearts. It spread like scent on wind, water through roots. Love, the All That Is, flamed within them, painting each stone and clod of earth with perfection. Untouched by small desires, impervious to fear, joyful and sacred, love wedded them one to another, and neither time nor space could ever sever that bond.

Rosie and Browser turned toward the forest. They were gone.

www.ingramcontent.com/pod-product-compliance
Lightning Source LLC
Chambersburg PA
CBHW021309250626
47155CB00002B/456